THE
ART OF
BREAKING
ICE

Rachael Mead is a writer living on unceded Peramangk country in South Australia. She's had an eclectic life, working as an archaeologist, environmental campaigner and seller of books both old and new. Rachael's work has been widely published, including four collections of poetry: *The Flaw in the Pattern* (UWA Publishing 2018), *The Sixth Creek* (Picaro Press 2013) and the chapbooks *Sliding Down the Belly of the World* (Wakefield Press 2012) and *The Quiet Blue World* (Garron Publishing 2015). Her debut novel, *The Application of Pressure*, was released by Affirm Press in May 2020. When not in rehab for her addictions to op-shopping and books, Rachael lives in the Adelaide Hills with her husband, animals and a ridiculous collection of vintage overcoats.

PRAISE FOR *THE ART OF BREAKING ICE*

'Rachael Mead has imagined the Antarctic voyage of Nel Law with such vivid strokes that I feel I too have seen the blue-white of icebergs and felt their exquisite cold. Even more than a great read about a remarkable pioneering woman, this is the story of a continent and the men who tried to keep it all to themselves.'
Pip Williams

'Mead's stunning portrayal of luminous icescapes sheds light on an unrecognised female explorer overshadowed in Antarctic history.'
Karen Viggers

'Simply put, it's stunning. One of Australia's finest writers, in her element and at the height of her powers.'
Laurie Steed

'Rachael Mead shines her own poetic light on this impressive, unsung heroine and her influence on a generation of young women who followed her path to the frozen south.'
Robyn Mundy

'Mead has written a beautiful, powerful, gem of a book that captures a search for freedom that still eludes us today.'
Sarah Sentilles

'Against the drama of cracking bergs plunging into ocean, Mead untangles the longings of Australia's first woman to set foot in Antarctica. In her inimitable poetic and measured style, Mead navigates tensions between science and art, a husband and wife, the Antarctic cold and rising heat.'
Rebekah Clarkson

THE ART OF BREAKING ICE

RACHAEL MEAD

affirm press

affirm
press

First published by Affirm Press in 2023
Boon Wurrung Country
28 Thistlethwaite Street,
South Melbourne, VIC 3205
affirmpress.com.au

10 9 8 7 6 5 4 3 2 1

A catalogue record for this
book is available from the
National Library of Australia

ISBN: 9781922848529 (paperback)

Cover design by Andy Warren
Typeset in Garamond Premier Pro by J&M Typesetting
Proudly printed in Australia by McPherson's Printing Group

MIX
Paper | Supporting
responsible forestry
FSC® C001695

For Andrew & Ron

Author's Note

This novel was inspired by real events, but at heart, it is a work of imagination. I have used real names for many characters, but their personalities, dialogue and many of the scenes have been invented. Some of the paintings and artworks described in the book were invented. While informed by the writing and art of the historical figure of Nel Law, the character who appears in these pages is my imagining of her. I took many creative liberties in the writing of this novel. While the work is based on the events recorded in Nel and Phil's Antarctic journals, I have attempted to write into the many gaps and spaces left by these source materials. For narrative purposes, I've also altered dates and locations to fuse Nel's separate journeys to Macquarie Island (November – December 1960) and Antarctica (January – March 1961) into a single voyage.

Map of the Antarctic travels of Nel Law, as described in *The Art of Breaking Ice* – November 1960 to March 1961 (see Author's Note)

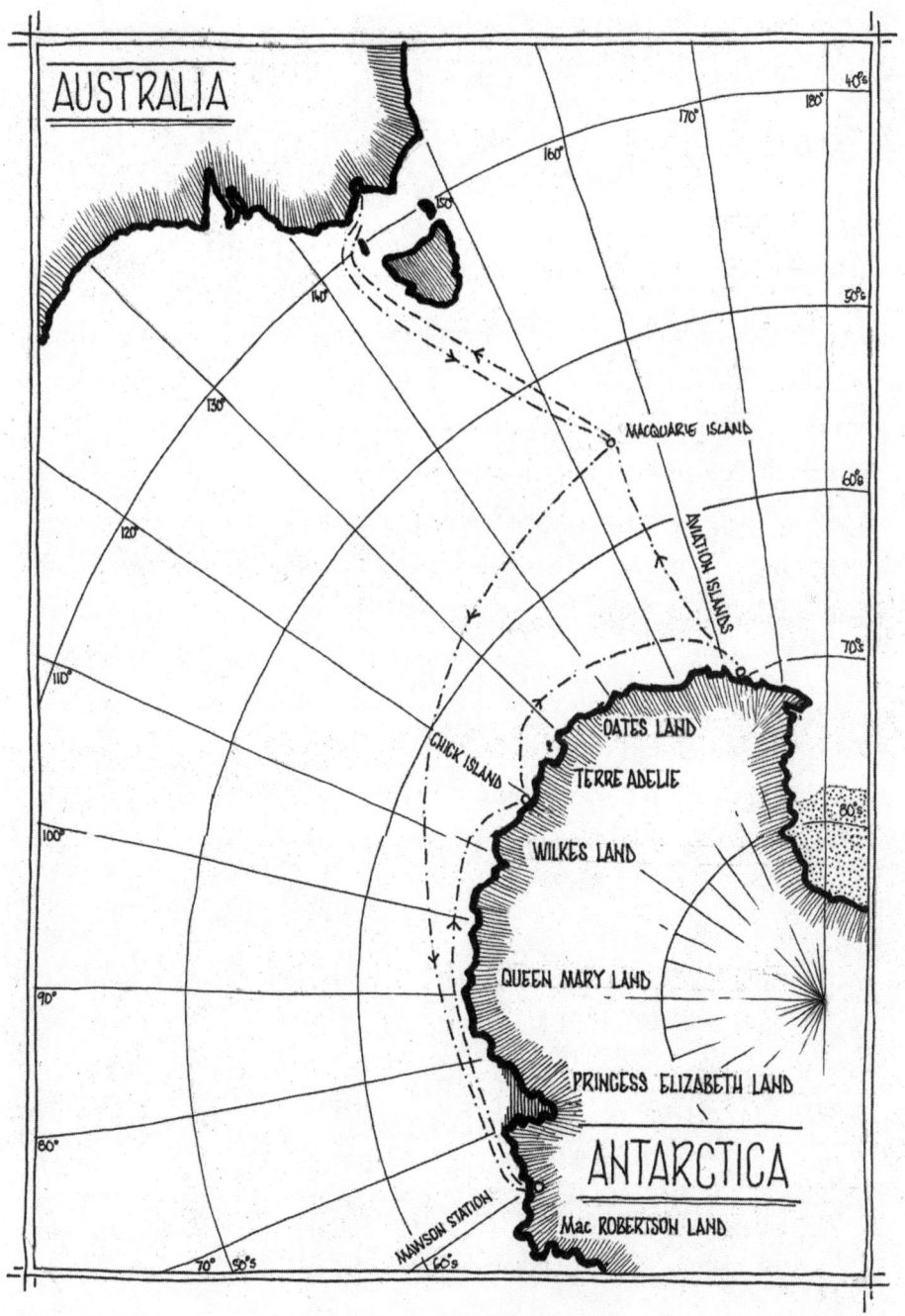

What a man is is an arrow into the future,
and what a woman is is the place the arrow
shoots off from.
Sylvia Plath, *The Bell Jar*

~

The universe is made of stories, not of atoms.
Muriel Rukeyser, *The Speed of Darkness*

Prologue

Mawson Station, Antarctica
June 2011

The south-westerly sliced across Cass's cheekbones in the slim gap between her goggles and the neck gaiter she'd pulled up to protect the tip of her nose. Her view was rimmed by the edge of her hood; icy gusts buffeted the grey fur and cracked the Australian flag planted beside the cairn. This was not the place to go bareheaded as a sign of respect.

The winterers stood in a shallow curve in front of the pile of grey stones, their backs to Mawson Station's metal sheds, which squatted like bright biscuit tins on the far side of the ice coating Horseshoe Bay. The sun had dipped below the horizon a fortnight ago and would stay there another month yet. It was beautiful, though, the dim polar dusk, the ceiling of cloud glowing like the inside of an abalone shell in the low-angled light.

The slope-sided cairn matched the three other memorials sitting side by side along the granite stretch of West Arm. Although only just

1

completed, all it needed was a tall white cross to be indistinguishable from the older memorials.

Graves, Cass corrected herself. The crosses marked the burial sites of expeditioners who'd died in the 60s and 70s, before the 'leave nothing behind' rules of the Madrid Protocol. Back then, dying down here had meant never going home.

Cass shuffled her boots, trying to force blood into her toes. Snow had fallen since the cairn was finished, dusting the top and gathering in a drift around the base. The wind whipped ice into the air, pitting sharp as sand on her Ventile parka.

Mark stepped forward, pushing back his hood to expose a cobalt beanie, cheeks ruddy with cold. Gloved fingers fumbling to unfold a sheet of paper, he cleared his throat. Gomble moved behind the cairn, camera in one hand, the other cupped to shield the mic from wind-roar.

'We are gathered today to lay to rest Nellie Isabel Law and Dr Phillip Garth Law.' Mark paused, glancing at the camera. Carefully, so as not to move the lens, Gomble jerked his thickly bearded chin. Mark straightened and kept reading, pitching his voice to carry and somehow managing to sound even more formal.

'We pay homage to Phillip Garth Law – truly one of the great men in the rich history of Australian Antarctic exploration. His indomitable will, humorous disposition and adventurous spirit set high standards for those of us who follow him. A minute's silence, please.'

Cass lowered her head, but not her eyes, surveying the uncharacteristically sober figures of her companions. For a memorial service, there was very little black. The bright and bulky department-issue parkas disguised all shape, leaving only height and her familiarity with her colleagues' taste in beanies and gaiters to tell everyone apart.

Too much room between us all, Cass thought. *If we were smart, we'd be huddling like male emperor penguins.*

No one was timing the silence, so when someone cleared their throat and Sorels began to shuffle in the snow, Mark got on with the speech. The wind wrestled with the paper and he gripped it with both hands.

'Phil Law spent his life in the pursuit and promotion of many scientific fields.'

As the long list of the man's polar achievements whisked from Mark's mouth, Cass's attention drifted back to the research paper she'd been trying to work on that morning, her lips tightening as she thought about the white screen and the judgemental flash of the cursor.

A wind gust slammed into her, thumping her back into the moment. Mark almost lost his grip on the notes. 'As testimony to his extraordinary service, he will always be remembered as Phil Law – our man in Antarctica.'

Our man in Antarctica. Cass rolled her eyes and shot a look at Rory. She was hunkered deep in her fur-rimmed hood, but Cass glimpsed the arch of an eyebrow. There wasn't much at the crux of language and feminism that slipped past her friend.

Cass hadn't taken to Rory when she'd first encountered her in the ship's dining saloon, only a couple of days into the voyage to Antarctica. One of the people Cass was sitting with had pointed out a short brunette reading by the light of the window beside her. She was a writer – a poet, in fact – accompanying them to Mawson as part of the department's Artists in Antarctica program, the expeditioner said.

One of the men in their group, a young physicist, had tried to spark a conversation with the poet. 'So – you're a doctor?' he asked, leaning across the aisle with a wave. 'Of what?'

'Literature.'

He murmured something to the guy sitting beside him, who ducked his head to hide a chuckle.

'Sorry. Missed that,' the poet said.

He hesitated. 'Just complimenting your fabulous earrings.'

She barked a laugh, cold and sharp as an icicle. 'Fellas, you disappoint me. Resurrecting the old arts/science binary? With jewellery shaming?' She shook her head. 'That's just intellectually lazy. And outdated. Honestly, I expected a bit more. Aren't you meant to be cutting-edge thinkers?' She pinned them with a steely look. 'I'm happy to debate the hierarchy of knowledge with you. But next time, please, bring your A game.' Then she turned back to her book, leaving the men shifting uncomfortably in their seats.

Cass had been impressed by the takedown, but it'd left her wary. She'd never met a poet, and wasn't quite sure one belonged down here, getting in the way of the real work.

Thank Christ she'd never let that slip. They'd ended up sharing a Googie, a field accommodation module resembling a huge scarlet egg, for several weeks. Rory had managed to finagle some time out in the field with the Adélie penguin team doing ecosystem monitoring on Béchervaise Island and proved a natural at bird-tagging, dodging pebble nests and shepherding penguins over the weigh bridge. In a backflip worthy of a rom-com, Cass had gone from eyeing Rory with wary suspicion to counting her among her dearest friends. It was almost a cliché of life down here that close-quarter living pressure-cooked a level of intimacy that would otherwise take years to forge.

Shoving the paper into his pocket, Mark stepped up to the cairn. Reaching over, he removed the lid of a neat wooden box set into the top of the monument. The shape reminded Cass of those old microscope cases from high-school biology. Appropriate, she thought, given Phil Law's significance to Antarctic science.

Cradling the lid, Mark stepped back, making room for two men who were each carrying a square bronze canister, the ashes of Nellie and Phil Law sealed inside. They placed the pair of urns side by side within the wooden box and Mark clipped the lid back on.

Picking up a stone from the small pile of rocks at the base of the cairn, Mark gently placed it on top of the box. The urn bearers followed his lead, then stepped aside for the other winterers to do the same. One by one, they added to the cairn, burying the honey-toned box in grey.

Last in line, Cass clinked her stone down, its mica glittering in the watery light. Behind her neck gaiter, her nose was starting to run.

Duty done, the winterers turned for whisky and warmth, trudging back across the iced-over bay, chins tucked against the wind.

Cass let them go, lingering before the two brass plaques on the face of the cairn.

Here lie the ashes of Nellie Isabel Law 1914–1990 and Phillip Garth Law 1912–2010 of Melbourne, Victoria, Australia.

The second plaque was larger and packed with words. *In memory of Dr Phillip Garth Law. Explorer. Scientist. Polar Medal Recipient. Director of ANARE. Founder of Mawson Station.*

Beyond the pale arms of the three crosses, a full moon sat like a muted sun in the western sky.

Cass brushed her gloved fingertips over the raised line at the bottom of the plaque, as if reading braille. *May he rest peacefully with his beloved wife Nel.*

There must've been more to her life than this, she thought. She ran her fingers across the brass letters one last time before turning to follow her colleagues. The rippled cloud over the station was now ablaze with orange and pink.

Quickening her pace, Cass drew alongside Rory, and the pair linked arms.

Cass elbowed her friend where her ribs would be under her thickly insulated jacket. '*Our man in Antarctica.* Wonder how the wife feels about spending eternity down here. She didn't get much airtime.'

Rory shot her a sideways glance. 'Surprised?'

Cass snorted. 'Curious. Just made me wonder who she was – other than Australia's longest-suffering Antarctic widow.'

Rory shoulder-bumped her with a chuckle.

'What?' Cass looked at her blankly. 'My guess is a housewife who lived in the shadow cast by her "Antarctic hero" husband.'

'Spent the years of her life in her husband's shadow, then the years of her death in six months of darkness. Nice image. I'm definitely using that.' Rory grinned at Cass. 'Now get a move on, woman. I'm fucking freezing.'

Stepping into the airlock of the Red Shed, the women stripped away layers, stomping ice from their boots, stuffing gloves and beanies into pockets and hooking up parkas. Rory grabbed Cass's arm, tugging her through the inner door and across the rec room before jerking to a halt where the library merged with the lounge. The space next to the shelves was crammed with photos – breathtaking icescapes, auroras, sled dogs, hairy-faced explorers. Cass had examined the photos when she first arrived, scanning for her grandfather's face, hoping his career as a ship's captain ferrying Australians to and from the ice had earned him a place in the gallery. Failing to spot her Farfar's beloved face, she hadn't paid it any more attention. Rory jabbed her finger at a portrait high on the wall.

'There she is. Your woman of mystery. Don't say I never give you anything. If you'd like to reciprocate, there's always whisky. Double. Speaking of which ...?' Rory raised her eyebrows, but when her friend failed to respond she moved away, towards the light and laughter of the bar.

Cass stared at the black-and-white photograph. She'd been here for three months, passing the photo countless times without noticing it once.

A man and a woman smiled down from the wall, both in the hazy zone where late middle age bleeds into old. They looked formal yet stylish, as if at an official event, with the governor and several heads of industry just out of frame. The man was short and bearded, with a sharp-witted air, while the woman beside him smiled as if well accustomed to cameras.

Cass leaned in to read the caption.

Phil Law, founder of Mawson Station, and his wife Nel, the first Australian woman in Antarctica.

Aureolin Yellow

Camberwell, Melbourne
November 1960

Nel stabbed the roasting penguin breasts with a skewer, feeling a jab of satisfaction as they bled thin juice into the tray. You could always count on scientists to be punctual. To the minute. She slammed the oven door, its hot breath sighing into the kitchen, and blotted her forehead with the edge of the oven mitt, trying not to smudge her foundation. As a firm advocate of fashionable lateness, Nel found this scientific compulsion for punctuality infuriating. These men may have devoted their lives to studying the laws of space and time, but surely the world would not halt on its axis due to giving their hostess a few minutes' grace between the kitchen and the arrival of guests?

Nel stretched her back with a half groan, half sigh. Lying in bed that morning, she'd felt crushed by the thought of tonight, as though the dawn air had the weight of several atmospheres. It wasn't as if Phil had sprung the dinner on her. She'd had plenty of notice. But on days when getting out of bed was a major achievement, pulling together one of her husband's 'Antarctic Feasts' made her feel as though she deserved to find herself on the Queen's Birthday Honours List.

These evenings weren't necessarily boring affairs. Usually, she relished entertaining, and being the wife of the man responsible for Australia's presence in Antarctica meant she was usually just as well informed about the next expedition as her guests – sometimes more so. But this didn't change the fact that these meals ended with her alone in the kitchen scrubbing penguin fat from saucepans while the men held court in the lounge, drinking whisky and trying to outdo each other with tales of polar exploits. Every year she noticed it more. The slow greying out – as if with each dinner she was fading, painted into the scene with watercolour rather than oils, and never quite able to hold her visitors' focus. At first she'd found it enraging. Now, she was surprised how draining invisibility could be.

The doorbell chimed. Catching her reflection in the kitchen cabinet, she grimaced at the exhaustion in her eyes, the weariness held deep in the bones of her face. No time to fix her melting makeup now.

Today had been touch and go. That morning, after Phil delivered her cup of tea in bed, she'd scrawled out her list of tasks for the day. The length of it had made her limbs leaden. But she'd done it, with barely a second to spare. Nel patted the heat-frizzed waves of her hair back into a semblance of the style her hairdresser had achieved that morning and slipped into the hall.

Phil was shaking hands with their two guests, a couple, as she joined him at the front door. Both were tall, making her husband's lithe body seem even more compact.

'Darling, this is Andy and Pamela Gressett. Andy's the entomologist heading down to Macquarie Island with me next week,' Phil said as he ushered the pair inside. 'Let me fix some drinks. Gin and tonic?'

'Ooh, please.' Pamela looked relieved as she stepped out of the evening sun, fanning herself and patting the base of her modest beehive, her brow damp with sweat. 'Just Pam,' she said to Nel with a smile, handing her a bottle of white wine, the green glass slick with condensation.

Andy's freshly shaven cheeks were shining, his skin ruddy where it bulged slightly above his tie. 'This heat feels specifically designed to protect Australians from us New Englanders. I'm amazed I convinced Pam to leave the hotel lobby.' The vowels of his Boston drawl sounded oddly Australian.

Nel closed the door behind them, keeping her surprise at Pam's presence from showing on her face. Phil must have told her dinner for four meant a married couple rather than the usual guest ratio of three male scientists to one hostess. It wasn't the first time her memory had failed her lately.

Nel trailed the group into the lounge room, her eyes lingering on Pam's back, trying to guess the younger woman's age from the presence of any silver hairs and the texture of the skin on her elbows. Late thirties, maybe? Despite the merciless heat, her guest looked fresh from the pages of *Vogue*. Her light cotton shift and dark upswept hair seemed futuristic compared to what passed for fashion in this staid Melbournian suburb. Only last Sunday, Nel had seen women stepping from the shaded entry of the local church wearing gloves, despite the state being in the grip of a heatwave. She looked down at her house dress and sighed. It had been fine for the hairdresser and grocer, but she'd run out of time. Her sleeveless coral sheath was still laid flat on her bed, matching shoes waiting for her feet.

In the lounge, Phil gestured for the Gressetts to sit while he poured a round of drinks at the trolley in front of the picture window. The low sun through the crystal decanters threw rainbows against the walls. Backlit, Phil's Brylcreemed hair gleamed, and with his sharp widow's peak and dark goatee he looked to Nel like a cool, calm devil mixing himself a drink in front of a fresh batch of over-heated souls arriving in hell.

Pam positioned herself directly in front of the fan, the fluttering geometric pattern on her dress roiling like an optical illusion. She took the glass Phil offered with barely a glance, her attention focused on the paintings hung against the white walls.

'I love this room,' Pam said. Nel wasn't sure if it was her American accent or her tone that made the statement feel more judgemental than complimentary. Pam was looking at the abstract landscape – *her* landscape – stretched above the pale blue couch. Nel's gut tightened as she tried to read Pam's face.

'It felt as if the temperature dipped several degrees the moment I stepped through the door and saw this,' Pam said as she leaned closer to the large canvas, a jagged geometry of blue and white representing a birds-eye view of an ice sheet. 'Who is the artist?'

'Forgive my wife,' Andy said with a grin, stretching to place his glass on the coffee table. 'She's an art history professor who can't turn it off, even when she's meant to be on sabbatical.'

An academic. In art. Assessing her paintings. The muscles around Nel's rib cage froze. Phil often laughed at her, saying how ridiculous it was to be so nervous of others' judgement, but she'd flip his argument back on him. Wasn't he more concerned about the opinions of his peers in Antarctic science than of those who asked him about encounters with polar bears?

Pam snorted indulgently at her husband. 'Like you've ever met a bug you didn't immediately befriend.' Drawn once more to the artwork on the walls, she stepped back as if she was standing in the National Gallery of Victoria instead of the Laws' living room.

'These oils are interesting. A little O'Keeffe in style but cooler. More crystalline than organic.'

'They're all Nel's,' Phil said, the sweep of his hand taking in the room. Every wall was hung with canvases, polar icescapes slashed with deep blue crevasses and black nunataks knuckling out of vast expanses of white.

Pam and Andy turned to Nel, who blinked in the beam of their attention. She stiffened. If this professional critic called her work a hobby, Nel felt she might fold in on herself so completely she'd compress down to a grain of sand – tiny, yet incalculably dense.

'You've been to Antarctica?' Pam's eyes were wide.

Nel shook her head. 'I paint from Phil's photographs.' She was about to go on when Phil stepped in front of her to collect Pam's glass for a refill.

'After twelve expeditions, I've got a trunkful of photos in my office. Nel's spoiled for choice when it comes to subject matter.' Phil smiled as he moved to the drinks trolley. Nel compressed her lips, swirling her glass to create a tiny whirlpool, the tinkling ice loud in the room.

'Well, I can only imagine what you'd produce if you were actually there – seeing it with your own eyes, framing your own scenes.' Pam sipped her drink, eyeing the painting.

Blood rushed through Nel's body in a flood of heat, self-consciousness pricking her skin, her cheekbones burning like the bars of tiny radiators.

Andy grinned apologetically at Phil. 'Look out. It sounds like my wife is about to climb on her soapbox.'

Pam huffed, keeping her back to her husband.

Turning to Phil, Andy continued in a conspiratorial tone, 'Sorry to inflict our domestic squabbles on you, but Pam is constantly incensed about a vast array of subjects. The latest is women not being allowed down South. Not that she wants to go herself. She's just outraged on behalf of all those women lining up to be included on polar expeditions. You know, that unruly crowd of female scientists on the dock, all clamouring to spend six months trapped in the dark with our body odour and smelly socks and swearing. And God forbid all the toilet seats left up.'

'Sarcasm is the last refuge of the defeated wit.' Pam shot an affectionately scornful look at her husband. 'The Heroic Age is over, darling. Women are making names for themselves in all fields of science. There's no rational reason they can't do the same in Antarctica. Just because something has always been a certain way doesn't make it right.' She waved her glass, clearly covering well-traversed territory. 'Look at slavery. Civil rights. The time will come when society looks back at us, unable to believe how stupidly conservative we were.' She glared at Andy in mock exasperation, then addressed Phil with a conciliatory expression. 'What *is* the Australian position on women in Antarctica?'

'No Australian women there yet. I think six ladies in total have been down so far, and only three of those actually landed. A Norwegian and two Americans.' Phil counted them off on his fingers. 'Mikkelsen's wife in '34, then Ronne and his chief pilot wintered over on Stonington Island with their wives in '47. That's it.'

'It looks like there's a precedent for the wives of expedition leaders, doesn't it? Bodes well for you.' Pam fixed Nel with a pointed look. 'Imagine what you'd paint,' she murmured and turned again to the art-lined walls.

~

Nel backed through the door into the pale blue dining room, four plates balanced on her arms.

'Penguins on horseback,' Phil announced from the head of the table, rubbing his palms together.

The penguin breasts, wrapped in shawls of bacon secured with toothpicks, crouched in their red wine marinade, looking lonely and forlorn on the large white plates. The first time she'd cooked them, Nel had felt her own chest compress with sympathy. Poor little things. How unimaginable, to live your life blissfully unaware of humans, only to end up as the exotic centrepiece of an Antarctic-themed dinner. She glanced at Pam. In her experience, scientists were likely to greet the dish with enthusiasm. Dissection was part of their training, after all. Wives, when in attendance, were harder to impress.

Phil topped up glasses. 'Mawson invented this dish himself on his 1911–14 expedition. Apparently, penguin was a menu staple on Mondays and Thursdays. Tuesdays and Fridays were seal.'

'Emperor?' asked Andy, poking his entree cautiously with a fork. Pam had yet to pick up her cutlery.

'Adélie.' Phil's tone implied this was an upgrade. 'Tastes like duck breast, but closer-grained. They can be a bit tough – like little hearts – but over the years Nel's developed a red wine marinade. Leaves them wonderfully tender.' Phil picked up his knife and fork and cut a piece off the breast, popping it into his mouth and chewing with evident enjoyment. He swallowed and continued, 'Weddell seal liver is actually my favourite. Nel cooks it up like lamb's fry. Delicious.'

Their guests exchanged a glance, before Andy took a deep breath and picked up his knife. He sawed into the pale meat, red wine oozing out to puddle on the white plate like diluted blood. Stabbing his fork into a bite-sized morsel, he raised it to his mouth, chewed thoughtfully, then swallowed. 'Not bad.'

Nel watched as Pam ate a wafer-thin slice of meat, immediately washing it down with a mouthful of wine. It was a little deflating. But

Nel imagined she'd feel just as much trepidation were the situation reversed, with Pam serving her a drumstick of bald eagle.

Pam glanced at Nel, then down at her plate with an apologetic smile. Nel grinned back and put down her own cutlery in a gesture of solidarity. Andy sawed another chunk off the hard little breast.

'Who knows when I'll have my next home-cooked meal?' he said through his mouthful. 'Now that's a great argument for women in Antarctica.' He raised his eyebrows and pointed his knife at his wife. 'The food would improve out of sight.'

Pam fixed her husband with a level expression, leaning back as Phil topped up her glass again.

'What?' Andy said. 'It's true. In fact, I think the improvement to morale would make an excellent case for your side.'

Pam took a long swallow of wine then shook her head. She turned to Nel. 'Unwitting condescension is my least favourite flavour of chauvinism.' Nel gave a snort of surprise and Pam grinned. 'Forgive me. *Of course*, the only reasons women would consider travelling South would be to cook and warm beds.'

'Hang on. That's not what I meant.' The bantering tone dropped from Andy's voice, but before he could mount a defence, Phil cut in.

'It's not a particularly pleasant environment down there, even for us.'

'Really? So hard it's physically impossible for a woman to survive?'

'Not physically impossible but—'

Pam was relentless. 'It's a social barrier, then? Maybe the answer is to allow some women down there. Let the men deal with it. Surely getting used to a few women on the base couldn't be as hard as doing all that *terribly complicated* science?' Pam laughed, raising her eyebrows.

Andy grinned around the table in a valiant attempt at restoring lightness. 'From my time on Macquarie Island, I've always felt some

of the blokes want to be down there *because* there aren't any women.'
Andy laughed. 'But not me, of course, darling. I can't get enough of
you. What man doesn't enjoy his every sentence being raked over for
accidental misogyny.'

'As long as it's accidental, darling. It's when I suspect it's deliberate, I
start cold-calling divorce attorneys.' Pam grinned back at her husband.

Phil said no more, but Nel knew that if there was one thing
guaranteed to raise his hackles, it was people who'd not been to
Antarctica having opinions about it. She took the opportunity to slip
away to the kitchen.

Ignoring the seal-liver pastries waiting in the oven, Nel leaned into
the open refrigerator, plucking the front of her dress away from her
damp torso and wondering if anyone would notice if she slipped off her
stockings. She looked down at her feet and felt a punch of grief at the
absence of Nefertiti's melancholic yowl and pale fur slinking around
her ankles. Her beloved cat would never have missed an opportunity
to emotionally blackmail her for a saucer of milk in front of an open
fridge.

Nel pulled the heavy salad bowl from the shelf and slammed the
door, feeling tears burning behind her eyes. Laughter floated in from
the dining room as though it had travelled a vast distance and, abruptly
aware that she'd been using the kitchen as a refuge, she swallowed back
her tears. She hastily dressed the salad, pulled the pockets of pastry
from the oven and arranged the food on the plates.

As Nel entered the dining room, two dishes balanced on each arm,
Phil recounted the meal's exotic provenance. For this course, he'd been
letting a Coonawarra merlot breathe, and now he poured it with a
flourish.

'Absolutely delicious.' Andy shovelled in a forkful, chewing
enthusiastically. As everyone focused on the food and wine, Pam

used the pause in conversation to put her elbows on the table and lean towards Nel.

'You have an amazing eye,' she said. 'A real talent for landscape.'

Taken by surprise, Nel gulped her mouthful, smiling and shaking her head as if refusing to let the compliment settle.

'Lately, I've been doing portrait commissions. Children mostly.' Nel's voice faded as she thought about the collection of sheet-shrouded canvases cluttering the corner of the laundry, accusing her like sharp-shouldered ghosts. The dusty, half-used tubes of oils, frozen in the same tortured positions for the last few months, ever since Nefertiti's death.

'Portraiture?' Pam frowned. 'I assumed you were a landscapist.'

Nel shot a glance at Phil. He met her gaze as if just as keen as Pam to hear her answer.

She took a gulp of wine. 'I can't say I love portraiture.' Nel gestured helplessly. 'But it pays. This doesn't.' She waved her glass at the polar seascape on the wall above the Danish sideboard. 'No one wants to buy paintings of places they know I've never seen.' She shrugged. 'I sell the odd work to scientists or colleagues of Phil's.'

'Huh.' Pam looked at the painting, head cocked. 'If I didn't *know* about using Phil's photographs ... And if you signed your paintings N. Law instead of Nel – I wouldn't have questioned they were painted on the ice.' She leaned in. 'What would you paint if you could do absolutely anything you wanted? Heart's desire material.'

Nel's eyes lifted to the canvas over the sideboard. She remembered chewing on the end of her brush, frowning at the photo she was working from. To her eye, the photograph's tones were over-saturated. Plus, the dramatic flash of lens flare made it difficult to gauge the clarity and quality of the light. But she couldn't quiz Phil on his memory of the scene. He'd been down at Mawson, still months from home.

Nel leaned forward, elbows on the table. 'I'd have to say *plein air* work. Growing up on a dairy farm, surrounded by the bush, I loved painting landscapes. The quiet and solitude. Being outside, nothing but me and the canvas. But these days, I do most of my painting while Phil's away. I can't just take off into the countryside on my own. So, I set myself up in the laundry and paint from photos.' She inclined her head towards the lounge room. 'Phil's photos are incredible. But not having seen it with my own eyes, I can't really tell how far I've missed the essence of it.' She trailed off, her cheeks reddening as she became aware of Phil watching her keenly, fingers plucking at the point of his beard.

Andy turned to him. 'Didn't some female scientists head down to Macquarie Island last year? So they can go halfway there, but they're banned from going to Antarctica itself?'

'It's the bloody department.' Phil's lips twisted in disgust. 'I'd give my eye teeth for Nel to come down with me.' He sat back in his chair, fingers fiddling with the base of his wine glass. 'Year after year, all she gets are the stories and the photographs.'

Nel stretched her hand towards him, patting the white tablecloth. 'Darling, it's fine.' She smiled consolingly at Phil before turning to Andy and Pam with a chuckle. 'No one is going to mistake me for Antarctic explorer material.'

'I just want them, the department, to acknowledge that the job has a ripple effect – they recognise the work is physically and psychologically hard. But what they don't see is how hard it is on those left behind. No one has been down there more often than me. Which means no one has been left behind more than Nel. All I want is for her to see for herself what takes me away for almost half the year, every year. To understand why I keep going back. I've told them I'd cover the costs. Food, berth, everything.' Phil spread his hands, before clenching them,

19

rapping his knuckles on the table. 'But according to the bean counters, if they let Nel go, everyone will want to bring their wives. "We're running a science division, not a tourist operation."' Phil's mimicry was acidic. 'Who do they think they're kidding? I can't even get them to fund the science properly. We have an opportunity to establish a world-class scientific facility down there. And all they want to pay for is someone to hoist the Australian flag every morning.'

Pam took another sip of wine. 'Sounds like you need a publicity campaign. Raise the profile of the science you're doing. Television. That's where the power is these days – that's where you need to be.' She waved a finger in Phil's direction.

Assuming her part in the conversation had ended, Nel began stacking empty dishes. As she moved to take Pam's plate the woman raised her glass in a gesture that looked like a private toast and she lightly touched Nel's upper arm with her other hand.

'An artist could be pretty useful in a publicity campaign,' she said to the table at large.

'Tried that.' Phil's tone echoed his weariness. 'We've taken photographers and filmmakers down there – made short documentaries to showcase everything we've achieved. And I still end up on my knees, begging for every shilling.'

'Hmm. I've seen some of those films,' Pam said. 'They're more anthropological records. Manly men doing manly deeds in the Land of Men.' She chuckled and leaned back in her chair.

Nel was entranced by this disdain for the rules. She saw Phil's chin tuck back towards his neck and widened her eyes at Pam. But the other woman was blind to the warning, and she swept back in before Phil could launch his defence.

'I don't mean it as an insult – that's just how those films come across. Occupational hazard.' Pam chuckled, even though Phil's eyes had narrowed. 'I'm a firm believer in the power of art to transform the way we think. And sometimes art comes dressed as advertising. Or propaganda.' Pam raised her eyebrows and pinned Nel with a meaningful look. 'Or someone who can show people the wonder of a place in a way that's not buried out of sight in a scientific paper or a textbook.'

Phil's voice had a cool undercurrent. 'But we're not down there because it's beautiful. We're there so we can understand how it works. I can't argue for more funding because it's pretty. It's all about the danger and difficulty.' Phil's gaze sliced away from Pam to Andy.

Pam was not so easily dismissed. 'Of course, the science is important. I'm married to the Emperor of Insects. I get it.' She laughed, slapping Andy on the shoulder a little too hard, so that a tiny wave of red wine sloshed over the rim of her glass to stain the white tablecloth. Pam mopped at the blotch with her napkin. 'Just imagine how the media would respond. A woman in Antarctica. Who paints. Who sees something more than the thickness of ice sheets or the exploitability of oil reserves.' She set her glass down with a *thunk*. 'Things invisible to science can be brought into the light by art. Imagine the Australian public suddenly captured by the romance of Antarctica. *That* would put your work on the map. Or at the very least in the news.'

Phil drummed his fingers on the stem of his glass. After a long moment, he wobbled his head. 'They'd never allow it. Officially.' He frowned at his wine before breaking into a devilish grin. 'As expedition leader, I have my own cabin. With two bunks. If someone were to sneak on board ... hide in the cabin until the ship was out at sea?' He looked across at Nel.

Nel's mouth dropped open. Was he *serious*? It was true, Phil had often said he wished she could come with him, but she'd always

21

thought it was just something he said to ease the separation, to reassure her that he missed her, that Antarctica was just a job – his version of scrawling *wish you were here* on a postcard.

Of course, she'd love to go. She swiftly corrected herself: she'd love to paint it. To see it with her own eyes, translate it onto canvas in her own style. But stowing away? How on earth would that work? Nel shook her head. 'You know I'd love it, but, darling, you'd lose your job.'

'As they say, it's easier to ask for forgiveness than permission.' Phil barked out a laugh. 'And sticking it up those stuffed departmental shirts has always been a dream.'

Pam leaned forward, pressing her glass into the table. 'This couldn't be more perfect. The first Australian woman in Antarctica. A female artist among a herd of male scientists. And a stowaway to boot. The headlines practically write themselves.' She threw back her head in a triumphant laugh. 'And they say art history is a useless discipline.'

'Thank God I don't let her travel with her slide projector anymore.' Andy chuckled. 'You can imagine the lectures. And lack of return invitations.' Pam grinned and Phil laughed good-humouredly, but Nel noticed calculation lingering in the furrow of her husband's brow. Was he seriously considering this alcohol-fuelled fantasy?

Phil pushed back his chair. 'Well, that was delicious,' he announced, rolling his shoulders and tilting his chin to the ceiling. He turned to Andy, raising his eyebrows. 'Whisky?'

At his guest's nod, Phil plucked two crystal tumblers from the sideboard, ushering Andy towards the lounge. Over the stained tablecloth and dirty crockery, the women's eyes met.

'Are you headed back home as soon as the ship sails?' Nel asked as she picked up the stack of dirty plates.

Pam collected the wine glasses. 'No. I'm off to Sydney to do some research while he's on Macquarie, then we'll sail home together. I've got a semester's sabbatical from the university, so I don't have anything to rush back for. The last few weeks have been a bit of a shock to the system, to be honest. All this free time and a husband always *there*.' Pam smiled, the glassware clanking in her hands. 'I love the man, but I'll admit to being quite keen to wave him off from the dock.'

Nel laughed in recognition, the uneasy mix of anxiety and envy that had been squeezing her chest all night finally releasing her from its grip. 'Are you free at all over the next few days? Have you been to the National Gallery of Victoria?'

'Thought you'd never ask!' Pam chocked the door open with her elbow as Nel moved into the kitchen. 'I had a quick nose around a couple of days ago, but the whole time I was thinking what I really need is a local. Someone who knows her stuff and who doesn't mind having her brain picked. You, my dear, would be perfect.'

Nel stacked the dishes on the drainboard and wiped her wrist across her damp forehead.

'These can wait. Let's head outside. I'm wilting. Drink?' At Pam's grateful nod, she took two fresh glasses from the cupboard and a bottle of wine from the fridge.

The pair made their way through the lounge, ignoring their husbands, now deep in conversation. Nel slid open the door and the women slipped into the backyard, the night air still thick with the last of the day's heat.

Pam looked at Nel, smiling widely as she sipped from her glass. 'Lady, we're getting you on that ship. Saturday – art gallery. Sunday? Reconnaissance mission. We're getting ourselves a tour of the *Magga Dan* and coming up with a plan. Looks like Phil's already on board. Next step? Charm offensive on the captain.' Pam fixed Nel with a meaningful look and clinked their glasses with more force than an ordinary toast. 'This is happening.'

Above the tree line, a flash of electricity split the sky and a wave of sound lumbered towards them. The patio door slid open but neither woman turned as the two men joined them.

Another flash, and as the thunder trampled across the sky, Nel felt the cool change roll in, chilling the sweat on her skin. She lifted her face to the breeze, the night's conversation playing through her mind. It was a terrifying thought. Going to Antarctica. The possibility had never occurred to her. She'd just blindly accepted it was a place she didn't belong. Where women didn't belong.

She looked across at Pam. Before tonight, she'd never thought to question the rules or why she obeyed them.

A wave of cloud reeled across the sky, and she felt the wind's cool breath against her skin. It wouldn't be easy. The plan was barely an hour old and already nervous dread was slithering through her gut. But she'd be with Phil. He'd look after her.

Phil squeezed her shoulders, and she leaned back against him, her arms prickling from the chill. Maybe this was what she needed to get her life back, leave this empty house behind and lever off the weight of grief. Maybe this was what would transform her from painter into artist. A real artist. The kind who had exhibitions. The fog that had been clouding her since Nefertiti's death began to thin, her vision sharpening to focus on a distant horizon.

'Sou'westerly,' Phil murmured in her ear. 'Straight from Antarctica.'

Nel closed her eyes, a smile curving her lips for an instant before the image of unwashed dishes rose behind her eyelids. Inside his arms, she held her ribs steady so he wouldn't feel her sigh.

Rose Madder

Camberwell, Melbourne
November 1960

Nel shifted on the parquet floor, easing the ache in her knees. She slid her bottom off the cup of her heels and tucked her legs to the side. Only a couple of years ago she could kneel comfortably on the floor for hours. These days, her forty-six-year-old joints complained with almost every movement. She swiped a cushion off the couch, tucked it beneath her hips and leaned into Phil's arm.

Sitting cross-legged beside her, he glanced over, eyes bright with mischief. In front of them, a huge map of Antarctica was spread across the lounge room floor, its corners held flat with four specimens from Phil's rock collection, mica and crystals glittering in the lamplight.

Even now, poring over this map of previously forbidden territory, surrounded by papers laddered with lists of all the clothing and equipment she'd need, she could feel the heavy lid of grief fitted tight over the excitement simmering in her gut. Nefertiti, her darling Siamese, would have approved of this floor-based activity. Nel imagined her padding across the map, tail swishing in their faces, before sprawling across the section where their attention was focused.

It was three months since her death. No goodbye. Thinking about it, the muscle of Nel's heart compressed into something cramped and black and infinitely heavier than her body could possibly hold. She'd been dreading Phil leaving on this voyage. Even his regular workdays at the office stranded her, the house so still and quiet her breath bounced off the walls. If she didn't go with Phil, these looming months would be the first time she'd been completely alone in twelve years. Nel took a deep breath, ticking her fingernail against the grey glitter of the Erebus feldspar weighting the map near her knee.

At the centre of the chart, Antarctica floated like a huge albino tadpole caught in the perfect net of longitude and latitude cast across the South Pole. The tail of the Antarctic Peninsula whipped west towards the tip of South America, but Phil's attention was focused on the opposite side, where the wedge of the Australian Antarctic Territory covered almost a third of the entire continent.

'So ...' Phil swept his hand across the map as if smoothing it, before tapping his finger on Melbourne at the very edge of the chart. 'The ship is scheduled to depart from Port Melbourne next week. November 29.' He looked across at her, an eyebrow raised. 'If you've got all your gear together, we can smuggle you on board at dawn. You'll stow everything in my cabin, making sure it's hidden, just in case anyone sticks their head in. We don't want your frocks and makeup giving the game away before we're at sea.'

The creases of Phil's face morphed from mischief into concern. 'If you're not ready, that's fine, too. There's no shame in shelving this idea for now and setting our sights on next season. That would give you until next October to have everything ready.' He cocked his head at her. 'But that vessel sails from Perth. You'd have to ship all your gear, and yourself, out west.'

Nel's eyes widened. 'I'm not about to sit for days on a train or boat all by myself, getting more and more nervous.'

His voice was carefully neutral. 'You could fly?'

'You know full well that is out of the question.'

Phil slipped his arm around her shoulders and pulled her close. She could feel his lips in her hair. 'When you think about it, darling, sailing is just like flying. All that space beneath you. It's just water rather than air.'

She pulled away from him. 'I thought you *wanted* me to come?'

'I do!' He seemed genuinely shocked. 'I'm only trying to show you how illogical it all is.' He took her hand and kissed it. 'I'm sorry, my love. You know I think you are one of the most impressive women in the world. But this irrational fear of heights holds you back. How are you ever going to see the art galleries of Europe if you won't fly? I'm never going to have the months of leave it would take to get us there by ship.'

Nel slipped out from under his arm. 'I know.'

'Honestly, when you've done it once, you'll wonder what you were ever afraid of.' He leaned his forehead against hers. 'And I'll be right there beside you. I promise.'

She swallowed, wishing she could say exactly what she needed from him, but not knowing how to put words around it. More than holding her hand when she needed it and less than trying to convince her she was being irrational. This was all such new territory. In their twenty years of marriage, they'd never been anywhere that couldn't be reached by car or train. And she'd certainly never travelled to a place that didn't welcome even the idea of women.

For years, she'd listened to Phil's stories of wild seas, blizzards and polar mountaineering, yet only now did it occur to her how much she didn't know. What would she need as the first Australian woman to reach the bottom of the world? Support, she guessed. For him to be there for her just as he was now – the way their marriage had been from the very beginning – leaning into each other, speaking the same language. Yes, he'd be busy, but she knew her husband skin to bone. She didn't doubt for a minute that, for him, she'd be the most important person on the ship. He'd be right there, whenever she needed him. Plus, she'd be surrounded by voices and energy and adventure. Not wandering around this silent house with empty arms and a weight in her chest.

There were many reasons not to go. Lack of preparation. Fear. The skinlessness of grief. And there were signs she was approaching the change. She no longer recognised herself; the mirror was no longer her friend, blunt to the brink of rudeness. And the changes were more than just weight gain, dry skin and hot flushes. Emotionally, she'd been on a hair-trigger for months, sliding from anger to sadness to anxiety to rage without warning or reason. Even before losing Nefertiti. She wanted to hide from the eyes of strangers, from Phil, from herself. At this moment, a sea journey as the only woman on board possibly wasn't the best idea.

Perhaps Pam was wrong and everyone else was right – women didn't belong down there. But she suspected her new friend had a point, and everyone else was lazily falling back on tradition and assumptions about women being too delicate and emotional. She'd been one of those lazy traditionalists. Recognising that truth was one of the reasons her brief time with Pam had moved her so profoundly. Perhaps now, weighed down with loss and not wanting to spend another minute inside this house full of absence and silence, was the perfect time to throw everything to the wind and step forward into strange, new territory.

She quashed the flicker of anxiety trying to spark itself into flame and leaned over the map. 'Show me where we're headed.'

To her surprise, Phil pushed himself off the floor, holding out a finger as he moved first to the radiogram and then the drinks trolley. Beethoven's Ninth and a gin and tonic. Nel smiled. How like Phil to elevate this into an occasion. She accepted the tumbler and waited for him to settle himself beside her on the floor.

She remembered the night, eight or so years ago, Phil had crouched on this very same bit of floor, Douglas Mawson perched on the edge of the pouffe, the two men poring over aerial photos of Antarctic coastline, choosing the best site for the first permanent Australian base. No music or drinks, that night, Nel serving and keeping Nefertiti from getting underfoot. Sir Douglas was more dog than cat person.

Phil had been devastated when the great man died, just over a year ago. In her less generous moments, Nel thought her husband had showed more emotion at the loss of his hero than of their precious girl. But she couldn't deny Phil had been unfailingly kind in the face of her grief – sliding a cup of tea onto her bedside table each morning, eating everything on his dinner plate, despite the meat being dry and vegetables boiled to mash, never mentioning the mountain of laundry, knotting his ties around collars left grimy and unstarched. And now, here he was, transforming this planning session into a tiny celebration.

Phil tapped Melbourne, where the south coast of Australia peeked from the border of the map. 'This will be the most important voyage this season. We'll get the resupplies done first, as quickly as possible, to give us maximum time for the exploration of Oates Land at the end.'

'How long?'

'A couple of weeks, I hope.'

'What? The whole voyage?'

'Oh. I thought you meant the exploration. All up? Three months. It depends on the ice conditions. By March, it's thickening fast. As soon as the sea ice starts building up, that's the end of exploring and we'll have to head home. Otherwise we risk getting trapped. And that would be a disaster. We'd be stuck in the ice all winter. Until September, maybe October.'

'*October?*'

'When the sea ice starts to break up again. But it won't come to that. Look.' Phil picked up a pencil and began tracing a trail of dashes from Port Melbourne past Tasmania and down into the great hoop of the Southern Ocean encircling Antarctica. 'First stop is Macquarie Island.' His dotted line stopped at the cigar-shaped island floating halfway between Tasmania and the Antarctic coast.

'That's where Andy and the four Macquarie women get off, right?'

'Along with the other scientists and mechanics and whatnot. We'll spend a few days unloading food and fuel and equipment – then we push on down to Mawson.'

Phil pencilled his line from Macquarie Island south-west across the Southern Ocean towards the dot of Mawson Station, just above the Amery Ice Shelf in Mac Robertson Land, at the most distant edge of the Australian Antarctic Territory.

Phil grinned at her. 'That's where you'll make your historic landing. First Australian woman to set foot on Antarctica.'

Nel bounced a little on her cushion. 'How long to get there?'

'It's a long push against the circumpolar current. Early in the new year, I'd say.'

'And I'll be able to paint once I'm there, won't I?'

'You'll have nothing to do *but* paint.' Phil stretched his back. 'Once *Magga* docks at Mawson, we'll be changing over men and supplies. It'll take a few days at least. The men we're picking up will have been down there for fifteen months and we're unloading supplies to last the new men through the winter and to the end of the year, just in case the next ships can't get through.'

Nel's eyebrows rose. Every year Phil was gone for months on end, some years as many as five months in twelve, but that was always through the summer season. He'd never stayed through a polar winter. Fifteen months. What would that do to a man? She pursed her lips. Well, she'd soon find out. She'd be sailing with a whole shipful of them.

'Once we've finished the changeover and resupply, there'll be a few days of the old hands training the newcomers. Then we'll head east along the coast, all the way to Chick Island.' Phil's pencil line traced a passage along the coast skirting the huge wedge of Australian territory made from Princess Elizabeth Land, Kaiser Wilhelm II Land, Queen Mary Land and Wilkes Land. He tapped a minuscule dot off the coast, so small Nel squinted to see it. 'We're building another automated weather station to send meteorological data back to Australia without having to have any men on the ground.'

Nel nodded, her eyes on the map. The dotted line was so long – this was a huge undertaking. What was she letting herself in for? 'Then we head home?'

'Not yet. This is the most exciting bit!' His eyes sparked with anticipation, yet Nel could see a tightening at the corners of his mouth. Of course. How could she have forgotten? Oates Land.

Phil's pencil line skipped across the thin sliver of French territory and drew closer to Oates Land, the grey of the line deepening to almost black with the pressure of his hand.

'Every minute we have left between building the meteorological station and the ice closing in we'll be using to explore this bit of coast. The Russians know time is running out before the Antarctic Treaty comes into effect next year, and they're putting men on the ground wherever they can, staking last-minute claims to as much territory as possible. This region ...' Phil pointed at Oates Land, the chock of terrain between the thin French slice of Terre Adélie and the larger

New Zealand wedge covering the great bite of the Ross Ice Shelf. 'This is what they're after. No one's managed to get close enough to even map it properly. I've tried. God help me. But every year something gets in the way.'

Phil tapped the end of the pencil on the map, a rapid staccato, his knuckles whitening. 'If it's not the ice conditions, it's the timing or some bloody piece of equipment fails. Or if I do manage to get an aircraft over it, I can't get them to land. But this year' – he expelled a breath like a pressure cooker venting – 'if I keep the men on a tight schedule, we can maximise our time there before the ice closes in. And ...' He stared at the map for a long second before looking up at her. 'I'll have my lucky charm with me.'

She smiled, hoping a glow of optimism lit her face. She remembered last year, the contrast between his excitement when she hugged him goodbye and the slump of his shoulders when she'd welcomed him home. Oates Land had eluded him yet again. At the end of each polar season, he had one run at it and every year something stood in his way. The ice had closed in early. The captain had lost his nerve. Equipment. Sea ice. Bureaucracy. Weather. It was his ultimate goal. The chance to be more than a leader. To hear his name spoken in the same breath as his heroes: Mawson, Shackleton, Wilkins, Scott.

She remembered when Phil had been offered this job with the newly formed Australian National Antarctic Research Expeditions program, the fire in his eyes at the prospect of fieldwork after the dryness of the classroom. Lecturing in Physics at Melbourne University, he'd had to steal moments of adventure during semester breaks hiking in the Snowies and Grampians.

In the blink of an eye, he'd been promoted from science officer to expedition leader to director of ANARE. He was in his element, bursting with drive and energy. He had such vision – Antarctica as a place of science with Australia at the forefront, a world-class scientific facility. But all that accomplishment happened against a backdrop of quiet stability. She left her job as a schoolteacher to create it, tending their home as he conquered the South. She didn't mind. Even when they decided children were off the cards, with so many months apart each year and Phil not just away, but completely beyond reach. It wouldn't be fair on her, he said, managing a household and family all alone. Or on the children growing up with an absent father. Left unsaid was that it wouldn't be fair on him to miss being at the helm of such important work. His would be a career for the history books. He bought her a cat, and they'd agreed their tiny household was complete. And now, with her body changing, the chance to edit this story had passed. *Too late for regrets.* Nel shook her head free of such thoughts, swirling the ice in her glass.

'Once we've spent as much time as possible in Oates Land – claiming territory, mapping, taking astro-fixes – we'll speed north before the ice closes in.' He took a long swallow of his drink. 'Then it's just a quick hop back up to Macquarie Island, pick up the scientists and the women, and home.' Phil slapped her lightly on the knee. 'What do you think? Sound exciting enough?'

Nel was quiet, staring at the spot where Phil's dotted line had stopped, in the ocean next to the coast of Oates Land.

'Look, I admit we'll be cutting it fine, but I'd never put you in any real danger. I've not been trapped in the ice yet.'

Phil pushed himself to his feet and paced across to the radiogram, flipping the record to side B. The stirring voices accompanying the final movement of Beethoven's Ninth flooded the room.

'And think of all the painting you can do. Seeing everything with your own eyes. Darling, you'll love it. I promise.' He crouched down beside her. 'If nothing else, I think it will take your mind off things.'

Nel pressed her lips together, gazing down at the map. She stood at the fork of two roads: one she knew, a well-worn path leading her through empty months in this house heavy with silence. The other led through the wilderness. Eyes unfocused, she took a deep breath, imagining herself returning home laden with art: oils, sketches, watercolours. It was almost like looking at a different person – a practising artist, someone sought after for newspaper articles, courted for exhibitions. She saw herself standing in a gallery, her paintings lining the walls, red dots glowing from the tiny labels beside them. She let out a long slow breath. 'All right.' She nodded, reaching for the equipment list.

Nel watched Phil as he drained his glass, tucking this night into her memory. Perhaps this moment would become the pivot on which her life turned to the sun, the shadow of Nefertiti's death stretching behind her – still there, of course, but where she would need to turn back to see it.

Phil hugged her, the breath gusting from her lungs in surprise at the vigour of it. She could feel his mouth pressing against her curls, kissing her hair, before he took her face in his hands and kissed her with more enthusiasm than she could remember over the past few months.

Releasing her face from the cup of his hands, he squeezed her again for a long beat. Then, glancing once more at the map, he picked up an eraser and began rubbing out the long pencil loop of their planned journey. When he'd finished, he brushed the soft rubbings away with the back of his hand, the map returned to pristine white.

Nel pushed the four rocks from their corners, the map immediately curling itself into a long roll. Snapping a rubber band around it, she carried it and the rocks across the hall. She left the map perched on top of the papers and files cluttering the desk in Phil's office, then slipped into the third bedroom. Flipping on the light, the crystalline glitter of mica and minerals leapt from the shelves lining the walls. Nel placed the rocks back in their spaces. She didn't need to check the neatly printed catalogue cards beneath each sample. She'd dusted this collection every week for years. In the kitchen, she could hear Phil rinsing the glasses in the sink, and by the time she stepped back into the lounge, it was as if the planning session had never happened.

Scarlet Lake

Port Melbourne
November 1960

Nel stood on the wharf in the granular dawn, gazing up at the red wall of steel. A bolt of excitement ripped through her, and she pressed a gloved hand to her chest, the crocodile-skin handbag banging against her hip. With its red masts and sea-silvered rigging, the ship looked cheerful among the grey military vessels and staid passenger liners moored along the piers of Port Melbourne. Far above her head, white letters glowed against scarlet on the ice-strengthened bow. *Magga Dan*.

She turned to Phil, but he'd moved further along the wharf, making sure the coast was clear for her to board. Keeping the whole plan hush-hush had been devilishly difficult and her nerves were wire tight.

Yesterday's heat still hovered in the air, ready to add itself to this day's blistering temperatures. Overhead, the bunting swayed listlessly; the dock was quiet and empty. It was hard to believe that later in the day the pier would be thronged with noise and people: well-wishers, reporters and people curious to see Antarctic explorers in the flesh.

How strange to think after all these years *she* was about to join that exclusive club.

Close to the wharf, the sea was glassy with a thick rainbow sheen, slugging against the great wooden pylons with dull claps. Nel took a deep breath of salt-tinged air, straightened her sunglasses and smoothed the red and white polka-dot silk scarf covering her dramatically trimmed hair. She wasn't overly keen on the effect, but she was sure she'd be thankful for the low-maintenance style when she found herself in a land without hair salons.

Nel could feel sweat dampening the back of her girdle and under her breasts. Despite the early hour, she was dressed for a full day of official events. It was imperative she maintain the illusion of being here to wave her husband off on this expedition. These dawn hours were her only chance to slip into their cabin and unpack her considerable luggage. Every item of clothing, plus all her toiletries and art supplies, had to be crammed into the drawers and cupboards, so should anyone peek inside while touring the ship, her belongings would be hidden or camouflaged among Phil's.

A seagull landed on a cleat securing the bow deckline to the wharf, balancing itself with wings outstretched like a disgruntled angel before folding them neatly away and opening its orange beak with a guttural squawk. Nel winced behind her dark glasses as she trotted to catch up with Phil, her heels loud on the wooden planks. It had been a hot, sleepless night and the gin and tonics she'd downed to steady her nerves hadn't helped. She touched Phil's arm, gesturing towards the slatted gangway with her chin.

She had imagined stepping onto the gangway for the first time as a stowaway with heady delight, the romance and adventure nestled in the word thrumming through her body. But now the electricity in her veins felt corrosive. This was it. The final decision.

Phil was putting on a great show of nonchalance, but she knew he must be worried about the potential fallout. The danger of being fired for smuggling her on board was real. But he'd kept all his worries far from the surface and answered her increasingly detailed questions with a limitless capacity for reassurance. She stepped onto the deck, leaning on the rail to gaze over the Yarra and Port Melbourne, the water sparkling ferociously in the increasing light.

Inside, *Magga Dan* seemed larger than she'd appeared from the dock. And air-conditioned, Nel noted with relief. The many floors, corridors and steep stairways linking everything made the interior feel expansive yet intimate. Phil directed her to their cabin, even though she knew the way from previous pre-departure tours. It was tradition for the expedition leader to entertain favoured guests before departure in the stateroom he used as his office. The cabin she'd be sharing with him was right next door.

Their berth was wood-lined and snug and Nel approved of the sleek Scandinavian lines of the teak cabinetry and the lovely little porthole with its circular brass trim.

'I've got some interviews to do before showing the minister around ... can I leave you to it?' Phil hadn't even made it the whole way into the cabin. He hovered in the doorway, the line between his brows telling her he had weightier things on his mind than helping her unpack. These final hours were always his least favourite. All he wanted was to make sure the expedition cargo and logistics were completely ready, yet he ended up dancing to the tune of the reporters and shaking all the right hands.

'Of course. Go. I've got my work cut out for me here. I won't show my face until this room is ready to pass inspection.' Nel gave a mock salute, kissed him on the cheek and pushed him out the door, closing it behind him with a businesslike click.

She threw her handbag on a slender bunk and plopped down beside it. Sweat pricked at her temples and dampened the fabric under her arms. If she wasn't careful, this sense of overwhelm was going to paralyse her. *Idle hands are the devil's tools, old girl.*

Not once in all these years had she ever truly considered this might happen. *I'd love you to come with me,* was something Phil said, but there had never been real weight behind it. Yet here she was, hiding gear in her cabin, the sentence now terrifyingly concrete. Everything was flowing around her. All she'd done was give herself over to the current.

With a shuddering breath, she plucked off her gloves, stripped the silk scarf from her head and flipped up the latch on the nearest trunk. Phil's kit was already stowed, so she forced his clothes as far along the wardrobe rail as she could. Her clothes looked ridiculously bright and new as she hung them next to Phil's dull, weather-beaten gear, so worn it seemed to hold the ghost of his body on the hanger.

She'd ended up with almost three times as much clothing as Phil. Hiding all her colourful shipboard wear behind Phil's was fiendishly difficult when her outfits outshone and outnumbered his so dramatically. She slid open drawers and stuffed her striped shirts and bright silk scarves behind Phil's dull long johns and thick skivvies.

Next she stacked her folded underwear and jumpers in the drawers as quickly and quietly as she could. By the time she reached the last pieces, she was cramming them in, pressing everything extra flat to slide the drawers shut. Fear of discovery was playing havoc with her coordination. *Hasten slowly,* she whispered to herself, stepping lightly around the cabin, trying not to bang cupboards or clank the lids on her trunks.

Finding appropriate clothing had been such a challenge, and not just because she was searching for winter wear in the height of summer. Female equivalents to Phil's extreme-weather gear simply did not exist. She'd ended up purchasing a series of layers and suspected that out on the ice she'd probably be so solid and weighty that movement and flexibility would be seriously hampered. The one positive was that everything was nylon, except for her gorgeous new angora turtleneck and cotton brassieres. While she wasn't wild about the feel of these newfangled synthetics, they were quick to dry. The cabin would probably look like a laundry within the week, but at least she wouldn't smell fusty.

At the bottom of the hanging space, Nel pushed Phil's mukluks to one side. The boots' fleecy lambswool lining, hard soles and waterproof outer layer made them so bulky she wondered how on earth he managed to walk. She slid her own version into place beside them: a pair of two-toned golf shoes that looked more like spats than expedition wear. It was ridiculous, really. The thought of her crunching through snow or across slippery ice floes in only woolly socks and a pair of golf shoes! But these were what Phil recommended – to her and the four Macquarie women. At least they were more stylish than Phil's footwear. She'd just have to hope they provided some insurance against frostbite and landing on her bottom. At the thought of the ice, her smile faded, all the lounge room horror stories of death and frostbite rushing in. The skin on her forearms knobbled, the hairs rising. Sporty was hardly a word anyone would use to describe her. Was this madness?

She sat back on her heels. There was no denying the danger. Men died down there. She took a steadying breath. There was no one more experienced than Phil. And he'd never put her in danger. Besides, she was there to paint – sitting behind an easel was hardly as perilous as dog-sledding or mountaineering.

The drawers and cupboards were full to bursting and she had yet to unpack her art supplies and toiletries. Her most obviously feminine piece of luggage, a burgundy cosmetics case the size and shape of a hatbox, was so full the brass clasp was straining with the pressure. She shoved it deep into the space beneath her bunk and arranged Phil's photographic equipment in front. The rest of Phil's gear – flash bulbs, tripods and rolls of film for the Leica, battery rechargers for the walkie-talkies, rolls of maps and cartography supplies – she left in boxes, stacking them neatly under his bunk and the small writing desk.

The last set of items to hide, her sanitary cloths and belt, she tucked at the back of the bottom drawer. At home, she used a special bucket in the laundry and hung them to dry on a short clothesline well out of sight of neighbours' eyes. She wasn't quite sure how she'd manage the soaking and drying in this tiny cabin – she'd have to make do. If Phil came face to face with a series of flannels hanging in the bathroom, he'd just have to be understanding. Thank goodness her monthlies had become less frequent. The downside was her cycle had gone from dependable to completely haphazard, so she had no idea how many times she'd need the cloths during the journey.

She sank down on the bunk, folded her hands in her lap and surveyed the cabin. The place was still a dog's breakfast, but at least nothing obviously signalled the presence of a woman.

~

Nel paused on the threshold of Captain Pedersen's stateroom, smoothing her dress against her thighs. The teak-panelled room was airless, the men's shirts damp beneath their arms and down their spines, faces gleaming with sweat above buttoned collars and ties. She needed a drink. Keeping a smile in place, Nel moved towards a well-dressed group clustered near the porthole. Captain Wilhelm Pedersen – or Bill, as he insisted – moved to her side, handing her a crystal champagne saucer, which he immediately filled.

Nel nodded politely as Bill introduced her to the group. Gripping the stem of her glass, she realised she'd missed every name except that of Mrs Gorton. This name had stuck because Senator Gorton, the Minister for External Affairs, was the man holding the power to grant or deny any request Phil made for additional funding or equipment. And decide the severity of Phil's punishment once Nel's presence on the voyage was revealed. Nel cast around the room for her husband. He was caught in conversation on the far side of the captain's desk with the premier and the lord mayor, both recognisable from their regular appearances on the front page of *The Age*.

'I can't imagine how hard it must be. Three months without your husband!' The long vowels of Mrs Gorton's soft Canadian drawl took Nel by surprise. The dark-haired woman leaned close. 'Although some days, I definitely envy you.' She chuckled, nodding towards the senator.

Nel smiled, as much for herself as for Mrs Gorton. 'Right now, I wish Phil was waving *me* off, if only to escape this heat.'

'Ladies, may I interest you in a tour of the ship?' Bill Pedersen appeared at her elbow. He topped up the women's drinks, then gestured courteously for Mrs Gorton to precede him towards the door. Inclining his head down to Nel, he murmured, 'Phil told me you're accompanying us.'

Nel stiffened. Her eyes darted around the room. Had anyone overheard?

He lifted his palms as if gentling a skittish deer. 'I just wanted to let you know you have my blessing.' He gestured up towards the deck, his Danish accent clipped yet soft. 'Now, let's proceed as if nothing is out of the ordinary. Shall we?'

Over the next couple of hours, Nel trailed the captain as he led a sweaty conga line of dignitaries through the ship, from the deepest hold to the broad-windowed bridge. Ensconced in the air-conditioned comfort of the wheelhouse, Bill pointed out all the newfangled technology: the double radar, gyro compass, windscreen demisters and smoke detectors. The group traipsed back along the corridors and through the heavy door to the forward bow, huddling in any shade they could find as Bill pointed to the crow's nest and explained how the tiny capsule could be accessed from within the hollow mast, so that in bad weather, he could steer the ship through cracks in the ice while perched aloft.

He left the most popular spot, the kennels, until last. The dogs were already locked inside their individual cages, barking and leaping against the bars as they clamoured for attention.

Nel crouched beside the last cage in the long row of kennels and tugged off her gloves. The husky was wagging its tail so energetically its bottom was practically bouncing from wall to wall, the water bowl at risk of spilling its precious contents. Nel reached through the mesh, sinking her fingers into its fur. The dog's coat was so thick she could barely worm her fingers deep enough to feel skin.

'You poor, poor loves.' Mrs Gorton was patting the next dog along, its pale eyes fastened on hers with an almost otherworldly intensity. 'I know just how you feel,' the Canadian crooned to the husky, who pressed its head against the bars, tongue lolling from the side of its mouth as her fingers scratched behind its ears. 'We're both snow creatures, completely out of our element in this heat.'

Nel straightened. Activity on the deck was intensifying, the crew bustling to stow and secure the last of the gear. It was clear the group of tourists were in the way, yet the men hid any impatience, smiling and nodding as they sidestepped the formally attired bystanders, now openly sweating in their suits and cocktail dresses. It was a relief when the captain finally shepherded them all back inside for last drinks. Nel let herself be carried along with the group, grateful to have got this far without being challenged, or telling an outright lie.

Too nervous to read or sketch, Nel slumped on her bunk, waiting for Phil. Her gut churned as she listened to the laughter and deep voices rumbling through the wood-panelled wall from the stateroom next door.

The cabin door opened and in the split second it took to recognise her husband, it was all she could do to smother a shriek. But instead of closing the door behind him, Phil held it open – for Senator and Mrs Gorton. Nel leapt to her feet.

Mrs Gorton edged past her husband to embrace Nel, whose eyes widened over the woman's shoulder, darting between the two men. The senator smiled, not appearing the least shocked at her presence.

'Phil explained everything.' The senator's smile was gentle as he ran a finger under his collar. 'We were discussing ways to make ANARE more relevant to the public and protect it from bureaucratic negligence, when he dropped your little bombshell. Of course, I was shocked at first, but I think it's just the thing we need to shake things up.' The two men shared a wry glance before the senator continued, 'I'm sure there'll be a bit of heat from the department. As you know, they don't like to pass up any opportunity to put your husband in his place. But rest assured, you have my official green light. I'll tell them I knew all about it from the beginning, and you'll be sharing his cabin, which has an extra berth that would've otherwise been unoccupied.' He turned to Phil. 'That should put them back in their box.'

With a cry of relief, Nel flung her arms around Mrs Gorton, and only just kept herself from doing the same to the senator. 'I'll paint you a landscape. And Phil will name something after you, won't you, Phil? Something important. An island. Or a mountain range. Once we get to Oates Land.'

Phil smiled, relief in the lines of his body.

The close air of the cabin and *Magga Dan's* looming departure brought the meeting to a swift end. Once the door closed behind the Gortons, Nel turned to Phil, who took her hands in his and drew her down to sit next to him on the bunk. She listened in a daze as he recounted the conversation that had led him to confide in the senator. It had been a risk, he said, but also too good an opportunity to pass up. Now they could embark with easier minds.

Nel nodded in agreement, and was relieved when Phil said he had to make an appearance on deck. She needed to lie down. She might have official approval, but, aside from Phil and the captain, her presence would still be a shock to everyone else on board.

The bedside clock ticked loudly as she lay on her bunk, shoes still on her feet, nerves stretched to snapping, champagne roiling in her gut. The cheers of the crowd gathered on the dock filtered in through the porthole, but she stayed low, too anxious to peek out in case she was spotted.

Finally, *Magga Dan* moved beneath her, the engines thrumming up through the mattress as the ship, oh-so slowly, moved clear of the wharf.

The horn blared one long, magisterial note and as she lay on the bunk she could hear the cheering from the wharf fade to silence.

~

Beyond the portholes, open water. She was at sea. Not yet in international waters, but beyond the reach of the department. She should feel relieved. She should be floating on air. But propped beside Phil in the dining saloon, she felt hollow, only her bones and self-respect holding her upright in the booth. The long hours of tension had run her emotional batteries dry. The room was hot and close, the smell of

45

sweat, cigarettes and Brylcreem making her light-headed as deep-voiced banter filled the air.

A steady flow of men trooped in, boots muffled on the carpet. This was the first time Nel had seen the entire ship's company in one place. It was easy to tell the ship's crew from the expeditioners, even without the distinction of the crew's uniform. The Danish seamen were all tanned and well muscled, and, while jovial with each other, they held themselves slightly apart from the other men with a proud Viking air. The expeditioners were all neatly dressed in grey trousers and short sleeves. To a man, all were clean-shaven, which Phil assured her wouldn't last long – shaving being the first habit to fall away down South. But there was something about the way the groups spoke and carried themselves that made Nel suspect a divide existed between the scientists and the crew that went deeper than clothing and facial hair.

There was one thing that appeared to unite the entire company – shock at her presence. No one would meet her eyes, yet she felt scrutinised. It was the strangest feeling – as if she was both invisible and under a microscope at the same time. She kept her head high, smile perfectly calibrated as she scanned the saloon, the men's gazes slithering away as her own approached. Her cheeks ached from keeping her facade in place. She took a sip of her drink.

The room was nearly at capacity when four demurely dressed women slipped through the door: the female scientists travelling to work on Macquarie Island. Holding themselves stiffly, eyes levelled above the heads of the seated men, the four exchanged a brief glance before separating and moving deeper into the room. People's conversation dipped, heads swivelling. Even at Nel's table, Phil and the captain broke off to watch as the four women slid into seats at four different tables. *Odd*, Nel thought, looking at the women perched straight-spined at their separate tables, yet she felt Phil relax beside her.

From hearing Phil debate their inclusion in detail and at length, she knew three of them were scientists: Isobel Bennett, a marine biologist from Sydney University, Hope MacPherson, the curator of molluscs at the National Museum of Victoria, and Elise Wollaston, who was a specialist in kelp and seaweeds from the University of Adelaide. The fourth woman, Ann Savours, was an historian on sabbatical from the Scott Polar Research Institute in England who'd been included to help the three biologists with their fieldwork. Nel couldn't tell the historian from the scientists from looking at them. All four were conservatively dressed, with hairstyles Nel thought should be easy to manage during their months without a salon. She leaned over to murmur in Phil's ear. 'Why aren't they sitting together?'

'I asked them to spread out.' Phil shifted as if to turn back to his conversation with the captain, but Nel caught his arm.

'Why?' Nel kept her voice pitched low.

Phil frowned at the question and his terse reply hissed below the room's rumble of conversation. 'The men might be daunted if they appeared in a block.'

Nel's mouth dropped open. Did he honestly have no idea how that must feel? Walking into a room packed to the walls with masculinity. *Polar explorer* masculinity, at that. Before she could say anything further, Phil rose to greet Andy Gressett, looking much more at home in civvies and an air-conditioned environment than the last time she had seen him.

'Room for one more at the head honcho's table?' Andy grinned, plonking down his glass. 'Shove over, fellas. Madame Leader.' He gave a mock doff of an imaginary cap to Nel and perched at the end of the booth opposite Phil, shunting his bottom more fully onto the cherry-red cushion and forcing the captain and the other men to shuffle along the U-shaped seat. 'Welcome aboard. I see the plans came together swimmingly. Brava, my dear. Brava. I've never had the excitement of sailing with a stowaway before. Feels like we're in a Stevenson novel, doesn't it, chaps?' Andy grinned, looking around the table.

Silence, but for the awkward squeak of legs shifting on vinyl. Beneath the table, Nel felt Phil's thigh tighten.

The captain broke the tension. 'It's a delight to have you on board, Mrs Law. I'm sure our dinner conversations and evening entertainments will be enriched by the culture and refinement your presence will bring.' Bill raised his glass to Nel, chinking it gently to hers, then turned to the rest of the table. Bob Dalton, Phil's second in command, scrubbed a hand through his bristly salt and pepper hair before leaning in to touch his glass to hers, his smile more confounded than welcoming. One by one, each of the men at the table followed suit. Nel smiled, meeting each man's eyes as their glasses chimed. Only Harold James, the young supernumerary, seemed free from any offence or confusion at being left out of the loop. As Phil's administrative jack-of-all-trades, Nel guessed he was probably relieved to find someone below him on the ANARE ladder. She grinned at the fresh-cheeked and healthily freckled young man.

Clearing his throat, Phil stood, his glass held in front of him. Nel felt all eyes turn her way. It took all her strength not to wither under the beam of scrutiny.

'Welcome, everyone, and many thanks for all your hard work to get us underway on schedule. A good omen for all we want to achieve this season.'

There was scattered applause. Nel shifted in her seat. Under her dress, her girdle gripped her like a giant sweaty hand. Beneath the table, she dug her nails into her palms. Once this night was over, she could happily sleep until they dropped anchor at Macquarie Island.

'Tonight, we sail on an auspicious date. Fifty years ago, to this very day, Sir Robert Falcon Scott sailed from New Zealand on the *Terra Nova*, bound for the South Pole. We all know what happened, and I don't want to quash the mood. But let's be upstanding' – Phil paused until the noise of scraping chairs and men lumbering to their feet died away – 'and pay our respects to those great men who travelled South before us, paving the way with their heroism – and, in the tragic case of Scott, Wilson, Evans, Bowers and Oates, their ultimate sacrifice. To Scott and the *Terra Nova*!' Phil raised his glass.

The room thundered. 'Scott and the *Terra Nova*!'

There was a hush as the room drank in unison, then he continued, 'And to Her Majesty the Queen, long may she reign!' Phil raised his glass, and the deep chorus rang, 'To the Queen!'

Phil cleared his throat, ready to continue, when from the back of the room a deep voice rang out, 'To King Frederick! *Skål*!'

A hearty chorus of *Skål!* rang out from the Danish crew who were leaning against the bulkhead on the far side of the saloon. At Nel's table, the three Danes – Bill Pedersen, Bend the first mate and Hugo the chief engineer – all took a long draught and banged their glasses on the table.

There was an awkward pause before Phil's voice rang out again.

'For those new to ANARE, and those with selective memories, I'll now run through the rules.'

The answering rumble was far from enthusiastic, but Phil squared his shoulders and launched into what was clearly a well-practised briefing on the rules and regulations of shipboard life.

Nel looked down, drawing her finger through the damp ring her glass had left on the tabletop. Heads were leaning together, the muttering a steady undercurrent to Phil's interminable list. She'd bet money that they were talking about her, based on the number of thunderous expressions directed her way. She shifted, trying to ease the tension strung between the crown of her head and the blades of her shoulders. Surely they must know she wasn't a threat. She wasn't taking their jobs or changing the way things were done. She was just along for the ride. Heat began to build in her core, and she felt the unwelcome blast of a hot flush wash from collarbone to hairline.

As Phil's speech droned on, Nel couldn't stop thinking about the four women. When she tried to catch their eyes, the youngest shot her a friendly smile, but the eldest woman, Isobel, met Nel's gaze with an even expression. All four, at their separate tables, were sitting up straight with tight smiles, dressed in tweed skirts and short-sleeved shirts, as if trying to strike a balance between respectability and invisibility. The two younger women were wearing the barest gloss of makeup. None wore jewellery.

Nel watched them, feeling overdressed as she nervously twitched her wedding ring. The best word Nel could muster for what lay beneath those four polite smiles was stoicism. Their expressions only cemented Nel's opinion of her husband's thoughtlessness. For the life of her, she couldn't fathom why Phil was worried about the *men*. If Nel felt as if she was under a microscope, it must have been a thousand times worse for them. While they were all clearly objects of scrutiny, at least Nel had privileged status. As Phil's wife, she was untouchable.

There was a pause and Nel felt Phil's body turn towards her.

'Now you may have noticed, we have some special guests among us.' Phil smiled down at her, before turning back to the company and raising his glass.

Silence fell so heavily, Nel could hear the faint barking of the dogs. 'For the second year in a row, we are joined by four ladies who will be disembarking once we reach Macquarie Island. They'll undertake fieldwork there until we pick them up again on our return journey in March. Welcome, ladies.' Phil raised his glass in a sweeping toast to the women scattered across their various tables. 'But even more exciting is the fact that this voyage is destined for the history books. When we arrive at Mawson Station, my wife will step ashore as the first Australian woman to set foot on Antarctica.'

'So much for the Heroic Age.' The muttered words were gruff and low, yet clearly meant to carry. 'Scott must be turning in his grave.'

In the abrupt silence, men at the nearest tables froze, heads down but eyes angled to catch Phil's reaction.

Nel stared at her drink. Beside her, she felt her husband stiffen. Murmurs leaked across the room. Her clothing felt welded to her skin. Waiting for the flush to pass, Nel kept her eyes down, willing away the shiny blush of heat.

Phil bent, placing his glass down with slow, deliberate precision. He braced his hands on the table, fingertips white with pressure as he fixed the room with a sweeping glare. The silence tipped from uncomfortable into awkward.

'You will make my wife welcome. Gentlemanly conduct is not only expected – it is non-negotiable. Should anything to the contrary reach my ears, it will signal that you are no longer interested in employment with ANARE. Clear?' A beat stretched into a pause. '*Are we clear?*'

'Yes, *sir.*'

Around the room, men shifted in their chairs, lit cigarettes and topped up glasses. Nel stared at the dancing pattern of light made by the low sun angling through her glass. In her opinion, there were four women in this room who proved the Heroic Age was alive and well. The noise of the room flowed around her as *Magga Dan* pitched almost imperceptibly beneath her feet.

Ultramarine Violet

It was the loveliest kind of smugness to upend everyone's assumptions. Nel tottered along the passageway, burdened with a tray bearing a huge teapot, five cups and a plate of biscuits. For the first few days at sea, the ship kept itself busy with energetic pitching and rolling, but Nel had barely seen any of its human population. The dining room remained empty except for a few intrepid souls who thought they might try keeping something down, but within minutes she would see them turn a washed-out shade of sage before staggering back to their bunks and bathrooms.

She'd not spotted Hope, Isobel, Ann or Elise in the dining room since that first night. Assuming they'd been brought low by the high seas, she thought she'd lay the first stone of friendship.

She made tentative progress to the women's cabin. It was like learning to walk on a new planet. The rolling between port and starboard, and the pitching from bow to stern (she was trying to learn the nautical terms) meant the ship was constantly swinging in three dimensions, shifting under her feet in ways that, for a first-time sailor, proved impossible to anticipate. Her body was clouded with bruises from being slammed against walls she now knew to call bulkheads. Moving down corridors, she would find herself either hanging in space, quite unaffected by gravity, or hurtling into an unforgiving surface. She'd developed a technique she'd dubbed the 'bum-bolster' when flying towards a hard object at speed. It involved a nimble twist in the moment before impact, her rear end taking the brunt of the collision.

Nel found this method especially useful when she had her hands full, delivering cups of weak, milky tea to her nauseous husband. She realised now that Phil had seriously downplayed his susceptibility to seasickness. Several times over the past couple of days she'd found him curled and cold on the bathroom floor, not daring to crawl even the few feet back to his bunk.

For the first few nights the rocking and rolling had been grim, sleeplessness from pitching back and forth across her bunk leaving Nel feeling as woozy as she imagined seasickness would have, had she been in the least affected by it. But she'd soon figured out a system of wedging herself into bed with several pillows between the bulkhead and her bunk's slim wooden rail, and she'd slept well ever since. In fact, she was beginning to enjoy the wild ride, much to Phil's envy-tinged astonishment when she checked on him, bringing tea and dry biscuits.

At her knock, the cabin door swung open. A waft of vomit rolled into the corridor and Nel took a step back, flinching in revulsion. Above the lapel of her dressing-gown, Isobel's pale, haggard face and black-bagged eyes told a tale of sleeplessness and nausea.

'Oh, you poor dears.' Without waiting for an invitation, Nel slipped into the cramped cabin and cast about for a bare surface for the tray. 'I thought you might be suffering, not having seen any of you at dinner.' She slid the tray onto the small table between the two sets of double bunks, pushing aside journals and field guides. 'Would you believe, I'd gone down to the galley and was collecting the ingredients to make you a big pot of chicken soup, when I was chased, *literally chased* out the door by that burly chief steward.' Nel sank down onto the nearest unmade bunk, eyes wide. 'He informed me, in no uncertain terms, that for the duration of the voyage, the kitchen was no longer my domain. His exact words.' She shook her head, throwing open her hands. 'Can you believe it?'

Isobel was standing beside the open door, lips compressed in a tight smile. Elise and Hope, who'd been lying in the two top bunks, sat up, their faces wan. Elise rubbed her hands over her face, one cheek creased with the imprint of her pillowcase. From the bathroom came the sound of retching.

'That's very kind of you, Mrs Law,' Hope said, wearily straightening the silk scarf protecting her curls from frizzing against the pillow. She nodded towards the bathroom. 'But I doubt Ann will be having any.'

Isobel closed the door but continued to stand, her expression tired as she leaned against the frame to keep her balance. 'None for me, thank you. I'm not sure I can keep anything down.' The three women were quiet against the background noise of Ann's distress. The cabin was close and warm, reminding Nel of the time her sister Joan had been bedridden with scarlet fever as a child.

Elise began to yawn, whipping her hand to her mouth, then patting the base of her throat as if concerned she might exhale more than air. 'Pardon me,' she said, swallowing hard. 'I expected to be worse off – Isobel and Hope went through it last year and Annie's fresh off the boat from England. But it seems none of us are immune.' Her smile didn't quite reach her eyes. 'You seem very chipper, Mrs Law.'

'Oh, it's Nel. Please.' Nel flapped her hand with a smile. 'We're all in this together.'

Isobel pushed away from the doorframe and tottered to her bunk, arms outstretched for balance, sinking onto the mattress with obvious relief. 'You seem to be weathering this like an old hand.' She tightened her robe. 'For a marine biologist, it's a little humiliating, to be let down by my body. You'd expect I'd have my sea legs by now. But every time I set foot on a boat, it's the same story. Three days, three nights. I can set my watch by it.' She gave a grim smile.

'You'd think we'd be used to it.' Elise swung her legs to dangle from the top bunk. 'Being let down by our bodies, I mean. Or at least the things about our bodies we can't control.' She raised her dark eyebrows at Isobel, giving Nel the impression this was the continuation of a previous conversation.

'Ah, yes.' Isobel nodded.

There was a pause, in which Nel darted looks at Isobel and Elise. She noted Elise's eyebrows were a little unkempt, as if she'd neglected plucking them for considerably longer than the few days aboard ship.

'It's the old equation. We've all had to spend many years proving to our *esteemed* peers that our brains are more valuable than our wombs.' At Elise's emphasis, all three women's mouths tightened.

Hope huffed a mirthless snort. 'Spend twice as long, working twice as hard to become twice as good, before receiving half the respect offered to our male colleagues.'

'That's a generous valuation.' Isobel settled herself on her bunk, thumping a pillow before wedging it between her lower back and the bulkhead.

'I know what you mean.' The moment this was out of Nel's mouth, all three women turned to her, eyebrows raised. In the silence, Ann retched. Nel rushed on, 'My friend Pam – she's an art history professor in Boston – when she married, they expected her to leave. They wouldn't give her tenure and wanted to promote a less qualified man over her. She'd had an almighty fight with the university. Ended up having to show them the medical records of her hysterectomy. So unfair.' Nel shook her head. On the day she'd spent at the National Gallery of Victoria with Pam, her friend had had a great deal to say about the 'marriage bar' and the injustice of forcing women out of work once they had wed. Nel hadn't minded giving up teaching. In the years of being engaged but not yet married, she'd felt strained beyond her strengths, the war leaching staff and those remaining stretched too thin. She'd been expected to teach maths and geography as well as her specialities, English and art. And the students had sensed her lack of confidence. Besides, she and Phil had been engaged so long, waiting for the war to end, all she wanted was to finally start their life together, build a home. And she'd had her own art to concentrate on. It hadn't bothered her that society took the choice out of her hands.

'Yes. Well. Your friend is fortunate.' Elise straightened her shoulders.

Nel's mouth dropped open.

'I can tell my superiors until I'm blue in the face that I have no intention of marrying or starting a family. If I hear "just wait until you meet the right man" from one more supercilious dean I may very well explode.' She pinched her fingers together at her temples then splayed her hands, widening her eyes. '*Boom.*'

Nel didn't know where to look. She'd heard Phil express that exact sentiment back when the departmental debate over allowing women to work on Macquarie Island was still raging. While he appreciated their expertise, he also assumed it was just a matter of time before female scientists married, leaving their research unfinished and, to his mind, wasting departmental money. She had nodded, her hands hot inside the rubber gloves as she scrubbed at a burned pan. Now, Nel's face reddened at the memory. These women were outstanding researchers and to have progressed so far in their fields meant they'd actively chosen their careers over love and family. That was how they came to be on board this ship, four women among sixty-odd men, their unattached status flashing like neon.

Nel slapped her hands on her thighs. 'Well. All I can say is I'm incredibly lucky. First time on a ship, and here I am with my sea legs already. Now I've been chased from the kitchen, I have all this lovely time on my hands to get on with my work.'

With the wild weather making sketching on the deck quite impossible, she'd taken to spending time on the bridge, chatting with Bill and the sweet, sandy-headed first mate, Bend. So as not to be underfoot, she'd found a comfortable spot up and off to one side, perched on the soft casing of an inflatable life raft. Tucked aloft on her raft, she'd spent hours each day with her sketchbook on her lap, the motion of the ship making her feel very much like she was riding a great sea-beast that was porpoising through the waves in slow motion.

When the women remained silent, she rushed on, 'It's been wonderful to get a head start on the work. I've finished a couple of watercolours already.'

'Lovely,' murmured Isobel in a tone Nel read as laden with either disinterest or extreme fatigue.

Pushing to her feet, Nel began to fuss with the tea tray and held up the pot to Hope and Elise. Hope shook her head, but Elise reached for a cup, which she held on her lap, untouched.

Hope sighed. 'That *is* lucky. I can't even read. The moment I try to focus on anything my head starts to spin.'

'We've all been trying to distract ourselves but even illustrated field guides are setting off the nausea. You're lucky your work doesn't require any reading.' Isobel's delivery was clear of sarcasm, yet the inference was clear. Nel bristled, bustling to cover her dismay by pouring herself a cup of tea.

So, this is what they thought of her being on board. They were professionals. So well regarded in their fields as to have elbowed out a space in this male-dominated world. Science was a man's game to begin with. But fieldwork on a subantarctic island? To them, she must seem the worst kind of tourist. A housewife. Worse, a housewife with artistic aspirations. *A dilettante.* She took a sip of tea and swallowed hard. It was only now, looking around this cabin stuffed with scientific journals, notebooks and field equipment, that she felt a bite of shame. What right did she have to be the first Australian woman in Antarctica? Feeling a wave of heat begin to build in her chest, she set down her cup and stood.

'I'll leave the tray with you, in case you feel up to nibbling something. I hope you're all up and about soon.'

'Thank you, dear. That was so thoughtful. We do appreciate it.' Hope smiled at Nel apologetically, flicking a frown at Isobel, who had risen from her bunk and was holding open the door. 'Despite not being at our best.'

'Yes, thank you. It *was* very kind. Perhaps we'll see you at dinner.' Isobel gave an embarrassed smile and closed the door, leaving Nel alone in the passageway, her farewell still in her mouth.

~

It didn't seem to matter how many layers she wore; the wind still muscled its way through her clothes. Nel crossed her arms over the sketchbook clasped against her chest, trying to use it as a windbreak, and tucked her gloved hands into her armpits. Her woollen cap was pulled down over her ears, but there was no protection from the sound of the ship, the percussion of wind through the halyards, clang of metal brightwork and slap of waves on the hull as sharp and atonal as anything Stravinsky could compose.

'Almost done,' Andy assured her, noticing her hunch and stamping feet. He clipped the last cone-shaped insect net onto the line and hoisted it aloft. Once out of his hands, it caught the wind, filling like a long, soft dunce's cap. Andy winched it up the red mast to join its fellows, fluttering among the rigging like fat pennants.

'If I'm honest, most of what I catch are paint chips from the masts,' he chuckled, head tipped back to check the position of the nets. 'But if I know one thing, it's this – the day I can no longer be bothered will be the day an insect unknown to science decides to drop by for a visit.' He grinned at her, giving his knots one last inspection. 'Hot chocolate?'

Before Nel could reply, a thump, squawk and shouts of surprise had her spinning to spot the source of commotion. She could only make out two grey woollen beanies before the ship's medico, 'Doc' Soucek, and a young ruddy-cheeked man stepped out from behind one of the helicopters lashed to the aft-deck. The doctor was holding an enormous bird at arm's length, his hands gently but firmly tucking the bird's black wings against its snowy sides.

'Bloody hell,' said the young man, backing away to stand well beyond the reach of its long and rather dangerous-looking yellow beak. 'Sorry, ma'am,' he added, catching sight of Nel. The ruddiness of his cheeks intensified.

'It's not struggling,' Doc said, examining the bird. 'Must've stunned itself. Damned heavy, though.' He began to move towards the door, the bird held out in front of him. 'Get the door would you, Gressett? Moofty, leg it up to the bridge and ask whoever's on watch to make an announcement. I'll take him to the mess. While he's getting his wits back, we can all have a bit of a look.'

Moofty dashed for the stairs, leaving Nel and Andy to trail the doctor as he made his way inside, stabilising himself against the roll of the ship with careful, wide-legged steps. The large bird preceded them down the corridor like a proud ship's figurehead.

In the mess, Doc set the bird down on a table in the middle of the room. It stood quite still for a moment, then, with a slight ruffle of feathers, peered curiously about. Diners clustered around the table, close enough for a good look but giving the bird's long yellow beak, with its vicious end-hook, a respectful radius. Bend's calm voice crackled out of the loudspeaker and immediately doors banged, footsteps pounding on the decks above and below. A dozen or so men crowded in, jostling for a view. Nel flipped open her sketchbook and fished a stick of charcoal from the tin in her pocket, standing firm in her front-row position.

She'd just swept the first dark lines across her page when a tall red-headed man burst through the door wearing a heavy weather-proof jacket with binoculars hanging from a harness fastened around his chest and neck. He wove his way, polite but firm, through the crowd. Nel had noticed him before, always either out on deck scanning the distances with his field glasses or sitting with a group of men Nel assumed to be scientists.

'Which sort is he, Dr McCallum?' Moofty had made excellent time, delivering his message to the bridge then legging it down several flights of stairs swiftly enough to secure a place at the front of the throng.

'She's a black-browed albatross. Not quite full-grown.' Dr McCallum crossed in front of the bird with slow, even motions, and the albatross cocked her head, following him with her eyes.

The name made perfect sense to Nel – the bird's eyes were captivating, the elegant marking on her brow looking as if she'd applied a smoky smudge of eyeshadow. Nel tried to replicate the bird's exquisitely graduated shading with a thumb-blurred charcoal line as the man kept talking.

'You can tell by the way she still has some brown on her plumage. If she were fully grown, she'd be perfectly black and white.' He stretched his hand towards the bird. The albatross looked at his fingers, clapper-clapped her long beak and took a small step backwards on the table, cautious yet still remarkably unperturbed by her strange surroundings. 'Good girl,' Dr McCallum said with soft affection, and then, to the rest of the crowd, 'She's moving well and in no distress. Just stunned, I think.'

Nel kept sketching, flicking her gaze between the impressive bird and the page. She worked quickly, trying to capture the sharp contrast of pure white body, soot black wings and the eyeshadow smear that lent her an air of elegant disdain.

Having filled one page with swift sketches, she turned over to the next, the sound and action catching the attention of both the albatross and the scientist.

Nel shot him a quick smile before turning back to her work. 'She's so glamorous with that eyeshadow. A Joan Crawford of birds,' she laughed, looking at the albatross but pitching her voice to Dr McCallum, who smiled back, raising his pale eyebrows.

The albatross shook herself, a ruffle that began at her neck and shuddered down her body, black tail feathers the last to settle into stillness. The shake had loosened the bird's pure white chest feathers, and a light rain of tiny dark specks pattered onto the table surface. Nel leaned in. The dots moved.

'Ew!' She stepped back in alarm. 'They're alive!'

A laugh rumbled through the crowd. She shot a glance at Dr McCallum as heat rushed to her cheeks.

'Now we're talking!' Oblivious to her discomfort, Andy fished several tiny bottles from his pockets and stepped forward to squint at the specks scribbling panicked paths across the teak surface. With practised ease, he brushed the tiny specimens into various bottles, and stepped back with a Cheshire cat grin. 'All this fuss over a bird! She's just the aircraft. I'm sorry, Harry, but the only interesting thing about this old girl is her passengers.' He grinned at Dr McCallum, brandishing his bottles.

'Each to their own, Andy.' Dr McCallum shrugged with a smile, but stepped forward to inspect the tiny passengers. 'What are they?'

'Feather lice and fleas. The fleas are probably *Parapsyllus magellanicus magellanicus*. And the lice, *Philopteridae* family, I'd say at first glance. But albatrosses can host up to six different species, so I'll have to pop these beauties under the microscope to be sure.'

Trying to quash her repulsion, Nel kept sketching, concentrating on getting the sweep and shading of the brow just right. The albatross's demeanour was self-possessed and curious, yet the natural contours of her head and swoop of shadow feathers across each eye gave her a concerned frown. Nel was desperate to convey the exact effect, swiftly outlining head after head on the page until she got the expression just right. She could feel the men watching her and her subject with equal interest.

'Not game to sketch the critters?' The dark-haired, thickset man on her left looked down at her series of albatross heads with poorly disguised disdain.

Nel straightened her back and took a step forward, keeping an eye on the hooked end of the beak, before leaning closer to inspect the insects on the surface of the table.

Andy smiled encouragingly. 'The lice are the larger, long-bellied ones. The fleas are smaller but can leap further.'

Nel held her ground, determined not to flinch, even if within landing distance of a flea. At this range, she could see the distinct feathers within the curve of the albatross's chest, the white not as pure as it appeared just two feet further back, but ever so slightly dappled with a shade a whisper closer to grey. Entranced, she stared at the interlocking pattern, wanting to imprint the complex repetition in her mind's eye.

She noticed movement. Clearly, not all the insects had jumped ship. The albatross's chest was alive with a significant population of lice and fleas.

'She's just like Gulliver in Lilliput.' Nel smiled until struck by a sudden thought. She looked up at Dr McCallum with concern. 'She's not ill, is she?'

'No, this is a normal level of insect life, wouldn't you say, Andy?' He looked over at the entomologist.

'Well, I don't often get this sort of close-up view of wild albatrosses. But she's not infested, by any means. Seems healthy – just being a great host for my little friends here.'

With that, the albatross released a prodigious squirt of faeces onto the tabletop. As one, the crowd recoiled in disgust, laughter reverberating through the room.

Nel felt a jolt of connection – she too was an oddity on this ship, an object of scrutiny. Each time she left her cabin, no matter how pleasant or inconspicuous she tried to be, she felt like this albatross standing on the dining table. Every tilt of her head or stretch of her wings reinforced her difference. And from the tone of the crew's laughter, it was as though they'd been waiting for the bird to disgrace herself. Nel couldn't help but think that this was just one more parallel.

The bird lifted her head, lengthening her neck towards the ceiling, and made a strange clacking, whirring sound in her throat. Then, almost in slow motion, she opened her wings.

A collective intake of breath. It was as if the bird had transformed into a creature from mythology, the great wings unfolding, arching to the ends of the table, then beyond. She flexed, beating softly at the air, her dark wingtips stretched so far across the room she parted the speechless crowd. Nel gaped at the clean architecture of her wings, broad as the height of a man. The sight reminded her of the quiet glory of the angel shining above the stable on her mother's mantelpiece nativity set.

A flash and pop of a box camera burst from the back of the crowd. The albatross clacked her beak, shifting from one pinkish-grey foot to the other, then closed her wings, settling them against her sides with a neat shiver.

Dr McCallum moved to stand behind the unsettled bird and lifted her gently from the table. 'Come on, beautiful. Let's get you back where you belong.'

The crowd began to drift away. The heavy-set man beside Nel threw one last scornful glance at her sketchbook, then moved to join a group of men at a window-side table. His voice was low, pitched only to his companions, but Nel could still make out every word.

'Save it. Kill it. Does it matter? So much bad luck on board already, we're lucky to have made it this far.' The jibe was met with a murmur of agreement, but Nel didn't trust herself to face them. Any sharp retort they'd see as shrill. If they saw they'd wounded her, they'd label her unstable. Whatever she did, she'd lose. *They wouldn't dare if Phil were here.*

Nel flipped closed her sketchbook and, with chin high, began to make her stop-start way down the pitching corridor, catching up with man and bird at the door to the deck. Dr McCallum glanced behind him.

'Would you mind?' he said, nodding at the portal.

Nel sidled past, the bird thankfully too nonplussed by her predicament to wield her beak as Nel brushed by within striking distance. She unlatched the heavy door, holding it open as the pair moved past, then scurried to keep up as Dr McCallum strode along the deck towards the stern.

On sighting the water, the bird began to shift and fuss. Dr McCallum lengthened his stride, struggling to keep his grip. Reaching the stern deck, he heaved the bird up and over the rail with one smooth motion. For a long second, the albatross plummeted towards the ocean. At the last moment, as if intending to build suspense, she unfolded her colossal wings. The great bird sailed into the open air, her glide clean and easy over the angry roil of the ship's wake.

Nel pressed her stomach against the rail. The albatross hung in the air, gradually gaining height as the wind rushed beneath her wings.

Nel flipped open her sketchbook and traced the twin dark curves of her wings against the sky. Dr McCallum rested his forearms on the railing and glanced over, taking in the swiftly sketched studies of the albatross's head on the opposite page.

'You've really captured her expression. Somewhere between curious and disapproving.'

She laughed. 'Thanks. I'm Nel,' she said, holding out her hand.

'Harris.' His fingers were strong and warm. 'I don't know about you, but I could do with a cup of tea. Let's head back in. I think she's none the worse for her little adventure.' He took one last look at the albatross, now a tiny scratch of black ink hovering high and alone on the vast canvas of sky.

Back in the deserted dining room, Nel made a pot of tea while Harris collected cups, milk jug and sugar. As the tea steeped, Harris pointed at the sketchbook. 'May I?'

At her nod, he opened it, examining the albatross sketches.

'I heard some gossip you're an artist. I must admit, I took that with a grain of salt.' He shot her a smile. 'But you are. The real McCoy.'

'Landscapes and portraits, mostly. She's my first attempt at a bird portrait.'

'Pretty good for a first go.' He paused, watching as Nel poured tea into his cup. 'Do you do more ... realistic work?'

The teapot hovered in midair.

'I've put my foot in it. I'm sorry – these are good, really. But they're ... I don't know ... more impressions of the bird, than ...' He waved his hands as if hoping to fish the right words from the air. 'What I mean is, you've captured the spirit of the bird rather than something anatomically accurate. And I realise you were working quickly, so I was wondering ... if you do both?' He rushed on. 'The reason I'm asking is totally selfish. I can't draw to save my life. And I'm also a terrible photographer.' He shook his head self-deprecatingly. 'And I desperately need help illustrating my research. So, if you were interested in some more wildlife portraits ...? How do you feel about penguins?'

His irises were French ultramarine with a touch of cerulean. 'Uh, sorry,' Nel said, realising he was waiting for her response. 'I have very strong feelings about emperors. Far too haughty for their own good.' His eyes widened and she laughed. 'I'm teasing. I adore penguins. Not that I've met one yet in the flesh. Honestly, who *doesn't* like penguins?'

'You'd be surprised.' He raised one rose-gold eyebrow. 'There are ornithologists out there ... very prejudiced against birds who can't fly.'

His grin told her she was the one now being teased, and she smiled back at him as she replaced her teacup in its saucer with a decisive *clink*.

'Well, I can't promise perfect realism. But I'm happy to try.'

'Brilliant.' He rapped his knuckles on the table, then shot her a serious look. 'I'll talk to the chief. See whether he's happy for you to come out in the field. Maybe we can do a trial run when we get to Macquarie? I'm planning on heading to a royal penguin rookery once the resupply's squared away. You could tag along, see if you like it? And if the chief's happy, then we can think about you helping me with my Adélies when we get to Mawson.'

'Sounds like a plan.' Nel straightened in her chair. Being out in the field, taking part in research? The flash of purpose warmed her for a long second, then continued to rise, morphing into the onset of a hot flush. She drained her tea, eager to draw this to a close before she visibly began to sweat. 'I'll speak to Phil.' She put out her hand again and Harris took it. The shake felt binding as a vow. 'Lovely to meet you, Harris.'

'Likewise.'

Nel sat for a while after she got back to her cabin, pushing back the tide of dread that always flooded her when she flushed, wafting air down her décolletage and blotting her face with a handkerchief as she tried to cling to the elation of her encounter with Harris. She flipped open the sketchbook to her albatross studies, attempting to see them with Harris's eyes. While her drawings were a far cry from the precise scientific illustrations that might appear in a field guide or textbook, they captured something deeper. Her black lines blazed with the *presence* of the bird. She flicked to a fresh page and selected a piece of charcoal from the tin in her pocket.

As she worked quickly and steadily, time telescoped until, at last, she tucked the charcoal back into the tin, unsure how many minutes or even hours had passed. She took a great breath, relishing the flex of her ribs as she stretched her arms above her head.

Satisfaction seeped through her as she examined the finished work – a full study of the albatross standing on the table, wings outstretched, its puzzled frown perfectly rendered. She was particularly happy with the bottom right-hand corner. Inside a square she'd drawn a magnified section of the bird's chest, the overlapping feathers rendered in precise detail. The final touch was the cluster of tiny, multi-legged dots and darting scribbles illustrating the panicky scuttling of the lice and fleas. Andy would love it.

~

Nel dabbed perfume on her wrists and behind her ears, breathing deep of the familiar floral scent. She tucked the square bottle back into the drawer, bolstering the crystal with neatly folded girdles and underwear to cushion it against the movement of the ship. Two bottles of Chanel No. 5 were travelling with her on this journey, just in case one broke in rough seas. Her sister Joan had also given her a bottle of Raphael's Réplique the night before departure. There was no risk of running out of scent.

Looking in the mirror, Nel smoothed her silk shirt, tucking it more securely into the waistband of her slacks. It would do. At home, Phil was adamant about dressing for dinner. It was his way of showing appreciation for the work that had gone into preparing the meal. It was one of the many things she loved about him. Not just the consideration of her labour, but the fact he enjoyed making an occasion of the time they spent together. He'd select wine and music to complement her cooking. And it was a custom he'd brought to every expedition, one that wasn't universally appreciated by the men, apparently.

Nel tugged the knot of her red neck-scarf so it sat at a natty angle, the ends trailing over the shoulder of her blue-and-white shirt. Choosing lipstick to match the scarf, she coloured her lips. There wasn't much she could do about her hair. She patted the short waves, sighing inwardly as her fingers brushed the brittle texture. The day before sailing, she'd spent the whole morning at the salon, where Yvonne had raised her perfectly shaped brows at Nel's request for a short cut and hard set. The second day out of Port Melbourne, Nel had been standing near the bow with Andy, revelling in the sounds and scents of the sea, when a wave had taken them both by surprise, slapping them straight in the face. Andy roared with laughter but Nel shrieked, hands flying to her hair as she raced back to her cabin. She tried to rinse away the salt, only to find that at sea, not even a shower is simple. Standing naked in the alcove, feet braced, the shower water was the only thing in the room unaffected by the ship's yaw. Clinging to the shower rail and laughing helplessly at her plight, she waited for the water to pass over her, the shower hitting her body only when the ship's roll passed her through its fall. The damage was done. Her set was ruined. But the short style was growing on her, each day making her more appreciative of the reduced maintenance time.

The cabin door opened, and Phil strode in, tossing a clipboard onto his bunk, the paper almost invisible behind the densely scrawled lists and notes. He leaned in to kiss her as he shrugged out of his insulated jacket.

'You smell delightful. A breath of fresh air after the bowels of the engine room. Do I have time for a quick wash?' He looked at his watch. 'Face and armpits in the sink, I think. Our little secret.' He grinned, unbuttoning his shirt, and dropping it on the floor before stepping into the tiny bathroom. As the water ran in the basin, Nel picked up his discarded clothing, stuffing the grimy shirt into the laundry bag and hanging the jacket on one of the ship's fancy coat hangers, the gold of the J. Lauritzen logo gleaming on the scarlet wood. She debated telling him about the albatross and Harris's invitation. No time. Phil hated being late.

Within minutes, her husband was freshly kitted out, tie knotted, hair slicked back. He held the door for her as she grabbed the folder with Andy's drawing tucked inside and, side by side, they made their way to the dining saloon.

She was glad she hadn't brought up the albatross and penguins, as they were the last to take their seats at the cadmium-red booth around the captain's table. Her stomach fell when she saw that the heavy-set man from earlier in the day had claimed a seat at the booth's far end, his face stern under thick, dark brows as Bob Dalton and Harold James talked across him. She smiled politely in their direction and turned immediately to Andy, who, thankfully, was seated opposite.

'I have something for you,' she said, pitching her voice so that it didn't interrupt the discussion slinging between the men in the curve of the booth. She slid the drawing of the albatross towards Andy, careful to avoid staining the work with the damp rings from the glasses dotting the table. His eyes widened and, after a long second of scrutiny, he hooted with delight.

'Magnificent!' He leaned closer to take in the detail of the insects. 'It's going to be a battle to keep Pam's hands off it. But I shall prevail! This will have pride of place in my study.' He grinned. 'Thank you, my dear. I shall treasure it.'

The men at the table craned to see, and Andy slid the drawing towards them. At Phil's quizzical look, Nel explained.

'We had a visitor today. The poor thing stunned itself on the deck. Doc brought it inside so we could all have a look, close up. I was sketching it ... then all these creepy crawlies suddenly popped out of its feathers. Andy was very excited. So, I did this for him this afternoon.' Nel gestured at the drawing and Phil pulled it closer, turning it to face him, a smile pulling at the edge of his beard when he saw what she'd done with the lice and fleas.

'Harry was in his element,' Andy chuckled. 'If the old girl hadn't left a rather ripe note of displeasure on the table, I think he might've kept her.' He swivelled in his seat, scanning the room. 'Harry!' he called, catching sight of red hair a couple of tables away. When Harris looked up, Andy waved him over.

The ornithologist made his way to their table and Andy passed him Nel's drawing.

Harris examined it. 'Beautiful,' he said, then looked down at Nel. 'And more realistic than the other sketches. Practising for the penguins?'

Nel gave him a tight smile and turned to Phil, opening her mouth to explain.

Phil was looking at Harris. 'Penguins?' he asked. Silence stretched a beat too long.

'I saw your wife's work earlier today and I wanted to ask if I could possibly borrow her. On occasion.' She heard Harris's deferential tone with relief.

Nel felt the muscles in Phil's thigh tense.

Harris went on, 'Her skills, I mean. You have no idea how much an illustrator would help me with the Adélies. No idea,' he laughed, shaking his head. 'The last paper I submitted, the editor said my illustrations looked like black-and-white flour bags sitting on nests of bread rolls. And frankly, my photographs aren't much better. My worst fear is going home with rolls of over-exposed negatives and having to rely on my powers of description alone.'

Nel said nothing, confident Phil would know from her body language she was happy with the idea. She was a little taken aback by Harris. It wasn't every day that she met a man quite so open about his failings, especially in front of a table of peers.

Harris went on, 'On Macquarie, I'll be heading out to a royal penguin rookery. Mrs Law could come along and try her hand at penguins. See if she's suited to fieldwork? If it's fine with you, of course.'

The man at the end of the table snorted and took a long pull of beer.

'Something you wanted to say, George?' Phil asked, fixing the dark-haired man with an even look.

'That sounds like a fine idea, Harry. If you want your paper to look like it was illustrated by Picasso.'

Across the table, Andy snorted with laughter.

'Here we go,' he said, winking at her before pinching the bridge of his nose. 'I foresee someone in the very near future uttering those immortal words *I don't know much about art, but I know what I like.*'

George frowned, his brows almost meeting. 'For your information, Gressett, I know enough to understand a scientist would benefit from the assistance of a *representational* artist, rather than a modernist. Or, God forbid, an abstract expressionist.' He shifted his disdainful glare to Harris. 'Or perhaps *Penguin descending a staircase* is exactly what the editor of *Nature* is after.' He placed his glass down with a bump, scanning the faces around the table as if expecting laughter. 'But what do I know? I'm just a geologist.' There was a long pause, only the men's eyes moving as they exchanged glances. Nel was glad the ship's glasses didn't have stems since, at this moment, her grip would've snapped one in two.

'Duchamp.' Nel said to her tumbler of wine.

No one moved.

'Pardon?' George leaned his forearms on the table.

Andy broke the tension with a wry smile. 'Not quite sure where you're going with this, George, but "Nude Descending a Staircase, No.2" was by Marcel Duchamp. And I think you'll find all artists learn the basics of representation. You need to know the rules to break them in the cleverest of ways. So if push came to shove, I'd put money on even Jackson Pollock being able to deliver a recognisable penguin without so much as a paint splatter in sight.' He leaned back in the booth, leather upholstery squeaking companionably. 'We all talk ourselves up with exploration and science. But, historically, artists are the backbone of polar expeditions.' Nel knew this must be familiar ground for Andy from debates with Pam.

There was a pause. 'Is that so?' George's voice was almost musical with sarcasm.

'Indeed, my good man.' Andy took a sip of beer. 'I'll happily take all comers on this one.' He winked at Nel, then raised his eyebrows as if asking a question for which he didn't already have the answer. 'How do you think expedition costs are recouped?' He paused for dramatic effect. 'Selling the art. Ponting? Hurley? You think they were only included to document the expeditions? No, sir. They were there to take photographs that could be *sold*. Scott. Shackleton. Mawson. All of them took artists. Right back to William Hodges on the *Resolution* with Cook – 1772. Tell me I'm wrong, Phil.'

'I can't. And I wouldn't dare, since I'd have to answer to both your wife and mine on that count.' Phil laughed. 'It's true. Selling photos and paintings was how Scott and Shackleton paid back their financiers.'

'And those *artists*.' The scorn was clear in George's voice. 'They were chosen for their sensibility? Their *interpretation* of Antarctica?' He shook his head and took a swig of beer. The whole table seemed to be holding its breath. Nel's ears felt hot. She made herself loosen her grip on her glass.

Unbelievably, George ploughed on. 'I doubt Picasso or Pollock or *Duchamp* would be high on the list of expedition candidates. If we need artists, surely they're a particular kind? Ones that are dedicated to accuracy, who help science – not make art a laughing-stock.'

Harold James shifted in his seat, loosening the knot of his blue striped tie as he swallowed hard, darting looks between Phil, Andy and George. 'Well, when it comes to painting penguins – I don't think you can go past Edward Wilson.' He nodded at Nel. 'Stick with Harry, Mrs Law, and you might find yourself hailed as the next Doc Wilson. Explorer *and* artist.'

George didn't look up from his drink, but his voice was clearly directed at Harris. 'Or Harry could just learn how to use his bloody camera. It's not rocket science.'

'Language.' Phil's voice was low. Nel froze, a flush of heat rising to her cheeks. She tried to cover it, sipping her drink, the muscles in her arm taut as wires. She could tell Phil wasn't angry; he relished robust dinner-table debate. But if George pushed it much further, Phil might feel the need to put a stop to the conversation to protect her. And she didn't want another black mark against her name, the men thinking she needed Phil to fight her battles.

Andy scowled theatrically down the table. 'Good grief, George. With those diplomacy skills, I suddenly understand why you work with rocks.' Laughter broke out around the table just as the rumble of conversation in the rest of the room fell away. The doors leading to the kitchen had swung open and several white-coated staff began loading trays of steaming food onto the buffet table.

Harold slid from the booth, relief on his freshly shaven face. 'Grub's up, chaps.'

Nel could hardly believe how happy she was to see yet another bain-marie laden with roast beef and vegetables.

~

Kicking off her shoes, Nel stretched out, ankles crossed on the rounded arm of the couch in Phil's stateroom, an ornithological field guide propped on her chest. The bird illustrations were magnificent. But far too small. She wanted them large, dominating the page. Not cramped beside all that text: names, measurements, distribution, the colourings of male and female, summer and winter plumage. The italicised descriptions of the calls, ineffectual attempts to wrangle bird language into English, made her laugh. But the glory of each bird was dwarfed next to the block of information. She wanted *detail* – the exact shade of the plumage, the wing structure, how the feathers lay against each other. She flipped through the pages from skua to petrel to penguin. How much did the printing process dilute the colour intensity or shift the palette? At least this wouldn't be such an issue with Adélie penguins. Most of her work could be done with either pen and ink or charcoal.

Nel stared up at the ceiling, letting the book fall onto her chest. She could do this. It would be a challenge. But wasn't that what she wanted? To be stretched? If she was honest, this wasn't quite the stretching she'd had in mind. She'd imagined sitting behind her easel out on a vast expanse of ice, surrounded by cold and silence, pushing herself away from realism and impressionism towards something new, something more like expressionism, but her own version of it. Translating onto her canvas something more than how the scene looked – how it *felt*. She was itching to start. But the thought of her art being useful was tantalising. It would be just like being employed.

A wave of engine roar rushed in as the door opened, and Phil bowled into the room. Fossicking among his folders, he unearthed a clipboard, flipped over some pages, then glanced at Nel, now sitting up with the book in her lap.

She held it up. 'Research. Do you have any that focus on penguins? Like the one Harold mentioned at dinner by … who was it? Wilson?'

'You're serious about this? You weren't just humouring him?' Phil looked at her closely. 'Because I can make your excuses if you were being polite.' He dropped the clipboard on the desk and perched on the edge.

'I think it sounds exciting. And challenging.' Nel held the field guide out to him, open on a spread of albatross species. 'Look at this. The realism – it's extreme.'

She turned it back to face her, brushing her fingers over a fluffy albatross chick. 'Imagine the hours of observation and discipline that went into creating these images. The commitment to getting it *exactly* right. It's something I've never tried, and I'd like to.'

Phil moved to sit beside her on the couch.

'You're sure?'

'Of course, I'll still be doing my own paintings too.' She leaned against him. 'But this will keep me out from under your feet. You can get on with your work without having to worry about me.' She gave him a playful nudge. 'And I'll be contributing. Like a real expeditioner.'

He looked down at her, his brow creased. 'Well, if that's what you want ... But I thought you wanted to be close by, seeing what I do?'

Catching the disappointment in his tone, Nel paused. She'd thought he'd be happy she was mingling with the men, being independent and not relying on him to entertain her.

'Just keep in mind you can always say no. There's no shame in changing your mind. You're here with me.' He squeezed her hand, then stood up, retrieving the clipboard from his desk. 'If you're serious about being a *contributing* expeditioner, I have plenty of projects to keep you occupied.' Phil ticked off a list, finger by finger. 'You could do paintings of all the stations on the itinerary. And the automatic meteorological station – a visual record of all the stages of construction would be wonderful. Then, once we reach Oates Land ...' He straightened, his excitement at just the thought of reaching that elusive coast threading his voice with electricity. 'I'll need maps and sketches of the new terrain. Plus oils and watercolours. Portraits of the men who make landfall. How does that sound?'

'Instead of the penguins?' She wasn't quite sure the buildings and maps sounded as appealing as the penguins, but she didn't want to disappoint him.

'You could try your hand at the penguins, but if the fieldwork proves too much we can revert to the original plan.'

'Original plan?'

'Of just being here, with me. Seeing what I do. And doing some painting, *your own* painting, while you're here. Our lounge-room-floor plan.'

Nel made her face stay soft.

'Darling, of course I'm still on board with all of that.' She turned to the bookshelf and slid the field guide back into place, forcing herself to loosen the tension in her jaw. 'But now that I'm here, and opportunities are popping up, maybe I can at least try? My own work as well as helping with the penguins. And, of course, I'd be happy to paint the stations for you. And Oates Land. Why didn't you mention it before?'

She sat down on the couch, crossing her legs and draping an arm across the back as she watched him. It was a habit, this vigilance – a continual scanning of his emotional temperature, assessing what he needed, calibrating her response.

Phil placed himself on the couch, back straight, knees angled towards her. 'Well, you didn't mention you were looking for extra work. I'd assumed you already had more than enough on your plate.'

It was suddenly clear to her that what he truly wanted was for her to see him at work – her role more appreciative audience than independent artist. It was sweet, in a way, this desire for her to witness him being Phil the Antarctic explorer. The leader. Yet, their whole marriage, he'd been the one in the spotlight; she'd been standing in his shadow. And now, here she was with this chance to show herself to be more than the boss's wife, someone with skills and ambitions of her own. She'd thought Phil understood, until this conversation.

She chose her words carefully. 'Darling, this is a whole new world for me. I really had no idea how much time would be freed up without housework.' She made herself laugh, watching his expression. 'How about we just see how I go?'

Phil slapped his hands lightly on his thighs and stood. 'Let's table this for later. I need to post tomorrow's schedule.'

As he moved towards the door, she stifled a sigh. Even she didn't know exactly what she was capable of now all domestic duties had evaporated. Sometimes she wondered, if she died – or, heaven forbid, just stopped – how many days it would take for all her work to become visible. Dishes in the sink, laundry in the basket, dust and cobwebs and dead indoor plants. What did Phil really know about how she spent her days? They rarely talked about the minutiae of her life. She was proud that he spoke with her about weighty things: funding applications and logistics and federal resistance to science. If they did discuss her day, what could she say? That she set up her easel, only to stand in front of it for an hour? Then the phone rang, and she needed to hang the laundry and she never went back? That the butcher gave her an extra kidney and the milk delivery was late? That she missed Nefertiti so much she spent long minutes with her face pressed into a blanket she still hadn't washed? That she felt frozen? That now her fertility was ending, she'd begun to wonder if they'd made the right decision? But she always allowed the conversation to dwell on the next expedition, on equipment and choices, and everything seemed chummy and fine. Maybe she hadn't seen that her silence was reinforcing the idea of her as no more than a wife. And when she did speak, it was to say she was fine, it was fine. Everything was always fine.

Phthalo Green

Macquarie Island,
December 1960

She was wearing so many layers her joints couldn't bend properly. Added to that, the bright orange Mae West made her feel ridiculous. The lurid life vest jutted out so far, she had no idea where she was putting her feet. Thank God everyone else going ashore was wearing one too. But possessing a healthy set of breasts beneath the thick foam padding added inches of encumbrance none of the men understood.

She moved to the side of the deck away from the rail, shuffling her canvas knapsack between her feet. Last night, she'd timed the conversation perfectly: Phil was so harried with the changeover and keen for her to stay out of the way, he'd agreed to let her accompany Harris without so much as a raised eyebrow. He'd barely glanced up from the typewriter. He probably assumed she'd baulk at the steepness of the terrain and this one jaunt would see the end of her naturalist aspirations. Nel smiled to herself, a wire of determination steeling her spine.

Phil had barely slept, and she'd woken this morning to find his bunk empty and the sheets cool. Commandeering his knapsack, she'd crammed the canvas bag so full of sketchbook, watercolour block, charcoals, pens, brushes and paints that she now dreaded having to carry it. She'd wanted to add an easel and oils, but, looking at the steep green slopes of the island beyond the porthole, she knew she'd never manage it. She'd need a mule!

After so many days of nothing but blue stretched across the horizon, catching sight of the tiny island that morning had been like finding a lost world at the edge of the earth.

Macquarie Island jutted from the ocean so intensely green that Nel became aware how far the spectrum of her world had skewed to blue and grey. Prussian blue, French blue, Persian blue for the glittering ocean. For the vast bowl of sky: gentian, cobalt, azure and turquoise. And on those days the sky was bullied by clouds, Payne's grey, Davy's grey, indigo, almost perylene black. But Macquarie Island was a green that declared *life*.

When the main station came into view, with its listless Australian flag slumping against the flagpole atop Wireless Hill, the decision was made to take advantage of the extraordinarily favourable weather. Rather than begin the station changeover immediately, they would speed down to Hurd Point, at the very bottom of the cigar-shaped island, where conditions were notoriously difficult, and unload supplies there first.

Last night at the post-dinner briefing in the saloon, Phil's agitation had been palpable. It was crucial that the resupply run swiftly and smoothly. If they fell behind on the vast list of tasks on the schedule, the delay would begin to eat away the days available for the exploration of Oates Land at the journey's end. She wanted that for him, just as much or even more than she wanted to be the first Australian woman in Antarctica. Caught up in the current of Phil's drive, she was being carried towards her goal, washing up on its shore not even out of breath, while Phil had been swimming hard, every muscle straining, his dream just beyond his fingertips, for years.

Macquarie Island was renowned for inclement weather, and Phil had been dreading the prospect of ferrying cargo ashore in one of the island's legendary squalls. He'd read out the changeover itinerary in excruciating detail: the landings, the unloading of supplies – even which gloves were to be worn and the exact procedure for boarding a DUKW. The 'ducks', as she'd heard them called, were strange amphibious trucks that looked like dinghies with wheels, but Nel couldn't for the life of her remember what the acronym stood for.

Despite some furtive groaning over Phil's gruelling schedule, those due to disembark were brimming with cheer at launching into their work, and even those still with weeks ahead at sea were in high spirits at the prospect of a few days on solid land.

When dessert was laid out, Nel made for the buffet. With the steady cooling of the weather, her appetite, particularly for sweets, had grown. She'd just dolloped her bread-and-butter pudding with cream when Harris appeared at her elbow.

'How do you feel about finally getting off this bucket?' He spoke without looking at her, scooping a large spoonful of golden pudding into his bowl. 'You, me and a few thousand royal penguins.' He put down the jug of cream. 'Interested?'

'Sounds like you have the chaperones sorted,' she laughed. 'I'll have to clear it with Phil. But I think so long as I'm not in the way, it should be fine.' She paused. 'So ... this will be my trial run?'

Harris shrugged. 'To be honest, as much for me as for you. I've never been in the field with a ...' His pale eyebrows almost disappeared into his hairline.

'A *woman*?' Nel loaded the noun with mocking emphasis.

'An *artist*.' He laughed, matching her tone.

'We are a completely distinct subspecies, you know.'

'And here I thought that the penguins would be the most interesting thing on Macca. Looks like I might need an extra notebook for field observations of the female artist in the wild. There could be a paper in that,' he added. 'After breakfast tomorrow?'

Nel nodded and he bowed lightly before heading back to his table.

Now she gazed across the sparkling water at the island. It was breathtaking, its two steep-sided peaks making her imagine that below the surface of the sea, a whole mountain range must be lurking, secret and silent. On the bridge, the consensus was that this weather was almost miraculous. Not even a whisper of wind. But even in the still, clear air, the day brimmed with drama – surf smashed against jagged rocks, cliffs plunged into ocean marbled with foam, the white flecks of gulls and albatrosses wheeled and screamed against the dark backdrop of volcanic rock.

She'd thought she was ready, but her first sight of Hurd Point struck her dumb. The mountainous terrain, carpeted with a lumpen blanket of tussock grass, tumbled down to black sand. At least, Nel thought it was black. It was hard to tell as every available inch was occupied by penguins. Thousands upon thousands, their black-and-white bodies pressed so close together Nel could not understand how any individual penguin found room to raise a flipper. Grey blobs of sea elephants spattered the strand, and Nel spotted the odd penguin perched atop a seal in what must have been a desperate ploy for personal space.

This was what people meant when they said *wilderness*. It was wild and rugged and teeming with life. If not for the tiny research huts, she could have easily believed humans had never touched this place.

The 'ducks' and inflatables buzzed across the swell between ship and shore all morning, unloading drums of oil, fresh food and all manner of subantarctic field equipment.

Nel kept herself occupied at the kennels while she waited for her turn to go ashore. The dogs, finally able to smell land, could not contain their excitement. As usual, Nel had loitered over breakfast, waiting until the room was clear before pocketing all the leftover bacon. The dogs could never replace her darling girl, yet she was drawn to them. Their clear delight each time they sensed her approach was a trickle of joy dropping into the great well inside her that craved wordless love. She wandered along the row of wooden, crate-like kennels, slipping the rashers, one by one, between the bars, tears pricking her eyes. The dogs conveyed their thanks in whimpers and warm tongues sucking every molecule of salt from her fingers.

Magga Dan maintained a cautious distance from the shoals and reefs fringing the shore, made visible by a creamy lather of lime green and white. Supplies for the scientists staying in the six tiny wooden field huts were given precedence on the first dinghies to make their way through the reefs. Several boatloads of biologists followed, as well as the four Macquarie women and the physicists studying auroras and magnetic fields.

Eventually, Harris came to find her, smiling excitedly. Leading her through the pack of men waiting to go ashore, he eased her into a small gap at the rail beside Moofty.

'Beautiful, isn't it, Mrs Law?' Moofty said.

Nel answered him with a broad smile, lifting her face to the sun and letting the breeze thread her hair.

'Couldn't ask for better weather,' Harris agreed, leaning over the side to see how many seats were yet to be filled in the dinghy below.

'Almost no wind at all,' Moofty said, lifting off his beanie as if to double-check his statement using his bare head as an anemometer. 'I don't care what anyone says, Mrs Law. Seems to me like you're bringing us good luck.'

There was an awkward pause, all eyes swinging to Nel.

Nel squared her shoulders. 'A day straight from God's top drawer,' she said, smiling gently at Moofty, noticing that his cheeks had intensified to alizarin crimson.

She leaned over the bulwark. Far below, the dinghy bobbed and wobbled like a child's shoe bouncing on a vast and treacherous floor. Waves slapped the red steel. It was a *long* way down.

'Easy,' said Harris, putting his hand over hers.

Between the rail and the tiny vessel stretched a rope ladder with thin wooden slats. An extremely flimsy rope ladder.

Moofty straddled the wide lip of the ship's wall and disappeared down the rungs, quick as a possum on a powerline.

It was her turn.

'Come on, love. Get your leg over.' A rash of sniggering.

Her breath echoed in her ears and the edges of her vision began to crawl with tiny dark spots.

She gripped the rail and leaned out.

Moofty peered up at her from the dinghy. 'No worries, Mrs Law. I've got you from this end. It's easier than it looks.'

'Ready?' Harris slung her backpack onto his shoulder and took her left arm in both his hands.

She was about to say *Not on your life* when she caught sight of George, watching her from the back of the crowd.

George shook his head, smirking. He called to Harris, 'Good luck, mate. You've got yourself twenty pounds of grief in a ten-pound bag, I reckon.'

Sensing the surge of tension in her forearm, Harris moved closer, blocking her view of the men behind him. 'Two minutes,' he said in a low voice. 'That's all – and you'll wonder what you were ever worried about.' His clear blue eyes looked straight into hers, his grip steady and firm on her arm. 'I've got you.'

Nel took hold of the top of the ladder and, resisting the impulse to throw a haughty look at George, hitched her leg over the side of the ship. Harris kept a grip on her arm as she groped for footing on the slick wooden rungs.

'Got it?' Harris leaned out to make sure both her feet were secure as she clung to the sides of the ladder with a death hold. Her heart hammered beneath her Mae West, heat radiating from her bones, the air on her hot cheeks not enough to cool the internal roast.

It was excruciating. One flailing step after another, she inched her way down, grasping the rope, so treacherously slick under her thick gloves. No matter how hard she gripped the ladder, it didn't feel tight enough to stop it slipping through her fingers. She was hot. So hot. As if a furnace had ignited deep within her body. Sweat funnelled down her back and she had to swipe her forehead against her sleeves to stop perspiration running into her eyes. Her makeup must look a fright.

The Mae West jutted so far in front of her she couldn't see past it to the rungs. All she could do was fish in the air with her foot until it caught a wooden slat, then slide her grip down the rough rope, one handhold at a time. Her cheeks stung in the cold, the temperature of her blood under the skin close to sizzling.

The further down she stepped, the further the steel wall of the ship curved inwards, so by the time she was a third of the way down, she was dangling in midair, swinging wildly with every movement. She clung to the rope ladder, completely at the mercy of the wind, gravity and the ship's rollicking motion. Her throat was tight and dry. Even if she called for help, she feared all that would emerge would be a croak. She forced herself to breathe, then couldn't stop, hyperventilating like the sled dogs scenting bacon.

It would've only been minutes, yet it felt like hours. A voice spoke from just below her feet. 'Almost there.' It was Moofty. She was close. The ocean was just below her. Heaving. She could taste the spray on her lips. Two steps and she felt a touch on her ankle, guiding her down, placing each foot on the last of the rungs. Moofty grasped her waist, one more step, and she felt the dinghy, solid beneath her feet. As she sank onto a bench in the rocking vessel a cheer floated down to her from the ship. She tilted her head back to see a line of grinning faces atop the looming red wall. It was several minutes, her eyes searching for the horizon as the tiny boat lurched, wobbling atop the vast green swell, before she managed to control her breath.

~

The waters of the bay were thick with giant kelp, its sinister, oily tendrils pulsing with the swell, as if its sole desire was to pull everyone overboard and strangle them in the dank depths of the bay.

And, once they reached shore, the *smell*. There were no words. Like a presence. No – an assault. Everyone else was entranced by the surging mass of penguins and seals, but all she wanted to do was press a hanky to her face and step right back into the boat. She didn't know where to put her feet. Every inch of the beach was covered in excrement of some kind or another. Or vomit? She'd seen krill in some of the deep-sea sampling the biologists had done on board *Magga Dan* and these orange streaks among the pale guano were a similar shade. Absolutely revolting. And the *noise*. It was as if every single living thing on this beach was yelling at her. If someone told her the tussock grass was screeching, she wouldn't have doubted it for a second.

Penguins were everywhere – wave after wave of them swimming in from the shallows, clapping each other with flippers, beaks clacking, bustling across the crowded beach to the tussock-grass slopes or heading back out to the deep.

Harris took her arm, his eyes alight. 'Amazing, isn't it? A wonder of the natural world.' He started moving through the seething crowd of penguins as if he was politely making his way through a mass of shoppers on Christmas Eve. 'Excuse me ... pardon.' The penguins showed him no such respect, nipping at his legs with sharp beaks.

Nel adjusted her knapsack and followed him into the crush, holding her breath and seeking clean patches of sand like stepping stones. It was impossible. Within minutes, her legs were smarting from multiple beak nips, she was light-headed from the ammonia and the soles of her golf shoes were weighted with crud.

She wove her way deeper into the morass of penguins, doing her best to keep up with Harris. The penguins were not in the least afraid; most of them were curious and only those with chicks still not totally fledged reacted to their presence with any trepidation. *Ugly little tykes*, she thought, looking at the odd chicks still ragged and patchy with brown fluff they'd yet to shed. For babies, they really were quite homely, and seemed to know it, their posture hunched and expressions almost comically downhearted. When she put aside the nauseating stink and the ear-splitting sound, the adult penguins waddling about were quite adorable. She thought they resembled quaint gentlemen with questionable taste in eyebrow grooming. In fact, it was hard to notice anything *but* the extravagant yellow and black brow-feathers sweeping out and back from the centre of their foreheads in luxuriant, citrus plumes.

Nel saw an opening and took a step forward, only to find that a penguin had had the exact same thought. She looked down into the upturned face of a bird that was now standing on her golf shoe, balancing precariously and a little pigeon-toed on its pink, healthily clawed feet. She let out a snort of laughter, but the penguin, tottering to keep its balance, looked up at her with a rather baffled expression.

'That hairdo! How can anyone take you seriously?' she said, looking at the penguin but speaking loud enough for Harris to hear over the cacophony of penguin conversation.

Harris grinned. 'Quite the monobrow, isn't it? I've always had a soft spot for crested penguins. So much character. They look a lot like the macaroni and rockhoppers I worked with on Heard Island, but these royals are larger with white faces, not black.'

'Lovely to meet you, sir – may I have my foot back? Please?' Nel jiggled her shoe until the penguin raised its little black wings for balance and hopped off the red and white leather, not giving her another glance as it waddled into the throng.

'Let's head for that hillside.' Harris gestured at the tussocky slope beyond the beach, where the ground was steep and clear of penguins. 'That should give you a good vantage point.'

~

Gasping for breath, Nel sank onto a tussock. Her heart thundered from the climb, and she suspected she looked every bit as red-faced and graceless as she felt. Had she been alone, she'd have been tearing off layers, decorating the tussocks with discarded clothing. She was so *hot*. Harris was doing a gentlemanly job of looking everywhere but directly at her, stamping his feet and flipping up his hood. When Nel's deep breaths showed no sign of easing, he pulled the canteen from his pack and offered her a drink.

She'd gulped too many mouthfuls before she remembered to leave enough for him. How stupid to pack hot chocolate and not even think of water. Field-assistant black mark numbers one and two.

'That was quite a clamber,' Nel said, when she'd caught her breath enough to speak. The last thing she felt like doing was work, but Harris seemed even more energised than when they'd landed. He'd pulled out his notebook and was squinting at the penguins massed below, holding his fingers in a square before his eyes, his lips moving silently. Several minutes passed as he counted without sound, Nel using the opportunity of his turned back to admire the breadth of his shoulders. When he eventually spoke, she startled and quickly began digging in her knapsack for her paper and ink.

'Three-forty-six,' Harris muttered, and jotted the number down in his notebook.

'If you're counting penguins, I think you may have missed a few ...'

'It's a technique for a coarse estimation of numbers. You make a square, count how many individuals in the square, then count how many squares fit on the whole beach – multiply the number of squares by the number of penguins per square and there you have it. The hard part is not losing count.'

Nel smiled. 'They're not being very helpful. You need to ask them to stand in neater squares.' Nel gazed along the coastline, thinking the huddled mass of penguins looked like television static when Nefertiti bumped the aerial, a deluge of it, flooding the entire beach.

'I've got ... 350,000. Which is pretty good considering the hit their numbers took back in the late 1800s and early this century.'

'Hunting?'

He nodded. 'When we head to Nuggets Beach, you can still see what's left of the refinery equipment. Apparently each one of these fellows boils down to half a litre of oil.'

Nel was speechless. It was incredible that humans had so depleted the world's whale and seal populations they'd turned on penguins. These cheerful little souls. Of course, she hadn't questioned their deaths when she'd put them on the dinner table. But she'd never thought about what it would take to actually walk up to one and club it to death.

'These penguins are only found here and on a couple of other islands close by. If these rookeries are wiped out, that's it. The royal penguin – gone forever.' He knelt on a tussock beside her. 'Do you have everything you need? Can I leave you to it?'

She felt a pang of disappointment but nodded. 'I was thinking I'd do a watercolour of the whole rookery. But I'm meant to be practising for the Adélie penguins. Shouldn't I be asking you what you need?'

'It's your first time ashore. You should enjoy it. Paint whatever strikes you. Later, if you have time, and you want to, a few pen and ink illustrations of penguins going about their business would be fantastic. But you're the artist. Your work comes first.' He smiled as he straightened up, his knees cracking audibly.

'I'm sure I'll have time. And if I'm going to be ready for your Adélies, I'll need all the practice I can get.'

'I'll leave you to it, then, Mrs Dr Wilson,' he said with a wink, shoving his notebook in his parka pocket, then clapping and shaking his gloved hands. '*Brr.* Yell out if you get too cold. Or if a sea elephant gets too close. You should be fine. Most of the big old bulls are out at sea this time of year. But the females and young'uns can still give you a bit of a fright if they take you by surprise.'

Nel gave him a brave smile she suspected didn't quite reach her eyes. Knapsack slung on one shoulder, he headed back down the slope, long strides quickly eating the distance it had taken her so long to climb.

Nel settled herself into the tussock, arranged her knapsack into a lap-desk and selected a fresh charcoal block. In front of her, the scene dropped away. She let it flow into her, the colours and contours forming in her mind's eye a plan of light, shadow and tone. She touched the charcoal to the fresh white page and began, blowing away the pieces that crumbled from the edge of the black.

Burnt Umber

Macquarie Island
December 1960

The sewing needle jabbed into the pad of her thumb and Nel thrust the snarled mess of wool and stocking off her lap, barely swallowing a curse. She moved to the porthole, sucking blood from the puncture. The resupply of the main station was almost done. Finally. The beautiful weather hadn't lasted, but the endless to-ing and fro-ing of the vessels continued regardless of the conditions.

It'd been blissful, at first. Every minute of Phil's waking life had been absorbed by the changeover and Nel had been free to spend all her time drawing and painting – either perched up on the bridge, in her cabin or, best of all, out on the island nestled among the tussock grasses, drinking in all the incredible *life*. After Hurd Point, it had been easy enough to just ease herself into any group of expeditioners waiting to head out to Green Gorge or Nuggets Beach. She just clambered down into the next available motor-launch or dinghy. No one questioned her. She wondered if Phil even noticed.

But as the days ticked past, she began to feel her husband's absence. She'd prepare for bed each night with the clack of his typewriter punching through the thin cabin wall. And in the brief moments she had him to herself before he dropped into his bunk, it felt as though he wasn't fully present. He was exhausted, his eyes red-veined and the black smudges pillowed in his sockets now permanent and tender. She was worried. This was only the first changeover of the voyage. How long could he keep going on so little sleep?

Nel turned from the porthole and sank onto the bunk, pulling the tangle of long black wool onto her lap. She held up her handiwork, trying to push down her irritation so she could calmly untangle the long strands of yarn she was trying to stitch onto the snipped-off foot of one of her nylons.

She'd hoped to spend this afternoon on Wireless Hill, just behind the base, painting a panoramic view of the main station for Phil. Her plans had gone awry before she'd taken her first bite of lunch. Colin and Smoky, two expeditioners who'd barely said boo to her, had approached the captain's table with a question for Phil about tomorrow's roster. It was a ruse. Their real objective had been securing her help with their costumes for the changeover party.

She could hardly say no. These weren't regular parties. The celebrations marking the changeover of staff on each station were a highlight of the Antarctic year. Full-scale blowouts. And, most strangely to Nel's mind, cross-dressing at these events was almost de rigueur. It was a tradition that went right back to Scott, Shackleton and Mawson – all the Heroic Age explorers seemed to enjoy a night of ribaldry and dressing up as women. So, when Colin and Smoky appealed to her, in front of Phil, for the loan of a brassiere and to make them a wig, she could hardly refuse. She knew this was an opportunity for her to bond with the men. But the last thing she felt like doing was wasting an afternoon playing seamstress.

She sighed, pulling the half-bald stocking cap back onto her lap and fishing the ball of black wool free of the mess at her feet. It was meant to be a beatnik wig for Colin. Nel wondered if his choice was due to a particular disdain for beatniks or whether a beatnik was a persona he felt comfortable inhabiting. The little she knew of Colin hadn't suggested counter-cultural leanings. But what did she know? Maybe this costume was a way of slipping into a skin he secretly admired without risking the ridicule of his friends.

What if she wore a suit? The idea halted her needle in midair. Would the men laugh it away? Think it a great lark? Or maybe it would pull them up short. Nel stood, the wig sliding to the floor. She unhooked one of Phil's suits from the wardrobe, then a shirt and tie. She laid them on the bunk, a flat idea waiting for her to flesh it into being. She'd need suspenders and a belt. Tuck the cuffs under. Brylcreem for her hair. An eyeliner moustache. Yes. If cross-dressing was acceptable for the men, let's see what they thought when the shoe was on the other foot. Pam would be beside herself. She must write her a letter. There was so much to tell her. The albatross. The penguins. All her fresh work.

Every spare space in the tiny cabin was crowded with artwork: watercolours of king penguins with their bright orange neck flares, sketches of sea elephants lolling like blancmanges and an oil painting she'd started of a tiny seal pup.

The wildlife still made her nervous. Especially the sea leopards and bull sea elephants. She'd only spotted one sea leopard, quite small with an injured flipper, but its snake-like head and mouthful of razor teeth was more than enough contact with the species. There weren't many bull sea elephants around, but those she saw were quite frightening, all red-eyed and bleeding from nasty bites, their moulting pelts so scarred and patchy from past battles they looked moth-eaten.

Yet it wasn't all alarming, and she was proud of her growing ability to see the humour in situations that would've previously tested the limits of her courage. At Garden Cove, she'd been happily sketching a family of royal penguins when, from less than a foot behind her, an ear-splitting *plaaart!* belched into the air with the reek of fish. Shrieking, she'd leapt up, art supplies tumbling, watercolour lost to the wind. Harris had almost toppled off his tussock laughing, only to be joined by the surrounding sea elephants, who all began to cough, bark and gurgle as if they too found the whole thing absolutely hilarious. Not so funny, in her shock she'd dropped a glove on a pile of penguin poo, and despite her best efforts with soap and scrubbing, the cabin still held a whiff of it some days later.

That must've been the last time she'd touched the laundry. If Phil had noticed in his fleeting visits to their shared space, he hadn't said anything. They hadn't been in the cabin together long enough for her to tell him about all she'd seen and done.

Outside, a door banged, and she heard Phil's footsteps receding up the corridor.

'Phil!' Nel flung open the door, just catching him before the stairs took him out of earshot. 'Come see. I'm almost done.' She shook the still incomplete wig into the corridor, waving him back.

Phil smiled, but as he strode towards their cabin, she noticed him sneak a glance at his watch.

'What do you think?' Nel pressed the unfinished side against her head, turning so that the stitched side of the wig faced him, and stroked the wool as if smoothing down long hair.

'Looking good. Very *cool*.' Phil clicked his fingers in beatnik applause, chuckling at his joke. Noticing his clothes laid out on the bed, he frowned. 'What's this?' Phil was usually self-sufficient when it came to choosing his wardrobe; Nel's input was usually restricted to, at most, a suggestion on tie colour or pocket square.

'My costume. For tonight.' She grinned, still buoyed by her flash of audaciousness.

Phil stood looking at the long shape on the bunk, the line between his brows deepening. 'Darling, I don't think so.'

'Phil,' she chided him, lightly. 'It's a costume party, isn't it?'

'I don't think the other women will be dressing up. Like this, I mean. They'll be dressed up, of course, but for dancing.'

'Oh, love. Don't be so fussy.' Nel put her hand on his arm. 'If men are dressing up as women, surely I can turn the tables. It'll be a hoot!'

Phil shifted from under her hand, but, seeing her crestfallen expression, put his arm around her, rubbing her shoulder. 'Just put on a nice dress and bring your dancing shoes. I'm sure tonight will be quite wild enough.'

Nel sank down onto the bunk and Phil moved in close, leaning so that her head was against his hip. 'I just don't think it's hitting quite the right note.' He gave her shoulder a pat.

Nel flinched. 'Not the right note? I think it's *exactly* the right note. ANARE would far prefer if I was a man.'

'Look.' Phil exhaled audibly, lips tight. 'You being on board is already a touchy subject. Not that it's anyone's business. You probably haven't noticed' – at Nel's scoff, he paused, raising an eyebrow – 'but it's caused some tension in the ranks. So you trotting out, wearing my suit, might be seen as rubbing their faces in it.'

'But, I think—'

'Nel. I said no.' He sighed. 'Look, I'm sorry, darling. I love that you're trying to get into the swing of things, and you know I hate to put the kybosh on your ideas. For a costume party at home, it *would* be a blast. But here? There's just more to consider. And tonight's all about the men's morale.' He patted her knee. 'All right?'

When she didn't respond, he stood up.

'Better keep moving. Still a few things to square away.'

Nel listened as his footsteps grew fainter, clanged on the metal stairs, then faded to silence. On one level, she'd known it would be like this. He was at work after all. The boss. Great White Chief, as they called him behind his back. But she hadn't been prepared for Phil at work to be so different from Phil at home. Less attentive. He had barely touched her since they left, when nothing would have stopped him at home. And when she did have his attention, he was listening with only half an ear. Her Phil, the husband who enjoyed theatre and opera and fine wine and wicked conversation, was being outshone by the Phil who drank beer, climbed mountains and laughed at bawdy jokes.

Nel tried to shake off her disquiet. He'd been doing this work for many, many years – it must've become second nature for him to morph into *this* version of himself while he was away. Still, she missed *her* Phil, the Phil now in the shadows, and she couldn't escape the sense that this turning to the spotlight of 'manly Phil' was a turn away from her. Nel slid the needle into the nylon and yanked the wool through.

~

She was dressed more for an evening at an ice rink than a party. So many layers. She'd stuffed a pair of lighter shoes into Phil's kitbag for the dancing. She wasn't exactly sure she felt like dancing but having to foxtrot in golf shoes was beyond the pale.

Stepping into the station's large mess hall, Nel was impressed. Coloured streamers and bunting webbed the rafters. The far end of the room had been set aside for the night's entertainment, the tables pushed back against the walls so that the radiogram and musical instruments held centre stage. Nel couldn't believe the amount of food. The tablecloths of the long trestle tables were barely visible between the steaming platters of roast meats, pies and vegetables.

The men drifted into the hall in loose groups. Nel's eyebrows felt pinned to her hairline. The expeditioners were almost unrecognisable. Since arriving, they'd been labouring from dawn until dusk, sweaty and caked with grime from unloading barrels of fuel and oil and seemingly endless cases of supplies. But here they were, stepping through the mess hall door in fancy dress or with hair slicked back, ties knotted and slacks ironed razor-sharp.

Phil poured her a glass of red and Nel sipped it as she accompanied him on his round of the room, the combination of polite small talk and her wine among the clanking pint glasses making her feel a little prim. Eventually, Phil pulled out a chair and they sat together, watching the festivities gain momentum. It was loud. Not the right moment to attempt a heart-to-heart talk about her concern over him being so different here.

It didn't help that some of the unease slithering low and greasy in her gut was the realisation that the time she was spending with Harris made her feel like a different version of herself too. A Nel she liked. To all these men, she was nothing but the boss's wife. Except to Harris. Sharing this secret self with him tinged everything about their time together with rose gold. Nel swallowed a generous mouthful of wine and crossed her legs.

A shout of laughter rang through the hall as Smoky made his entrance. Nel choked, patting her chest as her eyes watered. He had outdone himself.

Smoky strode through the room, grin as wide as his outstretched arms. The room erupted with raucous cheers. The man was naked but for a generously sized pair of fishing waders, his body moving freely inside the enormous rubber pants, the straps over his muscular shoulders the only part of the outfit in contact with his skin. The top of the waders came to just below his nipples, perfectly framing the sinuous blue-green bare-breasted mermaid tattooed on his chest. The finishing touches were a bowler hat and fat cigar clamped between his teeth.

Smoky climbed onto a chair and, with a flourish, announced the arrival of the evening's guest of honour. Miss Sonja stalked through the door as if on a catwalk. Nel stiffened. More vamp than beatnik, Colin's transformation into Miss Sonja didn't only involve the wig of black wool and the loan of her black jumper and brassiere. Given the number of pairs of woollen socks jammed into her underwear, Nel doubted her jumper would ever recover its original shape. She could smell Sonja's perfume from across the room, and a liberal amount of foundation and lipstick had been applied to her freshly shaven face. If Colin had brought the makeup with him especially for this transformation, why had he needed her help? Surely, he would've thought to bring a costume as well?

Colin paraded around the room as Miss Sonja, flirting in a Russian-accented falsetto as she sat on laps and planted bright lipstick blossoms on cheeks. The crew were in stitches, openly fondling her chest and propositioning her with increasingly lewd suggestions. The scientists were equally taken, laughing as they pinched Miss Sonja's bottom, plying her with drinks. Nel took a deep breath and hung a smile on her face.

The room was loud with radiogram music, clinking glassware and the rumble of men's laughter. The four Macquarie women claimed seats in a shadowed corner. Perching dinner plates on their plaid skirts and wine glasses by their feet, they leaned into their conversation, keeping an eye trained on the action. Sensible, Nel thought – she wasn't about to turn her back on the evening's festivities either.

Dinner plates cleared, the musical part of the night kicked into gear. Phil took centrestage with his accordion. Guitars and fiddles were picked up with varying degrees of skill, and those demurring had tambourines, triangles and maracas pressed into their hands. Musical requests were yelled from the audience, who then accompanied the musicians in an enthusiastic sing-a-long.

Keen to avoid being roped into judging the costume contest, Nel made her way to the women's corner, bringing a bottle of wine to top up their glasses. They thanked her, gesturing for her to pull up a chair, despite the room growing too loud for conversation. It was such an alien feeling – to be alone among so many people. And this was before she sailed away, leaving these women behind. They hadn't connected, not really. And if she was honest with herself, she'd taken their presence for granted, happy for them to deflect some of the attention. It hadn't struck her before now, sitting here in this tiny oasis of female understanding, what it would be like to be the *only* woman left on board.

She wished her sisters were here. Everything about this evening – her whole experience on the ship – was bottled inside her, the pressure mounting with each passing minute. She missed Gwen and Joan, the ability to talk and be heard; more than that – to be *understood*. What would Pam make of Miss Sonja? The thought almost made her snort aloud. What exactly was it about dressing as a woman that was so darned *funny*? Men had such strict expectations of how women should dress and behave. But when a *man* did it – well, that was so demeaning it must be a joke. The whole thing was insulting. Nel drained her glass.

Maybe I am a little like a scientist, she thought. An anthropologist observing a different culture. The Margaret Mead of Antarctic society. She scanned the room. Smoke had gathered in the rafters, forming a soft ceiling above the revellers' heads. A strand of bunting had come loose and slumped towards the floor; tablecloths were shadowed with dark patches of spilled drink – the room coming undone at a similar rate to that of the partygoers.

Her eyes came to rest on Harris. He was nursing an almost full glass of beer, leaning against the wall at the outer edge of an animated circle of expeditioners. As she watched, the group erupted in laughter. Harris smiled, his reaction perfectly timed yet less intense. As the laughter continued, Harris sipped his beer, the level barely dipping. There was something about the way he was part of the group but on its periphery, drinking but not obviously drunk. *Like me*, she thought, with a tender smile. *He's playing the observer.*

'May I have this dance?'

Nel jolted. George. She hadn't heard him approach over the musicians' upbeat rendition of 'Walking after Midnight'. There was no one in the room she wanted to dance with less – not that she wanted to dance at all. She would have preferred the party to flow around her as if she was a stone in a creek. She scanned the room, seeking Phil. He was watching her over the top of his accordion, perched on his stool amid the band, an encouraging smile on his face. One dance.

She pressed her lips into the semblance of a smile and placed her hand in George's. His face didn't even make that effort. *What is this about?*

George swung her into the middle of the room. His hand was slick, and as he placed the other on her waist, she could feel her shirt dampen between his palm and her skin.

'Boss's orders. Dance with the ladies.' He jerked his head towards the band. 'Since you're the only one who's not a spinster, my bet was you're the least likely to step on my feet.' His breath was a noxious combination of beer and tobacco. 'The Great White Chief's wife. I guess that makes you the Great White Squaw.' His gust of laughter made her lean back and angle her cheek away. He tightened his grip on her waist.

Nel locked her elbows, attempting to maintain an arm's length between them. The only positive thought she could muster was that at least this man was brave, or foolhardy, enough to make it clear how he felt about her being on board. The rest were mutterers, holding it all in their eyes. They thought they were being polite, masking it. But she could feel their disdain, disregard, derision, like a magnetic repulsion every time she approached a table, a cluster of men. The only time it eased was when she was with Phil or in the cabin.

George tried to swing her closer again, but she tensed her arms. 'Relax, Mrs Law. I don't bite.'

The song ended and she glanced over at Phil. The band was having a quick discussion over the next number. As they raised their instruments, Phil flashed a smile at her, clearly pleased she was mingling with the men.

'One more for luck.' It did not sound like a question, or feel like it, as George tightened his hold on her waist. Nel cast around, hoping someone would cut in and save her.

The band struck up and Nel found herself being whirled across the dance floor once more. She stumbled and George steadied her against his body. When she pulled back, she knocked into Hope MacPherson, also dancing.

'Sorry!' As Nel twisted towards her, she noticed Hope's partner had his hand not on her waist, but the small of her back. Low on her back. Hope was the mollusc expert, and reading the tension in her neck, Nel thought the poor woman would like nothing better than to retreat into a shell.

'May I cut in?' Andy appeared at Nel's shoulder, drawing himself up to his full height.

'You absolute darling,' Nel whispered as Andy guided her into a sedate box-step that moved them away from the music. 'Thank you.'

'My pleasure. Please feel free to relay my new-found "knight in shining armour" status to Pam, when next you correspond.' He smiled, using his back to shield Nel from the room.

'Actually, your gallantry has inspired me. Can you keep standing here for a second?'

Without waiting for an answer, Nel grabbed the front of her shirt and with a sharp twist, yanked the button off her collar. Andy frowned.

'*This* knight in shining armour needs a prop. Back in a minute.' Nel grasped the front of her shirt at her sternum as she threaded her way through the dancers towards Hope.

The poor woman was stiff, lips compressed as she swayed mechanically side to side.

'Hope!' Nel moved in beside the couple. 'Thank goodness.' She held up the button, theatrically holding closed the front of her shirt. 'Wardrobe emergency. I need your sewing kit!' Nel shot a look at the man. 'So sorry to pull her away.' She turned back to Hope. 'Is it in your purse?'

It took Hope less than half a beat. 'No. It's in our dorm. Let me fetch it for you.'

'You're a lifesaver.' Nel directed a hollow smile at the now empty-handed expeditioner, then followed Hope towards the door.

Out on the porch, Hope breathed deep in the cold night air. 'Thank you.'

Nel squeezed her arm and sat down on the steps.

'I'll be right back.'

'Wait,' Nel laughed, and patted the step, showing Hope the broken threads at the collar of the shirt.

Hope sat down, leaning back on her hands to look up at the sky. 'Good acting. I was convinced you had a cleavage situation.'

Nel gave a little mock bow. A blast of music washed into the porch as the door opened behind them. The women spun, shoulders relaxing as they saw Isobel, Ann and Elise slip from the hall to join them on the stairs.

'Everything all right?' Ann asked, scanning their faces.

'We're fine. Nel saved me from an expeditioner who had a little too much in common with an octopus.' Hope shot Nel a grateful smile. 'Fortunately for us, he's travelling on to Mawson. I'm sorry to say, he'll be your problem for the next few weeks.'

'I don't envy you,' Elise said. 'Being all alone. At least we have each other and the escape of days out in the field.'

'I think I'll manage. *Most* of the men are unfailingly polite. To my face, anyway. And I'm not alone. I'm lucky. I have Phil.' Nel shrugged, with a smile.

There was a long pause, Hope shifting on the step, Ann smoothing at the pleats of her skirt. Nel looked from face to face. The women were uneasy, darting glances at Isobel, who was staring grimly into the dark.

'You *are* lucky. You're married to the judge. Even though I'd not trade places with you for love or money.' Isobel met her eyes and Nel sensed she was striving to hold something back.

'The judge?'

Isobel sighed, clearly weighing silence against forthrightness. Finally, she leaned forward, her voice kind. 'Look. Our situations are very different. I was down here last year, one of the first women allowed. So, I can say from experience that, to most of the men, we're simply invaders in their world. Viewed with suspicion.' She gave a sardonic laugh. 'And that's fine. Irritating, but fine. We can handle that.'

Elise, Hope and Ann all nodded, not meeting Nel's eyes.

'But when it comes to your husband's attitude, well, that's a different matter. He's the one with the power. He decides who's included and who's not.' Isobel faced Nel squarely. 'Now, I don't know what he's said to you, but when we were interviewed for this voyage, your husband made it perfectly clear ...' She took a breath, as if steeling herself. 'We were told in no uncertain terms that the future of women on scientific bases – the future of women in ANARE as anything more than secretaries – depended on our behaviour. Or rather, the men's acceptance of our behaviour.'

Nel's eyes widened. 'Oh. I ... I'm so sorry.'

Isobel nodded, her expression softening as she read the shock on Nel's face. 'So, while we're ready to shoulder the responsibility – being ambassadors for our sex – I can tell you right now, we're not particularly amused by it.' She shrugged, a small smile easing the sting of her words. 'Which is why I think you'll have it a little easier. You're married to the judge.'

~

Phil stood on his chair, hands raised as he called for quiet to announce the winners of the costume contest. Nel recognised the tactic: her husband's voice was deliberately soft, forcing his rowdy audience into silence.

The final award, 'Best Dressed', went to Miss Sonja, much to the crowd's approval. She curtsied and simpered, then brought the evening to a riotous climax with her rapturous acceptance of an over-hammed wedding proposal from the bosun.

Just before midnight, Phil thanked the group for their hard work, said his goodbyes and picked up his accordion case. No doubt he was heading straight back to his desk; his days rarely ended at midnight.

The party sputtered out, the fresh Macquarie residents staggering to their new quarters and those headed back to the ship making their noisy, unsteady way down to the dock.

Nel let the first crush of revellers depart before making her way out of the mess hall. On the top step of the porch, she slipped off her dancing shoes, fishing the golf shoes from the bottom of the kitbag.

'Congratulations.' Harris's voice came from out of the shadows beside the hall. 'Miss Sonja may have been crowned queen of the evening, but I hear you were the real power behind the throne.'

'You know what they say ... behind every Russian beauty queen ... is another beauty queen past her use-by date, but without a five o'clock shadow.'

Harris chuckled and they lapsed into comfortable silence, walking side by side away from the lights of the station, their steps clopping on the painted wood of the boardwalk.

The night sky was clear, and the voices of those already at the dock carried back up to them on a gust of wind.

'We should make the most of this,' Harris said, pitching his voice low so as not to travel any further than her ears. 'Down on the ice, endless daylight really makes it feel like you're on another planet. You don't realise how much you miss the night until it's gone.'

Nel nodded, looking up at the sky. The moon had risen, but even with its light, the stretch of darkness was richly pocked with stars.

They reached the edge of the dock just as a full launch chugged away, its lights dancing across the ruffled surface of the water.

Nel guessed Phil was already back on board, brow furrowed over the details of the roster.

Pushing back her shoulders, she rolled her head to loosen the muscles of her neck, only to freeze, chin angled up at the dark.

A curtain of viridian light unfurled across the sky, as if caught in a celestial breeze. Around her, the world fell away. Filmy curtains of jade, pink and gold wafted across the dark, the great quiet suddenly singing with colour. Around the moon, a corona, the white face ringed with a halo of silver light. Nel held her breath, drinking it in. *This.* This was what Phil meant when he spoke about words failing him. When he told her Antarctica held such indescribable wonders that language and art failed. She drew herself up. No, it would not fail her. *She* would not fail *it*.

A clatter of footsteps rattled on the boardwalk behind them. The footfalls stuttered, followed by a sound like a sack of potatoes slumping to the ground. 'Come on, Jerry. Upsadaisy.' Raucous laughter.

Nel tried to ignore it, keeping her eyes on the sky. Beside her, she felt Harris tense.

'Hey, hey! Lovebirds.' Sniggers and shushing.

Nel stiffened, her throat tight and dry.

'Excuse me, Lady Law. May we join you aboard the next vessel? Or is it another *private excursion*?' The speaker slurred the last word, breaking down into helpless cackles as he heard himself.

Nel glanced behind her. Half-a-dozen men were bunched on the dock, leaning on each other, the whole group swaying uneasily as if already at sea. She didn't know any of them well enough to retort and wouldn't have trusted herself to speak even if she had. What did they mean? Was this the shipboard gossip? Anxiety rattled inside her, as if her whole body was a children's toy maze, tiny metallic balls crazily bouncing and rolling about, never finding her centre. If this got back to Phil, she could kiss her penguin work and time with Harris goodbye.

'Steady on, chaps,' Harris said over his shoulder. 'Don't want to say anything you'll regret tomorrow. Or for the rest of the voyage.'

'Who appointed you dep-yu-ty chief?' More laughter. 'Deputy,' the slurring man corrected himself.

'Simmons.' There was a world of weariness in Harris's voice. 'Just shut it.'

'Right. Yes, sir. Shutting it. Sir.' More giggling and snorting.

Nel kept her eyes on the sky, trying to steady herself with deep, even breaths. The drama playing out over her head suddenly seemed even more ethereal. The men behind them were so far gone they'd not even noticed it.

Behind them, a kissing sound, long and wet.

Beside her, Harris sighed. 'Grow up, lads.'

She couldn't breathe. Shame slithered in her gut. Nothing had happened. She felt herself start to heat, her cheeks burning in the cold air.

These men. These selfish, stupid, *vapid* men. *And they say women are the gossips!*

Out of the dark, the chug of motor, the lights of the launch sweeping the dock. Nel shook her head, teeth clenched. This once-in-a-lifetime night. These colours. Standing here with this solid, thoughtful man, who saw her as something more than Phil's wife. Who saw *her*. How *dare* these men ruin it. Why should this place be only for them?

Alizarin Crimson

Enough with this bloody weather. The ship lurched as another great wave smashed over the bow. The glass Nel was using as a water pot sloshed dirty liquid across her thighs. She swore under her breath. She'd reached the end of her patience with the heaving and juddering, never being able to walk anywhere without having to hang on for dear life.

Nel swiped her brush across the paper, washing a smear of cloud into the scene. The weather did hold a kind of beauty, but she was in no mood for it. The infernal reeling and plunging made it almost impossible to work. She gazed out the bridge windows at the white-chopped ocean broiling below a sky clotted with heavy cloud. A pod of sei whales slid past, puffing loud gusts of mist, their grey backs sleek and clean in the messy sea. Grey sky, dark water, grey whales. The tones matched her mood.

Since leaving Macquarie Island, everything had tested her patience. Enough with the broken glass and plates in the dining

109

room, enough with burned hands from spilled tea, enough with the books and equipment crashing from shelves in the cabin. She hadn't been able to shower in days. She couldn't draw – managing a steady line on paper was impossible, and even watercolours could be ruined with a single lurch.

Enough with grey. Enough with sea fog and wave spray and the terrifying phthalo green at the portholes when the ship rolled so wildly, she could see the void below. Enough with her cabin, the walls closer and corners sharper every day. She missed steadiness – steady steps, steady nib on the page. Steady heart. She missed Andy. Her sisters. Pam. The Macquarie women. She missed laughter. She missed sleep. She missed herself.

Enough! She ripped the paper from the pad and crumpled it, then grabbed her brushes and palette, awkwardly balancing the water pot so as not to spill any more liquid as she hopped down from on top of the raft.

Earlier in the morning, she'd made yet another uncomfortable entry to the bridge, silence falling the moment she stepped through the door. She hadn't realised how much attention the other women had diverted. Now she was the only woman on board, *all* the scrutiny fell on her.

Bill had tried to jolly her out of her funk. Seeing her struggle to capture the silvery tones of sea and sky, he'd attempted distraction, asking for her guess on where and when they'd sight the first iceberg of the journey. It was tradition. She'd leaned over the chart, gripping the table edge as the ship heaved and rolled beneath them. She had no idea, so she'd stabbed her finger at a random spot between Macquarie Island and the Antarctic coast. He'd pencilled the latitude of her finger on the list of guesses, waiting with kind patience until she'd also plucked a date and time from the air.

Nel shoved the crumpled watercolour into the bin, to join the jumble of previous failures, then stalked in her stop-start way back to the cabin, half hoping to crash into George or any of those gossiping busybodies with their flapping ears and overactive imaginations. Knocking one of them off his feet would be incredibly satisfying.

She saw the surreptitious nudges every time she and Harris spoke. Their meetings about her penguin sketches and plans for the Adélie work were deliberately public, a generous arm's length always separating them. But when she went to meet him at their booth in the dining saloon, she almost felt swept back to her university days, the glow of anticipation recalling the first months of Phil's courtship. She remembered her constant awareness of Phil's muscular boxer's frame, her wonder at the thoughts sparking behind the laser focus of his eyes. It was ridiculous. She was too old for this. Too married. And there was nothing in Harris's eyes or voice to suggest he was equally keen for her company. Yet when they were together, it wasn't all business. He was interested in her life, her opinions. He saw her as a friend. Nothing more. Hopefully, no one noticed the flush in her cheeks. They were unnerving, these relentless jitters she couldn't quite decipher as attraction or anxiety. And beneath it all, the constant dread that the men's smirking whispers would reach Phil's ears. No wonder she couldn't sleep.

Nel tossed her sketchbook and supplies on the bunk before throwing herself down beside them. Through the wall, she heard the rumble of conversation in Phil's stateroom, followed by a bang and footsteps down the hall. Nel put her fists on her knees and pushed herself to her feet with a sigh. She missed him. He'd be busy, but it was worth a try. She needed his company – that sweet, safe familiarity with its invocation of home.

Phil looked up as she opened the stateroom door, his frown softening a little the moment he registered it wasn't an expeditioner barging in without knocking.

'Darling. Everything all right?' Phil glanced back at the open ledger in front of him, jotting down several figures.

His desk was cluttered with notebooks and piles of paper, stacked like jagged bergs around the borders of the desk. In the centre, a map of Antarctica was held flat with fist-sized rocks. Nel pitched herself into a chair, facing him across his desk. Finally, Phil looked up, his expression expectant.

'Can't draw. Can't paint. And I've crashed into so many walls everything aches.' Nel made a face and laughed. 'That pretty much sums up my life at the moment.' She looked across at him, taking in the exhausted glaze and puffiness of his eyes. 'How about you, Dr Law?'

He expelled a long breath, pulled a telegram from the top of the closest stack of paperwork and slid on his reading glasses. 'A blizzard's hit Mawson. From the reports, it sounds more like a hurricane. The Dakota at the Rumdoodle airstrip? Gone. Just disappeared. Steel cables snapped and no sight of it. And the Beaver's wings were ripped clean off. Its tail's broken and the roof of the hangar's hanging on by a thread. No injuries, thank God.' He trailed off, his shoulders slumping. 'But it's a complete disaster.' He pinched the bridge of his nose. 'My plans for using the Dakota to explore south over the Prince Charles Mountains while we're at Mawson – buggered. And the damage to the Beaver means we can't use it in Oates Land. So now we'll only be able to explore with the ship – which means we're stuck with the coastline and maybe a little inland using the helicopters, if we're lucky with the weather. But no flights over the interior.' He smacked his pen off the desk with the back of his hand. 'Damn it.' He drew a deep breath, before leaning to scoop it up off the floor. 'I need to contact Mawson base. Send a search party after the Dakota. Might be salvageable. But I'm not holding my breath.' He pulled a notebook towards him and started writing.

His fingers gripped the pen, knuckles white, the pressure kinking the first joint of his index finger so that the flesh reddened around the edges of the nail. He had practical hands – short fingered almost to the point of stubbiness, yet surprisingly dexterous.

Nel was still looking at his hands as it began: another hot flush. The first part of her to heat up was always her fingertips. Then a moment of eerie quiet before the tide of thick unease rolled in. Like going down in the David Jones elevator. Her stomach dropped, leaving her weak as if her sinews had lost all their tension. Then the heat, every hair on her scalp hot as an electric wire. And finally – as if the heat ignited her nerves – the fear. Fighting the urge to fan her face, she balled her hands into fists and jammed them beneath her thighs. Phil didn't look up.

Nel wanted to ask him about what Isobel had said. But looking at the top of Phil's head, tension and disappointment straining his body close to breaking point, she didn't think it the right time. But when would it be? Finding him alone and willing to talk was so rare.

'Phil, I was wondering ... Back on Macquarie, I was painting that panorama of the base and I noticed ... the women. Their quarters, actually. That shed ... why were they put so far from the rest of the base?'

Phil frowned, then gave a snort of laughter. 'There's a big enough problem with rabbits on Macquarie. Lesson learned. Remove temptation.' He waggled his eyebrows at her, Groucho Marx–style, before shifting focus back to the ledger.

'That's disgusting. You can't be serious.'

Phil blinked, pen hovering.

'They are hardly inviting attention. Why punish *them*?'

His laugh was sharp. 'You have met men before, yes? If you'd seen a tenth of the things I have down here, you'd know even a toothless old hag would seem fair game after a few months. If women are going to insist on being included, they need to be ready to deal with the worst. Separate quarters? I'm doing them a favour.' He pointed his pen at Nel. 'If they can't handle that, they can't handle it down here.'

She opened her mouth, words bottling in her throat. So it was true. He *was* using them as guinea pigs, placing the future of women on scientific bases on their shoulders.

'And what about me?'

'What about you?'

'Well, if that's your attitude, I'm surprised you were so happy to have me come along.'

Phil looked at her as if she'd started speaking Finnish. 'But you're not one of them. You're my wife.'

She opened her mouth. No words came.

'Completely different situation. You're here with me – a guest – seeing what I do. All you have to do is stay out of the way. *They* are down here to work. If they want to continue being a part of it, they need to fit in. And by fitting in, I mean not disrupting the systems already in place. And certainly not parading around, getting the men all excited. Hence, the separate sleeping quarters.'

'So it will be the same when women are allowed on Mawson? Segregation?'

'Segregation?' Phil dropped his pen. 'Where on earth is this coming from? Women working in Antarctica?' He gave an incredulous laugh. 'I can't believe I need to explain this. You do realise that Mawson and Davis are still under construction? The men on these expeditions, the ones I handpick, they're not just here as scientists. Every one of them is a jack-of-all-trades. They erect buildings, wire up the electrics, maintain the vehicles.' He leaned back in his chair. 'You saw the changeover at Macquarie. How much work did the women do? See them carrying crates, rolling barrels of fuel? Piloting ducks or motor-launches? No. Frankly, it's a bloody stretch to have them at Macquarie when I could've had four more strong backs and capable sets of hands. To put it bluntly, I can't see women down here until the stations are completely up and running. They don't have the skills or the strength. Or the temperament, for that matter. And that's even before we get to the problem of sex.'

Why did it always have to come back to that? If Phil had taken even a moment to ask one of the Macquarie women what was foremost in her mind, it would never have been sex. Or men. It would've been *work*.

Too angry to speak, words caught in her throat. Back on the island, the Macquarie women were putting up with all manner of hardships so that other women could follow. And, worthy or not, she was going to be the first Australian woman in Antarctica. It hadn't occurred to her before this moment, but *she* had a responsibility too.

For the first time, she saw Phil not as her life partner, but as a man holding her future, and the future of women she didn't yet know, in his hands. Nel gripped the armrests of her chair. *Where is my husband?* The words caught in her throat were molten glass, her body burning with anger so hot she feared she might shatter as it cooled.

~

Finally, a day of sun; the sea ruffled as if stroked against the grain by the wind. Nel was standing at the rail when she saw it. To starboard, near the horizon – a chip of white. *Iceberg.* A moment later, the horn sounded, and she felt the ship shift beneath her feet.

115

By the time the iceberg was close enough to paint, the weather had come in. The sky was heavy with a great sweep of cloud and, as they neared the floating ice, a flock of snow petrels wheeled through the scene, so white against the dark sky it was as if she had taken a palette knife to an oil painting and scraped the grey back to clean canvas, their wings more absence than presence.

At first, she thought the berg looked like a skyscraper snapped off the edge of a city. It revolved in the dark sea, displaying every gleaming facet as the whole ship's contingent leaned on the railing, armed with binoculars or cameras.

It was so *white*. A white so pure it hovered on the edge of dipping into blue. Her teeth clamped together, as she assessed the floating island. So many hues and tones in what was meant to be an absence of colour. And she'd thought teasing out all the shades of blue had been a test!

Determined not to be daunted by this first inkling of the artistic challenge of Antarctica, she headed for the cabin and her easel. Disillusioned and still smarting from Phil's callousness, she was glad of both the distraction and the refuge. She understood he was under pressure. And exhausted. But for the first time on this voyage, she had no desire for his company. The dinner hour arrived. She paused, sable-tipped brush hovering as her attention expanded to take in the sounds of the ship. Hearing neither his footsteps nor the clack of the typewriter, she turned back to her canvas.

Staring at the painting, she felt the familiar flush of pleasure in accomplishment, tinged with dissatisfaction with the final image. At least she could keep tinkering. That was the beauty of oils. The pigments took days to dry, allowing the scene to be overpainted or scraped back and redone.

She squinted, swaying to take in the image from as many angles as the tiny cabin allowed. The problem wasn't the execution so much as the style. Even when she'd been painting from Phil's photographs, she'd never attempted an iceberg. Looking at this mammoth chunk of ice, her first real sighting of something quintessentially Antarctic, the only word she could think to describe it was *chaste*.

She'd felt lost, watching it floating there, so deceptively simple in colour and form. It wasn't *like* anything else. That's what she'd been excited to try to pin down on the canvas. But this painting? She sighed and shook her head. This was a vision from another time. Not the near future, which was how her paintings felt to her on the best of days. This was a painting from before her birth, something from a pioneer catching sight of a new world but only able to use the old, familiar world as a template. Her iceberg looked like a gothic castle. Its spires and turrets, while lacking medieval pennants, fluttered with a swoop of Wilson's storm petrels. Nel knocked the back of her head against the wall. She'd unwittingly channelled a Romantic version of the scene.

Still, it wasn't a total loss. The composition was fine, and she was quite happy with the reflected ice in the foreground. She tried to view it with Pam's eyes. *Forge something new.* Nel stretched and clambered off the bed with a groan. She turned the painting to the wall and stared out the porthole into the long, dim twilight. This world was so far from everything known and familiar. Out here, on this speck of a ship bobbing upon immeasurable depths, humans were small and strange and alien. *Even men don't belong down here.* She sighed. What she needed to do was leave behind everything she knew about how this place had been painted in the past. Antarctica didn't need humanity. Didn't need artists. Or scientists. That's what she needed to focus on. Nel picked up a 6B pencil, tapping her finger on the blunt point. With short strokes of her penknife, she whittled the graphite stiletto-sharp.

Manganese Blue

Southern Ocean,
January 1961

The sea was rough, but Nel had braced herself on the deck by wedging her folding stool between the rail and a tarp-lashed crate. Working swiftly, she stripped page after page from her watercolour block as each great crystalline chunk slid by, trying to bring the ice to the paper in a way that didn't immediately pull another style or time to mind. Waves lapped and foamed at the bergs' sides, wearing the ice smooth on the lower sections while the heights remained crisp and jagged.

She was lonely. With Andy gone, the need to maintain distance from Harris, and her anger at Phil still simmering, she woke each morning to elastic hours stretching empty and silent. Work. That was what she needed. Out on deck, in the bracing cold, she could focus. Be herself. Shove her disappointment with Phil and unnerving feelings about Harris to the back of her mind.

As if she had called him into being, she glanced up to find Harris leaning against the rail several yards away. Flinching, she cast around for onlookers. A few crew were on deck, and while they didn't seem to be taking any notice, she fumbled to gather her supplies. When she looked back up, Harris was still staring out to sea.

'Milestone day. Excited?'

She sighed, huffing a tiny cloud of exasperation. Couldn't he take the hint she wanted to be alone? Nel shoved her brushes into her knapsack and stood up, emptying the brush-water in her cup over the rail with a brisk flick. 'Bit hard to be excited when I don't know what for.' The words were more clipped than she'd intended. It felt as if she hadn't spoken to anyone for days. The Nel of a few weeks ago would've been tripping over herself to apologise. She kept packing, tucking her chin into the high neck of her jumper.

'Crossing the Circle. It's a big deal. Ceremony and everything.'

That was today? Phil hadn't mentioned it.

Harris hesitated. 'I guess Phil's done it so many times, it's lost its magic. But some of us still remember how it felt. The first time.' His smile was tentative in the face of her silence. 'You might want to dress up?'

Nel stared into the distance, then nodded.

'Nel, what's wrong?' Harris leaned forward, pressing his forearms on the rail. 'Is it the men? Those drunken louts back on Macca? There's nothing to be embarrassed about, we both know that. I doubt they even remembered it the next morning.'

Nel gave a grim laugh.

'I think you'd be surprised, actually.' He rubbed his gloved hands together. 'After the changeover ... that gruelling roster of Phil's ...' He trailed off. 'All I can say is since Macquarie, you're being looked at as more saint than sinner. Considering you've put in decades, while they've only experienced one changeover.'

'I can't say I've noticed.' Nel exhaled. 'Perhaps I'm being paranoid.' She stood up, gathering her things. 'He's not like that all the time. And anyway, they'll appreciate the extra time he's earned them when we get to Oates Land and they're standing where no one's stood before.'

'That's the problem. Most of these men won't. They're only going as far as Mawson. It's the over-winterers we're picking up who'll be making landfall on Oates Land.'

'Oh. Right.' Despite being angry with Phil herself, she still felt the men were being unfair. It was no secret Phil was a hard taskmaster. Everyone in ANARE knew what they were signing up for. But he never asked more of the men than he was willing to put in himself. 'Look, he's tired. I'm sure they think he's pushing them too hard, but, honestly, none of them has any *idea* about the pressure he's under from the department. And all he wants is enough time at the end to explore – it's …'

Nel stopped, sensing she was on the cusp of stepping over a line. 'I should go,' she murmured, 'if I'm going to be ready for this special dinner.' As she sidled past, the wind caught at the corners of the watercolour paper and, beyond the rail, drifting shards of ice jutted from the dark water like sharp tongues.

~

Nel was the first to arrive at the captain's table, and she wedged herself in at the apex of the curved booth, the thrum of the engine pulsing up through the soles of her feet. She'd been waiting for Phil in the cabin, pacing, streams of sentences spelling out her disillusion and anger running through her mind like tape through a telegraph. But he hadn't come.

In the late afternoon, the wind had escalated into a force-10 gale, punishing the ship with a screaming squall and 35-foot swell. Huge waves topped with long overhanging crests battered the ship, great patches of windblown foam streaking the deck.

They'd been hove to for a couple of hours, which meant that although they were stationary in the water, engines idling with the bow facing the gale head-on, every few minutes the ship would rear up onto a wave as if it was riding a stallion, then plunge down the far side. Inside the ship, all hell would break loose with chairs, books, ashtrays, bodies – anything moveable – crashing against the immoveable.

The dining saloon was subdued, more empty seats than men, only those with cast-iron guts making it to dinner. The kitchen staff were suffering too, and the sounds coming from behind the swinging doors were even louder than usual – the clattering intensified with random crashes, shattering and cursing.

Nel almost hadn't made it herself. She'd wanted to dress up, following Harris's suggestion, but the bucking ship made it impossible. Washing and makeup were out of the question, unless she wanted to risk broken bones. A colourful silk scarf knotted around her neck was the smartest look she could manage.

By the time dinner was ready, only she and Bill, Bend and Harold James had made it to the table. Phil slid in next to her with minutes to spare, offering her a smile and a confused look when she didn't respond. When Harris joined the captain's table, sliding in next to Phil, she pressed herself back against the booth's leather, using her husband's body as a shield.

The fiddles, those clever wooden slatted compartments fixed to the tabletops to stop utensils and condiments sliding around, were out for this dinner, which was of necessity a simple one: anything that could move from fridge to platter without needing the attention of knives or hotplates.

When the time came for the ceremony, Bill did his best to invest the occasion with the signature ANARE blend of humour, ritual and heroic tradition. He wore a thick green jumper, blue feather boa and a Father Christmas beard in an attempt to channel King Neptune. On his head was a crown of crumpled kitchen foil and he held a trident fashioned from a broom with three cardboard prongs lashed to the head, the whole flimsy weapon wrapped in foil. In the other hand, he held a clutch of certificates.

'We have among us several hardy souls, who today, for the first time, accomplished a feat uncommon among men.' He cleared his throat, then deepened his voice, eyebrows raised. 'I, Neptune, King of the Seven Seas, welcome you to join the rest of us in the elite club of seafaring heroes – men who have crossed the Antarctic Circle.' One by one, King Neptune congratulated the expeditioners who'd just passed below 66.6 degrees south for the first time, welcoming each of them with a certificate and a hearty toast of dry sherry.

'And last, but far from least, one intrepid soul in an even more rarefied club.' Bill turned to Nel with a gentle smile, holding up her certificate as she lurched across the room. Her parchment was inscribed 'The Little Mermaid'. She knew he meant it as an honour, alluding to the famous fairytale by Danish writer Hans Christian Andersen. Yet she felt a drop in her belly that the certificate didn't hold her actual name.

'To Mrs Law.' Bill raised his glass, and the toast echoed across the room with considerably less volume than for the previous 'heroes'.

She made her unsteady way back to the table, where Harris slid along the bench to make room for her beside him. As she perched on the edge of the upholstery, Harris raised his glass, looking pointedly at the rest of the men until they joined him in clinking glasses in her honour. Phil's smile as the rim of his glass chimed against hers was full of pride.

She pushed down the disillusionment and anger she'd spent the last few hours nursing. He looked so tired. Under pressure. How much did she really know about what he was dealing with? Maybe she had caught him at a bad moment, and had taken at face value comments he'd intended as flippant. Nel ran the conversation back through her mind for the hundredth time. No, she hadn't imagined it.

The discussion now turned to the delays caused by the foul weather, leaving Nel beached and silent.

Harris sat back against the booth, his sherry glass held steady against the ship's judder. He had outdoor hands, the kind in which a hammer or chisel would look at ease, with lean fingers and trimmed nails. It was rare for Nel to see him out of gloves, and she noticed that where his navy jumper was pushed up, his wrists were more tanned than she had expected, given his red hair. The soft skin inside his wrists was pale and blued with veins, while the backs of his hands were weathered, constellations of freckles smattered among the fine copper hairs. She remembered how nimble and gentle those hands had looked out on the beaches of Macquarie Island. He'd handled the penguins with such care, slipping the banding rings around their feet and folding them gently into the cloth sack to hang from the scales, before setting them back on their feet, smiling at their startled expressions and disgruntled air as they waddled out of reach.

Nel picked at her jelly. She wasn't nauseous but the motion of the ship wasn't doing her appetite any favours. The men were discussing the resupply logistics, the ship being due to berth at Mawson Station within the next few days, weather permitting.

Nel chased the jelly around her bowl with her spoon. Despite Harris's claim that the men now looked on her as an icon of patience and tolerance after enduring Phil's demanding changeover roster, she wasn't convinced. She wasn't imagining the whispers behind her back, the sidelong glances, or abrupt silences as she entered a room. Since leaving Melbourne, she'd overheard more than a few hurtful comments about her presence, and after Macquarie Island, some of them had taken on a lascivious tone. If Phil got wind of it, that would be the end of her work with penguins. And of time alone out in the field with Harris.

She pressed her lips together, looking down at the table. Next to her, Harris exhaled. They sat, not looking at each other, as debate about speed and bearing pinged back and forth.

'Look,' said Harris abruptly, in a low voice, 'you can't let them win. You're a symbol of a change they can see coming. And they're scared ...' He glanced at her. Nel kept her eyes fixed on the portrait of a bearded Danish shipowner hanging on the far side of the room.

'They're lashing out like little boys. Or teenagers, actually.' He shook his head as he sucked air back through his teeth. 'The newcomers are still getting used to' – Harris shot a glance at Phil, lowering his voice even further – 'life on board.'

Nel frowned, opening her mouth, then closing it again.

'And I really do need your help. If you like, I can draw you a penguin. Needle your conscience. Make you see that not helping me is striking a blow against science.' He leaned back and fished a small notebook with the stub of a pencil shoved into its metal spine from his trouser pocket. He flipped it open to a clean page and licked the tip of his pencil.

Bending over the page, he began to draw, pressing hard on the blue-lined page. When he was finished, he slid it over to her. She couldn't help but laugh, but stifled it swiftly, glancing around the room. Surely no one would think anything untoward was happening with Phil right there at the same table.

'I've seen better penguins when I was teaching kids.' Nel grinned at him, eyebrows raised. 'Is that even a bird?'

'Ouch. That's a bit harsh, coming from a nurturer of young minds.'

'Oh, I don't know – it's good to be aware of one's shortcomings.'

'Okay, maestro. Let's see what you come up with.' Harris pushed the pencil over to her.

Nel smiled, shaking her head as she picked it up. A minute later she slid the notebook back. Harris let out a bark of surprise.

'Well, that's just cruel.' He picked up the notebook, smiling as he held it out in front of him.

Nel had sketched a perfectly proportioned cartoon Adélie leaning against Harris's penguin, one flipper touching its misshapen comrade lightly on the shoulder, the other clutching its belly as it doubled over in laughter, tiny eyes screwed up in helpless mirth.

'I think you've just proved my point. The Adélies need you.' He looked at her, the next sentence not needing to be spoken.

She looked down at her glass, the fingertips of both hands resting on its base, as if she expected it to slip across the table at any moment. She gave a small nod, her eyes still downcast. Harris picked up his glass and chimed the rim against hers.

~

Nel was silent as they made their unsteady way back to the cabin after dinner. The ship bucked under her feet, and she found herself putting as much energy into staying upright as she did into avoiding contact with her husband's body. She made it to the cabin and, leaving the door open for him, placed the certificate on the desk. The cabin door clicked shut but she didn't turn, instead squaring the sides of the thick card against the edges of the desk. Behind her, the slide of silk as he loosened his tie.

'All right. I'll bite. What's this about?'

Nel turned and looked at him evenly.

'Right. The silent treatment.' He unbuttoned his shirt, jerking at the buttons through the holes. 'What astounds me is that you still

125

don't realise that for it to be fully effective I need to understand the source of the issue.'

'What astounds *me* is that you need to ask.'

He exhaled through his nose, audibly. 'Okay, Nel. Let's hear it.'

At home, on the rare occasions they argued, this was the point where she'd sigh, throw him an acidic look and stalk away. Only to find herself apologising sometime later, even when his behaviour had sparked the situation.

'I thought the story was that you wanted me here so I could paint. So, as you can imagine, I'm having a little trouble swallowing the news that, apparently, I'm only an appendage.'

'What on earth are you talking about?'

'You said it yourself. I'm *just* your wife. Even the Macquarie women get more consideration. And that's not saying much, since you made it quite clear you don't really think they should be down here either. You don't respect me. You don't respect my work. In fact, I'm beginning to suspect you don't respect women, full stop.'

'*This* is what you're being so uptight about?' He laughed sourly, yanking at the knot of his tie. 'I don't know if you've realised this yet, but I'm trying to run an entire ship. A whole Antarctic *program*. I don't have time to mollycoddle you.' He twisted his tie around his hands like a boxer's wrapping.

He'd been a boxer, back at Melbourne University when they'd first met. The spark had been immediate, even though she'd been the only one of her sisters to scoff at the notion of love at first sight. Back home, so many girls her age from neighbouring farms used to talk of working in Melbourne as secretaries or nurses, only to trip up before they'd made it as far as the railway station, pushing prams before their twenty-first birthdays. She'd kept her distance from boys, her eye firmly on the city and university. And she'd made it. Only to meet Phil, with

126

his boxer's hands and surprisingly heady mix of strength and elegance, intellect and drive. She'd been swept off her feet into a love strong enough to survive the austere years. The war. His masters in physics. ANARE. How could she have been married for so long, only to realise she'd never seen him clearly? How could a marriage work for so many years only to falter now?

Nel glared at him, so angry she could hiss. After a long beat, she folded her arms. 'You seem to be forgetting, this was your idea. You wanted me to be here. Yet you barely have time to *look* at me. Ask me how I am. Ask me about my work.'

'Work.' He shook his head.

'What's that supposed to mean?'

His neck shot forward, a turtle emerging from its shell. 'After working shift after shift, needing more hours than I have in each day, you honestly expect me to call these penguin sketches work?'

'And there it is.' She shook her head.

'What?'

'You don't think I can do it.'

'Wrong. I actually *do* think you have the ability. But ...' He stopped, shaking his head.

'Well?'

'You need me to spell it out?' The look he shot her told her he had every intention of spelling it out whether she wanted to hear it or not.

Heat began to rise, her cheeks burning and sweat prickling her scalp. She gripped the edge of the desk. 'Perhaps you don't know me quite as well as you think,' she said quietly.

'After all these years, I have a pretty good idea.'

She waited.

'Right now, it all sounds new and exciting. Tramping around in the snow, sketching cute little penguins. But we both know, after a few attempts, you'll be tugging on my arm, saying it's too hard, too cold or too dull. And you'll beg me to get you out of it.' He raised his eyebrows at her, as if daring her to argue. 'So, knowing this, knowing *you*, shouldn't we save everyone the bother, tell him no up front, and avoid the inevitable drama?'

Nel set her jaw, trying not to give away her frustration and anger.

He turned, looping his tie over a hanger in the wardrobe. 'If you really want to go traipsing about after McCallum, in the cold and the weather, don't let me stand in your way. Just don't come running to me to get you out of it when you're tired or bored or McCallum expected too much from you. And please stop calling it *work*.'

Nel took a great breath, unsaid thoughts dangling like live wires in the air.

Phil's gaze dropped from her face to sweep the room. 'This place is a sty. It's a bedroom, not a studio. You need to air it. These turpentine fumes are giving me headaches.'

'You'd need to spend time here for that to happen.'

Phil shook his head. She saw the exact moment he flicked his attention away, as if she were one of his men, an expeditioner disappointing him with substandard work. He strode through the door, leaving it open as his footsteps faded into the belly of the ship.

Flake White

Mawson Station, Antarctica
February 1961

Nel took a deep breath, the cold nipping at her cheekbones. The air was so clear she could see further than her eyes would normally allow. It was almost disorienting. She was tempted to run back to the cabin for her sketchbook, but didn't want to miss a second.

Phil appeared at her elbow. 'Ready for your big moment?' He smiled tentatively, giving her waist a quick squeeze. Over the past two days they'd reached a polite truce, one that allowed for conversation, yet stopped short of intimacy. The spines of her anger had blunted; he was as remorseful as was possible in the absence of a concrete apology. 'I've scheduled you on a duck leaving at twelve-thirty.' His excitement was as clear as the crisp polar air, yet she wasn't certain if it was for her, or Antarctica.

'You'll be there?'

'Miss my wife stepping into the history books?'

She wasn't going to let the splinters of the argument, still prickling between them, stop her enjoying this moment. 'You'll have your camera? I think I'll be a little too preoccupied with hopping out of the duck and not falling flat on my face to attempt a self-portrait while I'm doing it.'

'My Leica and I will be there to witness that first step. Twelve-thirty?'

'Copy, Dr Law.' Nel gave a mock salute.

Since they neared the sea ice, the waters had been calm, the icebergs, brash ice and bergy bits all dampening the motion of the waves. Although Nel hadn't been worried by seasickness, she wasn't immune to the pleasure of smooth sailing. It seemed incredible that even the famously wild Southern Ocean could be cowed to stillness by the presence of Antarctica. But as they neared the coast, the katabatic winds made their presence felt. They were a problem, and an ever-present one, at Mawson Station, where the air drained down off the polar plateau, the cold plummeting towards the sea.

The winds heightened the challenge of docking the ship, but Bill's hands were steady on the helm as he edged *Magga* slowly past the tip of West Arm to drop anchor in the slushy waters of the bay.

Onshore, a huge cheer went up. From the size of the group, Nel guessed that every one of the over-winterers had gathered to witness *Magga*'s arrival, their excitement spiced by the promise of mail, fresh food and the sight of the longed-for vessel that would carry them home.

These poor chaps had been down here for fifteen months. Nel wouldn't like to be in Phil's shoes when he broke it to them that their work was far from done. After the titanic workload of changeover, these men would still have to build the automatic weather station on Chick Island, then sail all the way to Oates Land, indulging Phil's hunger for exploration before turning for home.

Nel rested her forearms on the rail. Antarctica was so ... beautiful. It was hard to know where to look. Gazing across the huge sweep of bay and mountains beyond, she could understand the relentless pull of this place. Yet the base itself, nestled at the foot of a rocky hillside, was quite ugly. She'd never seen a mining site or a pioneer outpost, but she imagined that this cluster of metal buildings wasn't far different. Not that she'd ever say any of this in front of Phil.

Mawson Station was Phil's baby. He'd established it six years ago; the first permanent and continuously occupied station in Antarctica.

Hovering like the proudest of parents and never afraid to get his hands dirty, Phil had overseen every detail, from erecting the buildings to administration to politics, in Antarctica and in Melbourne. This place was his second home.

~

She grabbed Phil's hand and stepped down. Dark gravel crunched beneath her feet. A laugh bubbled through her, and she jumped, deliberately jarring her legs, relishing the resistance of solid land. Phil hooted and behind her she heard the muffled applause of gloved hands from the men still aboard the duck. She'd made it. She was here. Antarctica. Her smile felt as if it were hooked over both ears.

'Wait ... wait.' Phil released her hand and fumbled with the camera around his neck. He fiddled with the dials, then peered at her through the viewfinder, fingers twisting the focus. 'One, two, three ... *Antarctica*!'

Nel laughed and grinned, posing on the shoreline so that the shot could capture the red ship in the harbour over her shoulder.

'Now stand over there.' Phil pointed inland, backing towards the water so that Nel was between him and the continent stretching away behind her.

Nel smiled into the lens, hearing the shutter click and click. She wanted to spin and jump, grab great handfuls of snow, toss them in the air, put a chunk of ice on her tongue. She was *here*.

'It's one pm on Wednesday, February the eighth, 1961,' Phil announced, letting the camera dangle around his neck as he turned to address the men now scrambling one by one over the side of the amphibious dinghy onto the shore. 'And that foot right there' – he pointed at Nel's right golf shoe – 'is now famous. Because that is the foot of Mrs Phillip Law, the first woman from Australia – and the first female artist *in the world* – to stand on the great southern continent of Antarctica.'

Moofty crunched across the gravel, took off his beanie and shook Nel's hand. 'Congratulations, Mrs Law.' Then, with a cheeky grin, he bowed to her foot. 'I'm in the presence of greatness. The chief's wife's foot!'

Nel laughed, batting him away. 'Cheeky sod.'

He grinned at her and jogged away to join the crew heading towards the base. Nel's smile didn't fade as she looked down at her feet. She was here. Not for Phil. Not for artists, or for women or any of the people who'd love to be here, seeing this, but were still excluded. This moment was *hers*. The thought resonated in her, as if a beehive thrummed in her core. Bending down, she selected a slate-grey pebble, about the size of a penny, from the thousands of its almost identical, yet singular companions. She slipped it into her pocket.

~

The dinner was lively, once Nel and the thirty-three Mawson base inhabitants had recovered from their respective shocks. The term 'over-winterer' really didn't do justice to all that these men had endured.

Fifteen months. No wonder hygiene had long ceased to be a priority. All were bearded, some more wildly than others, with hair almost touching their collars. Nel's nose suspected that bathing might've become a special event during the long dark months.

At first, they gave Nel just as much distance as she was keen to give them. No one had warned them there was a woman on board. Or perhaps they had been told, but the jolt of seeing their first woman in over a year, in this unexpected place, was still too much. They stared. And stared. Thankfully, their stares eventually morphed into grins. But all the same, that first hour before the alcohol kicked in was less than comfortable. For goodness sake, she was old enough to be the mother of at least half of them! And married to their boss. Nel dreaded to think how she would've coped if she'd been twenty years younger and unattached.

One by one, the men introduced themselves, plying her with infinite refills of something they called 'Russian cognac'. Every expeditioner seemed to be known only by nickname, and Nel thought she had a better chance of memorising the order of a shuffled pack of cards than keeping 'Cheddar', 'Walter Mitty', 'Hudson Bay Trader' and the rest of their outlandishly named colleagues straight. As the atmosphere in the dining room thawed, they peppered her with questions about current events and the latest music, fashion, movies, cars – even motorbikes. By the end of the evening, she felt as though she'd been through the longest audition in history for Radio Australia. The men even told her she'd give radio host Jocelyn Terry a run for her money as the voice that 'warms the heart where the weather is cold' on *Calling Antarctica* – apparently the highest of praise.

While the enquiries about life back home were surprisingly varied, there was one question she must have been asked thirty-three times, one she would've preferred to avoid answering even once. *What's it like to be the only woman among so many men?*

Everything she wanted to say bottled up in her throat. How exhausting it was, the constant scrutiny, every action, every conversation watched and judged. And the weight of being the first, knowing that the abilities of all women would be assessed by how she handled herself. How the responsibility felt like one more heavy layer of clothing that she could only strip off in the privacy of her tiny cabin.

She hedged, taking a sip of cognac.

'Oh, it's thrilling. I can't believe how lucky I am. Not just to be here – which is just incredible, of course. But to see the amazing work that all of you do down here. After so many years hearing about it from Phil – to actually see it with my own eyes.'

I'm thrilled to be here. I'm so in awe of your work. The words must've left her mouth two dozen times.

'Isn't being alone with all these blokes a little ... intimidating?' a shaggy man with a blade of a nose and eyes like bitumen (was it Chompers or Monte or Pizza Pie?) asked, stretching eye contact beyond comfort.

Feeling like a specimen under a microscope, Nel held his gaze. 'Should it be?'

He stared a moment longer, then, without excusing himself, turned towards the bar. He didn't smell, yet Nel thought the air immediately freshened. This brace of new men would mean another knot of social tensions to unravel over the coming months on board the ship. She'd been focusing on the fact that the men she'd travelled down with would mostly be staying at Mawson. Foolishly, she'd assumed saying goodbye to George and the others who'd been less than welcoming would improve her situation. Clearly, no such luck. At least Bill, Bend and Harold James would be staying on board. And Harris.

The party was in full swing when Phil finally made his entrance. He grabbed a drink and climbed onto a chair, a curly strand of pink streamer brushing the top of his head.

'First, I want to raise a glass to all the winterers. Fifteen months. What an achievement.' He paused as a volley of insults bounced around the room with much back-slapping and laughter. 'You've all done an incredible job. The setbacks over the past season have been significant. Rebuilding after the power-shed fire last year. Then this bloody blizzard. But you held your nerve, pulled through. I've read the reports. Some of you risked your lives to save those aircraft. Damned heroic, chaps. You're a credit to yourselves and the whole of ANARE.' Phil raised his glass to a raucous cheer, followed by the silence of a room of men taking a long draught. 'And now for the bad news. Steel yourselves, lads.' Phil raised his voice to be heard over theatrical groans. 'This blizzard, it's complicated things. Losing the Dakota, well, it means the mission for the newcomers to take aerial photographs of over a thousand miles of Antarctic coastline is now cancelled. As well as the surveys and photomapping in the Prince Charles Mountains. With the Beavers we lost in '59 and now this – until I can get more funding for new aircraft, it's thrown a spanner in all our exploration plans, both south of Mawson and in Oates Land.'

Quiet fell across the room, smoke from cigarettes held in still hands twisting in lazy spirals towards the ceiling.

'Most significantly for those of you travelling home aboard *Magga*, our plans for exploring Oates Land will now be sea-based.' A rash of groans broke out, swiftly hushed as Phil's glare raked the room. 'Steady on.' He waited, demanding full attention. 'As you know, exploring Oates Land has been on my, and ANARE's, agenda for a long time. But with the treaty looming, sticking our flag in Oates Land before the Russians and Yanks claim it is a priority. With all our planes out of commission, we're a bit hamstrung. The plan will now be to get there asap, give ourselves as much time as possible before the ice closes in, and push as close to the coast as possible so we can map it from the ship. We can still try to get boots on the ground. It just means doing it from the ship rather than planes.' Phil paused, taking in the field of serious faces turned towards him. 'So, I've reworked the changeover roster.' At the surge of fresh groaning, he held up his hand. 'I know, I know. It's not ideal. But we need to give ourselves as much time as we can at the other end.'

'When will we get home?' a gruff voice called from the cluster of men leaning on the bar.

'You'll be home at the same time. All this means is we'll be working harder now to set sail earlier.'

Muttering flared across the room. 'Unless we get stuck in the ice.'

Phil drew in a deep breath. 'Drink up, lads. Tomorrow, the real work starts.' He stepped off the chair into a room that no longer had the sound or spirit of a party.

~

When the time came to catch a duck back to the ship, Nel was exhausted and more than a little tipsy. She climbed aboard and sat with her hand in her pocket, worrying the pebble like a bead on a rosary. Throughout the day, each time she'd reached for it, a warmth had spread in her belly, as if she'd breathed a fresh glow into an ember.

The sky was still alight at midnight, yet the harbour had the quiet stillness of the dark. Lines securing the *Magga Dan* were threaded between the ship and shore, forming a giant web of ropes across the harbour. Ice had washed in on the tide and banked up along the lines, creating beautiful patterns. Nel wished she had her sketchbook, and only realised she'd spoken aloud when she heard someone scoff behind her. George. She hadn't even noticed his presence on the boat until now. Russian cognac still humming through her system, Nel leaned towards him.

'George. I'm so going to miss the warmth of your company.' She'd intended to hit a chirpier tone, but once the words escaped, she could hear her mistake. The sarcasm was naked.

Silence fell like a guillotine, the men frozen mid-gesture. George glared at her, his contempt cold as the water beneath them. She attempted to hold his gaze, but within seconds the heat in her face and weight of his disdain were too much. She dropped her head and they continued across the icy bay with only the sound of the motor churning.

~

Finding a quiet spot on the outer rim of the station, Nel perched on her folding stool, examining the glacier tongue with its great ice cliffs protruding into West Bay. She could hear the sled dogs whining behind her, rattling their chains in excitement as they kept an eye on all the activity, the men busy as beetles between ship and shore. Now that she had a chance to really *look*, it all felt quite overwhelming. The subtle palette of white, the range of blues in sea, sky and shadows, the sheer immensity of the vista in every direction – where should she start?

She took her time scanning for the perfect scene. It needed to be right for her first artwork on the continent. A stiff breeze muscled inside her jacket as she bulldog-clipped the canvas to her masonite board before propping it on her easel. Then she lashed the board to the triangular frame with several tight bands she'd fashioned from dressmaking elastic. She'd come prepared for Mawson's famous katabatic winds.

In the pristine air, everything looked close and perfectly focused, the scarlet of the ship dramatic against the intense blue of the sky.

Needing to get the colours exactly right, she took off her sunglasses, then smeared white, cadmium red and mazarine blue across her palette. The harbour water seemed thick as syrup as it rolled without breaking, its surface spread with a raw-silk sheen, trapped in an uncertain state between solid and liquid.

Preparations complete, Nel got to work. The sun had lolled across the sky by the time she leaned back, rolling her shoulders and tilting her neck until her vertebrae cracked and popped. She held the board out in front of her. While she'd rendered all the visual elements of the scene, capturing the *feeling* of the harbour still hovered just beyond her grasp.

Nel pressed her lips together. Shaking blood into her stiff fingers, she fished her gloves from her pocket. She was freezing. It hadn't bothered her while she was working, but now all the discomfort she'd ignored over the last few hours came at her in a rush; her fingertips were red where they popped from her fingerless gloves and a headache was gathering behind her eyes. She shouldn't have left her sunglasses off for so long, but the nuances of colour were incredibly difficult. It felt as though she'd identified an entire spectrum of white.

She needed to warm up. Even a hot flush would be welcome. Nel looked over at the base, heart sinking. The solitude of the morning had been blissful. On the ship, this kind of seclusion was only possible inside her cabin, its porthole her sole window to the outside world. Venturing beyond her door meant opening herself to the constant scrutiny, curiosity and conversation of the men. But this morning she'd had silence, privacy and a white distance so vast and deep it seemed beyond measure.

She stamped her feet, the flush of circulation sparking a shiver that jolted her whole frame. Nel jammed what she could into her knapsack and made her way towards the base, trying to keep the still-damp oils from smearing. Hands full, she stepped carefully across the ice-clogged rocks.

Mawson Station was an oddly spaced collection of rectangular aluminium huts, the metal so reflective it made her headache throb in time with her pulse. The buildings appeared to have been positioned randomly across the rocky ground, the spaces between them stacked with oil drums, pallets of building materials, crates and piles of hessian sacks full of God knows what. The exception was a wooden building topped with a peaked roof that Nel thought looked vaguely Norwegian. In terms of style, Nel considered it the saving grace of the settlement. Without it, the base would have resembled a ramshackle accumulation of giant loaf tins.

Phil wanted a painting of the station. Nel could understand why he felt sentimental about the place, and she'd do it to keep him happy, but for the life of her, she couldn't see how to keep her word in a way that would make a good painting, rather than just a visual record of an important but hardly picturesque outpost.

In the future, she'd need to be more strategic about her painting plans. If the wind was up, she'd need a free hand to hold on to the 'blizz lines' stretched alongside every path. In a blizzard, when seeing the foot on the end of your leg might be impossible, they were the only way to be sure people weren't blown off course, never to be seen again.

The men were hard at work unloading the ship, creating neat stacks of building materials at the rear of the base and ferrying large orange crates of food and supplies into the storage areas beside the kitchen and new recreation hut.

Over the last few days she'd barely spoken two sentences to Phil. Or anyone, for that matter. With the never-setting sun circling overhead like a lassoed pony, the saying 'dawn to dusk' was meaningless. The concept seemed equally pointless for the men, who were hollow-eyed with fatigue.

Phil was working just as hard, hour for hour. Her presence hadn't lessened his work ethic one jot. Not to mention that seeing the head honcho knocking off early or having long dinners with his wife would've been disastrous for morale. Her only responsibility was keeping out of the way. She should have been revelling in this freedom, but the silence and space between them sat like heavy grey stones in her chest.

Threading her way through the station, Nel kept her distance from the communal area, choosing to explore the smaller workspaces and dormitories dotting the outskirts. The blizzard-proof doors took both dexterity and quite a bit of upper body strength to open, the great crank-handles making Nel feel like she was breaking into a vault. Inside, each building had an antechamber designed for stamping and shaking off ice and snow just before the main section. In the dormitory huts, she found cubicles for eight men, four on each side of a central passage, with a briquette stove at the far end. Each tiny curtained-off cubicle held a bunk with space underneath for a small writing table, drawers and hanging space for clothes. Poking her head inside each building in turn, she found the laundry, the huge engine hut and all manner of workspaces, crammed with desks, filing cabinets and arrays of scientific instruments and equipment.

Inside her gloves, her fingers were stiff with cold, and she began to doubt her chances of getting her paintings back to the ship without smearing the oil. Nel suspected they would take days to dry in these frigid conditions. But the air was also incredibly dry; her skin was in need of some Ponds. Perhaps the aridity would counteract the cold and dry her work more quickly? It would be her own scientific experiment.

She shrugged the knapsack higher onto her shoulder and adjusted her grip on the two artworks, ready to admit defeat and make her way down to the warmth of the communal recreation hut. She'd just stepped out of what she assumed was a meteorological workspace from the weird collection of equipment and maps marked with wobbly bubbles of barometric pressure, when she spotted a blizz line heading to a lonely building perched slightly higher up the slope. *Last one, then hot chocolate.*

Nel cranked open the metal door and was practically sucked inside by momentum and air pressure. The silence was lush and immediate. Her entrance into the main space set loose papers aflutter, and it took a moment for all the lists, photos and graphs to settle back into place.

The hut was clearly another workspace. The floor was crammed with tables and filing cabinets; every surface home to some kind of scientific instrument. Nel had no idea what they all were – a weird assemblage of metal boxes embedded with dials, round-faced gauges and needles skating across graph paper. Colourful wiring laced the walls, connecting instruments to their meters. Above waist level, the walls were almost invisible behind blackboards, maps with sticky-taped corners and photos of auroras snaking like colourful chiffon across star-speckled skies.

It must be the auroral hut. Nel stepped further into the room. Phil had told her about the work done here. Something to do with measuring the earth's magnetic field, photometers and a double telescope system that used mirrors and a beam-splitter. She remembered that because she'd misheard him when he'd first mentioned it and he'd choked on his tea, sputtering it across her clean tablecloth, when she'd called it a bean-splitter.

So where was this famous telescope? She'd already explored the building housing the two meson telescopes monitoring cosmic rays. Nel wandered through the hut, running her fingers over equipment, admiring the photographs and taking in the harbour view of the red ship framed by the small square windows. At the far end, she noticed a closed door, flanked on one side by a filing cabinet and the other by a clipboard hanging from a nail. She pulled off her gloves, balling them neatly inside each other with a deft tuck and stuffing them into her jacket pocket. Phil hadn't said any area was out of bounds. No one was around and she wouldn't touch anything. She opened the door.

Nel stepped into a great curved space, tilting her neck to take in the flood of space and light. Her mouth dropped open. It was a dome.

In the centre of the floor stood a tall apparatus that looked far too complicated and fragile to have its crown poking out of the top of the dome like a submarine's periscope. Nel stepped gingerly around the equipment cluttering the room – the body of the periscope that she guessed must be the prized telescope, a deck of controls jammed with dials and needles lying at zero in fan-shaped windows and a box mounted on a tripod that looked like something a surveyor would use. What fascinated her was not what was in the room but what she could see.

Above her, all was sky. The entire dome was constructed from great sheets of perspex. Nel pressed her nose to the hard plastic, drinking in the view: the ice-studded bay, the mountains, and beyond them the great, silent sheet of white rising and rising as it stretched out of sight all the way to the Pole. The *light*. And more than that – the *warmth*. Nel felt as though she was sitting in a scientist's version of a greenhouse. She slipped the knapsack from her shoulder and leaned the two completed paintings against the legs of a nearby chair. She had found her studio. Settling herself cross-legged on the floor, she opened her knapsack.

~

'Who let you in here?'

Nel flinched. The milky blue line of glacial shadow smeared into the titanium white of sunlit ice.

She would've leapt to her feet if not for the fact she'd been sitting on the floor for what must've been hours. Her legs were numb. She spun on her bottom, placing the painting on the floor beside her.

It was the man from the party. The one with the hard grey eyes. Monte, she had overheard one of the men call him. His lips were pressed together, and while his silver-flecked hair was Einstein-esque in its woolly unkemptness, his face held none of the famous scientist's mischief.

'No one.' She said it in a conciliatory way, trying to get to her feet. Her legs were so stiff. She felt a hundred years old. Nel tried to smile self-deprecatingly as she grabbed the back of a chair to lever herself up. Monte stared at her.

Having hauled herself upright, she went on, 'Phil didn't say there was anywhere I *couldn't* go.'

She was about to assure him she'd be out from underfoot straightaway when he cut in.

'So. You just assumed that meant you could waltz in. Take over anyone's office.' He gave a derisive laugh. 'Please, make yourself at home. Turn it into an art studio. It's not as if we're working on anything important.'

'I didn't think I'd be in the way ...' Nel trailed off as she looked down. Several paintings were propped against desk legs, and she'd spread the contents of her knapsack around her in a nest of paints, brushes and rags. The warm air stank of turpentine.

He continued to stare.

'Sorry. I'll be out of your hair in a jiffy.' She hooked a smile to the apology.

'Don't let me stop you.' His expression didn't flicker. The insolence was all in the tone and the slouch of his lean frame as he propped a hip against the nearest desk.

Chagrined, she knelt to pack her gear. 'So, you must be an auroral physicist? With the double telescope? Sounds fascinating.' Phil had told her all about the work that was being accomplished with this technology, but under this man's burning gaze, her thoughts failed to rattle themselves into coherent sentences.

'Ah. You're a scientist now too? Incredible. Is there nothing women can't do?'

She turned away, heat flashing to her face as she crammed the last of her supplies into the knapsack. Her knees were protesting, so she stood, bending from the waist, to collect the paintings. A long, slow whistle from behind her made her straighten swiftly and spin around.

Monte met her indignant frown with a cocked eyebrow, his gaze crawling over her body, lingering on her breasts and hips. She sucked in a shocked breath. His cold grey eyes made no effort to conceal his derision. She glared at him as she strode to the door, the gaping knapsack hastily slung on her shoulder, the still-damp paintings held like shields in front of her chest.

Cadmium Orange

Mawson Station, Antarctica
February 1961

Bacon in pocket, Nel threaded her way between the stacks of crates and barrels of fuel towards the kennels. She could hear the huskies before she saw them, the excited yips, rattling chains and paws crunching in ice. Someone was already there. She hid behind a pallet of crates lashed down with a tarp, and peered around the corner. That physicist. Monte.

He was kneeling before one of the dogs at the far end of the chain, offering it a piece of bacon, scratching its ears and rubbing its jowls as it gobbled the salty treat. Under the din, dogs bouncing on their front paws, whining for attention, Nel could hear him crooning, his sharp face soft and smiling. He gave the dog one final tousle behind the ears, then scooted on his knees to the next husky on the chain, fishing in his pocket for another rasher.

Seeing him kneeling before them, gentle-faced, and their reactions – pleading and pleased. They loved him. *Him*. It was the definition of unexpected. She could hardly believe this tender, soft-eyed man was the same person whose gaze had left her raw and trembling with rage. She watched him push his fingers through the coat of Bootsy, her favourite. The dog thrust her thickly furred muzzle into Monte's midriff, and he toppled backwards, face creased with laughter. This was a stranger. Or was the stranger the face he showed her, everyone else knowing this gentle, smiling man?

Nel drew back around the corner and leaned against the crate. She really didn't want to see him as anything except a foe – someone nasty and vengeful and bent on making her feel like an interloper. Yet here he was, drawn to the dogs just as she was – keeping his breakfast aside and treating them like treasured friends. She could still hear him, crooning their names, asking them sweet, rhetorical questions. Exactly as she did. She stared at the ice-sludged bay for a long minute before making her way back to the ship.

~

'Darling.' Nel stuck her head through the stateroom door. Phil was hunched over the desk, a blizzard of paperwork, open files and notebooks in front of him. When he glanced up, she didn't let his frown discourage her. 'Time for a cup of tea?'

'Not really.' His pen hovered over the page. 'Did you need something?'

Nel smiled, taking the question as permission to slide into the room. 'Only a little time.' She planted herself in one of the chairs across the desk from him, leaning forward to see what he was working on, despite not being able to read it upside down. After her encounter with Monte yesterday, a need for the comfort of Phil's company was hitting her with sudden and unexpected force.

Keeping her tone light, she said, 'You've been so busy. I've hardly seen you. And when I have seen you, you've been ... well, the chief, rather than my Phil.'

He pulled off his reading glasses, frowning as he massaged the bridge of his nose, before sliding them back on with a sigh. 'I'm not sure what you're getting at.'

'It's just that I'm seeing a different side of you. Which is good. Interesting, I mean.' She smiled, wanting to make sure he knew her delivery of this observation was intended to be stingless. 'But I'm here too, and I'd like my husband to come out for a brief appearance. I'm ready for a bit of quality time with him, rather than the boss.' She leaned back in her chair and was about to swing her feet up onto his desk but, catching his expression, kept them on the floor.

'We talk at dinner. I'm not working then. All we do is talk.'

'Yes, but it's still work, really, isn't it? Dinner conversation is with the men and Bill. Work Phil. Not husband Phil.'

He tipped back his head, raking his hands through his hair, and took a great breath, as if appealing to a higher power for patience. 'A, I don't see the difference. We talk about work at home, and I've never heard you complain that I'm "Work Phil". And B, I happen to be at work.' He enunciated each word, then shook his head. 'All the time. There's no clocking off.' He shook his head.

'Well, yes. Of course. I know that.' This wasn't going as planned. Nel struggled to keep her voice light and free of desperation. 'But you're exhausted. So maybe take advantage of me being here. Use me as an excuse to slip away a little early, every now and again. Then you get a break from the weight of being the chief. And I get a little time with my husband.' She looked at him, smile still stretched across her face.

Phil barked a laugh full of incredulity and empty of humour. 'You could not have picked a worse time to have this conversation.'

He picked up his pen. 'It's changeover. Between ferrying supplies, organising watches and work rosters, and making sure the old guard train the newcomers before we sail, I don't have time to scratch myself, let alone take a night off for some magical transformation from *this* Phil into *that* Phil.' He waggled his head, his tone mocking. 'Please. I need to finish this. I'll see you at dinner. And if you're awake when I make it to bed, we can talk more. But right now ...' He gestured to the chaos of paperwork.

Nel pushed up out of her chair, legs leaden. He didn't even look up as she closed the stateroom door behind her.

~

Nel had been working solidly for days. The air in the cabin was heady with fumes, and canvas boards still slick with oil were propped to dry against every wall and leg of furniture. Slumped back against the bulkhead on her bunk, she hugged her knees, mouth tugged to one side as she eyed her work. Her productivity gratified her, but if she was honest with herself, it was a matter of quantity over quality.

Phil seemed pleased, in the scant seconds she'd been able to grab his attention, so that was something. She'd painted him a view of the station, managing to compose something interesting by working from West Arm looking back at Mawson, with the scarlet of *Magga Dan* stealing attention away from the dull building blocks of the station in the background.

She'd alternated working in the protected comfort of the cabin with working outside, constantly worried about giving herself frostbite as she tried to capture the complexity of the ice cliffs, glaciers and mountains knuckling up out of the white. She'd braved the cold and katabatic winds for hours, trying to master the dramatic bergs in East Bay. She'd become a little obsessed with Castle Berg, a grounded iceberg of such size and grandeur that the tractor-trains coming back to base from up on the plateau used it as a landmark. Around the cabin, visions of this berg dominated the room, yet none totally satisfied her. Tomorrow. A shot of excitement tingled its way from her chest to her fingertips. Maybe tomorrow she'd finally find a way to get into the marrow of this place, rather than just painting what her eyes told her was here. Maybe tomorrow, out in the field with the penguins. With Harris.

It wasn't just the prospect of spending a whole day in Harris's company that excited her. Yes, the idea of it had her thrumming. But nestled within that excitement was also the anticipation of pushing beyond the limits of the base. She'd avoided trying to work at the station, not wanting a repeat of the encounter with Monte. Or any of the other men. The episode had made her gun-shy. And if seeing Monte with the dogs had taught her anything, it was that the winterers were still strangers, impossible to take on face value. She feared her instincts were out of kilter. All this time cooped up in a ship, surrounded by men, with not even her husband behaving predictably – no wonder her radar was off.

Nel slid off the bunk. Her hand was already on the doorknob when she remembered she hadn't checked her makeup since before breakfast. She hesitated. Since that first dinner on arrival at Mawson, she hadn't taken a great deal of care about dressing for dinner. Even Phil had mentioned the absence of her trademark accessories: perfume and silk scarves. Everyone was so busy with the changeover, dinners had become rather rushed affairs, the men less interested in meals than the activities rostered on either side – the resupply, training of the newcomers and sleep. No one had noticed she'd been deliberately avoiding the dining saloon. Avoiding Jefferson Montgomery. Monte. Some of the men called him Biscuit, but she couldn't think of the auroral physicist as anything but *Him*.

In the bathroom mirror, a tired face stared back. The morning's mascara and eyeliner had worn off, but she could still see traces of foundation. She needed to apply it heavily, as it served as both cosmetic and sun protection. The air down here was so cold it held barely any moisture and Nel could see the dryness had taken its toll. All those hours sketching and painting in the sun and wind, with the never-ending daylight bouncing off the ice, had left her with a tan. But her skin felt dull and tight rather than healthy.

She stuck out her tongue, then paused, assessing the face in the mirror as if it belonged to a stranger. Recalling the episode in the auroral dome made her shudder every time. It hadn't been her imagination. Monte had been undressing her, assessing her like horseflesh. What had he seen? She was nearly fifty, for goodness sake. Men had stopped looking at her with desire in their eyes years ago. Except perhaps Harris. It was subtle, yet recently she thought she'd caught the odd glimmer of something in his gaze. Something more than friendship. A mutual spark?

She looked at herself again, this time summoning some kindness. A woman with purpose. Someone delighted by the wonders of the world. And, yes, a woman who was not yet finished with desire. The prospect of accompanying Harris out on the ice had ignited something in her, something she hadn't realised had faded until it glowed back to life. It was pleasurable, undeniably so, to be in a man's company again, one who listened, enjoyed her conversation, made her feel seen. But it scared her, this warmth, the way she was suddenly more aware of her body. It felt dangerous, and in the hours after working with Harris her gut knotted with guilt and fear. Guilt that her body was responding to a man other than Phil. Fear that desire was written across her face for all to read. Especially Monte.

She needed to be careful. Control herself and her body – a demand more difficult now than ever, with unruly tides of hormones making her body a treacherous thing.

She leaned against the sink. She was lonely. She missed her sisters, her friends, her cat. Since Macquarie Island, she'd thought of Nefertiti less and less. Probably because she was so far from the myriad things that had sparked her grief at home, her darling's absence wasn't quite as sharp. And other worries had muscled in, competing for space in her sleepless, circling mind. Feeding the dogs had helped, but now worry over crossing paths with Monte had poisoned that too. Nel picked up a lipstick, glanced at the mirror, then placed the black and gold cylinder back in her toiletries case.

~

The ammonia stink sliced into her sinuses. It wasn't entirely unfamiliar. On returning home, Phil's clothes often held a whiff of it. A fist clenched around her heart as she remembered Nefertiti's wild delight at catching the scent of that supercharged catnip. But this stink was a level beyond.

The rocky shoreline they were tramping towards was still some distance away across the sea ice, yet already she was reeling from the sensory assault. *How can such tiny beings make such a tremendous racket?* Nel wondered as the penguins' trumpeting assailed her with both volume and stridence.

She raised her voice over the din. 'I'm sure a biologist once told me that penguins sing. If this is singing, I'll eat my socks.'

Harris, fumbling at the dials of his camera with gloved fingers, shook his head and smiled. 'They must've meant emperors, not

Adélies. Emperors are the singers, if you want to call it that. More like an off-key bugle, if you ask me. Makes your whole head vibrate.' The shutter clicked and he wound on the roll. 'Just wait until you see your first emperor. There's something ...' He paused, fishing for the perfect words with a waving hand. 'If Adélies are Charlie Chaplin, then emperors would be John Gielgud. Dignified. I almost fell to my knees in wonder the first time I saw one.' He smiled, his gaze soft and far away. 'They recognise each other for the rest of their lives by their song. It's romantic when you think about it.' He gazed into the distance and Nel wasn't entirely certain he was even talking about penguins.

Harris snapped back into his body, brushing his furry hat with its ludicrous ear flaps off his head and bowing with a grand sweep of his arm. 'Milady,' he said, offering her his thick sleeve. 'Might I escort you to the rookery?'

Nel took his arm as he helped her clamber the last few feet to the top of the rocky outcrop. Below spread the pungent chaos of the Adélie rookery. Harris stood on the ridge, smiling with deep satisfaction, as if pausing at his own front gate, taking in all that had changed in his absence.

Until this moment, Nel had thought of Antarctica as a place of astounding purity. All the vast stretches of ice, the great tabular bergs that appeared to have snapped off an ice cliff just moments before. Even the Adélie penguins she'd seen dotted along the edges of ice floes with their little white vests. All so pure. So *clean*.

She gazed down at the ragged expanse of windblown rock, her mouth hanging open. The great stretch of stony ground before them was completely free of ice and snow. Harris had explained that Adélies preferred to nest on exposed rock, which had made her assume that the ground on which the penguins bred and raised their chicks would be bare. But now, gazing down at the rookery, Nel thought if Hieronymus

Bosch had wanted to paint a penguin version of *The Garden of Earthly Delights*, this could have been the panel for Hell.

Beneath the achingly crisp blue sky, a great rabble of penguins peppered the slabs of earth-coloured stone, going about their rowdy business. The entire slope was pocked with rough-walled nests built from pebbles. These stony craters looked like the world's least comfortable places to lay eggs, but Nel guessed the penguins had little choice. It wasn't as if they had access to leaves or twigs.

The penguins waddled across the uneven surface, tottering, hopping, flippers waving for balance and squawking fiercely when they stumbled near each other's piles of stones. The birds were larger than she had expected; their heads around the height of her knees. Much taller than the little penguins she'd seen on Phillip Island back home.

Skuas lurked on the perimeter, scanning the rookery with sharp, predatory eyes, sporadically flapping into the air for an aerial view. Nel found them sinister, like enormous, dirty gulls with an appetite for fluffy chicks rather than hot chips.

Guano spattered every surface. *Forget Bosch*, Nel thought. *This is pure Jackson Pollock.* Compared to the other Adélies Nel had seen since crossing the Antarctic Circle, these penguins were filthy. The adults had sullied their clean vests, their bellies smudged with orange stains.

And the chicks! Most had reached that unfortunate stage of fledging when their soft down turned patchy and random, their mature coats sprouting beneath the fluff. The poor darlings looked like absolute frights. Harris had promised her chicks, but these fretting babies were as tall as the adults, and in their tatty suits of half-down, half-feather they looked mangy rather than cute.

'So I realise the white stuff must be their guano ... but the orange ...?' She trailed off, struggling to find the right word.

'Ah, yes. Delightful, isn't it? Krill vomit.'

Nel crinkled her nose. 'Charming.'

'Actually, I mean it's penguin vomit. Semi-digested krill. The krill don't vomit. Or maybe they do, but that's not what makes those orange stains.' Harris laughed. 'The adults feed the chicks just like regular birds back home – by regurgitating food. And since Adélies feed on krill ... Voila. Krill vomit.' He chuckled at his own joke again.

Thinking she was still confused when she failed to smile, he kept on, 'You've seen krill – those tiny, bright orange prawns? Well, that's what makes the stains.'

The silence lengthened. Harris looked at her, then the rookery, as if seeing it with fresh eyes. 'You're right. It *is* revolting. These chaps don't have the best table manners.'

She'd grown up on a dairy farm, so she'd expected to be fine among animals and all that came with them. This disgust was both surprising and, in front of Harris, embarrassing. But the problem wasn't just the smell and the mess. It was with the *art*. 'You want me to paint *this*?' Nel said, eyeing the rookery, wondering where on earth she was going to sit.

Harris turned to face her, smiling gently. 'Not if you don't want to.' He shook his head. 'Sorry. I guess I'm so used to it, I'd forgotten how overpowering it can be.' He eased her knapsack off her shoulder, doubling his own load. 'What say we find a good spot, set you up and then we can spend a bit of time meeting the locals.'

He started down the slope, hopping lightly across the rocks and avoiding cracks. A little like a penguin himself, Nel thought.

'Believe me, give these little fellows a chance to get to know you and by lunchtime you'll have your very own fan club,' he called back to her.

Harris made his way along the edge of the rookery, taking care not to disturb any penguin parents feeding their squat, raggedy chicks or damage any pebble nests. The penguins regarded him with more curiosity than fear, the odd parent lowering its head with a squawking hiss when he stepped too close to a chick. Nel thought she'd never seen anything manage to be so cute and malevolent at the same time. Like being sworn at by Mickey Mouse.

Harris found a spot on the edge of the rookery with a sweeping view across the rocky shoreline and put down their knapsacks, careful to place them on a clean piece of rock. He unbuckled her folding stool and popped it down, testing its stability before patting the seat for her to sit.

She was sliding her sketchbook from the bag when Harris put his hand on her wrist.

Her heart accelerated as if his fingers had touched her bare skin. She froze, sketchbook hovering awkwardly halfway between her knapsack and her knees. She tilted her head up towards him, and then realised his focus wasn't on her.

'Just watch,' he whispered.

Nel pressed her lips together and flipped the knapsack closed. Beside her, Harris sat cross-legged on the rock, leaning forward, elbows on knees, chin cupped in his hands.

Nel made herself concentrate on the penguins. This was his job, what he'd come all this way to do. How ridiculous to feel miffed because he was transfixed by something other than her. These penguins were his passion. Thank goodness they were alone, since she was sure that throb of disappointment had been painted across her face.

Nel resettled herself on the stool, trying to force her attention away from her body's response to his proximity. *He makes you feel as if you're more than just the boss's wife*, she scolded herself. *So act like it.*

Neither the penguins nor Harris noticed her inner turmoil, and after several minutes of silent observation, she too was entranced. Seated on her stool, she was down at their height, and soon found herself face to face with a highly curious and relatively clean-breasted Adélie.

It waddled up to her, looking for all the world like a sturdy little man in formal wear, and flapped its tiny wings. The pale undersides were neither white nor pink but a shade somewhere between. Nel's fingers itched to dig her watercolours from her bag. The penguin cocked its head, assessing the strangers with first one silver-rimmed eye, then the other. It toddled forward a few more steps on its pink-webbed, three-clawed feet and bowed. Nel could not help but snort with laughter at the grave decorum of the gesture, and courteously answered in kind, although being seated did make it hard to muster the same level of dignity.

'Does this mean I've been accepted?'

'Well, I'm not sure they're offering you citizenship, but you're clearly higher status than a skua.'

'That's not saying much.' Nel laughed.

'If one of them offers you a pebble, Phil might have to intervene. Males collect them to build their nests. The more pebbles, the bigger the nest, the more attractive the penguin. Can't have one of these lads using his pebble collection to tempt you away from the boss. I'd lose my job.'

Nel nodded, keeping her eyes on the little character. 'I think our vows would withstand the threat,' she murmured.

Harris continued, 'Don't underestimate these chaps. From the outside they're all adorable and dapper. Butter wouldn't melt in their beaks. But I wouldn't turn my back on one for a second.' He grinned. 'They're thieving little devils. Look at that.' He pointed to a nest about ten feet further down the slope. An adult penguin was feeding a chick. He leaned closer to her, still pointing. 'The time for nest building was over months ago. But they just can't help themselves.'

Her eyes followed the direction of his finger, but her body's attention was focused on the closeness of his cheek, the tilt of his body towards hers.

The large chick squatting inside the pebble nest was so hunched it appeared to have no neck at all. Its head was a weird mix of smooth black feathers and remnants of slate-grey down yet to be shed, giving the chick the look of a grumpy old man desperately clinging to the last of his hair. The parent, feeding finished, set off on the long waddle back to the sea. The moment its back was turned, another penguin darted in from the side and nabbed a pebble from the rear of the nest, the chick quite oblivious to the fact its father's hard-won collection was being pilfered. The thief, pebble lodged in his beak, quickstepped to the neighbouring crater, depositing his loot straight onto the wall of his own nest. Without pausing to consider the outrageousness of his actions, the penguin immediately headed back for more. This time the chick noticed, moving to protect its real estate with its sizable, fluffy bulk.

Aark! Arr-rar-rar-aah! The chick's throbbing bray sounded like a cross between a dog's bark, a chicken squawk and a seasick expeditioner.

'And that's just a run-of-the-mill argument over pebbles.' Harris nudged her and gestured across the whole colony. 'This racket? A symphony of Adélies fighting over pebbles, territory, mates. You name it.'

At the sudden contact, warmth flooded through her – not the anxiety-riddled heat of a hot flush but a mellow rush of delight. 'But they look so innocent. What about the ones on the ice floes? The way they waddle along after each other. That adorable tobogganing on their bellies. Please don't tell me they're chasing each other for a bit of biffo!' Nel looked at him askance.

'Not all the time. But those cute little fellows lining up on the ice floe? The poor chap who ends up closest to the edge will be hip-

157

bumped into the drink. Sacrificial penguin. First one in is most likely to be snapped up by the leopard seal or killer whale.'

Nel nodded. She'd heard similar stories many times from Phil. But the same tale from Harris's mouth, she absorbed like a thirsty sponge.

'Dastardly.' She laughed. 'I thought you said I'd be won over by them.'

'I thought women were supposed to love bad boys.' Harris grinned. 'Surely, charisma is more attractive than being staid and respectable. Like emperors.'

'Personally, I find the fact they mate for life very charming. Both Adélies and emperors, right?'

'Yep.' He paused, then looked sideways at her. 'Have you heard of George Murray Levick?'

Nel frowned. The name wasn't familiar.

'He was a scientist on the Scott expedition. Spent a breeding cycle with Adélies on Cape Adare in 1911.' He paused again. 'Apparently, he was so shocked by their behaviour he recorded his notes in Greek. To protect uneducated readers from the *horror* of penguin perversions.' Harris intoned the last sentence in a plummy accent. 'Well, he had a point, some of it was a bit off. Necrophilia. Paedophilia. Male penguins having their way with female corpses and chicks.'

Nel's eyebrows shot to her hairline.

He lowered his voice. 'So it's said, passed down in ornithological lore, that he wrote a book on Adélies, but the chapter on their sexual proclivities was deemed so shocking the publishers cut it out – to preserve decency or Levick's reputation, who knows?'

'Or the reputation of the penguins?'

Harris chuckled. 'Could be. Anyway, Levick apparently put the chapter in a pamphlet and sent it around to other penguin experts he thought could handle the shock. So, we know it existed. But it hasn't been seen in decades. Lost to science. All we know is Levick saw a side of Adélie behaviour he thought was – shall we say – less than charming.'

'Have you ever seen anything like that?' Nel was fascinated.

'Well ...' He looked at her, then away, gazing into the colony. 'I've seen things some people might class as perversions.' He let out a great breath. 'I'm not condoning necrophilia or paedophilia or rape, but working with other species, seeing all kinds of ways of living in the world can make you a bit more broadminded.'

Nel was silent, not wanting to move or breathe in case he stopped talking.

'I've seen males copulating with other males. Penguins making nests with mates of the same sex.' He didn't look at her. 'Some of my colleagues say they're depraved. Some say they're confused.' He stopped.

'What do you think?'

A long pause. 'Look, you may not agree with me. But these chaps live in a harsh world. Unforgiving. And I think it's not surprising that some are just happy to find someone to share a nest with. Share a life.' He held out his hands. 'You can't help who you love.'

Nel was aware of every second as silence stretched between them. She wanted to touch him, take his hand, lean into his shoulder. But despite the intimacy of this moment, instinct told her any movement would shatter it. She held herself still, hoping on some level he sensed the warmth and flow within the frozen shell of her skin.

They watched the rookery, the penguins bustling about their business, totally unperturbed by the humans sitting stiffly on the outskirts of their rocky village.

A throbbing squawk split the air. Nel jumped, almost losing balance on her stool. She spun around to see a queue of penguins snaking back towards the crest of the hill. Harris had inadvertently plonked them down in the middle of a penguin highway. Traffic was banked up. The penguin at the front of the line gave another screech, flapping his wings and looking so impatient with them Nel couldn't help but laugh.

Harris lumbered awkwardly to his feet, waving the penguins through with a sweep of his arm. Nel rose and folded her stool, unrolling her shoulders from their stoop as she watched the penguins waddle between them, hopping and swaying as they bumbled into the throng. 'Well, if the objective was to convince me that there's more to penguins than meets the eye ... you've done it. I probably should get to work. They may be eccentric little characters, but they are not going to sketch themselves.' Nel reached down to fish her sketchbook from her bag. This time he didn't stop her. 'What exactly do you need me to draw?'

Cerulean Blue

Mawson Station, Antarctica
February 1961

'How *dare* you?' The moment she was through the cabin door Nel spun towards him, a tightly wound spring, the words lodged in her throat since dinner now flying at him.

Phil's hand sliced the air. 'Keep your voice down.'

Nel's face heated as she fought for control. 'Can you imagine, for one second, how it felt to sit down at that table and realise every single man on this ship had the privilege of knowing your plans – your plans *for me* – before I did?' Nel's voice was low and tight, her jaw aching from the clench she'd maintained for hours. She knew from long experience that to allow her feelings free rein was to lose before she'd begun. Phil valued coolness and logic, and their marital battles could only be fought on that field. Any hint of exasperation or sentimentality or, God forbid, anger, and he would immediately disengage.

'You know how I am. If you think I'm setting one foot in that contraption, you are seriously misguided. I'm not doing it.' Nel folded her arms. The word 'helicopter' hadn't even been *mentioned*. Then tonight, she'd barely taken her first sip of wine when Harold James had asked her if she was excited. Of course, she had no idea what he was talking about. And when he'd explained it to her, Harold had laughed at the audacity of the Great White Chief slipping her name onto the passenger roster without warning or discussion.

And then, Phil joined in. *He laughed.* She still couldn't believe it. It was as if the floor had already swung away beneath her feet, panic blazing in her chest. He knew she was afraid of heights. But to keep her in the dark, then side with the men as they ridiculed her fear? Doubly treacherous.

At home, he'd happily do any chore involving ladders. Cleaning gutters, storing boxes in the roof space. Even the cobwebs she couldn't reach without a stepladder. And now he expected her to voluntarily step into one of those flimsy death-capsules? She'd seen them on deck. They looked like oversized toys clipped together from Meccano, with nothing between the humans and all that air but a thin plastic bubble.

She'd wanted to kick him. In fact, she couldn't remember ever wanting to physically hurt him until that moment. Throughout the meal, she'd stared at her husband, lips tight. He kept his body angled slightly away from her and towards the men filling the rest of the U-shaped booth.

Nel watched their faces as the conversation rolled on. Did they actually like him? Respect his authority? Or was all this hearty bluster just a facade, a necessity for getting along with the boss? What was said behind his back? Maybe she'd jumped to the wrong conclusion. Perhaps some of the conversations that dried up whenever she entered a room were not about her after all.

Through dinner and Phil's post-meal briefing, Nel observed the men the way Harris watched penguins – analysing every sound and movement, trying to see behind words and gestures. As Phil gave orders and issued directives, she detected a hardening of the eyes in one man, a twitch of the jaw in another. Tiny flashes of dissatisfaction. Phil was working them hard, and this drive for speed and efficiency wasn't winning him any popularity contests.

Now they were back in the cabin, and she finally had his attention, she remembered these observations and felt reinforced. She was not alone.

'How *could* you? Don't you think I should have some say in whether I'm happy to risk my life? On a joyride? This throwing orders about, expecting everyone to jump, may work with the men. But I'm your *wife*.'

Phil's jaw jutted towards her, his eyes narrowing. 'Darling.' He paused. 'Isn't seeing this place the reason you wanted to come?' The reasonableness of the words was undercut by his cold, measured tone.

'I am seeing it.' She glared at him. 'What I can't fathom is your sheer nerve – assuming I'm going to set foot in that ... that *thing*, just on your say-so.' Nel sat heavily on the bunk and wrenched off her shoes. 'You know I can't – I'd probably have a heart attack.'

'You're overreacting.' He glanced at his watch. 'This is a once-in-a-lifetime chance. We're leaving in two days – you won't have another opportunity. There are men who'd give their right arm for this privilege.' He crossed to the door and opened it. 'I was under the impression this is exactly why you came. I'll be honest, Nel. I expected more.' The door shut with a sharp click and he was gone.

I expected more too. Who was this man? After twenty years of marriage, she was no longer sure, but she did know she didn't like him particularly much.

~

Fumbling through her toiletries case, Nel found the small glass bottle labelled *Amytal* and shook a couple of bright blue triangles onto her palm. Phil and his blasted helicopter. Fear was a logical human reaction to threat. People had a horror of spiders and snakes – for good reason. Fear should be listened to, not taken as a challenge. The problem was that Phil had put her name on that damned list. If she backed out now, the men would know. Damn him, forcing her hand like this, making her choose between fear and humiliation. Why did he have to push her?

She'd lain stiff and silent when Phil finally came to bed. Through the night and long into the morning, she'd alternated between fuming and praying for deliverance. Frostbite, snow blindness, a broken bone, food poisoning. She wasn't fussy.

All these hours after the fight, anger still simmered marrow-deep. Nel looked down at the tablets in her palm, then cracked open the cabin door. The coast was clear. She padded up the passageway and bent her ear to the door of Phil's stateroom. Hearing no voices, she slipped inside, closing the door with the softest click she could manage. Making straight for the wet bar, she lifted the decanter of whisky from behind the thin wooden slat that held the row of heavy bottles in place.

Nel tossed the pills into her mouth, the bitterness barely perceptible on the back of her tongue before they washed down with a slug of peaty spirit. She slid the decanter back into place and within half a minute was back in her cabin, whisky burn still tingling in her throat.

A surge of heat flooded her, as if her bones were the glowing bars of a radiator. She yanked off her turtleneck and scooped up a sketchbook, fanning herself. She sank onto the mattress, waving the book in front of her face, plucking her long-sleeved spencer off her damp skin. Another hot flush. Great timing. Just when she needed to dress more warmly than ever.

She slumped on the bed, her thick windproof parka, snow-goggles, inner and outer gloves and warmest beanie a mountain on her lap. Her face flamed from the flush and fear. She checked her watch: 2.20 pm. Nel swallowed hard. She was not going to let them see her fail. She was shrugging into her clothes and parka as her husband stuck his head around the door. Or should she also start calling him Chief?

'Come on. Up we go.' The weeks on board had lengthened his goatee, making his face look even more devilish.

Nel trailed him through the ship to the rear deck, knees so rubbery she feared they might give way at any moment. She pulled her beanie down to her eyebrows and snapped her goggles over her eyes. *Do not cry.* Stepping through the heavy metal door onto the back deck, she straightened her spine and lifted her chin.

Now that the resupply of the station was finally complete, this would be the first flight out to Rumdoodle airstrip. In theory, it was to check on the damage wreaked by the huge blizzard. But any expedition off station was a privilege and the excitement was palpable. The rear of the ship was thronging with men – both expeditioners and crew, all there for the spectacle.

Phil strode to the front of the crowd, clapping the pilot on the shoulder and issuing last-minute directions. His parka was so well worn it looked moulded to his body, and standing there in his ice-bitten boots he looked every inch one of the craggy explorers he so admired.

Nel noticed he was holding his Wilkins gloves in one hand. Stiff with age and lined with moulting polar-bear fur, they'd originally belonged to Australian polar explorer Hubert Wilkins. *Sir* Hubert Wilkins, she corrected herself. The gloves were her husband's most prized possession – the first item into his duffel when packing for an expedition and the last to be put away when he came home. Right now, she was so incensed with him, she'd happily fling them into the sea. *Then we'd see who was overreacting.* Adjusting her goggles, she flipped up her hood and did her best to fade into the background.

The racket from the helipad was deafening. With the clamour of the engine – part roar, part whine – and the huge rotors bludgeoning the air, it was like walking towards a maelstrom. Nel pressed her hood to her scalp in the face of the turbulence. *Get me out of here.*

The crowd of men parted before her as she approached the helicopter. Neither George nor Monte was out on deck, much to her relief. Both, she was sure, would've seen straight through her veneer of bravado, immediately spotting her jelly legs and the tremor in her hands as she adjusted the knapsack on her shoulder. She'd applied an extra thick layer of makeup as protection against wind and sun, hoping it might also camouflage what must be a deathly green pallor. Where was Harris? Had he heard what Phil had done? Panic clattered in her chest.

The helicopter whipped the air into a miniature gale. Sitting on the pad, its feet replaced with plastic floats, Nel thought it looked like a plucked galah wearing clown boots. It did not inspire confidence. Phil finished yelling into the ear of his second in command, Bob Dalton, and held out his hand to her as casually as if he was helping her aboard a Melbourne tram. Every fibre of her being was telling her to turn and run, but she plastered on her best devil-may-care smile and took his arm. *You will pay*, she vowed, teeth gritted.

The rotors hammered the air. Phil leaned close to her ear and yelled, 'A big step up onto the platform, then I'll tell you where to put your feet.'

I'll tell you where you can put your whole damned helicopter. She gripped his arm so hard she hoped it hurt, although this was unlikely through the thick insulation of his jacket. Phil hauled her onto the platform. The whirring was so close, everything vibrated. She hunched her shoulders, fear twisting her innards into a fist. Inside the helicopter, the pilot was already in his seat, feet on the pedals and hands clutching a thin black handle, his helmeted head so out of proportion to the rest of him he looked like a being from outer space.

Phil pointed to where she should sit, beside the pilot, yelled for her not to touch anything, especially not the pedals, then gave her a push from behind. Nel perched on the rock-hard seat, jaw clenched so hard she feared she'd crack a tooth.

This was without question the ricketiest, most slapped-together contraption Nel had ever seen. And she'd grown up on a farm during the Great Depression. The dashboard looked like it'd been jerry-built using several clocks, all of them set to impossible times, every instrument lashed together with bits of wire and string and tape. *How on earth does this even get off the ground?* Panicking, she looked towards their destination, high on the ice.

Beyond the helipad, the side of the ship fell away to the choppy dark waves below. The body of this flimsy beast, as far as she could tell, was just a thin bubble of clear plastic. Nel gripped the edge of her seat and tried to steady her breathing.

Phil leaned over to strap her in. She couldn't hear a word he was saying. He was so determined not to see how angry and scared she was, she could have slapped him. Nel leaned forward and saw a couple of the men on the deck below clap or give her the thumbs up, then Phil crammed himself into the space beside her and she was hidden, smooshed between the pilot and her husband. Phil handed her a helmet, but, seeing that he scorned to put his on, she held it between her knees, ready to use as an emergency sick bowl.

The pilot glanced at Phil, revved the motor into a higher register of roar, and before she was ready, the whole contraption lifted. Then they were up and tipping like a picnic basket over a cliff. The sea rushed at her. Nel screamed and squeezed her eyes shut as her stomach flipped into her chest.

Oh Jesus, oh Jesus. She couldn't look. Nel knew she was moaning but the hammering rotor was so overwhelming she couldn't hear herself. Her eyes clamped so tight her eyebrows felt as if they were touching her cheekbones.

Never in her life had she been this terrified. The only thing between her and death was a scrap of clear plastic and the will of the gods. She wanted to vomit but found she couldn't loosen her grip on Phil's arm to clutch the helmet. Paralysed, all she could do was pant and keep her eyelids clinched tight.

'Open your eyes,' Phil yelled in her ear. 'You're missing it!'

Nel managed to shake her head and craned her neck away from him.

'Come on, the sea's gone now. We're over the ice. Look.' He squeezed her arm encouragingly.

'I'll fall out.'

'You're completely safe. Like being in an armchair over the world's most amazing view. Darling, come on. You really don't want to miss this.'

Eyes squeezed shut, Nel took a deep breath and yelled, 'You've strapped me into a flying eggcup. This is not how I want to take my last breath!'

'Well, if it's your last breath, at least take a peek before you go.'

Nel moaned, blew out a panicked huff and cracked open one eye. The entire world was halved: blue above and white below. She gulped a breath and opened her eyes, not easing her death grip on Phil's arm.

It was impossible to take it all in.

Spread before her was a vast panorama of ice, the great blue dome of the sky and the drama of black mountain peaks punching up through an immense white distance. Visibility was perfect. No haze.

No mist. Just space: smooth and endless, with nothing between her and the expanse of polar plateau, everything glittering as if dusted with diamonds. The mountains jutting through the vast ice sheet carried glaciers in their creases, frozen rivers etched with crevasses in shades of blue she'd never imagined.

The helicopter gained more height. Nel's grip tightened on the seat, her arms aching all the way to her shoulders. Below her spread a world of breathtaking simplicity, line upon line of meltwater lakes and windswept ridges of snow rolling across the ice sheet like waves on a frozen ocean.

Swivelling in her seat, Nel craned to look back towards the sea. The perfection of the endless distance was marred only by the unsightly jumble of the station and the red ship in the harbour. She turned back to the front and let the world unfurl under her feet.

The Masson Range loomed in front of them and, before she was ready, the helicopter dipped and hovered, its oversized shoes gently touching down at the base of the great wall of rock. The flight had only lasted fifteen minutes.

As the rotors slowed, Phil helped her down, steadying her on the hard-packed ice. With the jagged brown peaks of Rumdoodle and South Doodle at her back, their stone flanks striped with snow, Nel gazed out over the expanse of ice.

The only sounds came from the small pocket surrounding them: the tick of the cooling engine, *swoosh* of parkas and crunch of ice underfoot. Beyond, a vast and open silence. The clear air made the mountain range in the distance appear almost painfully in focus, although she knew it must be much further away than it seemed. Nel turned in a slow circle, eyes and ears straining to absorb an emptiness greater than anything she'd ever experienced. Even the open ocean was brimming with noise. This was a desert of sound.

The airstrip was a long stretch of hard, flat ice, with a fixed-wing aircraft lashed down to one side. She knew what it was before the helicopter pilot helpfully pointed it out: a De Havilland DHC-2 Beaver, its wings snapped, the poor thing sitting lopsided on the ice like a shattered toy. She also knew what was missing – the Dakota DC-3. It'd been damaged on its sea voyage south on *Thala Dan*, repaired, then moved out here only to be swept away by the massive three-day blizzard. The plan had been to use the Dakota to survey unexplored regions deep inland, and now that was out of the question, Phil was feeling even more pressure to explore the Oates Land coast by sea on the way home.

'You can set up over there.' Phil pointed to some rocks at the edge of the airstrip, in the shadow of the range, then reached back into the helicopter and handed her the knapsack full of art supplies. 'I'll be a while. We need to see if we can find where that damned plane ended up.'

Nel shouldered the pack and took a step towards the rocks. Her foot slid on the ice. She grabbed Phil's arm to stop herself from crashing to the ground.

'Ah. Crampons.' Phil fished a pair of the spikey foot-shaped metal plates from the helicopter and strapped them to the soles of his boots, slapping the buckles once they were secure. Nel looked over at the pilot, who had already lashed a pair to his own boots and was standing confidently on the ice.

'And mine?' Nel asked.

Phil looked at his watch and Nel was sure he was about to shrug until he saw the look on her face. 'How exactly am I meant to get around?' Harris had always made sure she had all the kit she needed to join him in the field. She'd assumed Phil would show the same thoughtfulness.

170

He had the grace to look embarrassed, and cast about in the footwell of the helicopter despite it being clear to all there was nothing there. 'You'll have to crawl.'

'You *are* joking.'

'Sweetheart ... I have things to do.'

'The first being helping me over to that rock.' She glared at him.

'Boss, I'll head over and check out the damage on the Beaver.' The pilot crunched away across the ice.

Nel took a tentative step. The ice was hard and slick. The slightest wobble in her centre of gravity would send her feet shooting from under her. She grabbed Phil's arm, steadying herself against him.

Phil took a deep breath, casting a look over his shoulder at the diminishing form of the pilot and the crippled Beaver beyond. 'Right. Let's get you set up. Where do you want to sit?'

Nel looked around, lips pursed with frustration. If left to her own devices and on solid footing, she'd wander across the ice until she found the perfect vantage point. And she'd be free to move whenever the urge took her to try a different angle or composition. Now she'd be stuck in a single place. From the look on Phil's face, it was clear she needed to choose swiftly. She stifled a sigh and pointed to a cluster of rocks on the far side of the ice runway, facing the black range rising up from the smooth flow of white.

As they made their way across the glassy cold, Nel forced her irritation down. She'd survived. More than that, she'd been awed by the experience. Yet she'd be damned if she'd admit to Phil he'd been right.

'This is how it will be when we're old,' she said, tottering along unsteadily. Her left foot shot out from under her. Only her grip on Phil's arm stopped her landing on her bottom. 'We should get used to it.'

'Or I could remember to pack extra crampons and we could stay young,' Phil said, hauling her upright and balancing her on both feet.

'That ship sailed years ago, my dear.' Nel gave him a squeeze that almost sent them both tumbling to the ice. They steadied each other and continued on their careful way, managing to reach their destination with dry trousers.

'One more thing before you go.' She watched Phil take a breath and smooth impatience from his expression. 'Could you fetch me a chunk of ice? Please?'

He raised his eyebrows. 'I reminded you to bring water.'

'And I listened to your instructions, O Mighty Chief. Part of the reason my bag is so heavy is that I packed water for drinking and for watercolours.' Nel shot him a level glance. 'The ice is for artistic purposes.'

He hesitated, looking back at the distant aircraft. Nostrils flaring, he fished out his pocketknife and crunched away, returning with a chunk of ice he'd chipped from an outcrop where the runway met the rise of the mountain.

Nel watched him stalk across the airstrip with swift steps, until he was a distant streak of grey on the white. She stretched her arms over her head and drew the cold deep into her lungs. The silence settled around her. Time to work. She arranged her easel and warmed up with a few quick sketches, her charcoal sighing across the page as she charted the stark lines of the landscape before her.

She sketched until the connection between eye and hand felt charged and effortless as an electrical conduit, then put down the sketchbook, readying her oil palette and her first board.

She closed her eyes and was back in the helicopter, the crumpled glaciers and sinuous lines of sastrugi unfurling in a vast sweep of white veined with blue. She opened her eyes and traced the patterns onto the board. The outlines done, she leaned back, stretching out the curve of her back and loosening muscles tensed with cold. This was it – her point of divergence. The vision she transcribed would not represent the world the way she'd always drawn it. She would reveal something else. Something new. Nel leaned down to where she'd placed the chunk of ice Phil had collected for her and picked it up.

Through her gloves, the damp reached for her skin and drew away the warmth. This ice used to be water. Before that, it was sky. She examined it like a jewel, watching how each facet caught the light and flung it back. She wondered if it remembered the pliancy and softness of being water. If it remembered falling through air. The feeling of being full of light and freedom and carrying life. Now, it was hardness and cold. Under her feet, layers of it. Pressing down and down until it was beyond the reach of the sun. Nel wondered how it felt to hold so much light, if ice felt alive, the way she imagined water would. And air.

Nel kept hold of the jagged chunk in one hand and readied herself to work with the other. She had the sense of the ice draining away, drawing colour and heat and texture with it. A presence making a statement through absence, describing itself by what it *wasn't* rather than what it *was*. Yes. That was it. That's how she needed to express it – by removal. Reveal its essence by paring everything back. Before now, she'd been layering it up – coat upon coat of paint and detail. The ice was telling her to do the opposite. She picked up her brush.

~

Before the sound fully registered, she thought it was the drone of an insect. She grinned at the ridiculousness of the idea. Engine noise. But not a kind she recognised. She scanned the cold, clean expanse before her, squinting against the glare. She couldn't see the source of the noise, but Phil and the pilot were making their way towards her from beyond the far end of the ice runway.

173

She kept painting. For the last few hours she'd been on *fire*. The painted boards propped to dry against the rock lit a glow in her chest. She'd experienced this a few times when she'd just finished a piece, the deep pleasure of thinking it might be the best work she'd ever done. When it had happened in the past, she'd sleep that night with images of the work spinning through her dreams. But the next morning she'd wake, look at the work again and it would be crushing, as if the cold light of dawn brought with it the artist's version of a hangover. She'd be mortified at the hubris of the previous day and turn the piece to the wall, too ashamed to even look. It would stay hidden for a week, perhaps longer, until she'd feel strong enough. Facing the work to the light, the shame would lift. It wasn't the worst piece she'd done – but it wasn't the best either. So, she'd prop it back on the easel, and try again. These pieces were different. Nel looked down at the boards, the geometry of white, blue and black like tiny abstract windows on a miniature world. Their style was unlike anything she'd done before. But it was more than that. They *felt* different. A tiny part of her suspected that tomorrow, perhaps, she'd look at these paintings and still feel pride. Perhaps.

By the time Phil reached her, the lush silence had been completely drowned by the rude roar of the strange, bottom-heavy machine approaching across the plateau – a Snow Trac. Below its cabin, the bright orange conveyance looked like a tank, the caterpillar tracks on each side powering it across the ice. But above the enormous belts, the Snow Trac looked like a regular car, with bucket seats, a steering wheel and a pair of bug-eyed headlamps, which Nel thought lent it the endearing expression of her favourite car, the Austin-Healey Sprite.

'Well, my dear, here's your ride,' said Phil.

'What?'

'We're going to be out here a while yet, and I thought you might have had enough of the helicopter for one day.' He gave her a wry smile. 'Besides, this will be another first for you,' he said, jerking a thumb at the Snow Trac, which had reached the smoother surface of the ice runway and picked up speed, its driver clearly relishing the secure surface and flooring the accelerator.

'What the hell?' Phil yanked off his beanie and scrubbed his mittened hands over his head before slamming the thick woollen cap back into place. 'He knows the engine's not run in yet.' He waved at the vehicle, swinging his arms in huge gestures, clearly signalling 'slow down'. The side window of the distant Snow Trac wound down and an arm waved back with no change in the speed of approach.

'Holy hell!' Phil waved more wildly, with even greater emphasis on the downswing. Still no deceleration. 'Harold bloody James! *Slow down.*' Phil kicked a rock, his jaw muscles ticking with anger as the bug-eyed vehicle raced towards them.

The Snow Trac did a flamboyant loop across the end of the runway before pulling to a stop. The door cranked open and Harold James leapt down, holding the door open as his passenger made a less ostentatious exit. Nel's gut sank as George climbed out and stretched his back, gazing up at the Rumdoodle peaks. It was as if she'd spilled ink on a perfect sketch.

'James. You sodding leadfoot. I told you the engine's not run in yet.' Phil's voice was burred with anger and cold.

'Sorry, Chief.' Harold looked down at his boots, his expression shamefaced, until Phil turned to speak to George. Then he shot a wink at Nel, and walked carefully across the ice towards her.

She grinned at him. 'Didn't you bring crampons?'

'Don't need them. I'm just the taxi service. Delivering one geologist. Collecting one artist. Can I have a look?' he asked, reaching down to pick up the closest painting.

'These aerial views are great. You opened your eyes on the flight, then?' At Nel's nod, Harold turned to George. 'Ha! Hear that, George?

You owe me two bob,' he called to the geologist. George's expression turned sour. Harold beamed at Nel, the brightness making his freckles stand out against his skin. 'Never doubted you for a second.' He reached for Nel's knapsack. 'Righto. Let's get you packed away. We want to make it back in plenty of time to get spruced up for the party, especially given the *speed limits*,' he said, waggling his brows theatrically.

The changeover party! Nel had forgotten all about it in her all-consuming anxiety about the helicopter ride. She groaned inwardly, wanting nothing more than to curl up in her cabin and contemplate her new work. Still, she was more than happy to take the land route back to Mawson. The adrenaline had ebbed from her system hours ago, and the sleepless night and Amytal were catching up with her.

The route back to the station was only twelve miles, but this time Harold obeyed Phil's decree. The Snow Trac grumbled across the terrain, careful never to exceed fifteen miles per hour, its progress loud and rough. Before long, Nel's whole body was sore from bracing herself against the motion of the cabin as she attempted sketch after sketch.

The late-day sun stretched shadows over the glistening ice, the whole world aglitter. It was dazzling – nothing but stretches of open ice for miles, each crystal a brilliant pinprick. The snow, blown by crosswinds, lay across the ice, scalloped and smoothed into striations of shadowed blue. She'd barely swiped an outline across the page before the next vista presented itself.

The colours. The blues – so beautiful and terrible. The crevasses shimmering down to almost inexpressible intensities. The milky blue of snow bridges. The crystalline blues of pressure ridges buckling against each other. The bumpy ride meant watercolours were out of the question, so she had to pencil in descriptions of shades and tones to complete them later. It was infuriating and exhilarating.

When Harold stopped the Snow Trac, Nel looked up to see the station, still some distance away: the tin sheds lashed onto the ice and, beyond the cluster of buildings, ocean all the way to the horizon, all of it besieged by a great phalanx of icebergs gleaming in the sun's low rays.

'I thought you might need an extra moment to sketch the view. All the winterers who're leaving tomorrow should be up here.' Harold waved his hand at the vista. 'This is the way to remember Mawson.'

'Everyone who's staying on should see it, too. Before the winter dark closes in, and all they can see are the walls.'

'True.' Harold nodded, staring out to the horizon, clearly in no hurry to return to the station himself. 'Well, we'll have a whole host of new faces for the rest of the voyage. Faces that are probably sick to the back teeth of icebergs and penguins.'

'It'll be so strange to be back on our cosy *Magga* with a horde of shaggy strangers. And sad to say goodbye to the new winterers. Although, to be honest, some of them I won't mind seeing the back of.'

Harold turned to face her. 'Look' – he hesitated for a second, then plunged on – 'I know George gave you a hard time. Having a woman on board took a bit of getting used to and you probably overheard a bit of what was being said among the rank and file. Not making excuses for it. Or for George. But I'm not sure you know the whole story.' He turned back to stare out at the view again. 'He lost his wife last year. Cancer. And he's got two kids. Little boys. Can't imagine how hard it was. Is. And to make it worse, George's life's work is out here. He can't do this research back home. It's Antarctica or nothing.' Harold grimaced. 'He's having a pretty hard time of it. He has to leave the boys with his sister. And he's a great dad. You should've known him before. He'd stick photos under your nose every chance he got. It's tragic. And I guess he sees you, here. With the chief. And it just reminds him of what he's lost. So don't take it to heart. It's not you.'

Nel was silent for a long moment. 'I had no idea.' She let out a breath as they both stared across the berg-studded bay. 'Poor man.' She hesitated, then decided if there was ever a moment to share, it was now. 'Being away for so much of the year – that's the reason Phil and I don't have children. First there was the war. We were engaged but then had to wait so long to be married. By the time we felt ready, Phil was in charge of ANARE. He knew it meant nearly half a year away, every year. And if he was going to be a father, he didn't want to be an absent one. He thought it wasn't fair – on the children. Or me, being the one who'd have to cope for so much of the year on my own.' She shrugged and smiled. 'And I agreed with him – and was happy, really. I had my painting. And my cat.' She laughed softly. 'But having your family destroyed like that. Poor George.'

Harold glanced over at her. 'You didn't know. George plays things close to the vest.' He shifted in his seat, drumming his fingers on the dark plastic steering wheel.

Sensing his discomfort, Nel closed her eyes. He'd only wanted to let her know the background against which her obvious dislike of George was playing out. And she'd responded by oversharing about the private life of his boss. A fist of embarrassment clenched in her gut. She'd never missed the company of women more.

Harold threw the Snow Trac into gear. 'Ready to head back and gussy up?' At her stiff nod, they lurched into motion, churning down the track towards the base.

~

Nel couldn't shake the cringe in her gut. She'd been lying on her bunk for over an hour, trying to get some rest before the party. But it was no use. She sat up, rubbing her tired eyes, before swinging her feet to the floor and standing up resignedly. She ripped a shirt from a hanger, wrenched a jumper from a drawer. In the bathroom she stared at her reflection, leaning on the edge of the sink, before applying her makeup swiftly, her past attention to such details long gone. She didn't like George any better, she decided, but she had an opportunity to make things right before never seeing him again.

Nel moved to the desk, and began rummaging through a stack of sketches and watercolours. There was still time. She skimmed through her illustrations of all the penguin species she'd seen so far: Adélie, king, gentoo, royal, chinstrap. None of them was quite right.

She could do it if she hustled, she told herself, filling a glass with water and throwing open her paints. She plonked into her chair, pulled out a sheet of watercolour paper and set to work.

Nel had just laid down her brush when a crash shuddered the wall of the cabin. She rushed next door, expecting to find Phil lying helpless and bleeding. Instead, her husband stood behind his desk, head down, leaning on his hands, the carpet on the far side of the room glittering with shards of broken glass. Scanning for blood, and finding him unhurt, she pressed her lips together and began carefully gathering the sharp slivers. The air was fumy with whisky still dribbling down the wooden panelling.

Phil stared sightlessly at the point of impact. 'That's it.' His voice was hollow. 'That blizzard wiped out our last chance of getting far enough inland to stake a proper claim.' Nel kept gingerly gathering pieces of glass, until, with a single great swipe, Phil dashed the contents of his desk to the floor. 'For a whole *year*.' He raked a hand through his hair. 'You know where we found the Dakota? Ten miles away. The only thing that stopped it just skating off to oblivion was banging into a huge bloody cliff. The damned thing was lashed down with steel wire that had a breaking strain of fifteen tonnes.' He shook his head, still gazing into the distance. 'Fifteen tonnes! I just cannot bloody *win*.'

'Darling.' Nel pushed herself up from the floor to perch on the edge of the couch. 'You'll get planes down here again. It's frustrating. I know. But you've overcome so much already. It's like you always say – patience and persistence matter more than luck and talent.'

'*Pfft*.' He fell into his chair. 'And now I have to go crawling back to the department begging for more money. Again. Explain why I can't do the things I've promised. No airborne exploration. And I have a whole contingent of RAAF personnel down here but *no bloody planes*. It's a complete goddamned *disaster*.'

'But, darling, you knew the Dakota was likely to be unsalvageable, and the Beaver unusable this season. Like you told the men – you can still explore Oates Land from the sea, can't you?'

Phil exhaled, a gust of air heavy with disillusionment. 'Yes ... but it's a poor version of what I could do with a plane. Seeing the Dakota just brought it all home to me, I guess.'

Nel nodded sympathetically as she folded the shards of glass into some paper she'd fished from the wastepaper basket and tucked them safely back into the bin. 'Here.' She poured him a fresh glass of whisky. 'The changeover's gone well. There's no reason putting up the weather station on Chick Island won't be just as speedy. If there's one thing I know, it's that you don't give up. You still have weeks up your sleeve. You'll make it work. I know it.'

Finally, he looked at her. 'Thank you,' he said, throwing back the contents of the glass in a single gulp. He pressed his lips into a line that was barely more than a grimace, then pushed to his feet. 'I'd better make an appearance. The party's probably kicking off. I'll just get out of these clothes and make a quick stop on the bridge.' Phil shrugged out of his polar jacket and headed for the door. 'Coming?'

Nel nodded, then held up a finger. 'I'll follow you across in a minute. I just have to get something from the cabin.'

~

The party was bowling along by the time Nel stepped into the recreation hut. She hovered near the door, getting her bearings, then made for the drinks table, careful to avoid catching either her clothes or the manila folder in her hand on the lit cigarettes being waved about.

Her skin prickled. He was watching her. She hadn't even poured herself a drink and already Monte had poisoned her night. Clenching her teeth and holding her empty glass and folder before her like Joan of Arc with shield and sword, she turned to face the crowd.

Monte was propped against the wall on the far side of the room, watching her with hooded eyes. Nel met his gaze with a stiff face, then cut her eyes away. Instinctively, she noted a flare of red hair. Harris was standing with a group of men, laughing at some wild story, but on the outskirts, his body angled slightly away, eyes on the game of darts as he sipped his drink.

Nel looked back at Monte. Watching her watch Harris, he had lifted one side of his mouth in a smirk. She shuddered and poured herself a drink.

The men were well sozzled, the room loud with raucous advice: returning over-winterers offering pearls of hard-won wisdom, fresh expeditioners offering suggestions on where to shove them. She downed her first wine standing in front of the drinks table, then made her way towards the door carrying her refill. She hadn't intended to stay late, but now she felt too far behind to join in. And too unnerved. Just sensing Monte's eyes on her body made her want to flinch, like she'd walked through a cobweb.

The one person she couldn't spot was George. She scanned the room once more, then slipped out into the enclosed porch for a lungful of smoke-free air. The door clicked behind her, dropping the din to a muffled rumble of male voices and the baritone of Perry Como. She gave an exaggerated sigh of relief.

'Thought you'd be right at home in there.'

George was sitting on a bench under a rail of coat-pegs, partially hidden by the puff of insulated jackets. A sharp retort rose up and then died on her tongue.

'George. Glad I found you.' She stepped towards him, clocking the wary expression in his eyes. 'Here. A going-away present.' She held out the manila folder and the wariness morphed into outright suspicion. 'Totally non-explosive. I promise.'

He looked at her for a long moment before reaching to take the folder. He held it in his lap for a moment, then flipped it open.

Inside lay a watercolour of a small group of emperor penguins: a tall male, his chest the unadulterated white of the paper, contrasting with his black cape tinged with blue and his lemon neck cravat. His neck curved downward in a graceful arc and his flippers were open, as if reaching to embrace the pair of fluffy chicks cavorting at his feet. Their soft down was exquisitely rendered, slate grey around their white faces and chests; their tiny black eyes bright and full of joy. At the bottom, Nel had inked the title 'A dad with two beloved sons'.

He said nothing, staring down at the painting. The muffled sounds of revelry contrasted so awkwardly with his silence, Nel rushed to fill it.

'I'm no expert – on penguins or parenthood – but from what I've learned about emperors, they do an amazing job in the worst possible conditions. Especially the fathers.' She faltered. She'd overstepped. It was really none of her business. This was meant to be an apology but all she'd done was reveal that his situation had been the subject of shipboard gossip. 'Well, anyway.' Nel stepped back, took a long swallow of wine and raised her glass as she nodded towards the door. 'Must get back. Just wanted to say goodbye and good luck.'

'Thank you.'

She looked back but his head was down, still examining the painting held in his lap. 'You're welcome.' Those two words held more kindness than any she'd spoken to him before. He looked up, his expression free of the hostility and disdain she usually read in his face. It felt as warm as a smile.

Yellow Ochre

Mac Robertson Land to Chick Island (Wilkes Land)
February 1961

The world was crammed with sound. A halyard chimed against the mast like the tongue of a bell. Beyond the engine thrum and slap of waves on the metal hull, the sea ice yawed and creaked, grinding and grating against the jagged edges of the pack. Fingering the Antarctic pebble in her pocket, Nel leaned against the starboard rail, her breath puffs of vapour as she watched Mawson Station disappear into the vast grandeur of the mountains.

It was delicious to be moving again. She was hungry for it. New scenes. She crossed to the port rail, unable to decide what to tackle first. The corridor of icebergs? Or the glaciers so milky blue in the soft morning sun? The light was perfect, everything glitter and sparkle, and the air still. Perfect conditions for watercolours – no flapping paper or her palette taking wing. She pulled out her block of watercolour paper and strapped it to her lap-easel with the homemade elastic bands. Then she tipped hot water from her thermos into a mug, adding two drops of ox gall to stop the water freezing and the sable brush sticking to the paper when the paint turned to ice.

Arching above the corridor of bergs, the sky was a pane of blue so piercing her eyes began to water. Her goggles were tucked into her knapsack – she wanted to see without anything between her and the colours.

Choosing an approaching berg, she had mere minutes to sketch its basic facets and features, then quickly wash and daub patches of colour so she could finish the work later in the cabin. Then the ship was past, the next subject looming beyond the bow.

She was aflame, all eye and mind – the rawness of her skin, the ache in her fingers all at a distance, like sympathy for the discomfort of an acquaintance. To be here, in this glorious, secret place; she felt lost among all this wonder, but also somehow found. The ocean sparkled with ice, and a small flock of birds wheeled, sweeping shadows across the vast bergs.

Harris joined her, leaning his forearms against the rail. She looked back over her shoulder, scanning the deck in both directions. They were alone. She forced herself to relax. She deserved to appreciate this grandeur with someone who wanted her company. They glanced at each other, sharing a smile, then stood gazing out at the scene gliding past. There was no need to speak.

She was brushing a swoop of bird shadow across the shining face of a berg when Harris leaned in, his upper arm brushing her shoulder.

He cocked an eyebrow at her. 'Know what they are?'

She laughed. 'Snow petrels. I seem to have picked up a thing or two about birds lately.'

He chuckled, following the snow petrels with his eyes. 'Beautiful, aren't they? Like angels.' The birds swung across the face of a vast block of ice, plumage invisible, only their shadows and onyx legs, beaks and eyes stark against the white.

'Of course, you imagine angels as birds,' she laughed.

'Snow petrels are *like* angels,' Harris said. 'Of course, the real angels are penguins.'

'I hate to break it to you, but I suspect angels don't waddle.'

'Have I taught you nothing?' Harris shook his head at her, then leaned back, tapping his palms on the rail. 'Actually, I *have* neglected something in your penguin education.' He stood up straight. 'All right. Pack up your gear.'

Nel looked at him incredulously, torn between annoyance and curiosity.

'It's important. Honestly, you need to see this.' He reached down and flung the water from her mug overboard. He picked up her knapsack, Nel still shoving brushes and paints inside, and strode for the metal stairs. Nel trailed behind as they climbed to *Magga*'s highest deck. The spark of irritation at losing a painting now an ember of anticipation.

It was colder up here, more exposed. Harris dropped her knapsack at his feet and propped himself against the railing. From this height, the view was even more impressive.

Enormous icebergs studded the water to the horizon: great tabular slabs larger than the ship, castles spiked with turrets and pinnacles and, most spectacularly, crowns of glittering ice, their centres hollowed away by waves.

The abundance of life was astonishing. Out at the Rumdoodle airstrip she'd only been twelve miles inland, but she couldn't remember seeing a single skua. Once Phil and the pilot were beyond sight, she'd been completely alone. More alone than she'd ever been in her life. But here, on the edge of the pack, the ice was thronging. Below the wheeling snow petrels, seals sunned themselves on ice floes and penguins punctuated the skirts of the bergs.

Harris nudged her. A large berg drifted past the ship. A line of Adélie penguins queued along the broken lip of ice. They seemed to be chatting among themselves, looking up and down the rank as if trying to decide who was to go in first. The furthest to the right peered into the water, presumably checking for orca or leopard seals. All at once his neighbour gave him a solid bump. The little chap squawked, teetering, flippers beating the air as he toppled. Nel gasped as the penguin executed a gymnastic twist, entering the water in a smooth dive. His comrades shuffled nervously until they saw their companion bob to the surface. Head up and alert, he paddled away from his friends, looking for all the world like a short-necked duck.

One by one, the tiny penguins dove into the ocean with barely a ripple, the last one tobogganing along on his belly the length of the ice before slipping into the sea.

The cold, clear water at the berg's edge glowed like turquoise glass. The moment the penguins touched the water, all their awkwardness vanished. Free and sinuous, their trails illuminated with bubbles, they zoomed beneath the surface, either in pursuit of prey or from sheer joy, it was difficult to tell.

'They're flying!'

'See? Angels.' Harris sounded as full of wonder as she felt. 'Anyone who calls a penguin a flightless bird has never seen them in water.'

'To see them bumbling about on land, you'd never believe this.' She leaned further out. 'What are they chasing? Or are they just having fun?'

'Fish? Or krill, most likely.'

'It's like underwater ballet. Esther Williams could take lessons.'

Harris laughed. 'Wait until you see the emperors. I'll be mapping the positions of penguin colonies on the way to Oates Land, so we'll see some in the water. You wouldn't think such a bulky barrel of a bird could be so graceful.' He paused, lost in thought. 'Can you imagine being able to watch them from under the water? One day we'll be able to do that. Swim with them. Study them in the habitat where they're most at home. As birds.'

'You'd want a thick pair of full-body togs!' Nel laughed. 'How did you come to penguins, anyway? You're from Sydney, aren't you? From the subtropics to the ice? There must be a story there.' Nel started pulling her gear from the knapsack as she spoke, one part of her mind playing over the problem of how to draw the penguins in flight.

When Harris did not reply, she glanced at him.

He leaned against the rail, his eyes tracking the penguins. 'It's a long story. Short version – I got the chance to go down to Heard Island as a field assistant. Years ago, studying subantarctic avian species.' He took a deep breath. 'Light-mantled, sooty and black-browed albatrosses, macaroni and king penguins. And I fell in love.' Harris stared into the distance.

The *scritch* of Nel's pencil on the coarse paper was the only sound. Eventually, she looked up and said, 'So who was your first love?'

Harris stood as if frozen, his knuckles white on the rail.

'Before penguins,' Nel said teasingly. 'You must've had a favourite. Before Heard Island?'

Harris relaxed, but a small furrow creased the gap between his pale eyebrows.

'Lyrebirds.'

'Really?'

'Have you ever seen one?'

Nel laughed, even as her hand moved furiously over the page. 'I grew up on a dairy farm in Gippsland. The forests are teeming with the sneaky things.'

'*Sneaky things?*'

'They hide in the undergrowth pretending to be other birds!'

'Mrs Law, if you don't take that back immediately, I fear we may no longer be friends.' Nel looked up and caught his grin. 'They're exquisite creatures. Their tail plumage! And what you call sneaky is the cleverest of adaptations. Sonic camouflage. So flamboyant, yet they hide in plain sight. They are simply amazing creatures – and I will not hear a word against them. End of tirade.'

On a nearby floe, a leopard seal lifted its head as if catching a scent, then slithered over the edge. Harris stiffened, leaning forward.

The Adélies shot for the surface. Launching from the water, they landed awkwardly feet-first on the lip of the berg, then waddled back from the edge, their more elegant selves a memory.

The leopard seal slid past, an oily streak on clear blue. Its reptilian head struck Nel as an uncanny hybrid – part seal, part snake – chasing prey that was part bird, part fish. The seal ducked back below the surface and in a tailbeat was gone. Harris relaxed.

A throat cleared.

Nel jumped and spun around. 'Phil! I didn't hear you.'

Phil's eyes flicked from her to Harris. He wasn't wearing his outdoor jacket.

'I need you back inside.' Phil turned on his heel and headed through the door, holding it open as he waited for her to follow him, raising his eyebrows when he saw she hadn't stepped away from the rail.

'Just a minute.' She held up the sketchpad in front of her, showing him the half-finished berg.

'I thought I explained this.' Phil's voice was low and tight. 'This month is the most important part of the voyage. My only chance at exploration before the ice closes in. You said you want to be useful? I need you on the bridge, recording the landscape all the way to Oates Land. And once we reach Chick Island, sketching the building of the weather station. So please' – Phil jutted his chin towards her – 'enough penguins – back to the bridge.'

Nel pressed her lips together, stuffing her gear back into the knapsack, the force threatening to fox the corners of the paper block. A flash of homesickness tore through her. How could she be missing her husband when he was standing in earshot?

He turned to the ornithologist. 'Harris.' It was a dismissal.

Slinging the bag onto her shoulder, Nel stalked through the doorway, then stood aside as Phil closed the latch and started down the stairs towards the lower deck. Before he'd gone two steps down, Nel tapped him on the shoulder.

'Phil.' Nel stood at the top of the stairs, looking down at her husband as he turned to face her. 'Wasn't it clear to you I was working?'

He opened his mouth, but she cut across him. 'Haven't I completed all the sketches you've asked of me?' She rushed on, not wanting to draw breath and give him an opening. 'Honestly, Phil. I love you, but you're being a bit of a bully. I'm doing the work you asked for, but you're acting as if the penguins are just a lark. Or a distraction. But they're my work too.'

Nel folded her arms, keeping her chin high. Phil looked a little red in the face.

'I understand that.' Phil spoke slowly and carefully, choosing his words as if he was stepping across lava. 'What you don't seem to understand about work is prioritisation. You don't just get to spend all your time doing the tasks you enjoy and skimp on the ones you don't. Especially when the person you are working for is both your boss *and* your husband. You need to spend a bit more of your time on the tasks I've asked you to do.'

Nel's eyes widened. 'You think I don't spend enough time working for you?' She leaned forward, mirroring his careful tone to the very edge of mockery. 'Ask me about all the things I do for you. The cooking, the washing, the cleaning, the shopping. All the mindless, thankless, endless tasks – that anyone can do. Work that I'm not actually put on this earth for.'

'Correct me if I'm wrong, but didn't you tell me you wanted to be a contributing expeditioner? Well, my dear, real work isn't pleasant. Real jobs are just hours and hours of doing things you don't want to do.'

'Oh. Right. So, following your own logic, exploring is just something you do for work? You don't really want to be here?'

He gave a terse laugh. 'I'd love to just explore. But there's much more to it. Which I thought you understood.'

'Being the boss, ordering men around, building things, making decisions, establishing bases. Being important. That's not what you enjoy either?' Nel softened her expression. 'Because I love being your wife. But I can't honestly say that pushing the vacuum cleaner around or folding clothes fulfils me on any level. But this …' Nel reached down and took his hand, drawing him up the stairs towards her. 'Being the one able to do this work – both for you and for Harris – doesn't just satisfy me.' She squeezed his arm. 'It fires me. It makes me leap out of bed each morning.' Nel took a deep breath, looking into his face. 'And that's something that hasn't happened for a while.'

Phil looked at her, drawing in a breath as if to speak, then changing his mind. He opened the door and walked out onto the deck, gazing out to sea. She followed and leaned against him, unsure whether his silence signified agreement, acquiescence, or abandonment of the argument.

A crack, sharp as gunshot split the air. Beyond the railing, a great wedge of ice spliced away from the towering face of an iceberg, plunging into the sea like great arrowhead. They clutched the rail, transfixed. The mass of the remnant berg pitched to one side, then back, the whole berg rocking like a giant metronome. *Magga* barely noticed the wave from the calved ice. But the remaining berg rocked twice more, then toppled over, its secret underside suddenly exposed in a cascade of water, the scoured line where the sea and air had met now angled towards the sky. Together they watched in silence as the berg found its new centre of gravity, settling itself on the ruffled waters as if slowly catching its breath.

~

Nel looked around the deck surreptitiously – all clear – then grabbed the front of her clothing, plucking the warm layers away from her body. The inrush of cold air immediately helped to quench the flames threatening to engulf her from the inside out. Thank goodness Phil had relented about wanting her to work on the bridge all the time. It was far too stuffy and full of men when she was in the throes of a hut flush.

If anyone asked, she'd say that Antarctica could be the best place on earth to experience the change. On her mental pro/con list, access to freezing air whenever she needed it was clearly a pro. But no one was going to ask. That was a mark in the con column. Female companionship. She'd taken her sisters and her girlfriends for granted, so much a part of everyday life she hadn't realised how fundamental they were. It was the little things she wished she could share, and laugh over: the ludicrous amount of clothing there was to put on, how long it took to end up looking so comprehensively unappealing, how awkward it was to deal with feminine issues when living in a place without women's bathrooms. Whenever Nel suspected she'd need the toilet it was an operation in precision timing. She'd have to extract herself politely from conversation, make her way through the ship to her cabin, a journey that was longer or shorter depending on sea conditions, and arrive at her bathroom with enough time to unbutton, unbuckle and unzip all the layers. She'd almost needed to do extra laundry on several occasions.

She hadn't mentioned any of this to Phil. Back home, she'd always thought they could talk about anything. But broaching her concerns about heading into the change of life right at this moment felt like confessing to the boss that she didn't feel up to the job. Or at least she feared that was how he'd read it. These Antarctic men considered women to be emotionally unstable at the best of times. If only her sisters were here. Or Pam.

Nel sighed. A bathroom run would be a good idea, now that she thought about it. She packed up and made her way across the deck towards the heavy metal doors leading to the saloon. Juggling her gear, she paused just shy of the entrance, bundling everything into the crook of one arm to free the other for wrestling the stubborn door.

'He's a bloody fascist, if you ask me. What about that broomstick he's got lodged up his arse? Isn't that ANARE property?' The deep voice was clearly audible around the corner of the bulwark. 'No one's accused *him* of stealing *that* coz no one bloody wants it back!'

Laughter and cigarette smoke drifted around to Nel, and she shrank back against the exterior wall, curious to know who they were discussing. Bob Dalton? The captain? *Phil?*

'So, what did you say?' A different voice.

'Well, I told him he had no right to open my trunk. Personal property.'

'Too right. What'd he say?'

'The bugger said I'd signed a contract. Everything I'd been issued belonged to ANARE. So if he suspected I'd filched something, he had the right to check.'

'Christ. He pawed through all your stuff?' A pause. 'Find anything?'

'Just some sheets and a pair of boots Dalton issued me six months ago. I'd been wearing my old ones down to the leather, saving the new ones for home. You should've seen his face. Almost popped a vein. Said I'd *committed petty larceny*, and it was lucky he wasn't going to press charges. As far as he's concerned, I've done my dash with the department.'

Phil. They were talking about Phil.

The voice continued, 'Can't get off this tub a bloody moment too soon.'

'What made him go through your gear?'

'Turns out someone found the crate of rations stashed down in the hold and dobbed. It was only bloody biscuits and a coupla cans of potted meat. Now he's on the warpath. Heard him tearing strips off Dalton. Said he's going to do a "customs check" before we reach Melbourne.' The voice dripped with acid. 'If we declare what we've pinched and hand it over, they'll turn a blind eye. But until then, Antarctic Stalin is going to lock the hold so we can't get to our gear.'

There was a volley of expletives. Nel heard the snick of a match and smoke puffed around the corner. 'Antarctic Stalin. That's going to stick.'

'I reckon he's more of a Hitler.'

'Wasn't Hitler's wife an artist too?' There was a snigger. Nel felt her chest tighten.

'Photographer, I reckon.'

'Artist. Photographer. To*may*to, tomato. She was about as much of an artist as this one's wife is anyway.'

Nel's arms crushed her gear to her chest, lungs withering as heat rushed to her face.

'Why's she even here? Everyone says something different.'

'I heard the owner of the shipping line invited her. Then James said she's here as an official ANARE artist. Recording the coast from

194

Mawson to Oates Land or some rubbish. Someone else said the papers back home were saying she's here with the minister's say-so. But the fresh Mawson chaps say she stowed away. With *his* permission.'

'Rules for some, and not for others. Surprise, surprise. I'd like to read his contract. Pretty sure it doesn't mention bringing a wife as one of your personal items.'

Nel backed away with soft footsteps until she was beyond earshot, then made a beeline to the starboard door. Clattering down the steps, she couldn't tell if the boiling deep in her chest was the shock of humiliation or undiluted rage.

~

Nel took a sip of her rapidly cooling tea. It was peaceful here, perched on her lifeboat case, in the quiet warmth of the bridge. She was surprised at how relieved she felt to have Phil off the ship. He'd been raking his hands through his hair for days, desperate to get into the air to scout the pack-ice conditions between the ship and Chick Island. Finally, the conditions had relented enough to get a helicopter off the deck. Down here, the weather always had the final word.

The plan had been to anchor the ship near enough to Chick Island to ferry the materials across in the ducks. Bill had done an amazing job pulling *Magga* this close, forging a route between the pans of ice. He'd been working around the clock, worried if he brought the ship in too close, the ice might fasten around them, freezing them in place. They'd be stuck all winter. *If that happens,* Nel thought, *mutiny is assured.* Phil might even find himself a modern-day Captain Bligh, without the benefit of being set adrift in tropical waters. There was no love lost between Nel and the Mawson men, but even she could see that her husband was a difficult boss. Nel was sure she hadn't been alone in feeling the tension lift when the chopper clattered away with Phil in the passenger seat.

A dull throb in the distance, drawing closer, signalled the respite was over, too soon. Nel sighed and picked up her sketchbook. Within minutes of the helicopter's return, Phil was back on the bridge, the metal walls vibrating with the violence of slammed doors. The ice was too solid, the island too far away. He paced the bridge, his face dark as the cloudbanks beyond the window.

Nel scooted as far back on the lifeboat case as she could, leaning against the wall. Phil loomed over the chart table.

'What about skirting up and around to the north, then trying to break through from the east?' Phil's tone poorly concealed his frustration.

The captain looked him steadily in the eye. 'The ice is too thick. Too changeable.'

Nel saw the crew exchange glances. Everyone was frozen, Nel not daring to raise her mug to her lips. From the look on Bill's face, Nel could see he resented Phil's implication that it was his lack of nerve that stood in the way of success.

It was curious, this 'do or die' way of thinking. She must be missing something. Why did they need to be right next to the island? She'd watched the resupply of both Mawson Station and Macquarie Island. The ducks had done the lion's share of the ferrying of cargo from ship to shore. But hadn't they used helicopters too?

'Darling?' Nel's voice sounded high and light above the rumble of men's voices.

'Not now.' Phil didn't turn around.

Nel tightened her grip on the mug. 'It just occurred to me ...'

Phil leaned over the chart. 'I'll need a report of our exact position and a detailed account of the ice conditions asap. If we're aborting the mission, the department *and* the Bureau of Meteorology will demand a full explanation.'

'Darling, one second ...'

'I. Am. *Working*.' He spun around, his face stiff with anger. 'You wanted a role, I gave you one. Can you please *get on with it*?'

Nel's mug almost slipped from her fingers. The tea sloshed over the rim before she could right it. She jerked her legs, fumbling for a hanky and cursing under her breath as she blotted at her slacks.

Honestly. She knew he was under pressure, but he'd *never* spoken to her like this. The crew were looking everywhere but in her direction. Except Bill. He was looking at her with such kindness she felt tears building. *Do not cry.*

'I just wanted to know what's stopping you using the helicopters? Like you did at Mawson. With the gear dangling below.'

Phil's hands tightened on the edge of the chart table. He rocked forward a couple of times, eyes closed. Nel was frozen. She wished she could suck the words back into her mouth.

He straightened, tapping his index finger on the table. 'Actually.' There was a beat before Phil rapped his knuckles decisively on the wooden surface. 'That might just work.' He looked over at Nel and smiled for what she thought might be the first time since leaving Mawson. He stepped over to the lifeboat case and clapped Nel on the thigh. 'My brilliant wife.'

Bill raised his eyebrows. Phil strode towards the door, checking his watch, his energy completely transformed. 'Right. Bend, get on the loudspeaker and call a meeting in the saloon. All hands. If we get cracking, we can start by lunch.'

~

Below the bridge windows, the decks swarmed with men so well insulated against the cold Nel found it almost impossible to tell one from another. The only people she stood a chance of recognising were those who had a distinctive beanie or quirky gait, and had been with the ship from Melbourne. With the notable exception of Monte. Tracking the progress of his tartan flat cap across the lower decks had become instinctive, the way a penguin read the ocean for the presence of orca. Should the flat cap stray from its usual path or duck from sight, she'd freeze, paint drying on brush tip. If he wasn't on the deck, where was he?

Often, she'd glance up from her work and there he'd be. Watching. Always from a distance, never so anyone else would notice. She hadn't mentioned it to Phil. He'd say she was being paranoid. But she knew without a doubt that the physicist took great delight in unnerving her.

She was especially conscious of it when working with Harris. They'd sit on deck, Harris recording species sightings and behavioural observations, Nel diligently translating Antarctica into two-dimensional form, while their conversation ranged far beyond the white world in front of them. Before Mawson, time with Harris had been a solace. Now, under Monte's sly surveillance, it had been tainted. But even Monte couldn't quash her response to a glimpse of Harris's deerstalker on the deck below. Her heart would kick into higher gear as her eyes followed him.

It was really quite impressive how quickly Phil had rejigged his strategy from seaborne to airborne delivery of supplies and manpower. The wave of pride at her lightbulb moment had washed out quickly in the storm of activity that followed. And now, three days into the weather station's construction, she was still confined to the bridge by both the weather and Phil's decree that she record the whole assembly process.

Sitting up on her life raft, Nel could now make out the pile of rocks that formed Chick Island in the distance, the scaffold of the meteorological tower slowly taking shape. Once Phil settled on using the helicopters, Bill had been relieved to move the ship away from the sea ice and its dangerous grip.

The bow had cracked through newly frozen black ice, shattering it into thin, clear plates that slid over each other like glass windows pushed open over the dark water, as *Magga* moved to safety. Now she was anchored among a flotilla of majestic bergs and thick floes of bay ice, and throngs of Adélies watched as helicopters clattered between ship and shore.

It took all Nel's will to stop herself flipping the page to sketch the little figures dotting the floes in their freshly laundered dress shirts. She sighed. *No penguins for you until you finish this transmission tower.*

Nel swiped her hair off her forehead with her wrist and bent back to the task. Brown boulders, white sky, black metal skeleton. This felt more like visual journalism than art. *Just the facts, ma'am.* She stretched her back, straightening and twisting, trying to look as far over each shoulder as possible, towards the island with its new metal spire, then out over the fractured pack.

And there they were. Emperors. Less than fifty yards away. The painting clattered to the carpet. Nel grabbed her knapsack and rushed for the door, pushing out onto the deck. Even on this dull day, they shone. She felt wobbly, in danger of melting with awe.

There must have been two dozen, standing together like perfectly groomed gentlemen gathered for cocktails. The delicate lemon at their necks, bluish undertones to their dark capes, and perfectly white bellies – Nel put her hands on the bulwark and the cold shock on her palms made her realise she wasn't breathing.

One of the penguins dropped onto its belly, glissading across the floe, its long, powerful feet paddling the ice. It shot into the water, darting in and out as if stitching the surface, before flashing into the depths. Within seconds, the rest followed his lead, leaving a guard penguin at each end of the floe. Nel scrabbled for her sketchbook. Looking down on them from this distance, it was hard to gauge, but Nel estimated the penguins to be the size of primary school children. The group paddled on the surface like enormous ducks, then shot below, zipping under the ice, flashing back into view. Nel was unaware how long she watched, her pencil matching the penguins' speed and grace.

'You are a sly one.' Monte's voice was so close she could feel the moist huff in her ear.

Nel shied away, the pencil skittering a rude line on the page. *Damn it.* She spun to face him and backed up. The bulwark pressed against her waist.

'Just going to keep them to yourself, were you? Where's your *friend*? Not even sharing with him?' He shook his head, sucking on his teeth, as if he'd just checkmated an unworthy opponent. Nel's stomach churned.

'Don't worry. It'll be our little secret.' He grinned and moved to lean on the rail. 'So many secrets for such a little boat. As a scientist, I find it quite fascinating. What's the capacity of secrets for a ship of sixty-odd people? Sixty-odd *men*.' He raised an eyebrow, turning to face her, his hip against the metal. 'When do we reach secret saturation? At what point do secrets just start oozing up into the light? Where anyone can just slip on them.'

Nel accelerated the stuffing of her knapsack, edging away.

'Imagine that. Stepping out of your cabin one day. Heading down to dinner. Just going about your business and *whoops*. Down you go. Coming a cropper on a rude truth.'

Nel jammed the last of her gear in the knapsack and straightened, making herself meet his eyes. 'A rude truth like a steely scientist who goes downstairs to coo and slip bacon to the dogs each morning?' It was a gamble, but something told her Monte would want this information kept from his colleagues. She cocked her head, watching the fact she'd witnessed something private dawn on his face.

For a micro-second, shock and vulnerability flashed in his eyes. Then it was gone, his gaze hardening so swiftly that Nel questioned she'd seen it at all.

'Is that your attempt at blackmail? Alright, Mrs Law. Let's dance.' His slate-grey eyes narrowed. Nel hadn't thought his gaze could turn more frigid. She was wrong. Monte's narrowed lips curved to a smirk. 'I'm not sure you actually grasp the basics of this game, but I'm more than happy to teach you. I've always said failure is the best lesson.'

Nel glared at him. 'Perhaps the lesson you need to learn is not to underestimate people.'

'Oh, I'm not underestimating you. In fact, I'm giving you a great deal of credit. Not everyone would be so brave in your position. Actually, I think the right word is "cavalier". Sneaking around, right under the boss's nose. On a ship, no less. Some might say it's stupid. I disagree. I think it's quite an impressive level of hubris.'

'I really don't know what you're getting at.'

Her cheeks flushed with heat, as if his eyes could probe the depths of her imagination, condemning her fantasies and fears. To make matters worse, he'd caught her red-handed, sketching penguins when the whole ship knew Phil had been on her case to paint the weather station.

Monte reached towards her face. She shied away, so violently she almost lost her balance. He smirked at her.

'Relax, Mrs Law. You have a smudge. Here.' He touched his cheekbone, then laughed at her. 'Someone has tickets on themselves.'

With as much calm as she could muster, Nel turned and walked towards the portside door.

~

Back on the bridge, bent over her paper block, Nel replayed her encounter with Monte on a constant loop. What had he meant? Whose secrets had he been referring to? She was so wrapped up in her thoughts, she didn't hear Phil approach, and started when he appeared at her side holding two steaming mugs of tea. She smiled at him gratefully.

'What perfect timing. If I don't get down from here in the next minute, I might seize in this position.'

'You would make a very appealing figurehead for that lifeboat.' Phil held both mugs as Nel straightened her legs and slid stiffly off the raft case. She landed with a wince.

Wrapping her fingers around the blissfully warm enamel, she stood beside Phil, watching the bustle on the deck below. She'd missed this quiet familiarity, she realised.

It was lovely, to stand, not speaking, with Phil; almost as lovely as it was to find herself deep in discussion with Harris. With the biologist, there was a constant frisson, reaching to grasp her next sentence, next thought. With Phil, she was totally at ease, no electric jolt – just warm, comfortable acceptance.

She took a sip of tea, relishing the sweetness. Beyond the glass, the heavy oyster-grey sky reached down to touch the sea where it thickened into icy rubble around them.

'How much longer will it take?' Nel squinted into the distance; she could only just make out the tip of the newly erected transmission tower.

'Not much longer.'

Nel glanced at him, surprised to hear the concern in his voice. His eyes were scanning the ocean.

'What is it?' she asked.

'Come with me.' Phil moved to the side door of the bridge and held her tea as she stuffed her arms into her insulated jacket. Cupping her elbow, he guided her out onto the narrow deck. They stood for several moments at the rail, facing away from the ice-capped islands and out to sea.

'Look at the waves.' Phil tilted his chin at the view without taking his eyes off the ocean before them.

The motion of the waves was sluggish, almost elastic, as if the skin of the sea was slowly clotting with ice.

'Now look at the sky. Feel the air.'

'It's very still.' Nel frowned, looking at him in confusion.

He waved a hand at the ocean. 'See the way the surface is thickening? We'll need to move soon. Very soon. If we don't ...' He trailed off.

The cold was beginning to burn where it touched skin; her breath an exhalation of white. As they stood, the air grew even more still, the sound of helicopters and men's voices falling away.

A white flake tumbled out of the grey air. In the time it took Nel to draw a shocked breath, it was joined by another, and another, the crystals drifting through the air as if lost.

Nel held out both her arms. Snowflakes landed on the blue of her sleeves, dotting the bright fabric.

'Oh.' Nel stepped from side to side, waving her arms to catch more crystals.

Phil grinned, watching her.

Nel laughed in delight, bending her arms close to her face.

'Exquisite. Each flake is so intricate. And they really *are* all different.' She couldn't take her eyes off the tiny marvels. 'So much more beautiful than I ever imagined.' She looked at Phil suddenly. 'Did you know it was going to snow? How could you tell?'

He chuckled. 'This is my second home, remember?' He held out his palms, crystals snagging on the grey wool of his gloves. 'Second,' he repeated with emphasis, and paused. 'I'm reminding myself as much as reassuring you. I've been so swept up in the work. The pressure.' He gazed out over the pack ice. 'When I noticed just now it was threatening to snow, my first thought was the helicopters. Then I remembered, you've never been in a snowfall.' He waved his arm, encompassing the snow and the great expanse of sea and ice beyond the rail. 'And even after all these years I've spent down here, I can still feel the magic of it too.'

Nel looked up at him, grinning as a snowflake landed on the tip of his nose. The warmth of his skin melted it to a bead within seconds. 'I wish I could sketch these. Or photograph them.' She gave a frustrated growl. 'Capture them somehow!'

Phil turned to her, smiling. 'I used to think the most beautiful things – the most precious – were also the most fleeting.' He reached towards her face, his thumb brushing her cheekbone so gently she barely felt the graze of his touch. 'But if our years together have taught me anything, it's that the opposite is true.'

Phil held her at arm's length, before tucking her under his shoulder, his face pressed into the wool of her beanie. 'We've been like ships in the night lately. I miss you. Us.' He sighed. 'Once this is all over, I can't tell you how much I'm looking forward to everything getting back to normal.'

Normal. Nel put her arms around him, nestling her head into his chest so she didn't have to speak. In a few scant weeks, all she would have of these long, light-filled days would be memories – as precious, fleeting and unbelievably beautiful as the impossible sculptures tumbling from the heavens. How could she tell him that his normal no longer existed? That, in so many ways, she was no longer the same person who had stepped up the gangway? She closed her eyes. Snowflakes brushed her cheek.

Raw Sienna

Aviation Islands, Oates Land
March 1961

The wind had teeth. Despite wearing almost every layer she'd brought with her for the field, Nel could still feel its bite where it muscled between goggles and scarf. Forty knots, she'd heard bandied about. The wind carried so much ice in its grip the tiny island they were heading towards was only intermittently visible from the bridge. Down on the deck, she couldn't see anything past the fat cluster of parkas and beanies. Men lined the rail, watching *Lollipop*, the Mac Robertson motor-launch, as it was winched over the side and lowered into the waves. Nel hovered at the back, not sure how many were going ashore and not wanting to push forward.

Phil strode to the edge of the deck where the ladder down to the launch clanged ominously against the steel. 'Last call.' He scanned the cluster of men disbelievingly. 'None of you wants your name in the history books?'

No hands were raised.

Phil gave them a withering look. 'Really? No human has set foot on this section of the coast before. Frankly, I can't believe I'm standing here trying to convince you. My wife has more of an explorer's spirit than you lot.' With a look that held as much disgust as disappointment, Phil dismissed them, turning to the men in the landing party.

The contrast between the studied casualness of those staying behind and the cool determination of those in the landing party was stark. When Phil had pinned the sign-up sheet to the mess noticeboard, not one of the Mawson winterers had written their name. Phil was flabbergasted, but Nel wasn't surprised. As well as the conversation about the gear search, she'd overheard plenty of muttering when Phil was out of earshot. All these men wanted was to turn the bow north for home. The fact that Phil kept them working – first at Chick Island, erecting the automatic weather station, and now laboriously mapping coastline, with the ship in constant danger of being trapped in the ice – was draining morale at a dangerous rate. It was no shock to Nel that the only people willing to board the motor-launch were those whose work involved geographical surveying and sampling rocks. No one was in the mood for tourism.

She was torn about today. She wanted the landing to happen, for Phil's sake. The desire to be the first man on Oates Land, officially claiming the territory for Australia, had consumed him for years, and yet again circumstances threatened to stymie his ambitions. But Nel also wished the weather would demand an immediate turn north. Again, for Phil's sake. When she woke this morning at 5 am his bunk was already cold. How long could he sustain this workload? Her husband was exhausted. It had been obvious to her for days. But now it hung on his face for all to see.

Today was his last chance. If he didn't make landfall on Oates Land, he'd have to wait another year. She'd been on the receiving end of his frustration since *last* March. If Phil had to postpone this moment again it would mean yet another year of rehashing all that went wrong, planning the next attempt, and blaming whoever he felt had blighted his plans to be the first to set foot on this legendarily difficult stretch of Antarctic coastline.

If she'd learned anything about Antarctic exploration it was that weather was *everything*. Phil had taken to consulting the barometer as if he was praying to a tiny god, trying to gain its favour with his constant attention to its every twitch.

And this morning his prayer had been answered. A small lead in the ice had opened up. In the last few hours, Bill had manoeuvred *Magga* as close to shore as he dared. And now, with just enough time, a motor-launch could carry a party ashore. Not to the mainland, with its spectacularly jagged white line of mountains, but to the rocky outcrops just offshore. The Aviation Islands.

All at once, the woollen-topped heads swivelled to face her, and Nel heard her name whipped from Phil's mouth and away. She straightened and stepped forward, making sure her legs carried her with no suggestion of wobble.

Hefting her knapsack into position, she leaned over the ship's side. Below, *Lollipop* was bucking about, whanging into the red steel. Between Nel and the motor-launch stretched a steel ladder, its end held steady with great effort by Hank Geysen. Or someone who looked like an extremely well-insulated Hank. The rest of the party was already aboard, their faces looking up at her like tiny pink petals floating on a black sea.

Nel swung her leg over the broad sill, gripping a cleat for balance, the steel ice-cold between her thighs. She'd just placed her foot on the first rung of the ladder when a huge wave slapped into the ship, ripping *Lollipop* away from the hull and taking the ladder with it. Nel clung to the cleat, still astride the red steel wall, watching the men in the bucking launch scramble to get the tiny vessel back into position and return the ladder to where Nel was frozen in place.

It took forever. She could feel the laughter of the men behind her as she perched there. No one offered a hand to help her back onto the deck. She grasped the cleat, keeping her eyes on the launch far below, not wanting to turn back to the deck lest the men read the fear on her face. She could only imagine the things being said, and at that moment, she was glad of the wind in her ears and the crashing of the launch against the ship. *Louts.*

Finally, the call came from below and Hank gave her a wave. Nel took a deep breath, and began inching down the bucking ladder. The wind tried to wrench her knapsack from her shoulders and her gloves slipped along the ladder's steel with a terrifying lack of traction. By the time she felt someone grip her legs, then waist, her hands were frozen, aching claws. Nel sank onto a thwart, relief gusting from her mouth in a cloud of vapour.

The man next to her, McLeod the geologist, held her pack as she settled, shuffling to give her some extra room, his bag of tools clanking between his feet.

'Welcome to Oates Land, Mrs Law.' The voice snaked into her ear from the row behind.

Nel froze. Monte. She hadn't recognised him up on the deck with his parka hood pulled over the tartan flat cap.

'Happy to be here,' Nel said in a light tone. She would not let him see his presence had rattled her.

The man on her left – Parkinson, she thought – grinned. 'Lovely day for it.'

Nel balanced her knapsack on her feet; the bottom of the launch was already slightly awash. 'Can't complain. Geologists seem to make very effective windbreaks.' She smiled at McLeod and Parkinson, then hunched into her hood, trying to hide behind her scarf. She'd made it to sea level. Now she just had to survive a couple of hours in the presence of the man she'd come to think of as her nemesis. That was probably overly dramatic. *Irrational*, Phil would say. Nel set her jaw.

From the pilot's position in the motor-launch's tiny cabin, Harold James gunned the throttle and *Lollipop* swung her nose towards the closest and largest of the five islands. As they bucked across the chop for the shore, Nel felt as if she were riding a horse without reins or stirrups. Waves slapped the sides, sloshing into the open boat and pooling around their boots. Instinctively, she wanted to grip McLeod's and Parkinson's arms, but Monte's presence kept her hunched on the thwart, shying from any contact.

Harold found an ice ledge about five foot high that looked promising, and he nudged the launch in against it, the men rocking the small boat as they scurried to secure the ice anchors. Phil ordered Monte and Owens to stay on board, while the geologists and surveyors made their way onto the island. *Island?* To Nel, the place looked more like a large block of ice with some rocks jutting up from its middle.

Nel's relief at leaving Monte on the boat was so visceral that she leapt up and onto the ledge from the rocking craft, Phil's offer of a steadying hand left hovering in the cold air. She stood for a moment, catching her breath and getting her bearings on the blissfully stable ice. The relief lasted barely a moment. Her first step brought her crashing to the hard white ground. Once again, her golf shoes proved completely useless, the leather soles with their small rounded cleats unable to find any purchase on the ice.

'*Blast.*' Nel threw a dark look at Phil, but he'd already moved away, completely focused on directing the men in the myriad tasks involved in the discovery of new lands. Of course, he'd not brought her a pair of crampons. Again. *Next time, I'll find some myself.*

The understanding there would be no next time hit her like a blizzard.

Nel struggled to her feet, arms out for balance and teeth gritted. She scanned the rock and ice sloping up and away, keeping her back to the launch. Everyone had scattered to their various tasks, the conditions encouraging swift efficiency.

All right, then. You're the artist. Get to work. About fifty yards to her left, Nel spotted a wall of rock that might give her an excellent panoramic view of the island and shelter from the onshore wind.

She took a cautious step. The moment her weight shifted, her feet began to skid from under her. Scooting one foot after the other, she attempted a skating shuffle. The coarse ice, lumped with rocks and frozen hummocks of windblown snow, made it a painstaking process. Nel cast a look over her shoulder. Everyone was either out of sight or bent to their work. She could retain her dignity and stay put – which meant losing this chance to capture history – or do whatever it took to get to work.

Oh, to the devil with this! Pulling the sleeves of her jacket down over the heels of her gloved palms, Nel got down on her hands and knees. She crawled. It was neither fast nor elegant, but within ten minutes Nel reached the shelter of the rock wall and set herself up. She worked on several charcoals and pastels, but after half an hour or so the cold forced her to stop, her hands aching and unsteady. She groaned, pushing herself to her feet, shivering as the wind hit her. None of the exploring scientists were back at the *Lollipop* yet.

Nel's nose told her there was more to the island than she could see from this position. It was time to do some exploring of her own. She slung her knapsack onto her back and made her way further along the shore, at first crawling along the ice, then on foot when she reached bare rock. From her time with Harris, she knew exactly what finding exposed rock would mean – Adélies.

Her nose didn't lie. She rounded the point and there in the bay huddled a colony of penguins, flapping and gossiping, waddling and weaving between their rocky nests. *Harris should be here.* Nel sat down on the nearest, cleanest rock, and began to work, marking the position of the colony and a population estimate on a rough map before quickly moving on to broad views of the scene and a few individual character sketches. She inched along the shore, stepping carefully between nests, penguins eyeing her with keen curiosity. It amazed her how used to the smell she'd become – or *the reek*, as she'd called it just two months ago.

All the chicks had shed their fluff and it was challenging to distinguish the adults from their fully fledged young without Harris's commentary in her ear. She smiled, watching the interactions. Even without Harris, she could now interpret the meaning and purpose behind much of the penguins' behaviour. The end of breeding season had clearly failed to render pebbles any less valuable. Nel squatted down near a couple of males. The pair were so deep in conflict that they didn't register her presence as she swiftly sketched their quarrel over a rather nondescript pebble. Lowering their beaks, they hissed at each other across the contested stone with full-bodied malevolence. She chuckled, and set off on her walk/crawl back to the *Lollipop*.

A little over halfway, still on her hands and knees, she was making her way across a treacherous patch of ice when she stopped, one hand in midair. A small object was lodged in the ice. She prised it free.

Pushing herself to her feet, back to the wind, she squinted at the piece of metal. It looked old, like brass greened with age. She had no idea what it was. Smaller than her pinkie fingernail, it looked a little like a curved hinge with an old nail driven through it. *We're not the first ones here!*

~

By the time she arrived back at the motor-launch, the air between the men was electric with tension. Nel swallowed. What on earth had she missed?

At the highest point of the island, not that far inland from where the shore party clustered, Phil was standing over a scatter of rocks, holding a half-sized Australian flag and looking quite red in the face as he addressed Parkinson and Marshall.

'The whole *point* of a cairn is that A, it's clearly visible!' Phil shook the flag in the direction of the ocean. 'And B, it lasts for all time!' He took a breath and practically spat the next words in the men's faces. 'This is *Antarctica*.'

The men stood their ground, their expressions as stony as the pile of rocks at their feet.

'Exactly how long did you think that piss-poor heap of stones was going to hold up the flag? Until we got back to the ship?' Phil kicked at the rubble.

Oh dear, Nel thought.

'It's meant to be seen by ships offshore. So that when the bloody Russians or Yanks arrive, it's clear that *we were here first*. Got it?'

The pair gave small, grudging nods; the rest of the men had their heads down but were exchanging looks under lowered brows. Nel could see any respect they had for Phil had now evaporated. Understandably. In all their years together, she'd never heard him yell at someone that way.

'Do it again. With a broader base this time. And higher.' Phil shoved the flag at them and turned away, shaking his head.

Nel took a step towards him. 'Phil, really, I think ...' McLeod was looking at her, eyes wide. He gave an almost imperceptible headshake. She trailed off as Phil turned to her, his eyes cold. He was looking at her like one of his men, not his wife.

Nel was taken aback. This was a man they knew better than she did. McLeod had been with ANARE for several seasons. Clearly, what was atrocious, unfamiliar behaviour to her was something they'd witnessed before. Or, more to the point, endured.

She gripped the object in her pocket, suddenly unmoored. She knew how her Phil would react. But not this scowling man.

The whispers and nicknames suddenly seemed understandable. Standing here, witnessing his behaviour, she could see both sides – Phil had worked for this moment for so long, visualised every aspect over and over; any deviation from his dream scenario would be devastating. But from the men's perspective, it was inexcusable. This was not the way a leader should behave. Respect breeds respect. Nel had heard these words in her husband's mouth many times. She couldn't quite believe Phil had so much to say about the art of leadership when this was the kind of authority he practised.

She bit her lip. Perhaps, against every wifely instinct, this was the moment to show him the object? Even if it didn't work as a circuit breaker, at the very least it would divert his frustration away from the men. For a split second, she considered keeping mum, but the burn of conscience was immediate; she knew she'd be unable to live with it. If Phil claimed the place as Australian territory, then found himself in the humiliating position of needing to retract, he'd never get over it.

'Uh, darling?' Nel heard the quaver in her voice.

Phil frowned at her.

Nerves quivered in her throat as she opened her gloved fist. The brass thingamabob lay innocently on her palm.

'I found this. On the ice.' She glanced back over her shoulder, indicating the general direction with her chin.

Phil picked it off her palm, turning it over in his hands several times. She didn't think his frown could deepen. She was wrong.

'What is it, Chief?' Harold James stepped forward.

'Where exactly?' Phil took off before she could answer, the pack of men hot on his heels. Nel scrambled in their wake, stopping when she reached the treacherous stretch of ice. If he wanted her help, he could hold her steady. She was *not* going to crawl after him. McLeod was the first to spot her absence and trotted back, offering her his arm with a smile that held both gallantry and sympathy. She kept her chin up, wanting to march but only managing a dignified stalk. She halted at the spot, pointing down at the green stain on the ice.

The men passed the object between them, turning it over in their hands.

'Russian, maybe?' Cook guessed, eyebrows rising to shelter under the edge of his woollen hat.

'But there's no cairn. No one's marked these islands on their charts. If they'd been here, why no record of a claim?' Geysen looked perplexed.

'A shipwreck, maybe? Flotsam washed ashore?' Harold's voice was brimming with hope for this best-case explanation.

Phil looked close to punching something. 'Bugger it.' His teeth were clenched so tightly it came out as a hiss.

The small brass piece passed into the last hand. McLeod squinted at it, looked down at his boots, then turned to scan inland. 'Hold your horses, chaps.' He bent his left knee and, catching his foot at the ankle, inspected the sole of his boot as if he'd stepped in

214

something unspeakable. He did the same for his right and started to chuckle.

'Something to add, McLeod?' Phil's voice was tight as fence-wire.

'I fear I'm your mysterious explorer, Chief. Look.' He pulled his ankle higher, twisting it so everyone could see the hard sole, dotted with the metal spikes that gave him extra traction. 'It's the tip off one of my cleats. These old boots have served me well over the years. Until today, that is ... when they almost gave the boss a heart attack.' He chuckled, putting his foot back down on the ice.

'Bloody hell.' Phil let out a sharp snort, shaking his head in disbelief. 'Thank Christ. I really didn't want to have to go back to Parkinson and Marshall and kick over their cairn again.'

The men barked with laughter, more relief than mirth, and the party started back towards the landing beneath the peak, where they could see the two men still collecting rocks for the bigger, better cairn they had yet to stack.

Payne's Grey

Southern Ocean
March 1961

It should've been a relief that *Magga* had finally turned her bow north, but Nel was as confused about it as the ship seemed to be. The elation she'd expected from Phil on successfully claiming the Aviation Islands had swiftly dissolved in the face of the terrible conditions. No sooner had they set course for home, than the ice had closed in. For hours, Nel had been kept awake by the discordant rhythm of the engines thrusting forward, then falling into idle as the ship tried to break through the ice, the cabin lurching and lunging as if perplexed about where it was going, how fast, and if it wanted to move at all.

In the last twenty-four hours, they'd crept north far enough to rediscover night. Crew and expeditioners alike were desperate to reach Melbourne. But every degree north brought Nel closer to an existence she was no longer sure she wanted. Her art, her time working with Harris, this freedom from domestic duties had made her see what life would be like if she was a man. And she liked it. Going home to the stove and the sink and the shopping bags, to a routine of tasks as endless as they were meaningless – the thought of it made her soul shrivel.

As she lay awake in her bunk, split with uncertainty and indecision, the ship banged against something, the steel hull clanging like a gong. Nel felt the engines slip into an idle and, desperate to escape her own thoughts, tossed aside the covers. She threw on some clothes and made her way to the bridge, keeping her back against the bulkhead so as not to disturb anyone at their tasks. Phil was already there, feet planted, front and centre at the bridge window. Bend, the first mate, stood at the helm, a muscle ticking in his jaw.

Beyond the ship, all was blackness, sliced by the shocking beam of the searchlight. Nel froze, breath caught in her throat. The third mate, a burly young Dane with a blond crewcut so short it was almost transparent, directed the searchlight, which was mounted on the wing of the bridge. The dazzling ray swung back and forth, severing the dark. The massive bergs blazed as the light sliced across their jagged faces.

'Growler. Portside.' The captain's voice barked from a speaker mounted somewhere in the control panel under Bend's hands.

Nel joined Phil at the window. The air was taut as Bend steered *Magga* to starboard, the searchlight panning left, then down to illuminate a hard, chunky berg, the growler, as it slid by, the ice skidding past the hull.

'Where's Bill?' Nel asked in a whisper.

'In the crow's nest. Giving instructions to Bend.' Phil gestured upward with his chin, keeping his eyes on the otherworldly scene stretched in front of them. 'We only have a narrow lane. And bad weather ahead. If we don't move tonight, we could be stuck indefinitely.' Phil's lips were so tight his mouth disappeared into his beard.

Nel observed her husband for a long moment before turning back to the window. Six weeks ago, if someone had told her this trip would open fissures in their marriage, she would've laughed. Now, as she stood beside him, she couldn't quite believe how different it felt. That warm connection that had laced them together was frayed to strands. She wanted to clutch his hand, slip her arms around his waist, rest her head between his shoulder blades. But, seeing the tightness across his shoulders as he leaned towards the window, she knew in her gut that his reflex, at this moment, would be to shrug her off. And feeling him pull away would confirm all she feared.

Something had shifted in their marriage. There was still love between them – there had to be after all these years – but it had slipped off-centre. Although it felt easy to say he'd changed, she knew it wasn't that simple. It was more that this voyage had allowed her to see the side of him that had always faced away from her. Their lives together had a cycle, a seasonal spin. He would leave in November, return in March. Yet she'd always believed their marriage was the gravitational centre. Now she saw the truth. His job was the core. She was just another body in orbit around Antarctica. Her life, her art, their relationship – all just whirling out on the margins, insignificant as Pluto – leaving her feeling just as cold and alone.

Nel stayed at the window. There was nothing to say.

In the sharp beam of light, the bergs loomed. Stark ghost-like cliffs towered over the bridge as the ship slid past, so close she could almost feel their chill through the glass. And beyond the edge of the light, the vast pack stretched away like a pale shroud.

Not knowing what lay beyond the light gave Nel the shivers. Tension quivered in the air as the crew read the radar and echo sounder, then relayed the information to Bill on the intercom, thrusting the ship port or starboard on the terse orders crackling from the speaker.

Right now, she'd give anything for Phil to turn to her, her Phil, not the tense man standing beside her. She straightened her back as tears burned behind her eyes.

Magga crept through the pack, inching past the corners of cathedral-sized bergs, squeezing into narrow lanes between jagged white slabs, the inky cracks narrowing, ice grating along the hull of the ship as she tried to push it aside.

Dawn was pinking the ice when the order came to stop. Bend settled the engines to idle. Bill climbed down from his crow's nest perch, hollow-eyed.

There was no way through.

~

Nel lunged between stepping stones of bare carpet to sit at the small table, shuffling dry pages into a pile, making room to work on a sketch of some Adélies on a glacial shelf. Beyond the cabin porthole, plates of frozen sea pressed hard against the hull.

She'd been distracting herself from the fear of spending months stuck on the ship by using the time to catch up on her penguins for Harris. Her plan had been to have them ready for him by the time they reached Macquarie Island. With the ship stationary, she had been zipping along, the Adélies dancing off her nib.

She spent most of her time down here now. It'd started with avoiding the men. Then Monte, specifically. And now, with Phil's stress and constant foul temper, plus the dire morale in the saloon, the cabin had become her refuge, a cross between a cloister and an artist's studio. Phil only made an appearance late each night. More accurately, it was usually the early hours of the morning when he'd make the short journey from his stateroom office to his bunk.

Wrapped in her blankets, she could hear him sighing and sucking his teeth in irritation as he kicked easels and canvases aside. But, assuming she was asleep, he didn't wake her to complain. At least there was that.

The space was overwhelmingly hers. Clothes and artwork vied for every bit of space. A funk of turpentine and damp laundry hung in the air. A clothesline strung with brassieres, spencers and sanitary towels threatened to decapitate the unwary or off-balance. She was happier here than anywhere else on the ship. In the saloon, only the snap and shuffle of playing cards broke the silence. The clink of glass or thump of mug-bottom meeting table. No one wanted to give voice to the fear lodged in everyone's throat. A winter on this ship. Frozen in place. Unreachable until spring.

It felt as though she'd barely touched ink to paper when she heard a creak behind her. She swivelled to see Phil's head leaning around the doorjamb.

'Dinner.' His slight excuse for a smile dissolved when he noticed her long johns and pyjama top.

'Is that the time?' Nel looked at her watch. 'Blast.' She gestured at her work. 'I lost track.' Pushing away from the table, she cast about for a clean, or at least uncreased, shirt and slacks. 'You go ahead. I'll be right behind.'

The mood in the dining saloon was less muted than she expected. Glasses were raised. Bend's birthday. She'd completely forgotten. The watercolour of a blizzard she'd completed for him was still somewhere in one of the piles on her desk. She was about to sprint for the cabin when she saw Phil gesturing impatiently for her to join him at the captain's table.

Nel waved at Bend as she crossed the room, eyes widening as she saw the source of all the laughter. He'd shaved his golden beard, and with his pale chin and smooth cheeks he looked too young to drive a car, let alone pilot a ship across the globe.

The talk at the table didn't stray far from the weather. Tomorrow would be critical. If the conditions worsened before they could make a little more headway, preparations would need to be made for wintering on board.

Bill had spent the last twenty-four hours either on the bridge or navigating from the crow's nest. He was haggard with fatigue, yet Nel didn't doubt he would spend the next spin of the earth in a similar way.

'All right, say we're completely jammed in, no hope of breaking ourselves out until spring ... what's the worst-case scenario?' Dalton scratched his thatch of salt and pepper hair before reaching for his beer.

Phil placed his glass deliberately in the damp circle its base had left on the wood. 'Best option would be to radio the Yanks for assistance. *Glacier*'s an icebreaker, so it's possible they could bash their way in to us. Then we could follow her out.' Phil looked around at the grim faces. No one seemed very happy about admitting they needed rescuing. 'Alternatively, *Thala Dan* should've reached the Kerguelen Islands by now. She could sail on to Perth, dump her men and gear, then pick up extra supplies and full steam back down to us. If she gets as close as she can, they could ferry in supplies to us by chopper.'

Nel desperately wanted to ask about the possibility of ferrying passengers *off*. Her gaze slid across the room to Monte. He wasn't looking at her, but his snicker sounded in her mind just as clearly as if he were sitting beside her. *Damn it*. If the men were to be stuck here, she'd just have to stick it out too.

The conversation flowed past her, the men discussing plans to send out parties to hack at the ice, weakening the pack enough for *Magga* to ride up and crack it open with her weight. Harold could gather volunteers for a hunting party to shoot and butcher seals in the event of a food shortage. If no progress was made tomorrow, the ship would need to conserve resources. Power, water, heat and food would all be rationed. Nel listened, her pulse hammering as the list of restrictions grew.

By the time she pushed her half-eaten meatloaf away, she was pale, sweaty and desperately needed to take off her jumper. Bill eyed her gravely across the table as she gulped the dregs of her wine.

Bend's birthday couldn't have come at a better time for morale. Birthdays were a compulsory excuse for a party and a welcome break from the normal after-dinner routine of charades, sing-a-longs, housey-housey or reruns of films. The first mate blew out his candles to a great roar and Nel suspected the entire company was into the spirit in more ways than one, a bottle or two of contraband circulating under the tables, perhaps. Phil had strict rules about alcohol consumption. Only three allocated drinks over the course of an evening in the saloon and no drinking at all in the cabins.

Fortunately for the men, their boss was no longer around to object. Under normal party conditions, Phil wouldn't dream of missing an opportunity to lead the evening's merriment on his piano accordion. But tonight, both the captain and Phil had finished their pudding and excused themselves, Bill returning to the bridge and Phil to his stateroom.

Nel slumped against the cherry-red upholstery. How on earth was she going to manage being trapped here until September or even October?

The men still at the table were all keen to continue the revels and none of them glanced her way as she excused herself. Harris wasn't in the saloon and for the last few days she'd only glimpsed him from a distance at meals. She worried about how he was faring since, unlike her, he was forced to eat, sleep and work side by side with the gossipmongers. But what could she do? It wasn't as if she could ask after him without eyebrows being raised and the rumour mill kicking back into overdrive.

With almost the entire ship's company either celebrating in the saloon or on duty up on the bridge, Nel had the corridors to herself. Outside, the wind was roaring like an express train. Everything was pulsing from the gale and the vibration of the engine as the ship pummelled herself against the pack.

It was rare to feel as though the whole ship was hers. She wandered corridors she hadn't travelled since her excited exploration of the ship in her first days aboard. Before the feeling of not being welcome had gradually fenced her in. If the ship *did* become stuck, this might be her home for most of this year. The long rows of cabin doors never felt more tightly closed against her.

She dawdled down the thoroughfares, running her fingers along the white gloss of the walls. Each time she came to a stairwell she chose down, the growl of the engine growing to a roar she could feel in her teeth.

The deeper below decks, the closer the air, and the more the engine rumble mounted, until she felt as if she was in the gut of an enormous beast. The stifling atmosphere finally convinced her there must be nothing more to see than the engine room and cargo holds. She spun and made for the upper decks, as if swimming up from the depths.

She'd just reached the stairs a deck below her own, when she heard a door open behind her. Hand on the banister, she turned to see Harris framed by a cabin door halfway down the passage.

'Nel?' He checked the corridor. 'What're you doing down here?'

'Just some light exploring. Claiming new lands for womankind.' She grinned at him. 'Seems I've developed a taste for it.'

'In that case, let me assist. I was just about to head upstairs for a slice of cake. But if this voyage has taught us anything, it's that exploration trumps all.' He grinned and swept his arm towards the cabin. 'May I introduce you to the rarely seen shared habitat of the biologist and meteorologist.'

Nel hesitated, glancing at the staircase behind her, then the passage beyond Harris's door. All she could hear was the faint sound of men's voices and music from the saloon above. They were alone.

She walked towards him, relief and excitement beginning their warm throb. She took a deep breath and had to force it past the pleasurable tightening of her diaphragm.

Realising she meant to take him up on his offer, Harris ducked into the cabin. She heard bustle, but by the time she reached the doorway, Harris was standing at attention, as if she was a sergeant major about to inspect his quarters.

'At ease, soldier,' Nel laughed, shaking her head as she stepped into the cabin, her smile fading. 'You've been a man of mystery lately. I was worried.'

'Just busy.' Harris gestured to the small table. 'Writing up notes. Analysing field data. I like getting the work done while the observations are fresh.' He slapped notebooks shut and shuffled papers into stacks.

Nel looked around the tiny room. She'd fantasised about this moment, being alone with him. Behind closed doors alone. But this was a far cry from the cosy yet thrilling intimacy she'd imagined while lying in her bunk.

It was as though a line had been drawn down the centre of the cabin floor. On one side, the bunk was made up with hospital corners, blankets pulled coin-bounce tight, the pillow plumped and creaseless where it lay perfectly straight across the folded top sheet. Boxes of equipment were stacked with precision by someone with a keen eye for maximising storage. In the wardrobe section, all drawers and cupboards were clipped shut.

The other side of the room, Harris's side, was chaos. Inside-out clothes and splay-paged books carpeted the floor. The bunk was a riot of bedding. Blankets were crumpled where they'd been kicked aside, and the sheets were so grey Nel suspected they'd not been changed in weeks. Nel spotted the light plaid of boxer shorts peeping from under the bunk, where she was sure they'd been kicked just moments before. The bedside table was cluttered with empty glasses and a wonky spine of stacked mugs, the uppermost ringed with stains. The only thing that didn't conform to the hard division was the smell, a warm, close funk of damp wool, old socks and acrid penguin guano permeating all corners of the room.

Harris saw where Nel's eyes had fallen and slipped between her and the bunk, twitching the blankets up over the sheets and plonking himself up near the pillow end. He patted the space beside him. 'Can I offer you a drink? Finest contraband.' He reached under the bunk, extracting a half-empty bottle of whisky. If Phil knew Harris had smuggled a bottle on board for private consumption, he'd be banned from any future ANARE expeditions.

When Nel tilted her head in assent, he pulled out the cork and selected the cleanest glass from his bedside collection. She lowered herself tentatively onto the bunk, feeling the uncomfortable bump of bunched blankets. Harris slopped a healthy shot of the amber liquid into the tumbler and handed it over before repeating the action with another, slightly cloudier glass. He stoppered the bottle and rolled it to join the rest of the mess under the bed.

'To a morning thaw.' He clinked his tumbler against hers. 'If I'd known this bottle would need to last through the winter, I would've gone a bit easier on the nightcaps.' He slugged back a generous mouthful.

Nel sipped at the whisky, watching him over the rim of the glass. He looked nervous. Why on earth did he invite her in if witnessing this mess was going to make him so edgy?

'Who's your roommate?' Nel gestured with her drink. 'I've got to say, you don't seem entirely compatible.'

'Astute behavioural observation.' He gave a grim chuckle. 'I believe that once Missen's feet hit the dock in Melbourne, I'll not see hide nor hair of the man again. And neither of us will complain. We drive each other quite mad. Hence me lurking down here, snatching precious time alone while he's up top.'

Nel compressed her lips into a semblance of a smile. She didn't know quite what she'd expected, but seeing this slice of Harris's character – or the unruly evidence of it – unsettled her. Unfairly, of course. She was far from tidy herself. But for some reason, she'd assumed Harris was far more organised, more *collected* than this messy – no, the right word would be *filthy* – room revealed him to be.

'So ... how are you and the penguins getting along? Are they playing nicely?' Nel asked, her eyes still roaming the room.

'The paper?' he said. 'Uh, yes. Coming along.' He took another swig.

How long had he been drinking alone in his room?

Nel took another sip and stood, moving to look at the work on his desk. In the centre, like a calm eye in a storm of papers and notebooks, stood an olive Smith Corona typewriter. On the right, she identified what looked to be a draft of his Adélie paper, scribbled notes and editing notations cluttered in the margins.

Nel plucked the draft from the pile.

'Can I—' She broke off as Harris jerked to his feet, reached in and bumped her aside in his haste to snatch away the papers she had inadvertently uncovered.

In the split second before they were whisked out of sight, Nel caught a flash of Harris's handwriting.

With all my heart, H.

Harris held the pages to his chest as he rustled among the piles. Reefing out a grease-spotted manila folder marked *Adélie – Reproductive Behaviour*, he shoved the letter inside, then turned to face Nel, holding the folder behind his back.

He looked so much like a guilty schoolboy, Nel couldn't help but smile.

'A letter to your girlfriend?' she said, attempting a teasing tone. *Why didn't he tell me about her?*

A photograph slipped from the buff folder, landing face down. Nel bent to retrieve it.

Harris saw it a moment too late and ducked for it, his forehead smacking into the desk as he tried to whisk the photo from under her fingers.

'*Oof.*' He staggered upright, holding his forehead. Seeing the photo in Nel's hand he reached towards her. 'Please.'

Nel stepped back, angling away from him. She wanted to see this woman he'd kept secret.

The thick card of the black-and-white photograph was worn, the square edges rounded and soft with age. Inside the white border, two figures leaned into each other. They stood on a steep tussock-grass slope in front of a wild sea, the wind whipping their hair. Behind them, albatrosses hung in mid-flight. A younger Harris grinned out at her, his red hair dulled to ash, his arm slung around the neck of the young man beside him, their smiles so white they leapt from the photo. The young man had a strong, bony face, his grin bracketed with creases, his dark eyes squinting with the light, wind or joy. Or all three.

The pair were clearly in love.

Harris stood before her, hand in midair, as if she was a wild animal that any movement might startle into panic.

Nel swallowed the last of her whisky, then held out the photo. Harris took it from her gently, slipping it out of her hand and into the folder, his fingers brushing the manila cover like a caress.

'You could've told me,' Nel said, her voice soft.

'You know I couldn't.'

Nel frowned. 'You really think I'd tell Phil?' This time, she let disappointment flood her tone.

She waited. They stared at each other until she felt as though she was looking at a stranger.

She exhaled and set the tumbler on the desk. It made a louder *thunk* than she anticipated. She moved for the door, but he held out his hand.

'Wait.' He shook his head, sucking his breath in through his teeth. 'It's not you. It's ...'

She stopped. He gripped the back of the chair. 'You don't understand. You couldn't.'

Nel opened her mouth, but he held up his palm. 'That's not an accusation. It's just that I can't see how *anyone* could know unless they'd lived it. If it's your job at stake. Your freedom. Your *life*.' He closed his eyes, knuckles white against the wood. 'I'm sorry if I hurt you. I've let you further in than anyone on board. But you've got to understand, it's not just me I'm protecting. Alejandro ... We were on Heard Island together. He works at Sydney University now but ... if word gets out.' His face flushed and he drew in a long breath. 'Look, I read that paper Phil wrote on the psychology of life on Antarctic stations. About needing to be on guard against homosexual tendencies. Making sure mateship doesn't tip into *perversion*.' He spat a caustic laugh. 'I didn't lie to you. But I couldn't risk telling you the whole truth. I'm truly sorry, but there was so much more at stake than your feelings.'

Nel nodded, her eyes on the folder. It was taking every fibre of self-control she possessed to keep the tumult from playing across her face. Shock had quickly out-flamed jealousy. Now the low burn of humiliation was threatening to take hold. How had she not seen? She thought there'd been a spark. Had he *wanted* to make everyone think there was something between them? Had his interest in her, *in her art*, been merely a ploy to keep himself safe?

'You *used* me.'

'No.' He grabbed her arm. 'Nel. It was *never* that.' He looked her straight in the eyes. 'I knew back on Macquarie that we had something. A kinship.' He released her arm, gesturing up to the saloon. 'Out there, we share something the rest don't. We're outsiders. We keep our heads down, don't call attention to ourselves.' Harris paused, searching her face. 'Hiding in plain sight.'

'The lyrebirds.'

A corner of his mouth lifted. 'The lyrebirds.'

She nodded and, taking a deep breath, squeezed his elbow. 'Your secret's safe.'

She opened the door and stepped into the corridor, then turned back to say goodbye. He smiled, but she could see muscles ticking in his jaw.

'I mean it. You can trust me,' she said, as he leaned a forearm on the frame. 'And put some ice on that.' She touched the lump on his forehead. 'That's going to be an emperor egg by the morning.'

His smile failed to reach his eyes as he nodded and softly closed the door.

Nel leaned against the wall, almost dizzy with the shock and weight of the last few minutes. She held Harris's future in her hands.

Turning for the stairwell, she exhaled deeply – and then stopped in her tracks.

Monte. His long body made sharp angles against an open doorway, forearm up near his temple and ankles crossed. She would have to pass him to reach the stairs.

Steeling her spine, Nel strode down the corridor, making herself return his gaze with a cold glare.

'So. This is what goes on below decks when the chief is busy and there are no penguins available for *observation*.' He sniggered. 'I knew it. Thank you, darlin'. You've just made me a nice little packet.' He straightened, holding out a hand to halt her as she drew even with him.

Nel swerved away, but he followed, stepping out into the corridor to trap her against the far side, her back pressed to the wall.

'Dalton and McLeod had their heads in the sand. Moofty even had coin on the Birdman batting for the other side. But I could smell it on you. A bitch in heat.' He gripped her upper arm, tugging her sharply towards the open door. Off balance, Nel's hands instinctively braced against his chest, trying to keep him at arm's length. He leaned in, his breath sour with beer. 'So, *Mrs Law* ... How much is silence worth?'

She shoved at him, but his hand gripped her bicep so hard she could feel each of his fingers like steel bands. She pulled back, trying to prise herself free. Monte smirked, then yanked her – hard. As she toppled against him, to her horror, she felt his hand squeeze her breast.

'Get off me, you *pig*.' She rammed her forearms against his chest, levering her body away. He released her so abruptly she staggered, slamming against the bulkhead.

He stepped forward, no part of him touching her but his height and proximity heavy with threat. 'Is that your final offer? I'm sure the chief will be very interested to hear my eyewitness account.'

'You saw nothing.' She narrowed her eyes at him, sliding along the wall, not daring to turn her back. 'Because there was nothing to see. And if it comes down to you or me – I know who Phil will believe.' The lowest stair knocked against her Achilles tendon. 'So *stay away* from me.'

She backed onto the staircase, climbing the first three steps still facing him. Then she spun and made herself climb slowly, deliberately, not trusting her voice or her body. Even out of his sight she could feel his eyes on her like an oily stain. She maintained her deliberate pace until the cabin door clicked shut behind her.

She perched on the edge of the bunk, forcing air into her lungs. A needle of rage lodged behind her eyes, awareness of the rest of the ship just beyond the door pressing in.

Nel gripped the edge of the bunk, rocking herself. He would tell Phil. She had no doubt. He held all the cards. He'd seen her leaving Harris's cabin. He'd seen her touch his face. And the only way to prove her innocence would ruin Harris's life.

Her stomach dropped; her legs were cold and trembling. She made it to the bathroom just in time, her throat aflame with the hot tide of acid. Then, she cleaned. Herself. The cabin. And only once the floor was clear, everything straightened and packed to its rightful place, did she turn off the light and let the tears come.

Carbon Black

Southern Ocean
March 1961

Nel swung her feet to the floor and shuffled to the porthole. For the last three days this brass circle had been her only view beyond the four close walls of the cabin. The ship was beset. Nel slumped into the chair and stared out into the white.

Ice axes chimed like tinny bells over the sound of the engine. The men were too close to the red steel hull for her to be able to see them, but she could hear their voices and the strike of tools as they tried to chip away at the ice jammed against the ship.

They were stuck, the frozen sea like a huge shattered plate, edges grinding with the tides, currents and wind. The captain must've been awake for days, keeping watch for leads in the ice, trying to use the bow like a huge wedge to ram the cracks apart.

A shadow moved across the edge of the porthole's round frame. Nel leaned forward to see, only to rock back in horror.

Harold's hunting party. They were using one of the dog sleds to transport the carcasses; the bodies of crabeater and Weddell seals lay heaped upon the wooden slats, as if they'd fallen asleep in a great pile. If not for all the blood. Three men were strapped into the harnesses like dogs, hauling the sled across the ice, leaving a swathe of scarlet on the white – as thick and vivid as the stroke of a Japanese calligrapher's brush on rice paper.

Nel crawled back beneath the covers. She imagined the next task would be the butchering and she had no desire to witness any of it. *Hypocrite.* She groped under her bed for a magazine. She'd cooked more seal meat for Phil's Antarctic dinners than she could recall. Where did she think it came from? Her hand touched glossy paper, then a hard spine. She fished the lot out. Several extremely well-thumbed editions of *Harper's Bazaar* and *Vogue* and a paperback book, *The Autobiography of Alice B. Toklas.* Who on earth had given her that? Right now, she'd use anything to keep her mind from the grip of the pair of vortices trying to drag her below the surface. Monte and Harris. Nel thumped her pillows and yanked the covers to her neck.

She managed only a few paragraphs before her thoughts returned to the first source of pain. Under her incandescent rage at Monte's behaviour lurked a cold dread that refused to burn away. Would he tell Phil? She couldn't help teasing out the possibilities, as if she was trying to remove the label from an empty jar, jabbing her fingernail under the edge again and again, hoping to find the point of release, that place where the whole thing would peel away cleanly, leaving no evidence it was ever there. But there was no clean solution. To exonerate herself would mean exposing Harris.

Harris was a friend of Dorothy. Of course he was. She felt such a fool. There'd been many moments when she'd entertained the possibility there could be more between them than friendship. She'd lain awake in her bunk replaying their conversations, analysing his tone and gestures, trying to untangle what was actually there from what she wanted to see. Yet all the while, some intuitive part of her had known that her attraction was not about physical desire. Or her disillusionment with Phil. She was in love with the way Harris made her feel about herself. As if she was desired, not only – or even – for her body, but for her mind. Her company and conversation. Her art. Harris *saw* her. *That* was what she was in love with. And that was what he'd taken away.

She knew she should be more understanding. Harris clearly had no idea about the scenarios that had been whirling through her mind. But underneath it all – the hurt and confusion – she felt betrayed. It was irrational. But knowing that didn't stop her feeling as if Harris had broken a promise. How could she have been so sure there'd been a spark between them when his orientation meant it was impossible? He hadn't lied. Looking back, Nel had to admit that he'd never given her any incontrovertible sign of physical attraction. But had he led her on, or at least not set her straight, as a form of protection? Had he used her?

If he'd been pretending to enjoy her company as a front, protecting his true self with misconceived rumours of romance, then even their friendship was a sham.

She scrubbed the sheet across her face, realising she was still staring at page one of Gertrude Stein. She was grieving. She recognised the lead in her gut, the long shadow across her thoughts. Grief for the death of the person she'd been when she was with him. The woman she recognised as most authentically herself. The woman who'd hidden within the Nel who was Phil's wife. Finally, that woman had risen to the surface, taking great gulps of air and revelling in the light.

Beneath the blankets, she stewed, turning memories of her time with Harris over and over, as though there was an angle from which the truth hunkering inside them would be revealed. As she lay there, humiliation and betrayal simmering in her chest, she could feel the witty, talented, enlivened version of herself she'd been in his presence dissolving. Now she was back to being Mrs Phil Law, wife of the Antarctic explorer. And Harris was not the man she knew. Perhaps it had been a kind of love, but if it was, it was between two people who had never really existed at all.

Nel flung the book across the room.

~

'It's been three days. You must get up.'

Turned to the wall, blankets yanked to her chin, she could hear the clank of Phil gathering teacups and coffee mugs, crumb-laden plates and bowls crusted with dried porridge. 'The men have noticed you're not about. Everyone's worried.'

'You mean everyone's talking.'

'No. When I say they're worried, they're worried. *I'm* worried.'

Nel was silent. She heard Phil put down the tray before his weight dipped the bunk behind her. She felt his hand on her shoulder as he leaned in, trying to hug her, his chin hooking into the curve of her neck. 'I thought we'd put this sadness behind us.'

She shook him off. 'It's not about Nefertiti.'

He drew back at her hiss.

'I just ...' Nel closed her eyes, unsure how to explain it even to herself. She took a deep breath, willing herself to calm down. She'd been on a hair-trigger for days but, even caught in the grip of this sudden fury, she had enough presence of mind to know that exploding at Phil would be far from the wisest move. 'Please, darling. I honestly don't feel well. And I'm just not up to parading myself around right now. All I want is a little peace and quiet.' She turned to look at him. 'Of course, I'm still sad about losing Nefertiti. But it isn't that.'

Phil's eyes hardened. 'You're ill.'

'Yes.' Nel glared at him before throwing herself back against the pillow.

Phil's lips tightened to a thin line as he continued stacking crockery onto the tray with a force that made the ceramic rattle and clack. 'Interesting. I wasn't aware it was possible to catch a virus out of thin air.'

Alarmed at the change in tone, she turned over in bed, propping herself up on one elbow.

Phil stared down at her, eyes like wet stones beneath his dark widow's peak.

'To be honest, darling, feeling the men's eyes on me, watching every move I make ... it sets my teeth on edge.' She tried to smile. 'You'd think I'd be used to it by now. But I'm tired and under the weather and I just don't have the *energy* for it.'

Phil's face remained stony. 'So that's your story. You're ill. You don't like to be watched. Which is a first, by the way.' He raised an eyebrow. 'If asked, I would've said it was what you lived for. I can produce my chequebook stubs as evidence of your love of dressing for the spotlight.' Phil slammed the tray down on the desk, the stack of dishes threatening to topple. 'Perhaps this lack of energy for facing the men is something else?' He leaned over her. 'Guilt, perhaps? Maybe it would be more honest to say you're *embarrassed*. Perhaps I should tell you how I feel, up on the bridge, with my men looking at me with pity.' He cocked his head. 'Well, I'll tell you. Humiliated. That's how I feel. And then you lie there, a sack of self-pity, with the gall to tell me you're *sick*.'

Nel pulled herself into a sitting position, meeting his eyes as calmly as she could, despite the hammering in her chest. 'I *am* sick.'

'Would it surprise you to know that the only other person who's claiming illness right now is Harris McCallum? Any theories on why it is that the only person he appears to have spread this virus to is *my wife?*'

Nel was silent, meeting his gaze.

'Do you have anything to say at all? Because, quite frankly, it's all the ship can talk about. You and McCallum. And the stories are quite detailed. One wonders how the imaginations of so many men just happened to invent the same tale.'

Monte. That adjectival degenerate. If he was standing in front of her right now, she'd slap him in the face with Gertrude Stein.

Nel forced herself to remain calm. 'Darling, I swear to you. There is absolutely nothing going on. Yes, I spent time with Harris. A great deal of time. *Because I was working.*' Nel pointed to the great stacks of watercolours and sketches piled on the desk. 'That is all I was doing. Talking. Working.' She held her gaze to his, trying to expose every particle of sincerity within her. 'Nothing more.'

He stared back at her and Nel was shaken by the distrust in his eyes. 'I want to believe that. In fact, I *have* been believing it, for weeks now. You think this is the first I'm hearing of it? The snide jokes, the sniggering, every time my back is turned? How foolish do you think I feel? *No, not Nel. Impossible.* I've been telling myself that for weeks.' He shook his head, unable to look at her. Nel caught her breath, sensing the immense hurt barricaded behind the fortified wall of his anger.

Here it was, the moment. She could tell him it was impossible. She could tell him why. Surely, Phil wasn't the sort of person who would ruin a man's career because of his sexual orientation. She could trust him. Couldn't she? Wouldn't he be relieved that his wife's honour was unblemished, and leave it at that? Just one sentence could fix everything.

A vision of Harris's face, eyes sad and wary, flashed into her mind. No. She would keep her word.

'There is nothing between us. I swear it.'

Phil expelled a breath, the pain she'd seen hidden as swiftly as it had appeared. Muscles flexed in his jaw. 'I'll be up on the bridge.' Turning on his heel, he moved to the door, refusing to look at her as he balanced the tray on one knee and reached for the handle. 'I expect you for dinner.'

The sound of her husband's footsteps trailed away, leaving only the intermittent growl of the engines as the ship continued to try to butt its way out of the pack.

~

Magga was moving. Slowly. Every inch they cracked through the ice brought Nel closer to the moment she could escape this ship.

The engine had settled into a steady grumble by the time she slipped onto the bridge, holding her big sketchbook in front of her chest like armour.

No one said a word to her as she climbed up to her place on the life-raft case. The crew, all stiff-backed, didn't acknowledge her presence, other than by casting sidelong glances at Phil. Standing front and centre before the broad sweep of glass, Phil stared fixedly out the bridge window, hands clasped behind his back. Only Bend, at his post behind the helm, nodded in greeting, but he didn't meet her eyes.

The silence was broken by the captain's voice crackling out of the intercom as he issued directions from his position in the crow's nest. Nel wished Bill was down here, certain of his intrinsic kindness if not his allegiance, given the apparent damage to her reputation. She straightened her spine. This was the right decision, to spend some

238

hours up here, sketching and getting reaccustomed to being under scrutiny before braving the full company of eyes over dinner. She couldn't stay in the cabin indefinitely, especially since she could no longer rely on Phil with his trays of food. And she'd missed this view. Beyond the stretch of window, *Magga* was squeezing her way down a jagged ink-black crack in the white. After the pinhole vista from her porthole, this felt panoramic.

She'd intended to sketch, but her energy had deserted her and she simply stared out at the brutal, broken world, her stick of charcoal hovering over the unsullied page.

The bergs were unworldly: huge, sterile slabs pressed so close to the ship it was as if *Magga* was sailing along a narrow street in an alien metropolis, towering blocks of ice rising like jagged cliffs on either side.

Between the press of icebergs, the avenue of water in front of them was ink-black. Bend urged the ship on, pushing forward on the throttle, steering to starboard to ease around the face of a large berg. Once past it, *Magga* was in a bay of open water, surrounded by huge, splinter-spiked bergs. There was no exit. The bay was a cul-de-sac.

Bend muttered something in Danish, and threw the ship into reverse, backing out and turning to another open lead that had offered itself, just beyond a looming berg to the port side.

Bend jammed the ship back into forward gear, giving the throttle some extra juice. *Magga* powered towards the huge berg. The captain's voice crackled out of the intercom, static scrambling the order. '*St—y ... app—ch.*'

They were headed directly for the berg, narrow leads of open water on both sides. Bend looked around at the bridge crew. 'Which side did he say?' The only responses were shrugs, headshakes and upturned palms.

'Captain? Repeat?'

The intercom speaker let loose a wild blast of static, the only intelligible word coming at the end. '*Now!*'

Bend stared out the window for long moment, a rabbit caught in the glare from the berg's bright face. Then he hauled the helm hard to port.

'Rotten ice!' Phil yelled from his position against the bridge window. 'That whole face is rotten! Hard astern!' He turned to Bend. The young man was hauling on the helm with his whole weight. 'Pull up!' Phil spun back to the window, gripping the handrails with such force his hands looked white. 'Reverse, goddamn it! *Reverse.*'

The ship swept towards the face of the berg, the bow curving to the left but clearly, at this speed, a collision was unavoidable. Cliff crammed the view. Nel could see the rough, raw-silk texture of the face, as if the bridge window was the lens of a great microscope. Bend wrenched the engines into reverse. From below, the shriek of machines.

This close to the ice wall, Nel could see exactly what Phil meant. The face *was* rotten. What had looked solid from a distance was half-melted and unstable, the structure honeycombed and on the brink of crumbling in a great avalanche.

The bow peeled across the front of the berg, clearing it with mere inches to spare. At the window, Phil had jammed his right foot hard into the wall, unable to do anything to avoid catastrophe other than instinctively slam on the brakes. The ship swept past the berg, the deck so close to the ice Nel thought a person at the rail might be able to reach out and touch it.

With a gunshot crack, a giant shard broke away from the face; it hovered for a moment and then fell, leaving a gaping blue chasm in the ice. Plunging into the ocean, the ice dagger pierced the space where *Magga* had been moments before.

'Christ Almighty.' Someone swore, but Nel couldn't tear her eyes away. The colossal needle of ice plunged into the water with a sound so deeply resonant it seemed to rumble up from the very core of the earth. The shock wave doused the starboard deck, tilting the ship and washing it sideways on its surge. Nel rushed to the wing of the bridge just in time to see the massive upswell catalyse an ice-slip, the entire face of the berg plummeting into the sea with a roar.

The tsunami passed under the ship, and *Magga* settled slowly, oh-so slowly, washed away from the remaining tower of ice. Its new surface glowed, pure white and shining, as if innocent of almost sinking them.

Nel heard running footfalls in the corridor, and a moment later the door banged open. 'Bloody hell, Bend! Who taught you to drive?' Hugo Larsen, the chief engineer, broke into the room, out of breath and possibly on the brink of cardiac arrest. 'I need to change my trousers!'

Bend chuckled, managing to look both shocked and shamefaced at the same time. 'What's the problem? In Denmark, we drive on the right.'

Nel laughed, a bray of fear and relief, letting go of a breath she'd not known she was holding. Death had passed so close she'd felt its gooseflesh chill. Instinctively, her eyes sought out Phil, needing to share this moment with him, to see him safe, as she was.

He was looking at Bend, shaking his head in disapproval, arms crossed. Feeling her eyes on him, he shot her a cold look, then turned to the window, hands gripped behind his back.

Terre Verte

She hadn't realised how much she missed the colour green until it was there, pulsing lush and verdant in the middle of the ocean. Nel had scented the island long before it surged out of the horizon. It smelled like escape. As the mountains took shape and stippled themselves with detail, she stood at the rail and stared, mixing the exact shades of green and grey on the palette in her mind.

As they'd finally cleared the ice and headed north, the Mawson men had grown rowdier, sensing the proximity of home. Now that the tension between her and Phil had boiled over into the public sphere, the men were less cautious about hiding their sentiments. Nel felt the heat of their judgement every time she stepped beyond the cabin door. For dinners and evening festivities, she slipped on the mask of ship socialite, refusing to let them see the damage.

But behind the facade, she was feverishly cycling between anxiety and rage. Before Antarctica, if someone had asked her who she was, she would've answered *a wife*, with no hesitation. Yes, she was still a wife – but she was no longer willing to push down her artist-self while walking around in her wife-skin. No one ever called Phil a husband first and Antarctic explorer second.

Phil was coolly courteous to her in front of the men, but she was in no doubt their marriage was in dire trouble. Her new-found determination to honour the artist part of herself over the wife might prove to be less of a choice than a default position if Phil was considering divorce.

When they dropped anchor at Macquarie Island, Nel was one of the first to disembark. She flung her leg over *Magga's* side, mounting the salt-silvered ladder down to the duck with no trace of the wobbles that had plagued her months before. Once on board the bucking vessel, she squeezed herself into the thin space between two of the Mawson men, gently encouraging them to narrow the spread of their knees. They obliged, yet their avoidance of eye contact spoke volumes, and they continued their conversation across her as if she were a piece of baggage on the thwart between them.

Shadows flashed across the face of the sun. Birds. Harris would know what they were. Harris. Her head dropped, cheeks burning at the injustice of it all. She wondered how he was faring. As far as she was aware, he had been keeping a low profile. Or at least avoiding the places she was likely to be. He was probably coping better than she was. Shipboard opinion seemed to have coloured her as the adulterous temptress, Phil the betrayed dupe and Harris just a regular red-blooded man indulging his natural male impulses. For him, being accused of cuckolding the chief must have been far preferable to the men knowing the truth.

The duck throttled through the breakers and kelp, and Nel raised her face, revelling in the strange freedom of being hatless outdoors. The wind lifted her hair, the air ripe with the scent of green.

243

On the shore, a tall figure paced the dark sand. Andy. She'd barely put her feet to solid ground before she was swept into a mighty hug.

'My saviours! Not a moment too soon!' He released her and stepped away, arms held wide to reveal a figure that was almost svelte. Nel dove back in for another squeeze, not willing to give up the sanctuary of the embrace of a genuine ally.

'*Andy.*' She released him from her desperate grip. 'Where's the rest of you?'

'Sweated away, my dear. I've lugged this caboose high and low, on the hunt for my tiny elusive friends.' He threw an arm around her shoulders as they made their way up towards the station buildings. 'Insects don't like to fly too far unless absolutely necessary, but get one of these infernal roaring westerlies under their wings and the next thing you know they're circumnavigating the globe.' He squeezed her shoulders. 'So, I've been plodding up and down, fossicking in every tussock. Shaking down the odd penguin.' He stopped, as if struck by a thought. 'What am I saying? They're *all* odd penguins!' His laugh boomed out. 'And what about you? Our intrepid exploratrix.'

'My adventures had the opposite effect. I've put on fourteen pounds!'

'Ah. Too many expeditions past the buffet.'

'The life of an Antarctic explorer has quite ruined me for the real world, I'm afraid.'

'Pleased to hear it. If I'm to believe everything I hear from my wife, the real world doesn't have much to recommend it for the fairer sex. You should compare notes with the Mac ladies.' Andy gave her a shrewd glance before squeezing her shoulder. 'I'm sure you'll have a great deal to talk about.'

~

Nel ran her thumb under the waistband of her woollen trousers, trying to ease the pinch. She'd been holding in her stomach for the past hour, worried that at any moment the button might shoot across the room, bringing down a random expeditioner like a prize stag. Even before Harris's revelation and the shipboard fallout, she'd been eating for comfort. Nel shifted in her chair, trying not to eye the row of trestle tables laden with party food stretched across the far wall. Her diet started *now*. She wasn't even home yet, and the old concerns over face and figure were already returning. How stupid to have thought all that was behind her.

Though the temperature was not even in double figures, compared to Antarctic conditions, the air felt balmy. For tonight's festivities, she'd decided to relinquish the baggy comfort of her jumpers and attempt to re-establish her Melbourne persona by wearing a dress. To her horror, the new layer of insulation on her waist and hips quite ruined the lines of her frocks. By the time she'd settled on this shirt and trouser combination, almost every piece of clothing she'd brought with her had been tried on, the carpet barely visible under the litter of discarded options. She'd managed to button up the slacks, but as soon as she sat down the waistband bit into her with such ferocity she feared the circulation to her legs might be in danger.

Harris stepped into the recreation hall, brushing aside a loop of twisted streamer that had slipped its tape. Nel's stomach clenched, and she took a swallow of wine, averting her eyes. She tried to keep her face relaxed.

The effect was immediate. Across the room she could feel heads swivel in her direction. With the captain still on board *Magga*, Andy yet to arrive and Phil maintaining a stony silence, she felt as lonely and cold as that little dog Laika, circling the earth in *Sputnik 2*. How quickly would the rumour infect the Macquarie Islanders? Across the

245

room, the Macquarie station head was drinking with Phil, trying to maintain high spirits despite Phil's reserve.

Nel knew his bad mood was not solely directed at her. It was true that the rumours about her and Harris, and the days spent stuck in the ice, had helped to erode Phil's elation after making landfall in Oates Land. But now the relentless toil of the voyage was taking its toll – and there was still some way to go. The transfer of cargo, research materials and luggage from the island to the ship had not progressed with the desired efficiency, and Phil was worried that the Mawson men's low morale was translating into an unenthusiastic approach to the day's work.

His concerns were well founded. After fifteen months at sea and on the ice, Nel could completely understand how sunshine and greenery could overpower any sense of duty. Most of the men had deserted their assigned tasks in favour of photographing seals and penguins. Phil was fuming.

At the door, Nel caught a flash of colour among the white shirts and staid ties. The moment Hope, Isobel, Ann and Elise entered the room Nel felt it deep in her body – a delightful lightening of atmosphere. Compared to the women in the streets of Melbourne, the four were hardly fashion plates, but after the last few months of overalls, dungarees and enough white to last a lifetime, even a dash of lipstick caught Nel's eye. Macquarie Island was practically jewel-toned.

The women were dressed for the celebration in plaid skirts and cardigans, and looked far more at ease than when Nel had seen them in December. They moved along the buffet, filling their plates and pouring drinks, before settling around a table in a corner.

Nel excused herself from her table and wandered over to the impromptu bar, where she slipped behind the trestle and pulled a full bottle of wine from one of the tubs. She approached the corner where the women were chatting and held up the bottle. 'Room for one more? I come bearing gifts.'

'Of course.' Isobel waved her fork at an empty chair at the next table. 'Pull up a seat.'

Nel reached for the chair while the women shuffled to make an opening between Elise and Hope. Now that she was close to them, the changes of the last few months were clearer. Under light dustings of powder, their faces looked tanned and slightly weathered. Unlike Nel, they were more svelte than when they'd last met, their wrists and the lines of their throats slim and lean.

'Lovely to see you all again. You all look so healthy! How did your work go?' Nel smiled at all four in turn before settling her gaze on Isobel.

'Very productive.' Isobel nodded, taking a sip of wine. 'Hope and I collected and classified some very interesting samples.'

Hope nodded. 'The weather's been very kind. We've identified some exciting species of crustacean. And the species we expected to find have shown fascinating variations when compared to their counterparts from northern waters.' She smiled at Isobel, adding, 'There's definitely a paper or two in this trip.'

'That's wonderful.' Nel leaned forward. 'But I imagine you're looking forward to going home?'

There was a pause, the women all glancing at each other, before Elise chuckled. 'Well, I'm looking forward to sleeping in my own bed. And wearing a regular nightgown rather than feeling like a caterpillar ready to burst its cocoon.' The others laughed in recognition.

'Those camp beds.' Ann gave a theatrical shudder. 'And I can't remember what it feels like to sleep without this wind. Our quarters – it's like sleeping on a freight train with the roar and shaking walls.'

All four laughed, Hope and Elise adding groans of agreement. Nel looked at them, a little envious. The bonds linking the group were clear and strong. Were they going to ask about her experience? Her work? She pushed aside the niggle of offence.

Nel leaned forward, and said in a low voice, 'You know, what I really want to ask you ... is how it went, you know. With the men.'

Isobel froze, fork halfway to her mouth. The other women shifted in their seats, and Hope shot a look across the room to where Phil was standing at the bar, holding court with a group from the Macquarie party.

Nel almost smacked herself in the forehead. 'No, no. This isn't official. This is just between us. As women.'

Isobel's expression remained slightly sceptical.

Nel continued, 'I'm asking only because ... well, when I joined the expedition, I thought I'd be fine. At home, I was happy on my own, with my cat.' She gestured helplessly, ploughing on. 'I enjoy being social, but when Phil's gone for months on end, I just get on with things. I like the solitude. I'm so much more productive. With my art.' She looked over at Isobel. 'And ... I assumed I'd be fine ... I don't know, I thought it'd be the perfect combination. I could be social *and* tuck myself away to work.' She uncrossed her legs and leaned in, adding in a lower tone, 'But I didn't realise that being the only woman would be ...' She shook her head and looked at the other women with a grave expression. 'I didn't realise how *alone* I would feel, even surrounded by so many people.'

They were silent, looking at her with softening expressions.

'It surprised me – even having Phil there with me – how much I missed the company of other women. And I thought about all of you. Often.' Nel smiled. 'With a great deal of jealousy.'

Eyebrows were raised around the table.

'You had each other.' Nel looked down at her drink, her mouth pulled to one side. 'I'm embarrassed to admit, at times I missed my sisters and girlfriends so much that I'd hide in my cabin, flipping through the fashion magazines I'd brought with me.' She chuckled. 'I can basically recite from memory the advice in *Harper's Bazaar* on teaming appetisers with cocktails.'

A smile from Isobel. 'Well, I can't say you'll find us as useful for the latest hostessing tips or fashion trends. The best we can offer is advice on how to strap plastic sheeting to your legs to protect from penguin bites.'

The group burst into laughter. Hope raised her glass towards Elise. 'I can just see you on the catwalk in Milan. Striding along in your brother's boots!'

'And your walking stick, Isobel!'

'The penguin trainer? I think I cut an extremely dapper figure, thank you very much!'

When the laughter died down, Nel took a sip of wine and placed the glass on the table. 'This is what I missed.'

The women fell silent.

'The men ... they were polite. Mostly. Or they didn't speak to me. But it was so wearing. Being watched, all the time. Not just how I looked, but what I was doing, who I spoke to, and how I spoke. It was exhausting. I felt like one of your specimens – under the microscope. For months.' She searched their faces. 'Don't worry. I'm not going to tell Phil anything you say. I just ...' Nel trailed off. 'I hoped it might've been different for you. Better. Since you had each other.'

Ann leaned over the table and rubbed her shoulder. 'That must've been awful.'

Nel smiled. 'Maybe I'm overstating it. Antarctica was breathtaking. I've been incredibly lucky. And I got an enormous amount of work done.'

Isobel nodded, pushing her plate away. 'It sounds very familiar, doesn't it?' The others nodded and Ann poured herself some more wine.

'Over time, it got better. The constant surveillance. But even after all these months, watching us work from dawn till dusk, they don't seem to understand we talk to each other about topics other than *them*.' Hope shook her head in disbelief.

'It's infuriating. The assumption we have nothing better to talk about.'

'They'd curl up in little balls of mortification if they knew how little attention we actually pay them.' The four cackled and heads turned across the room, initiating fresh laughter.

Isobel was the first to let her amusement fade. She gestured around her. 'They can't seem to get past the idea of us being invaders in their world.'

Elise cut in. 'We get through each day by being alert to how they perceive us. Always easygoing. Non-threatening. Taking everything as a joke.'

Nel shook her head, shoulders slumped. 'That approach didn't work for me, I'm afraid. My face ached from constantly smiling, yet I still found myself the butt of gossip.'

Isobel nodded, frowning at Nel. 'It's exhausting. Especially when there's nothing you can do or say. We're at their mercy. And I'm sorry to say, you don't even know the depth of it until you get off the ship. Prepare yourself. After getting home, I spend at least two weeks feeling like a sea slug.'

'For me it's a washed-up strand of kelp. No, an elephant seal! Cranky and with only enough energy to roll over every couple of hours.' Elise slapped her thigh, letting out a loud laugh that immediately had heads turning around the room. Monte's included.

Smile dwindling from her face, Nel leaned forward. 'Actually, it's been worse than just being talked about. And watched.' She paused. 'One of them. It was awful. *Is* awful. He really has it in for me.' Nel

250

lowered her voice, and the women leaned in to catch her words. 'He touched me. And keeps spreading rumours about me. It's like he's made it his mission to ruin my marriage.'

'Who?' Elise scanned the room.

'Don't look,' Nel said. 'I'm sure he's watching.' She tipped her head down. 'Montgomery. The physicist.'

Ann nodded, drumming her fingers on the side of her glass. 'I was warned about him by the secretaries in the department. More red flags than a crevasse. Confirmed bachelor. Used to be a bit of a ladies' man. Past his prime now, and a chip on his shoulder since the job title "Antarctic explorer" stopped working for him like it used to. And now we're edging in, diluting the virility of the label even further.' She frowned at Nel. 'Sounds like a piece of work.'

'It's not that it's a surprise – men behaving badly. Back home, I just deal with it. Avoid that shopkeeper. Ignore construction workers. Keep smiling and turn the other cheek. But here, it feels so personal. It isn't just that I'm a woman. He wants to humiliate *me*.' To her mortification, Nel felt her eyes start to burn and she blinked to keep the tears at bay.

'Power games,' Elise said, tipping her head to the side. 'You're the perfect target. Bring you down and he's not only defeated an "uppity woman", but he's scored against your husband, too.'

'I don't know what to do. Part of me thinks I should just grin and bear it. Boys will be boys, and it's just my bad luck to have drawn the attention of a particularly poisonous specimen.' Nel gripped her glass, leaning into the circle. 'But the other part of me wants to tell Phil.'

Ann and Hope were nodding, but Nel could see calculations running through Elise and Isobel's minds.

'But after what you told me about Phil's expectations of you ... I'm worried I may do more harm than good.'

'I'm guessing there's no evidence. It's just your word against his?' Ann raised an eyebrow.

Nel nodded, her mouth turned down. 'No witnesses. He was always very sly. And if I tell Phil, I'm worried it's going to come across as bleating. The last thing I want to do is give him ammunition that might damage your chances of coming back down here.'

Isobel sighed. 'Telling you that in a few days you'll never have to see him again feels totally self-serving – but it is the truth.' Her lips thinned to the point of disappearance. 'As you've learned the hard way, there's a different set of rules for us down here. The squeaky wheel doesn't get the oil. It gets replaced with a policy that rationalises why wheels weren't suited to the task in the first place.'

Hope muttered 'Amen' before draining her glass.

Isobel hadn't finished. 'That said, I do think change is coming.' She smiled at Nel's look of incredulity. 'Slowly. Too slowly for us.' She picked up the bottle and topped up the glasses. 'Look at all these men. They go through life putting themselves first. And as women, we're taught to put them first too. But what if we put *ourselves* first? Prioritise our own happiness, our goals and ambitions? We can't change these men, but we can change who we put first. And I firmly believe *that's* how we'll start to make a difference.' She raised her glass. 'We're playing the long game, ladies. We won't be around to see how it ends, but we can certainly make some moves.' The five women reached forward, solemn-faced as they chimed their glasses together.

Nel settled back in her chair. 'Maybe my nieces will see those changes. I can't wait to hug them. And my sisters.'

Ann said with a sly grin, 'I, for one, cannot wait to run a hot bath and stay in there until I'm as wrinkly as my grandmother. Imagine, not having to worry about using too much hot water or who's waiting outside the door. Luxury!'

'Ooh, yes. And playing records I haven't heard two thousand times,' Elise added.

'New novels.'

'Fresh fruit.'

'Underwear I haven't named!' Ann said to peals of laughter.

Nel looked past Isobel's shoulder, searching for Phil's dark head in the crowd. The large room echoed with men's voices, clusters of standing figures shielding her short-statured husband from view. She heard what she thought could be his laugh from a group of men near the drinks table. One flame-coloured head stood out from the crowd. Harris's pale eyes caught hers as the conversation flowed around him. He dipped his chin, raising his glass in the barest suggestion of a toast. Nel gave a slow blink, accepting his thanks, then refocused on the women at the table, praying no one had witnessed the exchange.

'Are you all right?' Elise looked at her with concern. 'You're white as a ghost.'

Nel pasted on a smile. 'Oh, I'm fine. Thank you. Just a little light-headed. After all that cold, this place feels almost tropical.' She gave a bright laugh, then broke off, realising she was overdoing it. She stood up, resting a hand on the chairback. 'A bit of fresh air should do the trick.'

Ann started to get up, but Nel waved for her to stay. 'Please, enjoy the rest of the party. I'll be fine.'

Outside, she breathed the night deep into her lungs. *It's all right. No one saw.* She swallowed her rising panic. *Phil didn't see.* In a few days it would all be over. She'd never see Harris again. And as she reminded herself multiple times a day – *there was no proof.*

The only evidence of what they *had* shared were the penguins. And those penguins represented far more than her friendship with Harris. They symbolised who she'd become. A professional artist. She would not let Monte ruin that. The women were right – once she was home, she'd never have to see Monte's vicious grin again. But until the day she stepped off the ship, he still had the power to poison Phil against her.

She was suddenly so *tired* of it all; she wanted it to be over. Right now. There was a launch waiting to take partygoers back to the ship. She could just leave, call it a night. The women would understand and Phil didn't care if she was around or not. Nel stepped off the porch, and started striding down the boardwalk towards the shore. Maybe she could even drop off the penguin artwork while Harris was at the party. And then stay in her cabin for the rest of the voyage. She'd never have to see him or Monte again. Nel's step quickened. Above her, a green ribbon rippled across the night sky, wafting a soft veil across the Milky Way's sneeze of stars. Nel glanced up, but didn't stop.

~

Nel stood outside Harris's door, clasping a thick folder full of intricately detailed penguin sketches. She knew it was some of her best work, and wished she could see his reaction when he saw it. But it was better this way. The last thing she wanted was for anyone to see them together. With any luck, Missen, Harris's introverted roommate, would be in, and she could give the folder to him for safekeeping. She rapped softly on the door. No answer. She tried the handle, hoping she could just leave the folder on his desk. Locked.

'So, it is true.'

Nel's gut clenched, a fist of muscle. Phil was standing at the end of the corridor, a roster in his hand. His eyes cut away from her and he turned to the noticeboard in front of him, stabbing the page to the corkboard before spinning away and marching up the stairs.

'Phil.'

His thumping cadence up the stairs did not slow.

'*Phil.*'

She ran, party shoes clattering on the treads. Reaching the top of the stairwell, she heard the door to the lower deck slam. *Damn these shoes.* Clutching the folder to her chest, she raced after him.

Nel found him standing at the curved white rail of the lower deck. He was stiff-backed, the tendons in his neck pulsing. Beside him, the Danish flag lifted and sagged, the pulley clanging as the crimson fabric rippled in the rising wind. She moved to stand beside him, facing the sea. The aurora throbbed across the sky as faint sounds of the radiogram and laughter stained the breeze. He didn't acknowledge her presence.

'Phil. I know what you think you saw. All I can tell you is what you *did* see was me attempting to deliver the penguin illustrations.' She offered him the folder, willing him to take it. He didn't move. She drew a deep breath. 'Nothing went on between us. Harris and I are friends. That's it. If anyone has told you differently, they are stirring the pot. Or being downright malicious.'

'In my experience, where there's smoke there's fire.'

'In my experience, knowing there's no love lost between you and the Mawson men, you should take any rumours with a grain of salt. Especially when weighing their words against those of the woman you've known for twenty-three years.'

'I *thought* I've known.' He looked at her, the chill in his eyes thawing just enough for her to glimpse the pain beneath. 'How do I really know what you get up to in the months I'm away?'

Nel's mouth dropped open. 'You're now questioning my fidelity for the last *twelve years*?' She leaned towards him, trying to keep her voice down, but anger was pulsing through her. 'Because some pig-headed lout who can't keep his hands to himself decides to keep the ship entertained by stirring up trouble? You do realise that this is all because he's against women, against *me* being on board? Threatening his men's club. Can't you see that for Neanderthals like him, if women show they are perfectly capable of working down here, suddenly he's not quite so heroic?'

He pulled his chin back towards his neck, the hurt she'd glimpsed once again concealed behind a flare of anger. 'You may not think I've been paying attention. But it's been very clear to me that you're not the same woman who boarded back in Melbourne. And listening to this hysterical diatribe, trying to shift the blame, I'm not sure who you are.'

'*Excuse me?*' Nel took a deep breath; she had to stay cool. 'Actually, you're quite right, Phil. It's true. I have changed. Because what was I before? What exactly am I to you? A warm meal at the end of the day and clean sheets? A soft chair? A bloody *pillow*?' Nel's fists clenched at her side. 'Frankly, I'm embarrassed at how long it's taken me to work out that I'm more than that.' She stared at him, making him hold her gaze. 'Much of that's my own fault. Women are taught to be soft, to not make noise, to smile. Work out what our husbands want and turn ourselves into it.' She narrowed her eyes. 'Well, I've worked out that I'm actually more than my interpretation of your image of the perfect wife. I'm also an artist. A wife and artist who feels underappreciated on both counts. So yes. You are quite right. I *have* changed. But if we're being totally candid here, I'm not sure who *you* are either.'

She thrust her rage down deep into her core, knowing her next words needed to be untainted by emotion. 'Whether or not you can love this new version of me, I'll say this one more time. There is nothing between Harris and me but friendship. I have been faithful to you. Always. Believe me, or don't. But if you continue to doubt me, our marriage is over.'

Phil looked at her as if she was speaking a language he didn't understand. 'But I always supported your art. I said that right from the beginning. You were here on this ship to do your own work. But all you wanted to do was *his* work.'

Wide-eyed, she looked at him. 'That statement proves how little attention you pay to me.' Nel shook her head in disbelief. 'The cabin, *our* cabin, is almost bursting at the seams with my work. If you bothered to look, you'd see I've used every page of every watercolour block I brought with me. The oil boards? All of them are painted *on both sides*.' She lowered her voice, using his own technique. 'I have done my own work. I did the work *you* asked for. And I have done the work for Dr McCallum. All of it. And I have loved every single second. But, apparently, you seem to be blinded by gossip.'

Phil stood in front of her, mouth slightly open. He reached for her hand. Thinking he was reaching for the penguins, she flinched, sheltering them with her body.

Shock and hurt flashed in his face.

She felt her mistake at the exact moment she saw him misread it. He thought she'd made a choice. To him, whether she'd flinched to protect her art or Harris, it didn't matter. All she read in his expression was loss.

This was the faultline. Under her feet, everything was unstable. With one sentence she could save her marriage. All she had to do was reveal Harris's truth. What happened after that was beyond her control. The surface of his world would be rearranged. But hers would be safe. It would be so easy.

She yanked the rubber band holding the folder of penguins closed. It snapped with a crack.

She flung the bundle over the water, the pages sailing apart, opening out like the wings of a flock of snow petrels taking flight. Just as the sheets began their fluttering descent, a gust of wind blasted in from the sea, flurrying them back towards the ship. The white leaves scattered across the deck, catching in railings, plastering against bulwarks. Nel turned her back on her husband to watch her penguins skate and wing along *Magga*'s decks and walls before disappearing into the night.

Naphthol Scarlet

Port Melbourne
March 1961

The final dinner. Sitting at the captain's table for the last time, Nel felt as though she had a painting still on the easel, needing more work, more time before she could step away and call it done.

The excitement in the room bounced off her as if she were glass. Bill was solicitous, refilling her wine, eyeing her with concern, but he said nothing. Phil's demeanour was thunderous, and the men at their table were stiff with discomfort. Dread began to pool in Nel's gut.

The dessert dishes were cleared and all around the room men made sure their glasses were full. This was the moment for toasts and thanks and the jokes that stood in for heartfelt farewells. Nel felt heat building, bone-deep, and sweat began to pool beneath her eyes. If she blotted it away it would look as though she was wiping tears. She took a sip from her glass.

Phil was staring at the grain of the teak tabletop as if trying to decipher an alien script, his lips a thin line. He pushed to his feet. The room stilled.

'Tomorrow marks the end of this Antarctic season. For us and for ANARE.' Phil paused.

Seated beside him, Nel could see many of the men sneaking glances at each other in the uneasy silence.

'This is my thirteenth season with ANARE. The twelfth as director. And setting out, back in November, I knew this voyage would be a standout for me.' He looked down at Nel, and she gave him a small smile. His expression remained as hard as the tabletop. 'And I was right. But not entirely for the reasons I imagined.' He stared out at the men.

'We made it to Oates Land. Finally.' Phil paused, gazing into the space above the men's heads. 'Circumstances were against us, yet again. But I want to thank those of you who came ashore on the Aviation Islands. While we didn't get as far inland as I'd have liked, we made inroads. And next year, we'll push further.' He raised his glass, his gaze seeking out the men who accompanied him onboard *Lollipop*.

A few glasses clinked.

'In previous years, at this point I'm usually making lists of men I want with me on future expeditions. What I didn't expect was to be making lists of men who will not be returning South.' The line between Phil's brows darkened. 'It has come to my attention that some of you have been helping yourselves to supplies.' He leaned forward, bracing his hands on the table, thumbs and index fingers cocked like guns. 'To say I am disappointed would gravely underestimate my state of mind.'

The only sound in the room was the dull boom of wave on hull.

'Those of you from the Mawson winter party will return to your cabins and prepare for a customs check. I want to see all your gear, unpacked and laid out for inspection.'

With those words, the freeze shattered. Disbelief and indignation surged through the room.

Monte stood up, anger creasing his face. 'Why only us? What about everyone else?'

Phil stared him down, before slicing his gaze away with a curt nod. 'Fair point. All expeditioners will present their gear for inspection. I'm offering an amnesty. Surrender any looted items now, and no charges will be levelled against you.'

'Charges?' The muttering rose in pitch.

'Yes, charges.' Phil leaned forward. 'This is theft, black and white. Which leaves me in the frankly appalling position of needing to write an ANARE policy on looting.'

'Excuse me, Chief,' a voice called from the back. Nel recognised the tentative shyness that could only be Moofty. 'We'd heard it was just small stuff. Biscuits and boots and the like. Are we ... does the amnesty mean ... if we surrender it, will we still have jobs next season?'

Phil's sigh was pure exasperation. 'Boots. Biscuits. Tools or gloves or even a bloody helicopter.' He jabbed a finger at the shocked faces. 'It's the *principle*.' He scanned the room. 'What kind of a man helps himself to property that is not his?'

Nel's breath jammed in her throat. Phil was glaring at Harris.

The biologist held his gaze, but Nel could see his knuckles whiten as they gripped his glass. It didn't seem possible, but the tension in the room amplified, heads swinging as if watching a tennis rally.

Harris cleared his throat. 'I think what the lad meant was that it's only small items ... everyone's a little worried about losing their job over what's really a victimless crime, since any loss would just be to the department ...' His voice trailed away, leaving the insinuation that Phil was taking this personally trailing in the air between them.

Phil's eyes did not leave Harris's face. 'I believed I'd selected a company of hard-working, honourable men who know right from

261

wrong. Men guided by a personal code, not by what they think they can get away with. Men who know that if something isn't theirs, they have no right to it. Regardless of *who* it belongs to.' His voice lowered but the entire room heard the steel threaded through his words. 'But it seems I find myself in very different company.'

Harris remained impassive. Monte, of course, was watching the fallout with proud fascination. But, to Nel's relief, the men seemed to be preoccupied with the threat to their future with ANARE, and no one else seemed particularly interested in the bitterness blazing from her husband towards Harris.

'Phil.' Nel put a hand on his elbow. 'Darling. I don't think ...'

He flinched, and Nel closed her mouth. She stole a glance at Harris. He was looking at her, worry forming a crease between his pale brows. She made her face relax, hoping the absence of alarm in her expression was enough to reassure Harris she'd kept her word.

'Head to your cabins. I'll be down directly for the inspection. Geysen, you're with me. Dismissed.' Phil stalked to the saloon door, yanking it open with such force it banged against the wall. For once, Nel and the men were as one, the entire company gawping at the dark, empty doorway.

~

Nel knelt on the floor, leaning forward with her whole weight as she smooshed the air from her insulated jacket, attempting to clip the trunk closed. The door opened. Phil looked around the room, taking in the thick stack of oil boards, the desk piled with stacks of watercolours, sketches and her hand-drawn maps and charts.

Nel grunted, bouncing on the trunk lid. He watched her battle with the luggage for a long second, then stepped inside and pushed down the lid so that Nel could snap the latches into place. She sat back on her heels, brushing her hair away from her flushed face.

Nel struggled up from the floor, knees creaking. Again, Phil watched her for a protracted second before cupping her flailing elbow. They looked at each other warily – trying to read the other's face while keeping their own illegible. He waved for her to sit, and she lowered herself onto a bunk that earlier that morning had been a miniature mountain range of clothing, Phil's photographic equipment and her art supplies.

She had often wondered how he felt in the final hours of a voyage. What was stronger: desire to be home or disappointment that the excitement was over for another six months? But this was hardly the way any of his other voyages had ended.

Phil hadn't returned to his bunk last night, and she guessed he'd slept in his stateroom. She wasn't exactly clear how she felt about the end of the voyage, either. The returning men all spoke of their homecoming as clipping themselves into a jigsaw puzzle where they were the missing piece. Nel had the uneasy feeling that she was now the wrong shape for the hole in the puzzle waiting for her at home.

'Before we reach port, we need to talk.' Phil looked at his shoes.

A band tightened around her forehead. *He still doesn't believe me.* She'd sacrificed her artwork and scuttled Harris's publication chances, all to make this grand gesture – tossing the work that linked her with Harris. Couldn't Phil see she was showing him she valued their marriage more? *He didn't understand.* She'd lost her penguins for nothing.

Nel closed her eyes. She wanted to tell him that if he ended their marriage, she'd be devastated, but she'd survive. Yet, if they kept on, she didn't just want to step back into her old life. She wanted something different. What she had, plus a future that was only just becoming clear. A new beginning.

'You're about to step into a media scrum. I just got a tip-off from a friend in the department with a contact at *The Herald.* I'll do what I can to divert attention, talk up everything we've achieved this season. But you won't be able to completely avoid the reporters.'

He hadn't said the word *divorce.* For several seconds, relief insulated her from what had been said. 'Oh dear.'

'Over the last few days, your trip's been in all the papers. The department's been flooded with requests for interviews and official comment. It appears you're about to become the face of the expedition. For better or for worse.' He cleared his throat. 'What you say to the media will have enormous ramifications. For everyone.'

He looked at her steadily, and Nel thought she saw a softening in his gaze. But when he sat beside her on the bunk, a hand's width of distance between their thighs, the space yawned wide as a chasm.

'In all the interviews, you'll need to make it clear you had Senator Gorton's approval. You contributed to the expedition with your artistic and drafting skills. And, this is the important part, you had absolutely *no adventures.*'

She lifted her chin. 'What on earth do you mean? That's ridiculous. Surely the entire trip was an adventure?'

'No. If you'd been injured or fell ill or needed rescuing, the department would've been liable. So, this is the most important part of the message to get across. You need to make it absolutely clear you were just a spectator, happy to sit back and watch while the men did all the work and took all the risks.'

She exhaled audibly, feeling the weight of every one of her forty-six years.

It was his turn to sigh. 'Here. Read for yourself.' He pulled a piece of onion-skin paper from his pocket.

Nel scanned the typewritten memo as Phil continued, 'So no

mention of helicopter flights. Or fieldwork. Or the landing on Oates Land. As far as anyone is concerned, you watched everything from the safety of the bridge.' He dipped his head towards her, his voice deepening with emphasis. 'This is what you have to say – exactly these words – *now I understand, first-hand, how important this work is and what keeps the men coming back.*'

Nel listened with half an ear as she scanned down to the bottom of the page. She stiffened, anger rattling in her stomach, hard as a nut.

The memo was from Phil's deputy at ANARE, the man holding the fort while Phil was down on the ice. She read the page aloud, as if sounding out the words might alter their meaning.

'*I think it advisable for her to complain, tactfully, that a voyage to the Antarctic, while just too* madly interesting, *is not nearly as adventurous as people think. Adventure comes to those allowed to do flying or shore operations – and these, of course, were banned to her on the grounds that she would be a liability if anything, however trivial, went wrong. She should convey, if possible, that she was irked by these restrictions upon which her master and commander was so insistent.*'

Nel's voice shook as she repeated, 'Liability? My *master and commander?*' She thrust the paper at Phil. 'This makes it sound as if the whole trip was one long "take your child to work" day.'

He sighed but made no move to take the paper back. 'That's the angle they want to stress. It's just for the press. Australia's most long-suffering "Antarctic widow" finally gets to see the place that steals her husband every year.' She refused to look at him.

'Nel. Please.'

The two words were asking for more than cooperation.

The thin page sagged onto her lap.

'I guess the underlying message is now I've got what I wanted, I should just shut the hell up? Do I get to say anything about paving the way for women to go to Antarctica? Scientists like Isobel and Elise and Hope?'

'Nel. We're in incredibly tricky territory. Worst-case scenario? I lose my position and the department makes us pay full-tote odds for your passage. I really don't think this is the best time to suddenly become a spokeswoman for female scientists. Especially considering you aren't one.'

She turned to him, anger burring her voice despite the assumption of a shared future woven through his words. 'You said you supported the idea. Eventually. When the bases are all set up.'

'I do. But when the time is right. Which, let's be honest, isn't this afternoon. Just think about it. I can only work towards that goal if I still have a job. Let the women scientists spruik for more women on stations. We're already up to our necks in hot water – let's not turn up the heat.' He ran a hand through his hair and, with a sigh, moved to the door. 'Please, just think about it. I trust ...' He paused in the open doorway. 'I trust you can handle this.'

Nel stared out of the porthole, unseeing.

She wasn't sure how much time had passed when she heard footsteps in the corridor. They stopped outside the cabin and a note shot through the crack beneath her door.

Nel froze, not daring to move until the footsteps had faded away. Gingerly, she plucked the small, folded-over page of notepaper from the carpet. It had been ripped from a field notebook, the torn perforations fuzzing the top. She unfolded it.

Inside, two pencil-sketched penguins. The pair of Adélies from the night the ship crossed the Antarctic Circle – Harris's lumpen flourbag and Nel's laughing cartoon. Underneath, two words. *Thank you.*

She slumped down on her bunk, the note pressed to her chest.

~

Under the bright afternoon sky, everything was so vivid Nel fished for her sunglasses in her crocodile-skin bag. The riot of colour. The blare of music and cheering from the wharf. Even the feel of the close, humid air on her skin. After the frigid dryness of Antarctica, Melbourne felt as though it should have palm trees and white sand rather than grey stone and concrete.

The berthing of *Magga Dan* had attracted quite the crowd. Phil and the captain were still who-knows-where with the customs officials. This was it. The end. She'd never have guessed she'd be sailing home feeling more alone than at any point in her life.

Nel found Andy pressed against the rail, watching as the thick salt-silvered ropes were slung between the ship and the dock, mooring *Magga* securely to the wharf.

She touched him on the shoulder, and he turned with a grin. 'Honestly, I'm as worried as I am excited about coming home – now that I'm only half the man she married.' He made room for Nel beside him, throwing a consoling arm around her shoulders. She'd told him as much as she'd told the Macquarie women: about the distance between her and Phil that had yawned wider with every passing day, her work with Harris and the blossoming of her artistic ambition, the rumours, Phil's cold response – everything except Harris's secret and her unreciprocated crush. He'd listened, his brown eyes warm with sympathy, before enfolding her in a comforting hug. He'd wanted to confront Monte, and it had taken all her debating skills to deflect him, finally convincing him she'd resolved to rise above Monte's guttersnipe gossip.

They fell into companionable silence, and Nel scanned the throng waiting on the wharf. Even from this distance, she could see that the horseshoe-shaped space where the gangway would meet the pier was ringed with men holding notebooks and cameras. Anxiety began to jangle in her stomach.

Andy, feeling her stiffen, turned to her with concern. 'Everything all right?'

She shook her head. Down on the quay, a reporter spotted her at the railing. All at once, the crowd was bristling with pointing arms. She stepped back, using the shadows and Andy's frame as cover.

She clutched her handbag against her stomach. 'There are so many of them.'

Andy took hold of her shoulders, speaking gently, as if to a scared animal. 'You, my dear, will be an absolute triumph.' He smiled, then paused, as if struck by inspiration. 'This is what's going to happen. I'm going to shoot down that gangway as if chased by an incensed colony of fire ants, into the arms of my loving wife. Then, I'm going to tell her the score – that she needs to sweep you up the moment your feet hit terra firma.' Andy nodded at her as if all this had already come to pass and he was merely recalling a pleasant memory. 'Believe me, she's a sorceress. The woman's done so much public speaking, I exploit her mercilessly at every faculty cocktail party. Five years ago, she had me sweet-talking the dean so famously, I got tenure. She's so good, it's spooky.' He squeezed her arms. 'Deal?'

Nel nodded gratefully, and when the gangway was finally secured, Andy took off, as good as his word. After his departure, the minutes stretched as Nel waited to disembark, standing well back to let the crush of Mawson winterers funnel down the walkway.

She could delay no longer. At the top of the gangway, Nel gripped the railing, her palms dampening the cloth of her gloves. Noise thundered in her ears. *Mrs Law. Over here. Mrs Law.*

Grey-suited men surged forward, waving notebooks, huge box cameras slung around their necks. She plastered on a smile, her sunglasses feeling like the only protection between her and the mass of sound and colour pressing in on her.

A tall dark-haired figure in an emerald dress appeared, elbowing her way between the suits, not stopping until she'd parked herself squarely at the foot of the slatted bridge. Pam. Nel's relief was visceral. She pushed her sunglasses to the top of her head and made her way down the long wooden ramp, the bulbs of camera flashes popping like fireworks. Nel stepped onto solid ground and was immediately engulfed in Pam's embrace.

'My incredible friend,' Pam said into her hair. 'Welcome home, darling.' Over Nel's shoulder, she called to the press of reporters, her voice warm and agreeable. 'Just give us one minute, chaps. Then she's all yours.' With one arm still holding Nel close, she moved slightly to the side so as not to block the men still disembarking behind them.

'Look at you.' Pam's face was alight. 'You did it.' She engulfed Nel in another hug. 'I'm so damned proud.'

Nel squeezed her in return. 'Pam. Please. Get me out of here. I ...' She loosened her grip, pulling her sunglasses back down and hanging her head to shield her face from the hovering crowd. 'I'm meant to say ...' She touched her forehead to Pam's. 'They want me to ... make myself *small*.'

Pam took hold of Nel's hands, keeping her forehead pressed against hers. 'Well, that's not what I see. I see a woman, whom I know to be a talented artist, stepping off a ship that sailed from *Antarctica*.' She squeezed Nel's hands. 'Have any of these reporters been there? Have any of these women?'

Nel didn't answer, her eyes shut tight.

'No. They haven't. *You* have.' Pam leaned back. 'Look at me.'

Nel opened her eyes.

'You, my friend, have done something amazing. Something most people will never do.' Pam looked straight into Nel's face, her smile falling away but the pressure of her grip emphasising every word. 'So, you're going to stand tall, lift your chin, smile – then turn around and *be* the strong, brave, talented artist that I *know* you are.' Pam moved her hands up to Nel's shoulders. 'And tomorrow morning, little girls all over the country are going to see you on the front page of the newspaper and know that they can grow up to be explorers too.' She gave Nel's hands one last squeeze. 'All right?'

'*Mrs Law, over here. Mrs Law, how did it feel to be the only woman among sixty-seven men?*'

Nel straightened her spine and turned around, her heart hammering as she stretched a smile between her ears.

'*Now* I understand why the men have been keeping the place all to themselves.'

Renaissance Gold

Camberwell, Melbourne
March 1961

Nel stepped out of the Red Top taxi, hooking her handbag over her arm. *So much to be done.* The unpacking and the mail and the unruly thatch of lawn. She hadn't even unlocked the front door and already she felt exhausted. Since facing the reporters at the pier, she hadn't been able to stop sweating. Air that three months ago would've seemed cool and dry was now so hot and humid her skin felt encased in Glad Wrap.

The taxi-driver had not stopped talking from the moment they'd left the wharf. He was perfectly amiable, but the sound of conversation, piled on top of the traffic and the radio, made her want to press her hands to her ears. The colours, the noise, the pine scent of air-freshener over base notes of nicotine and body odour. The whole world seemed so loud and fast and complicated, everything screaming *artificial* at a different pitch.

She waited as Phil and the driver pulled the luggage from the boot of the red-and-cream Holden, careful not to ding the chrome on the fins as they stacked the cases on the footpath. The rest of the trunks and all her paintings would be delivered over the next few days.

Nel picked up her cosmetics case and walked slowly along the path. The garden was bristly and dry. The flowering shrubs all needed deadheading; leaves curled at the edges and drooped on their stalks. She slid the key into the lock, the door swinging open into the cool, dim interior. The hallstand was furred with dust.

She stepped across the threshold, then paused, turning back to the light. She watched Phil pay the driver, then roll his shoulders, stretching as he took in the streetscape and state of the garden. Catching sight of her in the shadowed entry, his body stilled. They gazed at each other across the stretch of parched lawn.

Nel heard birdsong from high in the plane trees and, as she stood there, looking at her husband, she noticed how the earth felt stable under her feet.

~

The phone receiver clattered into its cradle. The spiral cord had twisted itself into a string of knobbles and Nel picked up the handset again, letting it dangle, the cord circling lazily as it unwound. The calls were finally trailing away. For the first two weeks the phone had driven her quite mad. The blasted contraption began ringing before the breakfast dishes were even in the sink. She'd spent so much time perched on the hard seat of the telephone table, speaking to reporters and giving quotes for magazine articles, in the end she'd had to move one of the comfortable television chairs into the hall.

The dial tone of the hanging handset changed from a buzz to more strident notes and she gently replaced the heavy plastic receiver. Her hand hovered for a few seconds, ready for another shrill ring, then she scooped up the pad and pencil she used for jotting messages and things to say in interviews and walked into the kitchen.

At first, being home had been absolute bliss. She blended in, could walk wherever she wanted without feeling eyes on her. It was like being invisible. If it wasn't for the infernal telephone, she would've been in heaven.

Phil had gone back to work, with not even a day of grace to settle himself in at home. She hadn't minded. They were wary of each other, and the solitude was both a relief and a balm. The issue of Harris was a wound, the flesh barely knitted. And being back in the house, *her* house, felt magical, a gloss bathing everything in wonder. All of its ordinariness had been washed away, revealing its hidden essence – its beautiful 'thingness' was the only way she could think to describe it.

She'd taken so much for granted. The washing machine was revealed as a marvel of engineering and ingenuity. Her wardrobe was stuffed with glorious dresses, masterpieces of fabric and tailoring. Even the toaster was a thing of beauty, its chrome sides a triumph of modern design. The warmth of the sun. The scent of her roses, the heads now blowsy and dry, were miraculous examples of nature's genius. She lived in a verdant wonderland. And the *trees*. The first morning at home had found her standing in the middle of her street, agape at the sheer magnificence of the plane trees, the early light slanting through their branches, so pale-barked and elegant, leaves just on the brink of mellowing from summer green to bronze. But now, after several weeks, the gloss was slowly evaporating.

Phil had been quiet since their return. They paced gently through the house, their spare interactions over breakfast and dinner immaculately polite. She saw him watching her, not with suspicion or anger, but in a way that reminded her of Harris observing penguins. And while it worried her, the lack of conversation had the surprising effect of turning up the volume on the rest of the world. Suburban sounds she'd been filtering out or ignoring for years, background noise she would've classified as 'silence', now filled the house with delightful music. Lawnmowers, barking dogs, footsteps on the pavement, the squeak of the postman's bike. In a way, she was like an explorer in her own home.

Nel slid into her chair at the kitchen table. The sunlight washing through the windows and across the formica top was gentle with the first inklings of autumn. Warmth still felt like a luxury.

She flicked the notebook to a fresh page. The day's list. They hadn't had beef Wellington since their return. She scribbled a quick rollcall of ingredients needed from the butcher and grocer. If she flapped the duster around this morning and nipped out to do the shopping by lunch, she might finally find a moment to sort through her artwork. She wrote *ART* on the list, the bottom rung of a ladder of tasks.

In the space under the list, a few deft lines and a snow petrel alighted on the bottom edge, wings slightly lifted as if just settling from flight. Nel tapped the pencil against her lips, eyeing the sketch critically. This little bird had promise. She'd been searching for an image that might serve as a logo.

It had been so disappointing. She'd honestly thought that her voyage on *Magga Dan* and the way she'd contributed to the expedition would show the world that women should be able to venture South. It was ridiculous. There was no reasonable argument against it. But there'd been no significant progress, as far as she could see. Of all the interviews she'd given, only *The Australian Women's Weekly* and *The Age* had taken any interest in her art. Most of the journalists had only wanted to know what it was like to live among all those men, and there had been a few annoyingly worded articles about female scientists threatening the 'exclusive men's club'. All those column inches wasted on such tripe. Did they really think the only reason women were so keen to go was just to irritate men?

Nel cocked her head, darkening the snow petrel's beak to black and thickening the leading edge of the wing. Given her apparent failure to spark any change for women wanting to go to Antarctica, an alternative idea had been taking shape. If her experience had taught her anything, it was an appreciation of the power, comfort and support of female companionship. Perhaps she could harness that, for the greater good. No other wife had endured anywhere close to the amount of time she'd spent alone. Thirteen Antarctic seasons. She'd stopped tallying the months years ago. No one understood the pressures and deprivations better. She could form an organisation to support Antarctic wives and their families. She had the time. And a brand-new determination to corral housework into a limited number of hours to free her for more important work.

'Yoo-hoo! Nellie!'

She hadn't heard Gwen's car. Nel flung open the door, enveloping her sister in a hug. Her enthusiasm bowled Gwen off the doorstep; the wicker basket and tea-towel-wrapped plate wide held wide as her sister struggled for balance.

'Gracious,' Gwen laughed, extricating herself.

'Just appreciating the women in my life,' Nel said, grabbing the handle of the basket and waving Gwen inside.

'Well, you don't have much choice. There's no getting rid of me.' Gwen nudged past her, holding the wrapped plate aloft, the full skirt of her pale lemon dress brushing Nel's legs with a *whisht* of stiff petticoat. It was the exact shade of an emperor penguin neck, Nel observed, following Gwen and the scent of warm scones down the hall to the kitchen. The pair bustled comfortably between stove and cupboards, making a pot of tea, setting out plates and butter for the scones, their silence warm and familiar.

Gwen sat down and slipped off her cardigan, arranging it so that her chairback held it like a pair of shoulders. 'Sounds like the phone finally stopped.' She patted her hair, then reached forward to unwrap the plate of scones.

Nel reached for one, breaking it open with her bone-handled knife then slathering the steaming faces with butter. 'I'm meant to be on a diet.' Nel glanced ruefully down at her capri pants. 'Thank goodness I only see you once a week.'

Gwen laughed. 'I've given up.' She gave a melodramatic sigh. 'Since turning fifty, I could starve myself but it doesn't seem to matter. Everything keeps expanding.' She took a bite of scone. 'Why fight it? I'm just making myself miserable.'

Nel fixed her sister with a serious expression. 'I thought I was just eating more on the ship.' She looked down at her plate. 'We were all eating more because of the cold. But maybe ...' Nel met her sister's gaze. 'I've started the change.'

Gwen tightened her lips in a sympathetic grimace and reached across the table, gripping her sister's wrist in consolation. 'Sweetie.'

'At least Antarctica is the perfect place to deal with hot flushes.' Nel chuckled and took a sip of tea, then centred her cup in the saucer, not meeting her sister's eyes. 'Actually, the worst of it is the moods.' She frowned. 'Not *moods*, really. More feelings.' She twisted the cup in its china circle. 'Everything has become so intense.'

She'd debated telling Gwen about her feelings for Harris. Gwen would still love her. There was no doubt about that. But her sister might not look at her the same way, and she wasn't sure she was quite ready to say goodbye to the old self she saw reflected in Gwen's eyes.

Gwen sat quite still, as if any movement might derail Nel's unusual frankness.

'Phil and I have always been so solid. I knew going down there wouldn't be easy. Phil would be busy, so I was ready to keep myself occupied. But seeing him at work ... he was a completely different man. I'd see him on the bridge or giving orders to the men, and I'd want to throttle him. It was as if I didn't recognise him. And ... some of the men were ... difficult. It made me so *angry*. I didn't recognise myself.' She shook her head, sketching a pattern with her fingernail on the brindled formica. 'And it ended up driving a wedge between us.' She gave a bitter laugh. 'I can't believe I thought going down there with him could only strengthen our marriage. It was almost the death knell.'

Gwen squeezed her hand. There was a long silence.

'Well, I'm glad you're both still here. And Ann and Gillian are so proud of their famous aunt.' Gwen gave her a rueful smile. 'I was surprised by the anger, too. I remember feeling like I was always on the edge of slipping out of control. I *lived* on that edge.' She laughed. 'To be honest, it was less anger than rage. Snapping at the girls for leaving glasses on the drainboard. Slamming doors. I even smashed a plate in the sink at something Fred did. I can't even remember what it was now.'

Nel smiled, wide-eyed. 'I can *not* picture that!'

'Fred was beside himself. He had no idea what to do or how to handle things. He even hinted I might have a brain tumour and insisted I see a doctor. He said it was like living in a house with three teenaged girls. There were times I thought he was on the brink of having me committed.'

Nel started to laugh, but at the look on her sister's face, it dwindled.

'But you get through it.' Gwen's mouth pulled to the side, and she helped herself to another scone. 'Now I'm out the other end, I can honestly say life is better. And not just because there's less laundry.' She lifted an eyebrow.

'Better how?'

Gwen cut a thin wedge of butter, her knife chinking against the crock. 'I guess I just don't care as much.' Seeing the confusion on her sister's face, she went on. 'Looking back, I can see I was a slave to my emotions, especially in the days before the visit from Aunt Flo. Always worried about what people would think. Of me. Of the girls. But now, I feel ... steadier. Less volatile. No – more insulated from outside opinions is a better way to describe it. It takes more to rile me.' She smiled reassuringly. 'Maybe the best description is I feel closer to being a wise old woman. Like Great-grandma.'

'Poor Fred!' Both women broke into laughter.

Nel selected another scone from the plate, breaking it open with her fingers. 'There was a moment, a day actually, just before we got home, when I seriously thought it was over. Each time I saw him, I thought the next words out of his mouth were going to be that he was done. And even though I was scared, it was exciting too. Because underneath the shame and embarrassment and fear there was this tiny thrill of freedom.'

Gwen reached across the table and gripped her wrist. 'Oh, love.'

'The voyage – it didn't just change me. It changed the way I saw him.' Nel looked into her sister's eyes. 'Once you've seen someone in a different light, can you ever see them the way you did before?'

Gwen's eyes slid away to stare at the pattern etching the glass of the kitchen cupboards. 'No.' Silence hovered over the table. She grimaced and met Nel's eyes. 'But people grow and change. Nothing is permanent. Wanting him to be the man you met at uni – it's a fairytale. If he was still that man, you'd be bored out of your mind. He's grown and changed. As have you.' Gwen tapped her fingernail against Nel's wedding ring. 'Marriage isn't just a bond or an institution. It's a living thing, and like any living thing, it flourishes and life feels easy. Then it falters and you think it's dying.' She rubbed the back of Nel's hand. 'I think that's exactly where you're standing for the first time. It's not menopause, darling. It's *life*. And Nel' – Gwen gripped her sister's hands in both of hers, squeezing to emphasise every word – 'honestly, after *twenty years*, if this is the first time you've seriously wondered if your marriage is dead, there's probably life in it yet.'

~

Gwen had stayed for lunch, then afternoon tea, leaving Nel barely enough time to dash to the shops if she was to have dinner in the oven by the time Phil's car pulled into the drive. In her haste, she'd forgotten her list, gathering the ingredients for beef Wellington from memory.

As she hurried back down the street, Nel's heart sank. Their two-tone blue-and-white Holden sat in the driveway. Putting her hand on the bonnet, it was cool to the touch. He'd been home for a while. There was nothing to be done; he would just have to wait for dinner.

At the door, she kicked off her shoes and hurried down the hall. Oil paintings leaned against every available wall; the dining table was piled with sketches and watercolours. It'd only been a few weeks, but already her blaze of artistic energy and ambition felt on the cusp of sputtering to ashes.

Nel lumped the heavy basket onto the kitchen bench, and looked around with a sense of shame. It had not taken long for the old routine to exert its pull. She was still here, in the same role. Still Phil's wife, despite his silence and the new distance between them.

Nel unpacked the shopping basket, piling the paper-wrapped parcels of beef fillet, mushrooms and bacon on the bench. Where *was* Phil? His office was empty. She poked her head into the lounge. The room was cool and still. 'Phil? Are you home?'

She returned to the kitchen and picked up the list from the kitchen table, scanning for missed ingredients.

Her lips thinned. Phil *was* home. He'd edited her list.

Her chores – breakfast dishes, spider-broom, dust and vacuum – had all been struck through with Phil's spidery biro. A long scribble like a cartoon tornado obliterated her shopping list. And at the bottom, the word *ART* was ringed several times, a fat arrow pointing to its rightful position at the top of the list.

'*Phil.*'

'I'm here.' Phil stood in the doorway gingerly holding a large cardboard box.

She eyed the box with alarm. 'Is this an early minute or did they ask you to clean out your office?'

'Early minute. They must still be gathering the signatures for giving me the boot. Wait a second,' he said, disappearing into the lounge. A moment later, he reappeared, his hands free. 'Come with me.' He plucked the list from her fingers, tossing it on the table, then led her down the hallway, past his office, stopping in front of his rock room. He turned the knob, swinging the door open.

Nel stood in the doorway, blinking at the space where, the day before, crystal and mica had flashed and sparkled in the light. The shelves were empty. By the window, positioned so the sun fell across the face of a fresh canvas, stood her easel.

Her heart fluttered, light as a bird, as she stepped into the room, the floorboards warm beneath her feet. She spun in slow motion, not quite believing her eyes. She'd assumed the hours he'd spent closeted in here after dinner last night were spent cataloguing and arranging his latest specimens – not doing this.

He'd given her this room. His room. She took a deep breath, hooking the scrim curtain up and over the end of the rod. Naked light poured in. A studio of her own.

'Phil' – Nel touched his arm – 'are you sure?'

'An artist needs her own workspace.'

Her voice caught as she whispered, 'Thank you.' Phil took her hand tentatively, and said, 'Before I lose you to your new studio completely, there's something else I need to show you.'

'One second.' Nel slipped her hand into her pocket. The Antarctic pebble was warm and smooth in her hand. She placed it reverently on the shelf of her easel. Splinters of mica glittered in the wash of sun.

Nel put her hand back in Phil's, allowing him to pull her down the hall to the lounge room. 'Close the door,' he said over his shoulder as he strode to the box, moving it to the centre of the floor. Phil perched on the footstool in front of his armchair.

He looked up at her and smiled, gesturing to the chair. 'Sit. Let me get you a drink.'

Nel caught her breath. It was his old face. No longer the chief – the man sitting in her lounge room was her husband.

She hovered in the doorway, worried any sudden movement might shatter the spell. She'd longed for this moment, to see love in his gaze again. For him to see her.

There was a long silence while he busied himself mixing drinks, then he handed her a glass, his mournful, anxious eyes looking deeply into hers.

'I owe you an apology,' he said. As if realising he was looming over her, he perched back on the footstool. 'These past weeks, it feels as if we've dropped back into the same routine. And that's not right.' He cleared his throat as Nel stared at him. 'What I'm trying to say is that coming home this time, I stepped into a house that was dark and cold and lifeless.' He gripped his knees, not meeting her eyes. 'At first, I thought it was because of this coldness between us. It took me a while to realise the reason it felt so different was because of you.' He looked up at her. 'All the other expeditions, I came home to a house full of life and warmth and you were so happy to see me. It never occurred to me to think about how life had been for you while I was away. As if you existed in suspended animation while I wasn't there.' He shook his head, eyes sliding away from hers in embarrassment. 'While I missed you, I'm ashamed to admit I didn't really think that much about home.' He took her hands in his. 'But while we've been away together, seeing you so deep in your work and free from the house, it's like you're a different person. And – I'm so sorry, my love – I didn't like it. That change. Because it was new and ...' Phil raked a hand through his hair and took a long swallow of his gin and tonic. 'I was being someone I don't respect. Someone selfish and afraid of change.' He gave a grim laugh. 'Basically, I failed to see that under the surface of the woman I love was someone who hadn't had a chance to show herself. I just left you alone with only a cat for company and expected to return home to the same house and the same person. And I'm so sorry.'

A small noise escaped her throat. He gestured towards the box.

'Open it.'

The floorboards were cool beneath her knees as she pulled open the top flaps. The box was half-filled with a messy nest of raffia fibres and shredded newspaper.

It rustled. Nel's eyes widened as she reached into the box, pushing aside the knotty mess.

Four eyes looked up at her. The blue of glacier melt.

Two Siamese kittens scrabbled in the box, claws like the finest needles, their pale fur so feathery it defined softness. They were creamy white with dark brown smudges across the nose and the points of their ears. Nel scooped the tiny cats from their nest, cradling them against her chest.

'Phil.' Her voice cracked. Two thin brown tails whipped against her belly as the pair began to mewl. 'Oh, my darlings. Are you hungry?

Do you want some milk? Let's see what we can find.' She struggled up from her knees, hands full of writhing fur, and paused to press her cheek against Phil's face before carrying the kittens into the kitchen, cupping both their skinny pink chests side by side in one hand. The tiny triangular faces craned upwards, wide blue eyes fixed on Nel's face.

Nel stepped over to the sideboard and, after a moment's hesitation, picked up a blue ceramic dish. It had been Nefertiti's water bowl.

Phil had followed Nel into the kitchen, and stood leaning in the open doorway as she placed the two little white bodies on the floor, then spread newspapers and filled Nefertiti's bowl with milk.

The sound of tiny lapping tongues filled the room. Kneeling behind the kittens, Nel looked up at Phil, a hand to her chest. *Thank you.* She mouthed it, not trusting her voice.

He smiled, at *her*. The woman who had returned home, not the woman who'd set sail. She stood up, slipping her arms around him, her cheek finding its familiar hollow between his clavicle and shoulder. He squeezed her, arms wrapped around her waist, his cheek gently crushing her curls. They swayed, back together, in a new, beautiful form.

Epilogue

Hobart, Tasmania
November 2011

Cass passed under the heavy stone arch into the courtyard of the Tasmanian Museum and Art Gallery, the shadow of the grey masonry immediately cooling her skin. The sensory overwhelm of Hobart after months on the ice took days, sometimes weeks, to fade, and visiting TMAG had become a ritual, her way of reacclimatising to life on land.

Aurora Australis had docked yesterday but Cass's first night back on solid ground in real darkness hadn't ensured a good night's sleep. She'd lain awake with every thought and worry she'd ever shoved away now looming over her bed. It was always like this: the cool, dry Tasmanian climate felt sticky and close; the white noise of traffic sawed at her nerves. And *all the people*. So garish and loud, walking around with their minds in their phones, not even noticing the world around them.

At the top of the stairs, Cass took a deep breath in the doorway of the Argyle Gallery. *Islands to Ice*. She always left this room to last, wanting its atmosphere around her like a cloak when she re-emerged into the city bustle.

Cass stepped inside, and the polar tones and soundtrack of seabirds and wind immediately cast their spell. Her pulse slowed. In this space, there was no need for methodical focus. Cass paced the curved photographic displays as if on a nostalgic stroll through her childhood neighbourhood – from embalmed snow petrel to prismatic compass, flensing knife to sea sponge.

She rounded the final display wall and stopped short. Rory. The poet had her back to Cass, standing in front of a painting in the furthest corner of the gallery.

Cass sidled up behind her. '*Boo.*'

The shorter woman flinched, before breaking into a wide smile. 'Are you stalking me? I thought we said our goodbyes yesterday?'

'Just getting my last taste of the ice before my flight tomorrow.'

'Same.' Rory nodded, turning back to the painting.

The women stood side by side in silent contemplation.

'This is my favourite. I visit it every time I'm in Hobart.' Rory cast Cass a sideways glance. 'You're the only other person I've ever seen looking at it.'

'I've got to be honest, I've been through this gallery countless times and never noticed it before.' The painting was tucked deep in the shadows of the furthest corner, but now that Cass was standing here, she couldn't believe she'd missed it.

It was a landscape in watercolour, just a little smaller than an A3 page. A muted wash of greenish brown hillside swooped down to a cold, grey bay, jagged with teeth of black rock. Macquarie Island. She'd recognise those windswept hills plunging into the sea anywhere. Cass could practically feel the slap of wet wind. But the evocation of the landscape was not what made the scene so extraordinary.

286

It was the penguins. Hundreds of them. No, thousands. Packed across every inch of grey sand, cramming every hillside crease. Each individual penguin was marked by its own strike of ink. The whole scene was painted from a distance, the artist's vantage point high on an overlooking slope, with the largest penguins crowded in the bottom right corner. The penguins were too small to tell the species, yet even so, those in the foreground were inked in such a way that each one was individual. Stance, beak tilt, flipper angle – each penguin's presence and attitude rendered with just a few strokes.

The sheer number of penguins sketched in this way was staggering. The perspective rolled back until penguins were only the tiniest dots in the furthest reaches of scene, yet it felt for all the world as if the artist had given each penguin individual attention, regardless of size. Cass realised her mouth was hanging open and shut it with a clack.

Rory grinned. 'Incredible, isn't it?'

Cass nodded, still speechless.

'It's like three-dimensional pointillism. You could stare at this for hours.' Rory stepped forward to squint at the tiny figures in the foreground. 'Can you imagine how long this took to paint?'

'And how cold it must've been on that hillside?' Cass shuddered in sympathy. 'You've got to hope the artist took a photo and filled in all the penguins later. Back in the dorm. The weather looks classic Macca – cold, wet and windy as hell. Diabolical.' She leaned in until her nose was almost touching the glass. 'You can't tell the species, but they must be kings or royals.'

'The first time I saw this, I was sure they were Adélies.'

Cass laughed. 'No Adélies on Macca.'

'I know that *now*.' Rory hip-bumped her friend. 'Since being taken to school on all things penguin.'

Cass lurched with the bump, but she continued to gaze at the painting. 'There's something about ...' She leaned even closer to the penguins at the bottom right. 'These remind me so much of my grandfather's penguins.'

'Your grandfather kept penguins?'

'Sketches my grandfather had when I was a kid.'

'Your grandfather sketched penguins?'

Cass chuckled. 'He didn't do them. They were in the spare bedroom at my grandparents' house. As a kid, I was obsessed with them. When I stayed overnight, Farfar would make up these amazing bedtime stories about them. He was a merchant navy captain. Migrated here from Denmark. His favourite voyages were the ones down to Antarctica. He regularly captained supply ships going down to the ice. And after one of those voyages he brought home these beautiful sketches of penguins. Actually, it's a weird story.

'One night, they'd docked at Macquarie Island and Farfar had stepped outside to watch the aurora. There was a gust of wind, and suddenly a flurry of papers blew across the deck. He managed to catch a handful before they all flew out to sea. When he looked at what he'd caught, the pages were these amazing pen and ink sketches of penguins. All Adélies. He brought them home and framed them. When Farfar died, Mormor gave them to me and now they're hanging above the fireplace in my house. Those sketches and Farfar's stories are probably what made me fall in love with Antarctica. And ultimately got me working with penguins.' She flapped a hand at the artwork. 'And there's something about this painting that really reminds me of those sketches.'

Rory cocked her head to one side. 'That's really cool. Counts as a definite win for the power of art. Could your Farfar's penguins be by the same artist?' She pointed at the interpretive panel. 'This was painted in 1960. By a woman. You know her actually – she's the one in the photo I showed you at Mawson.'

Cass frowned, moving over to read the interpretive panel.

Nel Law 1914–1990. Pen and ink and watercolour. Nugget's Beach rookery, Macquarie Island, c 1960.

Cass's jaw dropped. Nel Law. The first Australian woman in Antarctica. Wife of Phil Law. And now it turned out she was an artist too.

Hardly daring to breathe, Cass returned to the painting, eyes scouring the bottom left corner. There it was, almost completely disguised among the tiny pin-pricks of penguins: NL. The small, slanting signature she knew so well from Farfar's penguin sketches.

Cass felt something chime deep within her. It was that miraculous feeling of something falling into place, something longed for, like years of data finally validating a hypothesis.

Rory looked at her curiously. 'Are you okay? You get knocked for six every time you come across this woman.'

'It's just I'd always thought the first Australian women down there were scientists, back in late seventies or early eighties. But seeing this ...' Cass fished in her bag for her notebook and pen.

'The power of art, hey? I really have converted you.'

Cass didn't hear. She was back at Mawson, standing in front of the cairn in the midwinter gloom, her fingers running over the raised bronze of Nel's name. Casting around for a seat, she sank down onto the nearest padded cube. Beneath her feet, she had the sense of the earth turning, light falling at last on a place that had long been in shadow. She flipped to a fresh page and, notebook across her lap, she began to write.

Afterword

People who've been to Antarctica often say the experience changed their life. But when asked to articulate how the place wields such power, they struggle. Jon Krakauer, one of my favourite non-fiction writers, said, 'Antarctica has this mythic weight. It resides in the collective unconscious of so many people, and it makes this huge impact, just like outer space. It's like going to the moon.'

I'd felt that icy, mythic weight since I was a little girl, devouring those incredible stories of beauty and tragedy from the Heroic Age of Antarctic exploration – the *Boys' Own* adventure tales of polar explorers such as Amundsen, Scott, Shackleton and Mawson. Growing up in the late twentieth century and reaping the benefits of second-wave feminism, it didn't occur to me that being a woman might hinder my dreams of seeing Antarctica. By the time I was old enough to think about turning desire into reality, women had been included on polar expeditions for decades.

I've had the immense privilege of travelling to Antarctica

twice. For my first voyage, in 2005, I gave up my job working as a climate change campaigner for Greenpeace to enrol in a Graduate Certificate of Antarctic Studies at the University of Canterbury in Christchurch, Aotearoa. Part of the curriculum was flying to Scott Base in Antarctica, then camping on the Ross Ice Shelf within view of Mount Erebus.

That experience changed my life. Yes, I became one of those people. While down on the ice, I met New Zealand author Laurence Fearnley. She noticed my fledgling passion for writing poetry and gave me her copy of *The Ode Less Travelled* by Stephen Fry. That gift flamed a spark into a fire – every spare second, I scrawled poems in notebooks and scratched words on every piece of paper in my duffle, trying to wrestle the incredible scenes before my eyes onto the page.

Returning home, I kept writing, knowing deep in my bones that Antarctica had shown me a new, deeply satisfying path. Scientific knowledge helps us understand our planet and the ecological mechanisms that support all life. But environmental advocacy – encouraging humanity to alter its values and behaviour – that challenge needs the power of art and storytelling.

Antarctica steered me from environmental campaigning towards writing. Eventually, those early Antarctic poems formed part of my first poetry collection, and in 2013, as a fledgling writer, I travelled to Antarctica again. This time I travelled with my husband; I was a tourist, drinking in the wonder of the West Antarctic Peninsula and its wildlife from the comfort of a small ship.

Anyone who has stepped into a bookshop in an Antarctic hub city like Christchurch, Hobart or Ushuaia will know that polar literature is hugely popular. Generous stretches of non-fiction shelf space groan under rows of blue-and-white spines. Antarctica may be a continent devoted to science – and I'm not alone in my addiction to books on polar ecology and biology – but hands-down, the genre claiming the greatest stretch of bookshop real estate is Antarctic history. Exploration history, to be precise – biography after biography dedicated to the men who went South in the early twentieth century, that period we've dubbed the Heroic Age.

But it was the discovery of two books that broke me away from this unquestioning reverence for the Heroic Age. The first was Jesse Blackadder's wonderful novel *Chasing the Light*, a book that reimagines the Antarctic journey of the first Western women to reach the Antarctic continent. I devoured that novel, wondering how on earth, as a feminist, I'd managed to read so many biographies of Antarctic explorers yet failed to wonder where the women were.

Not long after that, I picked up *Terra Antarctica: Looking into the Emptiest Continent* by William L. Fox, a book exploring the ways in which painters and photographers have depicted the Antarctic landscape through history. In a chapter on visual artists, beside a colour plate of a stunning emerald-coloured iceberg speckled with rows of penguins like strings of morse code, I read a single sentence describing the artist Nel Law as the first Australian woman to set foot on the Antarctic continent. *Who?*

I searched for more information, only to find glimpses and shadows of Nel Law in the footnotes of weighty tomes about men. Yet with every mention of her name, my conviction that I was on the scent of my next book grew surer.

Nel was the wife of Phillip Garth Law – a name prominent in Australian Antarctic lore, yet not as well-known as other famous Australian polar explorers such as Douglas Mawson, John King Davis or Hubert Wilkins.

Phil Law was a man who combined great vision with incredible energy and drive. As director of Australian National Antarctic

Research Expeditions (ANARE) from 1949 to 1966, he was responsible for Australia's permanent presence in Antarctica. He established Mawson, Davis and Casey stations, and lead expeditions that explored over 5000 kilometres of coastline and approximately 1,000,000 square kilometres of territory. His vision was for Australia's presence in Antarctica to be more than a territory grab, and he fought long and hard to establish world-class scientific facilities there. He was a remarkable man, a hands-on leader who personally led twenty-three voyages to Antarctica and the subantarctic regions over his career, exploring the coast of the Australian Antarctic Territory from Oates Land in the east to Enderby Land in the west. Biographer Kathleen Ralston has written two extraordinary biographies of his life, which I highly recommend, as they shed light on a period of Australia's Antarctic history that is sadly overshadowed by the earlier exploits of Heroic Age explorers.

So it was no surprise that Nel Law's fame had been eclipsed by her husband's incredible career. My research uncovered three points that made me sit up and pay attention: she was the first Australian woman to stand on the Antarctic continent, she was also the first female visual artist to travel to the ice, and to get there she'd stowed away on a supply vessel. It felt like the bones of a good story.

Fortunately, Phillip Law donated his papers to the Australian National Library. This huge trove of voyage diaries, personal documents, correspondence, reports, navigational records, meteorological records, manuscripts, press cuttings, scrapbooks and publications fill 105 archive boxes. One of these boxes held material about his wife.

In 2018, I travelled to Canberra to look in this box. Inside, among the sketches, newspaper clippings and magazine articles (including one about her cooking penguin and seal for Phil's 'Antarctic Feasts')

I found the diary in which she recorded her journeys to Macquarie Island in 1960 and then Antarctica in 1961.

After Nel's death in 1990, Phil compiled a manuscript of her Antarctic and subantarctic travels, typing out her diary entries and interspersing them with his explanations of various details her diaries had glossed over. I read her original diary, her handwriting scrawled in her trademark green biro. Then I turned to Phil's more detailed manuscript, in which he situated Nel's journey and achievements in the broader context of Antarctic exploration. At the time, Phil recorded being aware of only six women who had travelled South before Nel, and of these only three had landed on the Antarctic mainland. Nel Law was the first Australian woman to do so, and the fourth woman in the world.

Travelling back to Adelaide, I plotted out my book, wanting to adhere as closely as possible to her experiences. But as I read the diary, I couldn't help feeling like something was missing. It described stunning landscapes, days full of sketching and painting, and evenings brimming with sing-alongs and parlour games. But there were huge gaps in the story, creating more questions than answers. Given the era, how had this shipload of men responded to Nel's presence? How did this 1950s housewife break free from the gender roles of her time? What was it like to be the only woman on a ship with nearly seventy men? Considering that a study published in 2022 reports that women on Australian Antarctic bases are still experiencing sexual harassment and gender-based discrimination, these questions felt more urgent than ever.

I returned to the National Library, this time to read Phil's account of the journey. This was a little juicier, hinting at ship-board tensions, the threat of becoming trapped in the ice, logistical issues on Chick Island, his desire to explore more of Oates Land and the discovery of looting among the men. But in terms of Nel's experience, there was nothing of note.

Only once I was home, gazing forlornly at my shelf of Antarctic literature, did I realise that Nel's diary could only ever have told a small part of the story. It wasn't a traditional diary – an intimate record of her thoughts, written for her eyes alone. It was composed with a readership in mind and was being shared with Phil, whose notations peppered its pages. Nel had even recorded Phil's excitement at the idea her diary would be published, one day taking its place beside other famous journals of polar exploration. The more I thought about it, the more I realised that all we had of Nel's writing was a highly selective account – a sensitively penned piece of propaganda. With her husband in charge of Australia's presence in Antarctica and his job on the line to bring her with him, it was understandable that her account would avoid any potential bad press. Even in her own diary, there could have been no escaping from the shadow of Phil's career. The reality of her experience remained hidden.

With this new-found perspective on Nel's diary, I put aside the desire to write a conventional biographic account and instead began to look more closely at the gaps and silences in her account. That was where the story lay. Not a biography, but a novel.

My plan had been to write a story about adventure. A feminist escapade about a trailblazing woman, forging a path for all the women who came after her. What I ended up writing was a story about love. A story about long-term relationships and living in a spouse's shadow. A story about mid-twentieth-century gender roles, about the art–science binary, about landscape and grief, and even a bit of perimenopause thrown in the mix.

That's a roundabout path to the heart of this note – which is making clear that this book is a work of fiction. This novel was inspired by real events, but while the plot uses events recorded in Nel and Phil's Antarctic journals, I have attempted to write into the many gaps and spaces left by these source materials. Dialogue, characters and scenes were invented for narrative purposes, as were some of Nel's paintings and artworks described in the book.

In trying to create a smooth and engaging narrative, I fused Nel's separate journeys to Macquarie Island (November to December 1960) and Antarctica (January to March 1961) into a single voyage, changing dates and locations. There were indeed four female scientists at Macquarie Island in 1960, and the experience of the first women to travel to Macquarie Island with Phil Law in 1959 is recorded in material available online from Mary Gillam Archive Project.

Though this novel is a fictional account, I believe it is true to say that going to Antarctica did indeed change Nel's life. Her Antarctic travels fuelled public interest in her art, and in 1964 Nel had her first solo exhibition at the Leveson Street Gallery in Melbourne. Although Australia stubbornly refused to change its policy on women in Antarctica until late 1974, Nel resisted stepping back into her husband's shadow, and instead made her own mark on Antarctic history. In 1965, she founded the Antarctic Wives and Kinfolk Association of Australia, an organisation dedicated to supporting spouses, relatives and friends of Antarctic expeditioners – people just like her who understood that the hardships of Antarctica stretched beyond the continent itself. ANARE expeditioners think of themselves as part of an enormous Antarctic family, and Nel's experience and vision extended this sense of belonging to embrace the actual families of Australia's Antarctic expeditioners. Nel was the founder, first president and later patron of this organisation, and it survives to this day as part of the ANARE Club.

So much has changed since the 1960s. Feminism has made great strides forward in the battle to win women the same rights and opportunities afforded to men, but there is still so much work to be done. Nel's willingness to break away from the strict gender roles and expectations of the post-war era continues to amaze me. And even though we live in different times, it is my hope that she inspires others as she has inspired me. To seize the moment. To not allow fear to hold us back. And to refuse to let the long shadows cast by history and tradition make us doubt ourselves or limit the scope of our dreams.

Acknowledgements

This project was made possible by the generous support of several organisations: Arts SA, for project funding; Varuna, the National Writers' House, for the 2021 Mick Dark Fellowship for Environmental Writing; Writers SA, for the 2021 Writer & Reader in Residence Program (Kangaroo Island); and the State Library of South Australia and Adelaide Festival Literary Awards, for the 2022 Barbara Hanrahan Fellowship. I'm incredibly grateful for the writing time and financial support afforded by these invaluable programs and fellowships.

Many thanks to the archivists and librarians of the National Library in Canberra for their deep reservoir of knowledge, kindness and support.

Thank you to Dr Mary Knights and the staff of the Tasmanian Museum and Art Gallery, who graciously assisted me with information on the artwork of Nel Law held in their collection.

Heartfelt thanks to the amazing writers and editors who have been so generous with their time and advice: Nadine Davidoff, Monica

McInerney, Robyn Mundy, Sarah Sentilles, Angela Slatter, Laurie Steed and Karen Viggers. I cannot thank you enough.

Many thanks to the writers of Laurie Steed's 2022 Subcommittee and Angela Slatter's novel writing class of 2020 with the Australian Writers' Centre. Thank you.

To Alison Flett, Katherine Tamiko, Narelle Hill and Shaine Melrose – deep thanks for your friendship and help with the challenge of keeping my butt in the chair.

For friendship, and always checking in on me when I disappear, thank you, Heather Taylor Johnson.

To Rebekah Clarkson, my sister in Strout-adoration and the other half of the tiniest bookclub, thank you for the best literary conversations and for setting my feet on this path.

To all the brilliant people at Affirm Press who have been so supportive – my heartfelt thanks. To Martin Hughes, the man who always has my back, thank you for your unwavering encouragement and patience. To my incredible editor, Ruby Ashby-Orr – you are simply a superstar – thank you so much. And many thanks to Laura Franks and Sonja Heijn for all your hard work and vision in trimming this behemoth down to size.

And, as always, Andrew Noble. Thank you, my love. You make everything possible.

Reader Questions

1. Nel was a housewife throughout the 1950s. Why do you think women of this era accepted roles so strongly focussed on domestic life?

2. In the 1960s, Antarctica was still a male-dominated space. How much do you think this has changed in the past sixty years?

3. What was your impression of Phil as a husband? How did that impression change across the book?

4. Many of the characters in the book viewed science and art as opposing ends of a spectrum. Do you agree?

5. How significant was Harris to Nel's transformation from wife to artist? Do you think this was a lasting change to her self-image?

6. What did you think about Nel's choice to avoid an ultimate confrontation with Monte? Have you ever chosen to avoid calling out sexism or misogyny as a means of self-protection?

7. What did you think of the choices Nel made about her future and her marriage? What would you have done in her situation?

8. During the journey there were many things Nel and Phil kept from one another and yet they'd had a remarkably close relationship before leaving home. Do you think a relationship can have gaps and silences, yet still thrive?

9. In 1960, homosexuality was considered a criminal act; the sentences imposed on those found guilty were serious. How well do you think Harris was hiding his orientation? Do you think he was using Nel as a 'beard'?

10. The novel's title hints at Nel breaking through the social and historical barriers standing in her way. Looking at the history of women in Antarctica, do you think she was successful?